JANE POLLER

OATH

OF

REBELLION

VINCI

BOOKS

By Jane Poller

Royal Oath

Oath of Rebellion
Oath of Revenge
Oath of Redemption

Dedicated to my hubby, who always shares his Pathfinder and DnD campaigns, includes me in his stories, and makes me want to be the best version of myself. I also want to see if he reads this, so yo, go read the second to last chapter and meet me in our bedroom.

Vinci Books

vinci-books.com

Published by Vinci Books Ltd in 2025

1

Copyright © Jane Poller 2024

A CIP catalogue record for this book is available from the British Library.

Paperback ISBN: 9781036708009

Trigger Warnings

Not sure how this trigger warning thing goes, but there's a lot of blood and gore in part of this, along with a rescue from a dungeon, some trauma from being a prisoner, poisoning of a family member, spider bites, snakes, etc.

Also, there's double penetration monster peen with slight non-consent vibes while in monster form. I'm warning you now, so don't come at me about beastiality because he's totally still himself, just shifted into a dragon. Please don't read it if this if these things trigger you.

Preface

Eirwyn is the darling drakin princess who just wants to escape the political upheaval the war has brought. But then her brother, the king and the most powerful drakin mage in the land, tries to have her killed.

Raised by druids with powers and abilities even they cannot explain, Knox the lumberjack is the unofficial protector of the Feral Forest. He's distracted from his work, robbing the king to feed the poor when a beautiful princess begs for his help.

He tries to resist her pleas for help to defeat her brother; however, if he helps, he might finally solve the question of who he is and where he came from. When fated mates and loyalties clash, he must choose whether to save the forest, defeat her brother, or rescue the damsel.

Contains mature content.

RINEWOOD   HARTSGROVE   DWARVES

E FERAL
FOREST

VIRELAND

DEIVE'S

DEMEREL   BUSPARIA

GROWLERS

ANGERWALD

MYRRVANE

GLATHEN

~CAPITOLS OF~
DOPHIAS

Chapter One

"The king's forces are pushing into the woods again. For what purpose this time?"

Knox frowned and leaned against the tree outside of the Robins' camp, pausing his spell to focus on his two best spies' weekly report. He took a drink of water from his flask, careful not to disturb his ever-present hood that covered his face.

Dirt clung to his brown pants, a constant side-effect of his job. His hatchet hung from his belt, ready to fight the Feral Forest's magic at a moment's notice. But on the edges of this little ragtag encampment of Vidrland, they were safe enough, and he had a job to do.

He flicked his fingers, crouching once more and setting his water aside as tiny vines began to grow at his feet. He wove them into a thicker rope while they talked.

Will nodded, shifting on the saddle as he looked down at Knox. "Aye, the bloody king's men are repeating the performance from when they tried to chop down the east side."

"Except now they're trying to build their own road instead of just taking the lumber for their war machines," Ashur added. "I guess the king is tired of paying the Robins for protection on the Lone Road, since it's the only route in and out of the forest."

Knox groaned and raked a hand over his face, careful to keep his hood in place. "That doesn't make sense," he said. "The king stopped trying to use the Lone Road years ago. He's refused to pay us since we shut them down from chopping down the east side. Why is he pushing into the Feral Forest now?"

Only the most desperate ventured onto the road between the kingdoms without the protection of the Robins. Or the most heavily guarded, and even then, only a handful of them had ever made it through without escort. The forest's magic worked hard to keep intruders out.

Knox frowned at the possibilities running through his head.

"The Southern Road is starting to fall into the sea," Will said.

Ashur nodded. "Plus, there's the Growlers that prey on the Southern Road."

"But that's still safer than the Lone Road. Do they have druids to keep the forest at bay?" Knox took his hatchet and chopped the rope, coiling it into a circle beside the four others. He wove his fingers and started the process over again.

Ashur uncorked his water and took a drink before saying, "He's the king. He has the best mages in the land, and if you listen to rumor, the king himself is the best mage on the continent."

"But sorcerers aren't druids," Knox replied.

Will shrugged. "Seems about the same to me."

Knox pursed his lips, reminding himself that Will was just a regular human, not magically inclined. Ashur was too, but he had worked closer with the two druids who lived in the camp known as Vidrland. Ashur had been around since almost the beginning.

He knew Knox had been raised by a third druid deeper in the forest. The three druids had long been the caretakers of the forest. They ensured the balance between life and death and claimed the forest's magic was because it was one of Gaiana's favorite places in the world.

Knox had wanted to be just like them when he was a boy, worshiping the goddess and protecting the forest. His magic was completely different though. While the Druids channeled Vitaron spells of protection that were as old as the forest itself, Knox had found a way to protect the druids without his presence. He'd magically branded them with runes which allowed them to move freely throughout the forest. Well, except for the normal assassin vines and killer plants. But he'd taught them how to avoid those dangers, just like he'd branded and taught the Robins that followed him.

"Do you want me to take a squad of Robins to stop the king?" Ashur asked.

Knox rubbed his bumpy head, careful not to move his hood. "The Robins have come a long way from our original purpose, if we're going to use guerrilla warfare tactics to stop him."

Will stroked the side of his horse. "It's what worked years ago, and it'll work again."

The Robins had started as a protection detail for any who wanted to travel the Lone Road through the forest.

Without the rune brand, the forest took care of those who tried to barrel inside without a path. Of course, providing safe passage from travelers was a relatively new endeavor for the Robins. Only in the past ten years since the start of the war had the Robins offered their services.

"Things have been steadily getting worse over the past two years, Knox," Ashur said softly.

Knox raked a hand over his temple and sighed. "So you've said, but their sorcerers have never been up to the task of finding a way through the forest. The Southern Road along the cliffs and the border of the forest has served them fine for the past decade. Why does he want a road now?"

Neither man answered, and Knox took a deep breath as he chopped another rope and coiled it tightly. He paused to look across the camp. People walked from wooden building to building, each with a purpose and goal. More and more civilians had joined them over the past few months. How was he supposed to support them all? Their numbers were almost to a hundred on any given day. And that didn't even include the Robins that infiltrated Busparia, collecting information and trading goods and secrets.

"Our sources haven't found the why yet," Ashur said. "But I have a theory."

Will looked around the edge of the Robin's camp. "The why doesn't matter right now. What matters is how to stop them. The forest and our spells are keeping the king's forces out for now, but what do we do if their sorcerers find a way through?"

Knox stroked his chin and looked up into the sky, barely visible between the green leaves of the trees swaying in the gentle breeze.

"Monitor the area without being seen. Do not let them

chop down more trees. Use magic or arrows, not close combat. I don't want anyone captured."

Will nodded, and Knox turned to Ashur. "What's your theory? Does it have something to do with the war front?"

Ashur straightened. "The Glathens finally reclaimed Auckwald from the Buspartans."

Knox's eyes widened, and his brows rose in surprise. "Interesting. So, the peace negotiations failed. Hm, are the Buspartans on the way home then?"

Ashur continued. "They are fleeing along the Southern Road to Busparia, and the Growlers are picking off the stragglers and wounded like always."

The Growlers and the cliffs made it a dangerous journey. There were choke points on the road that would collapse into the sea if they tried to crowd an entire army on it at once.

Knox pushed the thought away. The army wasn't his concern. He had taken an oath to safeguard the forest and its people. Nothing else concerned him.

Except, the war kept shifting how he could protect the forest and the people who called it home.

Ashur spat in the dirt and murmured. "About time those soldiers came home."

Knox had stayed out of politics until the king had chopped down trees in the forest. It was imperative that they maintain the balance of life and death in these woods. If they wiped out the forest, death would spread to the entire continent, according to Olive, and she would know.

Will grunted. "Agreed. Ten years is too long. We need to do something about the king, though."

The king was erratic. He had ruled for the past twenty years after his parents' deaths. But in the last decade, he'd banished those who offended him, executed those who broke his rules, and set fire to the houses who refused to pay taxes.

He had no concept of money or concern that he was bleeding the entire nation dry. The lavish parties with his closest confidants grew more frequent, causing the taxes to rise.

Knox frowned, his chest growing tight. "We need someone on the inside, an informant who can tell us what the king's next move is. I don't want to be surprised if he has some plan other than a road. Perhaps an insider can tell us the why."

Ashur nodded, "He's probably going to retaliate at the Glathens for reclaiming Auckwald. His pride will make him strike back."

Knox stroked his chin. "Hm, true. Either way, the forest needs to remain neutral and stay out of the bloody war."

A robin trilled above, and the summer sun filtered through the leaves, bringing peace to Knox's racing mind.

Will arched a brow. "You know I'm the best sneak here. I can infiltrate."

Knox sighed and rubbed the back of his neck as he straightened. "I know, but it's risky. I don't want to jeopardize you unless necessary. Start at the taverns and see what you can hear. If we can't glean any information from the drunken city guards, we'll see if we can bribe a noble or official."

Ashur shifted on his saddle. "You know Scarlet would be willing."

Knox glared. "She has to stay out of this. She decided years ago, and so did we."

He jerked his thumb. "Go on and get some decent rest. You've earned it. I'll be going to Olive's today, so Ashur, you'll handle camp?"

Ashur nodded, and both men touched the tip of their green hoods and rode into camp. Knox gathered the ropes and circled around the tents, wooden cabins, and tree houses as he patrolled, his mind swirling as he thought through every scenario.

Vidrland was originally a druid settlement that had fallen into disrepair. He'd spent a lot of time with the druids while he was growing up. They'd turned over the master warden job to him when the war had broken out, claiming to be too old to keep up.

Then Knox began bringing in the wounded and repairing the falling wooden cabins, building the structures by hand. The desperate and sick sought their aid for healing at the natural hot springs and had even started worshiping Gaiana at the druid circle.

He checked that the trees were nearly a solid wall to protect them, then strode into the heart of the Robin's base, the nest. He stopped by the lodge and checked in with their dwarven steward John, but all was well. He left the ropes by the door where people could grab them if they needed them. With all the construction, the ropes were in demand, especially for the tree houses. But he would leave that to the others. It was time to head to Olive's to seek her counsel.

It took a few hours, but Knox turned his horse down a well-worn path and whistled a seemingly innocent tune. He smiled as Olive's cottage came into view in a small clearing, one wall attached to a giant tree. He gestured, the air shimmering with Vitas magic as it interacted with the existing spell ahead.

The humans with magic could either go to high wizard

school or learn low magic by apprenticing with local witches and wizards, working for their limited education. Those who weren't inherently strong enough began using magic with the help of a magic item like a wand, dagger, stone, hairpin, or even a toy.

Knox had never needed a focus item, though, as he wasn't human. He'd only needed to point or wiggle his fingers. He rode through the protection spell he'd placed around the area long ago, then wiggled his fingers to close it behind him. The door opened at his whistle, but it wasn't Olive who greeted him. Scarlet stepped out with a smile.

Wearing leather riding pants and a green vest over her black silk shirt, Scarlet waited as Knox approached, her dark auburn hair piled high in a messy curly bun. Freckles dotted her nose, and her green eyes matched her vest and cloak. His sister had ignored the style of most eligible women in the nation for as long as he'd known her, rejecting dresses for pants. She'd always marched to her own beat and not caring what anyone said. He admired that about her, so free and open about who she was.

He pulled to a stop and dismounted Ryder, leaving the reins dangling as he bounded up the stone path to the door.

"Red, you're back!" He swept her up in a hug and spun her around, making her laugh.

She pounded on his back playfully. "Put me down, you big brute. I'm too old for that nonsense, along with that dumb nickname."

He released her, grinning. "Never."

She rolled her eyes, and he followed her into the cottage where he grew up. It was the only home he'd known but trying to settle in Vidrland and build it up the past few years had left him restless. He'd long ago stopped thinking of the druid's cottage as home.

Olive bustled around the kitchen, the familiar scents of herbs and spices mingling with the stew on the stove. She was cooking dinner or making some potion, or both.

She turned and smiled over her shoulder. Red hair streaked with gray, she had a few crow's feet at the corners of her eyes, but that was mostly where the differences lay. Otherwise, she could've been Scarlet's sister instead of her grandmother.

"There you are. Just in time for lunch, too," Olive said, turning back to the stove. Knox kicked off the mud on the front stoop and ducked his head as he entered.

"I would've been here yesterday, except the Growlers were roaming, and I needed to go to Vidrland first."

He and Scarlet sat at the small table, and she pushed a cup of water to him. He drank, the coolness was exactly what he needed after the hot ride.

"I saw their tracks too," Scarlet said, frowning at Olive's back. Their eyes met, and an unspoken worry was shared. If the wolves decided to, Olive would have no defense against them. Her potions would only last so long, and her wild shape form was no match for them.

The forest acknowledged the Growlers' inherent magic, so they'd easily get through Knox's protection spells. He'd learned all the druid's spells early on, also learning both high and low magic spells they'd collected over the generations.

Glathen had several shifter communities, including the wolf-like Growlers, but their magic and culture wasn't well known. It was part of the reason for the war. Most Buspartans feared the shifters because of the secrecy and insular nature of their packs. It was another reason most people avoided the Feral Forest. No one wanted to be caught by the Growlers, who were fiercely territorial.

It hadn't happened in his thirty years living in the forest, but the last attack had killed Scarlet's mother.

The Growlers normally stayed in their own territory, but Knox had to protect her. Half of that job was always being prepared.

The old druid bustled past them, grabbing a vial from a shelf and going back to the stove. "Psh, nothing to worry about, loves. They're just hot and cranky. You know it's mating season for them. If we stay out of the way of all those hormones, we'll all be alright. Now, how were the lads up north, Knox?"

Knox told of his visit to the dwarves' stronghold and the latest magical technology they'd shared with him. Scarlet's eyes glittered with excitement.

The topic shifted to politics and the ongoing war, and Knox shared what he'd learned so far.

Scarlet shrugged. "There are rumors of the king finding a new mistress too. Perhaps she will help calm him down from the blow of losing Auckwald and the troops running home with their tails between their legs. I heard that he lit the barracks on fire when he heard of the defeat."

Scarlet knew he traded with Vidrland but not that he'd become the unquestioned leader of the Robins. To everyone, including Scarlet and Olive, he was just a lonely lumberjack who lived in Vidrland and went to the city of Demerel every few months for supplies. No one knew Vidrland was the Robin's nest.

Still, he had to warn Olive. "Between the king's temper, mating season, and the full moon coming up? Olive, maybe you can come stay in Vidrland for a few days?"

Olive scowled as she sat a bowl of soup in front of him. "No, this is my home, and I'm not leaving."

Scarlet frowned, picking at her nails with a thin-bladed

dagger. "Grandma, a few days won't hurt. Consider it a vacation. Think of all the friends you can visit. Don't you want to see River and Oakley?"

The three druids now only got together once per year on the pilgrimage to the southern ruins. He wasn't sure how much they'd told Olive about the Robins' work, but Knox certainly didn't discuss any of it with her.

Olive set a bowl of steaming soup in front of Scarlet and then sat. "Perhaps, I'll think about it. Now, why don't you tell me why you're here?"

Scarlet shifted in her chair, her eyes downcast as she said, "What makes you think it's anything other than just a well-deserved break?"

Olive stared at her, and Scarlet blushed, then admitted, "The princess of Busparia might be traveling the Lone Road."

Knox's brows rose. His people hadn't mentioned the princess at all. "Why?"

Scarlet didn't question his demanding tone, thank the gods.

"After the peace negotiations fell through, she went to tend to the wounded and boost morale at Auckwald. She left, and not even a week later, Auckwald fell to the Glathens. The army is on the move back to Busparia, but the princess is not on the Southern Road. She followed the western edge of the forest to the Glathen's village."

Knox rubbed his chin, his mind racing. "Interesting."

Scarlet nodded. "The king sent me into the forest to see if she's on the Lone Road."

Knox nodded. "If she is, it'll be dark in a few hours. She won't make it in the dark."

Scarlet eyed him. "I was hoping you'd ride with me to find her?"

He raked a hand over the side of his head and sighed. She knew he could protect them all from the forest's magic.

He nodded and sat back in his seat, pushing his now-empty bowl away. "Whenever you're ready."

Soon, they were back in the saddle, riding swiftly on the faint path. He reactivated the spell behind him to protect Olive's circle.

The forest closed around them, the underbrush reaching for them. He waved a hand, and the vines and bushes went back, now not even touching their horses.

Scarlet asked, "How's the lumber and pelts business?"

Knox nodded, telling her about the last hunting trip.

His conscience nagged at him to bring Scarlet into the Robins' work. The fact remained that it would only put her in danger.

She hadn't visited Vidrland in ten years, not since he and the druids had grown it into a small village. Not since she'd become a Hunter at the start of the war. Mercenaries paid pretty well, thanks to the Hunter's Guild.

That was before the wounded and deserters and draft dodgers had begun to trickle into the forest seeking his protection.

Scarlet visited Olive once or twice a year but didn't go all the way north.

He couldn't share their plans with her, not when she worked for the king who kept threatening the forest.

Not that he didn't trust her. He absolutely did. She was the only sister he'd ever had. Many just assumed that because they both had the same sun-weathered complexion with a shit load of freckles, they were true brother and sister, but they were wrong.

No, only three people knew he'd been a giant egg that sat on Olive's mantle for her entire life until he'd hatched thirty years ago. He'd learned so much from Scarlet's ranger father. He'd died in the war, but Knox felt he owed the man. He would protect Scarlet.

And the less she knew of the Robin's work, the safer she'd be.

Chapter Two

Eirwyn lay on the top of the carriage with her hands behind her head. "That one looks like a butter churn. Do you see it?"

"No, I don't. I told you I'm not playing this time, and if you don't get back in this carriage this instant, I'm going to–"

Eirwyn snorted. "Do what? Tell Gastone? I thought we were beyond this, Helga. You promised."

Helga banged on the roof. "And so did you, but you forgot, didn't you? Again. So I'll bloody tell him if I think I should."

Eirwyn laughed. "We've been in the forest for hours, and nothing has happened. We paid the toll for safe passage, so we'll be fine. Did you really expect me to stay cooped up in that bloody carriage the entire drive?"

"Don't say bloody. You're a princess."

Eirwyn laughed again, weaving shadows around her hands and playing with them. With one hand, she focused a condensed ball of air, refracting the sunlight, and formed a

14

tiny point of light on her palm. It bounced off her palm and formed a projection of a tiny knight on her lap. She held out the other hand, and created a shadowy dancing princess, spinning circles around the knight with soft prismatic colors swirling.

"Helga, dear, you're the one who says bloody way more than I, or haven't you noticed? Should I tell Gastone where I learned to curse?"

Her nanny turned traveling companion and maid banged on the roof of the carriage before leaning her head back out the window. "I'll just point out all your tavern visits and tell him you picked it up there. Now get back in here. It's not safe out there. Haven't you heard the stories?"

Eirwyn nodded absently, her mind flitting to the stories of the Feral Forest. She slowly stood, widening her stance on the roof and spreading her hands wide. She threw her head back and closed her eyes, listening to the birds chattering and feeling her magic flare.

The wind swirled around her, and she smiled. It was almost like she was flying. This was something she did all the time at the top of the castle, imagining herself flying with the goddess Eirasil, whom they had named her after. Enjoying the wind through her hair, the rush of excitement from having nothing beneath her, the fear of falling.

The way the carriage moved... it added a whole new, more exciting layer to her daydream.

She opened her eyes, her head still back so she could see the faint light filtering through the trees. There was something about the forest that called to her on a primal level.

The carriage hit a rock, and she stumbled, sitting hard on one of their trunks strapped to the back half of the roof. She sighed and leaned back on her hands, her bodice stretching tight over her breasts.

Still, her mind wandered as she stared through the trees to the sky above. Stories of old told of humans flying dragons and even turning into dragons. Helga had tried to dissuade her from fantastical children's books, but it was one of her favorite obsessions.

Stories were so much better than reality. Realistic facts were dry and boring. And sometimes sad. One fact stood out among the others, and she asked, "Do you think my parents died around here?"

Helga's banging quieted, then she popped her head out once more. Her eyes were serious, and a frown marred her forehead. "If you come inside, I promise to tell you when we get to the site of the accident."

Eirwyn sighed and looked through the treetops once more, and then she stood and waved a hand imperiously. "Well, open the door then."

Helga harped on her even as she obeyed. "Don't you dare swing in here like a heathen. You're a princess, and it's high time you started acting like one. You're twenty, for gods' sake."

Eirwyn swung a leg over the railing and used the window as a ladder to get to the door. Helga was still ranting when Eirwyn landed inside, closing the door behind her.

The driver had insisted on no stops along the way. They went straight through, steady and sure. It was the only way she'd gotten him and the guards to agree to take this route. That and triple the normal pay.

The guards were on high alert. The Glathen royal escort had left them in a small village on the edge of the forest next to the Lone Road. They'd stopped for a few days to stock provisions, pouring over maps and planning for the dash through the forest, meeting with experts and hiring more guards.

Not that they were racing per se. That would've been fun, though, to sit on top of the carriage and let the wind rush over her face.

"Eirwyn?" Helga asked, pulling her back into the moment.

Eirwyn blinked and sat back on the well-cushioned bench, immediately picking up her sketchbook. She smoothed her features and looked up at Helga serenely. "Alright, I'm ready. You can continue berating me."

Helga rolled her eyes and picked up her long-forgotten embroidery. "You're riding the carriage like it was a jaunt through the countryside. You have to be more careful, Eirwyn. It's time to grow up now that you're of marriage-able age."

Eirwyn's parents had died in this god-forsaken forest. It's full of untold monsters and strange magic, yet Helga was right. She had just been daydreaming and playing around. Guilt stabbed her, twisting her stomach.

Eirwyn sighed and sketched the treetops and leaves, the light filtering through. The way the shadows danced between the light had always fascinated her, since the Nekrosan half of her magic was tied to it. Her drakin bloodline came from a black dragon, unlike her brother who inherited his power from some type of red dragon. She'd heard stories that the colors didn't matter to dragons and that's why they were different, but almost everyone in her family had traits of red dragons, while Eirwyn could barely create a spark. But wind and shadows... those were as innate to her as breathing.

She was almost finished with the picture when a shout

rang outside the carriage. Screams followed, and the carriage bounced.

Helga shrieked, and Eirwyn's heart thudded too fast. Dread threatened to drown her. Helga had been right. This wasn't safe.

But it was too late now. She threw her notebook into the corner of her seat and pulled back the curtain. She was about to stick her head out of the window when Helga grabbed her arm and jerked back.

"No, you don't, your highness. You'll stay right here, safe where you belong."

Eirwyn wrung her hands, light and shadows swirling around her in the dimmer light of the carriage as she prayed to the gods for safety for their guards. She reached out with her senses to see what the birds thought. Perhaps they could tell her what was going on outside.

She gasped, feeling their alarm as the vines jerked riders off their horses. The carriage jerked as the driver yelled. Panic raced through her as she worried for the soldiers outside.

They began to barrel along the road, screams and cries flitting from the left and behind them. The carriage swerved, and Eirwyn's heart raced with adrenaline. She gripped the window's edge as she slid over the seat and slammed into the other side.

The road became much bumpier. Eirwyn's other hand went to the roof, trying to protect her head as she bounced. If she could see where they were going and what they were doing, perhaps she could use her magic to help. But she was at the mercy of the forest now.

She gritted her teeth and took a deep breath, praying to the gods for safe passage through the forest as Helga cried and bounced on her seat.

Knox neared the section of the forest where the road almost met the river. They had left the game trail some time ago. The Lone Road was wider, so he and Scarlet rode side by side toward Glathen, following the winding path.

Different areas of the road were more dangerous than others, but not many people knew that. They passed the loudest part near the rushing river, and he sat up straighter as they neared one of the more perilous sections of the drive.

Screams drowned out the peaceful sounds of nature. He kicked his heels, and his horse shot forward.

He rounded a bend and saw body parts of men and horses lining the ditches in a trail of bloody gore and guts. Vines wrapped around the bigger pieces as they pulled the dripping twisted torsos and severed heads into the dark underbrush.

He let the forest take them. There was no helping the guards now, and he felt no remorse about it. The princess should've requested safe passage from the Robins in the village at the end of the Lone Road and paid the toll first. The guards' blood was on her head.

He inspected the road and listened for sounds of struggle. He pointed. "Carriage tracks."

Scarlet followed him as he waved his hand, the forest parting before them. He followed the tracks and trail of body parts to an overturned carriage. The front wheel had crashed into a tree, shattering into pieces.

The forest was already dragging the carcasses of two horses away. The other two screamed, their cries piercing the air as the vines wrapped around their stomachs and squeezed them to death, kicking the entire time. Their neighing grew fainter as vines wrapped around their heads.

A stab of guilt did hit him at their loss. He couldn't free the people in the carriage in time and the horses too. Knox waved a hand, and the vines and underbrush that pulled the carriage into the ground receded to create a grassy clearing.

He sighed and approached the carriage. "Hello?"

He leaned over to see into the window, coldly detached and not worried about what bloody sight might be inside. He'd seen enough of these accidents over the years that he'd become somewhat desensitized to it.

But this one took his breath away. He blinked and frowned, surprised for the first time in years. A plump woman leaned against one seat but appeared unharmed and passed out.

It was the smaller, petite woman that drew his attention, though. Her black hair was long, several braids at her temples pulled back and the rest hanging down past her shoulders.

Her red, black, and white dress hugged her curves, and the fabric screamed high-quality noble. But that wasn't what had him captivated. He had a direct line of sight down her ample cleavage. He blinked, forgetting to breathe as he stared at this vision of womanhood.

He shook his head and stepped back, blinking at the too bright light filtering through the trees. He'd been around women in town and in Vidrland. What was he doing, staring down her dress like a degenerate?

He took a deep breath to control his racing heart. It was safer to stay arm's length from women, and this one was no different. He glanced back inside as the beautiful woman checked on her companion. Interesting, he hadn't thought the princess would be selfless enough to care for her maid, but here she was, checking for injuries instead of being hysterical herself.

There was something about this woman that made him want to break his rule to stay away. He wanted to touch her, kiss her, hold her, and comfort her. He'd never had this visceral reaction to a woman before. He took a deep breath and tried to open the carriage door, but it was stuck.

The princess was panting, her eyes wild as she knelt on the side of the carriage and checked on the other woman. "Helga? Helga, wake up."

Her voice was a melody that he could spend hours listening to.

Scarlet broke the trance from behind. "Well? What are the injuries? No sign of Growlers."

He shook his head, but at the words, the black-haired woman looked up. Her gray-blue eyes widened, captivating him like she held all the answers in the universe inside her head. Light wrapped around her like a halo.

Her shoulders slumped in relief. Her rosy red lips sighed, pouty and lush. She looked at him with complete trust and hope, and it slammed into him. A pressing need that had been building for years crashed through him, threatening his carefully curated control. The need to protect, to love. *Mate*.

She reached up a hand. "Oh thank the gods. Will you help me?" Her sad eyes pulled him in.

Scarlet shouted behind him, and he looked back. Trees had shot up around him and the carriage, blocking Scarlet out like a wall. His tail was now lifted almost as high as his head, ready to strike, the barbs now visible with venom dripping from the end.

He whipped the cloak around and breathed deeply to control his emotions and body. He wanted to do more than help the princess. A clawing ache at his chest made him wa*nt* to protect her, throw her over his shoulder, and hide her from everyone else.

Curling his tail up around his shoulders, he safely hid it under his calf-length cloak, looked around at the tree circle, and waved a hand. The trees reversed back into the ground, turning back into acorns.

He'd lost control for the first time in years. Scarlet's brows rose as she pressed her horse closer to him, brows raised in surprise.

She asked softly, "What does *that* mean?"

He glared at her. "Nothing. It means nothing."

A scratching sound made him look back down, and the dark-haired beauty's head popped out of the window. She looked around and then waved at Scarlet.

"Oh, there's two of you, wonderful. My maid is injured. Will you help us?"

Her voice was lilting, like the water running through the creek, tumbling over the rocks. The worry in her voice drove him to action.

He grunted and said, "Watch out. I'm going to right the carriage."

She frowned, and her head disappeared as she replied. "How are you going to do that? It's heavy, and— oh!"

He straightened the carriage, and it settled upright on two wheels, leaning heavily on the broken axles but no longer on its side. Then he opened the door.

She was thrown against the side of the carriage now, then quickly scrambled to her feet, grabbing two bags. The glimpse of red stockings in her black boots blindsided him, and it made his blood boil for her. He froze in the doorway, trying to maintain his thin level of control.

She collected scattered pencils, notebooks, knitting, and

books into the bags. Her complete unconcern as she tidied up their things showed a level of trust that he wanted to honor. Or perhaps she was a nervous cleaner, too jittery to sit still.

He wanted to swoop her into his arms and carry her deep into the forest where no one else could find them. Shit, he couldn't. This was the *princess*. Instead, he stepped back, offering her a hand out the door.

Her soft fingers slid into his, and it was like lightning danced up his arm. He stiffened and had to consciously think to keep his tail down. Then he backed away as she jumped onto the ground. She shook out her dress and took a deep breath. Squaring her shoulders, she looked up at him.

"Thank you, sir. Much obliged. My maid, Helga–can you help her too? I'm afraid she'll be a little harder to get out of the carriage. But then again, it's probably a good thing she's passed out. The poor woman wouldn't be able to handle being in the middle of the Feral Forest with who knows what beasts. Are we safe now? Or is the danger still present?"

I'm the danger, wench.

He blinked, gripping his hands behind him to avoid reaching for her and to hold down his tail. What was wrong with him? He'd never reacted like this before, even when the hormones had threatened to drown him during puberty, and he'd been getting a handle on his abilities without accidentally killing anyone.

Scarlet saved him from answering as she swung off her horse and approached the woman. She bowed low, hand on hip as she said, "Princess, you're safe with us. We'll protect you from the forest's magic and the beasts that haunt it."

But who will save the beast from her?

He turned his back on the two as he looked back into the door of the carriage. Her maid was still unconscious, and he had to solve the problem of getting her out. It would be difficult to get her out at that angle.

He walked around the carriage, assessing the situation. He didn't think he'd be able to make two wheels and all the little pieces to fit them together to make the carriage work. When he came back to the door, he glanced at Scarlet and the princess.

The princess' arms waved animatedly as she talked. Scarlet was smiling, too, which gave him some relief. At least it wasn't just him who felt this excitement and joy around the princess.

Except it was more intense than any emotion he'd ever had before, even when he'd first met her as a baby. It was like he'd been punched in the gut and dragged through a swamp pit.

He reached for the door, ripping it off its hinges. Then he grabbed the frame and pulled. His muscles strained, but after a few seconds, it ripped, too. He tossed it aside, the vines already reaching for the door.

They grabbed for the small wall and dropped the door like a pack of dogs with a new toy. He reached out, making some safer vines grow closer. They wrapped around the door, lengthening it and creating a loop to form connected reins.

He reached inside and pulled the maid out, cradling her in his arms and turning to the other two women.

"Red, get on your horse and take the maid on the litter. I'll take the princess. We'll stop at Olive's for the night, then continue through in the morning."

The princess turned to eye him. "Red? She said her name is Scarlet."

"My brother has jokes. Ignore him, princess."

Eirwyn glanced between them, then pointed to Scarlet. "Why can't I ride with her? She's fun."

Scarlet walked steadily to her mount, her grin frustrating him into another scowl. He laid the maid gently on the litter, then pulled the reins to Scarlet, who looped the vine end around the pommel.

"Because her horse can handle the added weight of the maid. My horse is strong, but this is easier and more balanced."

She stopped, straightening. "Oh, that makes sense. You're not exactly a small man. Your poor horse must be exhausted after carrying you around."

She walked over to his horse, reaching up a dainty hand and petting Ryder's nozzle. He shook his head, then mounted with ease.

He reached out a hand. "He's used to it. Are you ready to go?"

Chapter Three

Eirwyn looked up at the giant man on the giant horse and blinked as the late summer sun filtered through the leaves. They hit his head to form a halo of light around him, but with the way his hood was pulled up, she could barely see his faintly glowing green eyes and the angular features.

His big frame caused his green shirt to bulge, the vee with the leather drawstring revealing a tuft of brown hair. Her fingers itched to touch him, and she waved her hand in a circular motion.

A small gust of wind pushed his cloak back, and she eyed the rest of him as he grabbed at his hood with the other hand, holding it in place. Gods, his thighs were as thick as tree trunks. The only drawback of this man was how dirty his boots and pants were. She wasn't a fan of dirt.

The magic faded as she wavered on her feet. She must be more exhausted from the carriage accident than she'd thought. She just hoped she hadn't used too much magic. It was a good sign that she could still stand and talk, though, so she'd probably be alright.

When the carriage had hit the tree, she'd used her Naturos wind magic to form a type of bubble around them until they stopped moving. Her heart had raced but not really with fear.

It had raced with excitement and magic flowing through her veins. She'd never formed a physical bubble before. All her projections were always just made of wind and shadow, as firm to the touch as waving your hand through the air, but this was tangible, thick, like being cocooned in feathers.

If only her fussy old magic teachers could see her now. She was soaking up every moment of this adventure and was slightly glad it wasn't over yet.

But now her heart raced with something more. She reached for his hand, then pulled back as she remembered.

"Oh, our bags. Let me put these with Helga. That way, your poor horse won't be overburdened even more."

She almost jogged over to Helga but stumbled as she reached her. She tucked the two shoulder bags around her to form a type of barrier to keep her from rolling off the litter. Then she turned back to the man.

He looked so mysterious in his dark green cloak with the hood pulled up. He stared at her with such intensity it made the hairs on the back of her neck stand up.

She was used to people staring at her. She was the princess, and her brother often paraded her out at court and at balls. And even when she went to the tavern to sneak out for a fun time, she was used to all eyes on her as she told shadow stories and entertained the people.

But the way he looked at her made her feel alive with desire on a level she'd never experienced before. And she was plenty experienced.

Hells, she'd even tried to seduce the prince of Glathen in order to negotiate the treaty. Ultimately, the Chancellor that had gone with them had shot down any chance of the treaty going into effect.

"Princess?" The stranger asked with his deep voice that felt like a caress on her skin. "I think you should ride in front so I can more easily protect you from the forest."

She blinked and realized she'd been caught staring at him, daydreaming yet again. She smiled and blushed, then she took his hand. A jolt of lightning shot up her arm, making her gasp. His eyebrows rose in surprise. Did he feel it, too?

Her hair began to stand on end, and she struggled to control her magic even as she stepped into the stirrup and climbed in front of him.

She sat side-saddle and wiggled to hook her knee around the pommel. She was the princess, for drake's sake. She needed to stop being a klutz, control her magic, and act like the princess she was.

Ugh, she was making such a bad first impression with this guy. She held herself stiffly as he turned the horse to follow Scarlet through the forest.

"This is awkward, isn't it? I bet you don't rescue a lot of princesses in the forest like this."

His voice brushed the hair near her ear as he said, "No, you're the first. But you can ride astride if it'll make you more comfortable."

She grinned and shifted, swinging her leg over the horse and exposing her calves. "Wonderful. I love riding astride!"

He made a strangled noise, then he cleared it. "You've ridden astride before?"

She nodded, smoothing down her skirts and trying to brush off the dirt. "When I race my horse. Can't do that side-saddle, of course."

"You race your horse?"

She nodded and shifted on the saddle, feeling his knife digging into her rear. "Yes, she's really fast and light-footed, not like this guy. He's a brute. What's his name?"

"Ryder."

"That's a good name. Nice to meet you, Ryder," Eirwyn leaned over and petted the mane of the brown horse. Then she frowned and turned back to face him, their noses barely an inch away as she stared up at him.

"And what's your name?" Damn, was that really her voice so soft and breathless? He was going to think she was a ninny, flirting like that.

His eyes widened, and he jerked away from her, turning his head and staring at her from the side of his eyes. "Don't get too close. Turn around."

Her jaw dropped at the command, and her back stiffened. She pointed a finger at him, which was awkward with how she was half-turned in the saddle to better see his features up close.

He had a strong, straight nose that was covered in freckles. She blinked, surprised by all the freckles. Even his forehead had freckles. His chin was covered in a five o'clock shadow of brown hair.

Those green eyes, though... they were more beautiful than emeralds. There was something about them that drew her in, and she tried to lean closer.

Then he eased his hold on the reins, grabbed her hips, and scowled as he leaned further away from her.

"By the gods, stop wiggling, Princess."

Her eyes widened as she realized. "Light, that's not your knife, is it?"

His lips thinned as he glared at her. "No, it's not, and if you'd stop wiggling, I'd appreciate it."

She wiggled more, her grin growing. "But this feels so

nice. My, that's quite a large *knife* you have, isn't it. Does it cut well?"

He blinked at her, frowning. She tilted her head and waited. Any other man would've been flirting right back at her, but not this guy. Why not? He obviously liked the feel of her ass riding against his dick.

He glared at her as Scarlet looked over her shoulder and laughed.

"He wouldn't know," Scarlet said with a grin.

Eirwyn's brows rose, turning to face Scarlet. "Wait, what does that mean?"

The man's growl behind her had her on full-alert as she stiffened in front of him. Scarlet just shrugged and turned back to leading them down the road.

"I still don't know your name," she pointed out, staring straight ahead as they rode. Eirwyn watched Helga to make sure she didn't fall off.

"Knox, the lumberjack and warden of the forest." His breath tickled the back of her ear again, sending a shiver down her body.

"Knox," she whispered, leaning back against him a little. He gathered the reins, cocooning her in between his big arms.

She could feel the heat of him, but he was a standoffish man whom she was determined to become friends with. She was friends with everyone. It was anathema to think she couldn't win him over.

He wasn't her brother, after all.

She cleared her throat, determined to get to know him. "Knox, it's nice to meet you. You can call me Eirwyn."

"Princess is fine with me," he said.

She shook her head. "That won't do. When you take me

into town, I will hail your name as the greatest guide and protector the forest has ever seen."

"You could've gone back to town with your guards and driver and carriage if you'd paid the toll to the Robins like the Lone Road demands."

She frowned and stiffened, leaning forward and trying to put distance between the comforting warmth of his embrace.

"I did pay the Robins. There were three of them at the tavern in the little village just outside the forest, the one in Glathen. I paid them well for protection. They said we wouldn't see them, but they'd be watching and guarding just the same."

He snorted, careful to turn his head away from her as he did so. "You were swindled, princess."

She frowned and looked up at the trees as her mind began to grow fuzzy. "Perhaps you're right. But it stands to reason there would be Robins in that village watching the entrance of the road."

He didn't respond, and her mind wandered to the way he made her feel. She felt her skin tingle in anticipation. She loved this stage. The flirting, the build-up, the accidental caresses.

With him, it felt different, though. Like she was on the precipice of the castle, about to jump off the edge and attempt to finally fly.

She was hot, frustrated, and her eyelids began to droop as they turned off the Lone Road.

She stiffened, watching and waiting for the forest to attack. But within a few yards of the road, she saw they were on a faint path. The steady pace of the horse lulled her into an exhausted sleep, and she sank against him.

When she awoke, dusk was falling around them. Her

head was groggy as they came into a clearing. There was a small cottage at the base of a giant tree with a barn peeking behind it.

No one came to greet them, but Knox walked the horse to the front door. He jumped off the horse, his hands never leaving her. Even with his hands, she still swayed in the saddle.

She pulled her head up and looked around before sliding off the horse. Her mind knew she was going to hit the ground and get dirty, but she couldn't stop herself. She felt like she was floating but being pressed down at the same time.

It was almost like being drunk. Gods, he must think she was a weakling. No wonder he wanted nothing to do with her.

Her body had entered the Edge. If she wasn't careful, she'd fall into the Beyond and never wake. That was what happened when someone used too much magic.

Before she hit the ground, Knox's arms swooped her up. He cradled her to his chest, and her head flopped back on his arm to look up at him.

The weight of embarrassment pressed on her chest. Only an untrained mage or a child entered the Edge. It'd been years since she'd been here. Why now? Why in front of him?

Oh yeah, because they'd almost been killed in a carriage accident and eaten by the forest.

"Come on, let's get you inside," Knox said, his deep voice almost as lulling as the horse. He strode to the front door of the cottage.

Eirwyn nuzzled into his cloak, the smell of morning dew hanging to him like a promise of adventure.

"I just need to sleep it off. I'll be fine in the morning," she said with a yawn.

Scarlet pushed open the front door, and Knox dipped his head and turned sideways to carry her inside. He looked around, a frown line between his eyes.

The light from candles and a fire finally illuminated more of his face, and she relaxed even more in his arms. She could stare up at him for hours if only her heavy eyelids would cooperate.

"Olive? Do you have a tonic? She's entered the Edge."

A bustling sound came from her right, but she didn't want to turn her head away from him. He held her like a child tucked to his chest as he walked to the fire and sat in an oversized chair, not letting her go.

She snuggled into him as he pulled his arm out from under her legs. "Sleep now. Need to recharge," she slurred with another yawn as she closed her eyes.

She could feel it. The Beyond called to her. She knew it was coming. The fast heartbeat. The shaking and dizziness. The clawing hunger that gnawed on her from the inside out.

"Shit," Knox said. "Olive?"

"Here, here," a breathless voice came closer as Eirwyn began to float away, her mind detaching as her body went limp. As if watching from above, she saw Knox's hand shake as he took the mug from the old woman.

A rustling sounded and she wanted to sink into the numbness of the Beyond as Knox lifted her body up slightly. He brought a warm mug to her lips and pried them open, pouring the foul liquid inside. She began to choke, and her spirit sank back toward her body. He closed her chin, holding her mouth until she swallowed.

Then she gasped, her eyes going wide as she jerked back to herself. As she exhaled, he poured more in, starting the process all over again. She gripped his shirt, her eyes flying open as the liquid burned her throat and settled in her stomach.

Warmth spread like a fireball, and her eyes connected with his, the frown marring his forehead still. His eyes searched hers as if looking for something, but her body was tense as she gripped his shirt. She whimpered at the burn.

She hated this. It brought back dark memories of her childhood, of all the tonics and potions she'd tried to get stronger. Her brother had been so disgusted with her sickly nature. He still was, if she were honest.

Tears stung her eyes, and her hands shook where they grasped his shirt.

Someone took the mug, and he smoothed the hair away from her face. "There, there. It's alright. It's almost over now."

His words were like a balm to her soul, and she slowly relaxed, going limp in his arms as her eyes rolled back in her head. This time, it was just sleep that claimed her.

Chapter Four

Knox looked down at Eirwyn, unable to stop touching her. "Is she going to be alright?" He didn't look up to ask. He couldn't stop staring at her, either.

She had this ethereal beauty that was the exact opposite of him. She had clean, pristine, smooth skin that was nothing like his own.

Tiny black braids extended from both temples to the back of her head like a crown. It was wild and tangled from her ordeal in the forest, though, and nothing like what he'd expect a princess' hair to look like.

She was a petite little thing, too. He could easily wrap his hands around her waist and pick her up. But the way her silk dress hugged the curves of her breasts... he somehow knew they would fill his big hands. The idea of throwing her over his shoulder and taking her into the forest to ravish her was more than intriguing.

The light from the fire and candles illuminated her pale face, giving her an ethereal satin glow. Her skin was flawless, and he marveled at the lack of freckles or sun spots. She had an elegant, swan-like throat. High cheekbones tinged with just a hint of peach. And those lips.

They drew his gaze. Tinged red, he wanted to taste her. He swallowed hard, trying to rein in his lust once more. It seemed to be a near-constant battle since he'd met her, and here she was passed out on his lap, and he could only think about ravishing her.

He was no better than the hooligans back at Vidrland.

"She'll be alright now. See her pulse? Steady and strong. Is this the princess?"

Olive asked as she took the mug back to the kitchen. Scarlet walked into the cottage and came straight to Eirwyn's side with a frown.

"Well, will she live, or will I be on the run from the king for the next century?"

Knox sighed in relief as he looked back down at her. "She should be fine. Let me take her upstairs, and then I'll go check on the maid."

Scarlet nodded, turning to the stairs as he lumbered carefully to his feet.

"That's a good idea. She's still out cold, but I have her and the horses safely tucked in the barn."

"There's another one? Light, child, and you left her in the barn?" Olive asked, wiping her hands off on her apron as she strode to the door.

Scarlet snorted and walked to the stairs. "Well, come on then. She can use my room. Let me just move my bag to Grandma's."

Knox followed Scarlet. She weighed less than he thought, and he had no trouble taking her up the stairs.

He strode to the right and laid her on the long bed in the center of the room. He brushed the hair back from her face and started to pull the blanket up over her.

Then he frowned and unlaced her boots, setting each one neatly at the foot of the bed. His hands slid over her tiny feet, and he took a deep breath at the feel of the red silk in his rough hands.

"Brother, we have got to get you laid," Scarlet said from the door.

He jerked back, pulling the blanket over her with a snap of fabric.

Scarlet playing with her dagger in one hand, her brow raised as she said, "Don't you think it's time?"

He sighed, turning to stare down at the gorgeous princess. She looked so innocent in her sleep.

"I've never felt the urge before. You know that."

He'd gone into the taverns outside the forest a few times. He'd even gone to a brothel twice, but none of the ladies or men had given him even an urge.

Not until the princess had looked up at him with that calm, happy smile in the midst of chaos. Not since she'd sat on his dick in the saddle and asked him how well he used his knife.

His lips twitched. She was feisty and a breath of fresh air. He'd expected the princess to be stuck up and arrogant.

But she was more of a go-with-the-flow kind of girl. It seemed like nothing bothered her. Not the carriage ride, not the threat of death from the forest.

She was a puzzle to unravel, and he loved puzzles.

Scarlet cleared her throat. "But you feel the urge with her? Is that why your tail popped up and you formed a wall of trees around the two of you?"

He rubbed a hand down his face then both hands over the scales behind his temples. He scratched them, the motion bringing some relief. The movement dislodged his hood, and he raked a hand over his pointed, scaly horns, smoothing down the single thick brown braid, hair only growing straight back from his temples and down the back of his head.

Scarlet used to make fun of him for having a mane like a horse. Between that and the scales and horns, he always wore his hood anywhere he went. He wasn't even sure how many of the Robins had ever seen his uncovered head.

He glanced down at the beautiful princess as she slept peacefully. There was no way someone as beautiful as her would go for someone as hideous as him. They weren't even sure what species he was, for drake's sake.

He shook his head slowly and sighed. "Fat load of good it does me."

He turned and strode back down the stairs, Scarlet's stare weighed on his shoulders as she followed him.

"I think you should woo her. Everyone knows she's promiscuous, much to the king's horror. You might have a chance to get laid after all."

Olive's head popped around the edge of the kitchen as they reached the bottom of the stairs, her eyebrows raised. "What's this?"

Knox took a deep breath and closed his eyes as a wave of frustration made him scratch at the scales on his head again.

"It's nothing," he said, striding to the hearth and glancing around. He quickly found the bowls on the sideboard and scooped up a generous portion from the pot over the fire.

He sank into the overstuffed chair again, hoping to smell her scent once more. It was like jasmine and honeysuckle and something else.

"It's not nothing," Scarlet said, grabbing her own bowl and following Olive.

"Well, out with it then," Olive said, spooning her stew into her bowl.

He growled and began to eat. Maybe if he ignored her, she'd forget about it.

Scarlet filled her own bowl as Olive sat in her chair directly in front of the fire. "Knox wants to fuck the princess," Scarlet said bluntly.

Olive's brows rose, but it was another gasp from down the hall that drew his gaze. The princess's maid stood at the door to the washroom, her hand clutching her neck as she stared in horror at Knox's head.

His fingers itched to pull his hood up, but he lifted his head instead, not looking away.

The maid blinked and frowned, storming toward him even as she shook in fear. "You will do no such thing," she said, waving her finger at him before dancing behind the other two women's chairs.

Olive waved to the sideboard. "Helga, there are bowls just there if you're hungry. Meet my godson, Knox, and my granddaughter, Scarlet. They're the ones who brought you both safely through the forest."

Helga eyed him and widened her feet. "You will not lay even a finger on the princess, do you hear? The king would kill me if anything happened to her."

Knox nodded slowly and turned his eyes back to the food, his cheeks burning in shame at being caught with his hood down. Her words were only slightly annoying compared to that.

He knew she spoke the truth. Only a few weeks ago, the king had found out Eirwyn had been visiting the tavern in Demerel and had tried to burn it down. The tavern owner had put the fire out, but it wasn't the first time he'd tried to burn something down in his anger.

Scarlet snorted. "If Knox were going to fuck her, he already would've. So there's nothing to worry about. He's incredibly disciplined. It's rather annoying actually."

Helga wavered, but Olive eyed him curiously.

"You—you will leave her alone?" Helga asked.

Knox nodded again, sipping the bottom of his bowl. When he put it down, he made a show of wiping his mouth with his sleeve like a peasant. Sure enough, the maid winced at his lack of gentility.

"After I escort you both into Demerel, you won't have to see me ever again. Regardless of how I feel on the matter, I know better than to go after the princess. So stop your worrying."

He stood and offered her the seat. "Here, you can have my seat. I'll be outside if anyone needs me."

Helga's eyes widened even more as he bowed perfectly, walked to the sink to drop his bowl off, then strode out the back door.

The nerve of the woman. Who was she to decide who the princess slept with or didn't? It wasn't like she was her mother.

A pang of remorse stabbed him, and his steps slowed as he entered the barn. He hadn't told her about her parents' accident. He frowned as he checked on the horses. Normally, the movements were calming, but not tonight.

He shut the barn and crept toward the house, his eyes trained on the upstairs window where Eirwyn lay. The giant tree that the cottage was built into lowered its branches for him, and he stepped onto one, his hand latching onto the rough wood as it took him up to the window.

She lay sleeping, now turned on her side. The tree obscured the moonlight, but he could still see her in the dimness. They were separated by more than just the glass window.

She was a princess, and he was a lumberjack. Leading the Robins didn't matter. The war didn't matter. All that mattered was that he didn't even know who or what he was. He was worse than a bastard. Besides, she was meant to be in a political alliance in some arranged marriage or another.

That she'd made it to twenty without being wed said little since the war had been raging for so long. She would probably make a politically helpful marriage soon. Much of the rumors in Busparia the past few weeks had hoped for a marriage with the prince of Glathen. A marriage uniting the two kingdoms would definitely have ended the war. She was a princess and destined to be queen. He felt it in his soul.

Whereas he lived in the woods and couldn't even offer her a home. The entire forest was his home, and he slept outside almost every night. To do otherwise was dangerous.

What princess would want to sleep outside with the bugs and insects and all manner of animals?

He sighed, a pressure growing in his chest at the futility of dreaming of a future with her. It was useless. There was no way it would work.

Tomorrow, he would have to say goodbye forever.

He waved his hands, and the branches formed a type of hammock. Then he laid down, the gentle breeze through the leaves lulling him to sleep as he watched the princess.

Chapter Five

Eirwyn woke to the sounds of birds outside the window. She yawned, feeling restored and only slightly sore from her trip to the Edge. She blinked and rubbed her eyes.

Thank the gods for the tonic from... who had given it to her? All she remembered was Knox. At a trill from a bird, she tossed back the covers and strode to the window.

She pushed open the glass and blinked. The birds settled on the window sill, each vying for her attention. But the beautiful peach, white, and blue flower bundle drew her attention first.

She picked them up and buried her face in it. The sweet scent helped her wake up with a smile. When she looked up at the birds, she pushed a question into their minds.

"Where did these come from?" she asked, glancing behind them and raising her brows. "And what is that hammock doing here?"

Almost as one, they pushed impressions back to her. The lumberjack had slept in a living hammock outside her window. He'd created it himself. He'd grown flowers and wrapped them in stems, leaving them on the windowsill.

She smiled, her heart flipping. He'd watched over her in the night and gotten her flowers? No one had ever been so thoughtful before. Not someone who wasn't a servant anyway.

She pushed another question to them. "And where is the handsome man this morning?"

Flashes of images burst in her head. He was checking the perimeter around the cottage, searching for any threats that might lurk in the forest. She leaned her elbow on the window sill and let the wind hit her face, lazily lifting the flowers to breathe in the peaceful smell.

She sighed and thanked the birds, listening to their chirps and seeing the impressions they sent. It was all inconsequential, such as where the best worms were to be found and which nest had the most hatchlings.

She laughed and let the proud mama bird perch on her finger. "Well, congratulations then. I'm thrilled for you."

The bird's chest puffed out, and Eirwyn stroked her feathers with a finger. A throat cleared behind her.

She turned to see Scarlet in the same clothes as yesterday, but at least her clothing was pressed now.

Eirwyn held out her finger to the window so the mama bird could fly home to her babies. Then she adjusted her own dress, wincing at the dirt and grime that made her feel so gross.

"Good morning," Eirwyn said, pasting on a smile and walking toward the bed. She spied her shoes and picked them up. "How are you today?"

Scarlet nodded and stepped away from the door, waving at Eirwyn. "Fine, thanks for asking. Olive is making breakfast, but I know Knox will want to get an early start. I was hoping you were awake."

Eirwyn went down the stairs in her stockings, shoes in one hand and flowers in the other. Helga sat by the fire with a steaming cup of coffee in her hands. She looked up, relief clear in her eyes. Then, her gaze narrowed on the flowers.

Before she could open her mouth, Eirwyn said, "Oh Helga, I'm so glad you're alright. I was worried about you when you hit your head. I'm sorry I wasn't able to cushion us more."

Eirwyn walked to the door and set her boots down.

"It's alright, child. I'm fine. Mistress Olive fixed me up in no time. How are you? Are you well? Where did the flowers come from?"

She turned back to Helga and tapped her chin. "I think I'm better than you. You look dreadful. Did you not sleep at all last night?"

Helga glared and pursed her lips, looking away.

But Scarlet leaned in and whispered loudly, "No, she didn't. She watched the stairs like a hawk to make sure Knox didn't take advantage of you."

Eirwyn's jaw dropped open, then she giggled, turning back to Helga. "I guess you didn't know that he slept in a hammock outside my window then, eh?"

Helga's spine straightened, and she spilled coffee on her dress, making her curse.

Eirwyn laughed, knowing her skirts were too layered for her to get hurt. Then she turned to the delicious aromas coming from the kitchen.

She went to Olive and said, "Hello, you must be Mistress Olive. I'm Eirwyn. I'm sorry I didn't get to introduce myself last night, but thank you so much for the healing potion. It was just what I needed."

Olive reached out a hand to shake and smiled. "I'm glad you're better, dear. Knox was concerned."

Eirwyn perked up. "Have you known him long?" She went to the sink and splashed water on her face, wiping it with a clean, folded rag. Then she found a mug to put the flowers in, filling it with water and setting it in the center of the table.

Olive nodded, bustling to pour the gravy into a bowl. "Since he was born. In fact, he was born right there by the hearth."

"Oh, are you his mother, then?" Eirwyn asked, turning to the kitchen table and beginning to wipe it clean. Nerves and curiosity ate at her stomach. Who was this man who was so gruff and quiet but fiercely protective and sweet?

"Heavens no. He's my godson. Oh, princess, you don't have to do that."

Olive set the bowl of gravy on the now clean table and turned back to the brick stove with a stone top and metal door on the side. The stone had perfectly circular holes bored into the top, and inside the brick was a raging fire.

Olive had multiple pans on the stone top, one covering each hole. Eirwyn's brows rose at the amount of bacon, sausage, porridge, potatoes, and vegetables.

Olive set a new pan where the gravy had been and paused. "Excuse me, dear, do you mind? I need to make the eggs. I'm not used to so much company and wasn't sure what you'd like for breakfast, so I made a little of everything."

"Can I help, Mistress Olive?" Eirwyn asked, stepping up to the hot stone top. She grabbed an egg and cracked it with a practiced flick of her wrist before the woman could answer. "I cook at the tavern in Demerel sometimes, but don't tell my brother," she whispered.

Olive beamed a smile. "Oh, how lovely. Yes, I'd love some help if you're sure you want to. But do call me Olive. Knox is the druid master warden of the forest now, so no more Mistress Olive."

Eirwyn's eyes widened in surprise. She'd surmised that they were druids, but the lumberjack was the leader of them? She opened her mouth to ask all her questions, but Olive beat her to it.

Olive asked, "Do you cook at the tavern a lot?"

Eirwyn shrugged. "Not as often as I'd like, but I've been going there for a few years now."

"Well before you should've been sneaking out," Helga said from by the hearth.

Eirwyn tilted her head. "Is there an appropriate age to sneak out? I thought it was forbidden no matter the age. Oh well, it's too late to put that bird back in the cage. How does everyone take their eggs?"

Olive flipped the bacon and said, "Scrambled but three fried for Knox."

Eirwyn nodded, grabbing a wooden spoon and spices to mix them with. "He probably needs a lot of food, as big as he is."

"Oh yes, he's always been big for his age, even as a baby," Olive said quietly. "I raised him here, you see, and it was very hard. His magic was wild and uncontrollable for a long time. Scarlet came to visit a few times a month, and the two of them were thick as thieves, practically siblings."

Olive pulled the sausage off the hot stone and onto a tray.

Eirwyn bit her lip, not sure how to ask, so she just blurted out. "Siblings? They're not together?"

Scarlet popped up behind her, stealing a piece of meat

and laughing. "Hells no, that's gross. Just brother and sister, thank you. The only one he likes is you, little princess."

Eirwyn blushed and put the eggs into a bowl. She took the sausage grease and poured it into her pan. "I don't know about that. I tried flirting yesterday, and it was like flirting with a brick wall."

She was afraid to read something into the flowers though. Maybe he did like her?

Scarlet snorted, leaning against the counter beside them. "That's because he's never flirted before. Or done anything else."

Eirwyn's eyes widened as she looked up at Scarlet. Scarlet's green eyes were calculating and watchful.

"Are you serious?" Eirwyn whispered.

Scarlet nodded. "Yeah, he's not one of your tavern boys, princess."

Eirwyn blushed harder, the heat on her cheeks making her groan. She looked away, cracking the eggs to fry them for Knox as her heart raced.

No wonder he hadn't responded to her attempts to cajole him. He probably didn't get into town much anyway.

Scarlet nodded to the flowers on the table. "He left those for you?"

Eirwyn nodded, unable to stop the smile from flowing across her face.

Scarlet continued, "Ask him on the ride why those flowers."

There was a meaning behind them? She knew the nobles often sent secret messages through presents such as flowers, but she'd never taken the time to learn what meant what. Plus, no one ever sent her flowers, presents, or messages. Her brother either intercepted everything or forbid it. She was sure he'd done something, as she had no friends of her own age and station.

Bella was the tavern owner and her only real friend. As well-read as she was, she would probably know what those flowers meant immediately.

Olive moved the meat to a tray. "Breakfast is almost ready. I'm going to get Knox. Flip the biscuits in the pan in three minutes."

She walked away, but Scarlet stayed, eying Eirwyn as she cooked. The awkward silence between them stretched, and for once in her life, Eirwyn didn't break it with mundane chatter.

Her mind turned back to what she'd said earlier. How could a strapping young man like Knox go his entire life without ever having sex? Hells, she hadn't even made it fifteen years before her first time, but he'd made it—gods, how old was he?

Eirwyn bit her lip, the questions about him piling up one on top of the other. She took a deep breath to ask Scarlet, but then he walked in the door. All the air rushed out of her in a whoosh, and wind lifted her hair slightly around her head before settling.

His eyes went immediately to her, the bright green distracting her from her task at the hot stone. His presence was like a shooting star, and she wanted to turn and chase after him, leaping into his arms.

He walked to the table and sat down at the head, and she blushed, turning back to cooking. She was such a ninny, getting this nervous. He was just a man, and she'd been with her fair share of men before.

She flipped the biscuits and eggs, watching carefully as they cooked. She wiped sweat from her forehead.

So what if she was avoiding his gaze? So what if she

wanted to teach this virgin lumberjack a thing or two? After today, she wouldn't see him again. It didn't matter what she wanted, really.

Her heart sank, heavy with disappointment. Disappointed in the missed opportunity with him and disappointed in herself that she wanted him so much. Normally, her hormones were just an itch she needed to scratch.

But Scarlet was right. He definitely wasn't one of her tavern boy dalliances. He was all man, and just the feel of his stare on her back made her shiver with awareness. It'd take more than a quick tussle between the sheets to put out the fire he was stoking within her.

She slid his eggs onto a plate and grabbed the biscuits. She set the plate in front of him, stepping close and inhaling his earthy scent.

His hood was up yet again, but none of the others said anything. She didn't want to point out his rude behavior, so she just turned back to the hot stone and began to clean it, moving the dishes to the sink.

"Dear, leave it until after you eat. You need a good meal for the rest of the journey through the forest," Olive said, sitting at the other end of the table.

Scarlet sat beside her on a bench, and Helga sat across from her on another bench.

Eirwyn took a plate and sat beside Knox, loading her plate full of all the delicious foods she didn't get to eat at the palace.

She bit into a piece of bacon and groaned. "Gods, this is delicious."

Knox's eyes were on her like an animal lying in wait for its prey. Still, she ignored his gaze.

"What can we expect from the rest of the journey?" Helga asked.

Scarlet waved a slice of bacon and explained. Eirwyn took a bite, savoring the taste yet somehow inhaling it, too. She ate faster than she should've, and it felt like a piece got lodged in her throat.

She reached for the pitcher of water from the center of the table and poured it into the mug. Then she chugged it.

She gasped in relief when she was done and wiped her mouth with a napkin. Helga's eyes were narrowed, and she knew she'd disappointed her.

But when she finally couldn't take it anymore and looked up at Knox, it was to see his emerald green eyes staring at her in contemplation.

She blushed and looked back down. "Excuse me," she said, eating slower and chewing more deliberately.

A faint twitch of the lips had her staring at him more intently. "Don't worry about it. The Edge will make anyone ravenous. Are you well this morning?"

She nodded, glancing back down in embarrassment. "Yes, thank you. And you?"

He nodded, taking another bite of his food.

Gods, she was such a ninny. She couldn't even carry on a decent conversation with him now because all she could think about was riding him for days.

It was going to be a long ride back to Demerel.

Chapter Six

Knox tied Scarlet's horse and the donkey to the front fence post of the cottage as Olive walked toward him. He had slept well but had woken up restless in a green cloud of poison, his dreams haunted by images of the princess.

He'd refilled Olive's wood stack by the back door, done a perimeter check, fed and watered the horses, and had been looking for something else to do when Olive had found him.

"Breakfast is almost ready," she said as he turned to walk back to the barn.

"Great," he said. "I'm almost ready, just need to grab my horse. I'm going to borrow your donkey for the maid, if that's alright?"

Olive nodded and handed over a list as she entered the barn behind him. "That's fine. Can you pick up these supplies while you're in town?"

He glanced down and nodded. "It'll be a few days before I can get back. Will you be alright to wait on the delivery?"

She nodded and fidgeted with her apron. She looked

toward the cottage and back to Knox. He inspected Ryder and let the horse's hoof drop to the ground.

"About the princess," she began.

He shook his head and tugged on the reins as he strode past her to the barn door. "Not you, too. Leave it alone, Olive."

"I'm just saying, she's a nice girl, and you deserve some happiness, Knox." When he didn't say anything, she continued. "You're having a reaction to her. That's not like you, Knox. All I'm saying is it's worth looking into. There could be something there."

He snorted and stopped the horse in front of the cottage. "Like what? It's just lust, Olive, plain and simple lust."

She shook her head, and he barely saw her eyes over the horse's back. "I'm not so sure about that. Why don't you try?"

He tied his horse next to the others. "It's just asking for rejection. I'm just a monster who roams the Feral Forest, Olive, and she's the most beautiful princess who's ever lived."

Olive swooped under the horse's head and stared up at him with worry. "Oh, Knox, you're not a monster. You're a lumberjack, an aspiring druid with plant magic, a drakin, and an honorable man who just loves the forest."

Knox looked at her, his eyes deadpanned as he replied. "Who has poisonous breath and a deadly venom tail? I almost killed you when I was a baby, Olive, and again and again as I grew up. We know what it would do to anyone I tried to be with. I'm not going to put anyone else in danger. Just because I think the princess is beautiful doesn't mean I'm going to pursue her and possibly kill her."

Olive rolled her eyes and crossed her arms. "I'm telling

you. If she's your true mate, she won't be affected by it at all."

Knox crossed his arms and widened his legs, facing her in a battle of wills. "And I'm telling you. True mates are just fairy tales. Do you know of anyone who has a true, fated mate? No, because they died out with all the other myths in the land."

Olive pointed a finger under his nose. "Mark my words, Knox, one of these days, you'll see that I'm right. I didn't get to the ripe old age of sixty without learning a thing or two."

He sighed and rubbed his forehead, then scratched the side of his head. The bumpy raised scales reminded him of who he was. "It's pointless, Olive. Let it go," he said softly, walking around her and to the front door.

When he walked inside, a halo of light fell on the princess at the stove. She looked up at him with those gorgeous gray-blue eyes, her mouth bowed in surprise. Eating was a blur. Most of the time, he just watched the princess like a wolf stalking its prey. Why had she sat by him at the table? He'd wanted to reach for her hand, touch her, lean closer, and smell her.

He barely tasted the food. This ride was going to be torture, but he would just have to maintain his distance and bear it.

He'd been through worse though. He could do this. When they were finally ready, they walked outside.

The maid frowned and looked from where he stood next to Ryder to Scarlet's horse to the donkey. He pointed to the donkey. "You're riding Herb."

He didn't wait to see her expression, but as he turned to swing into the saddle, he heard her sputtering in disapproval about the ill-treatment by the low-life lumberjack.

"Helga, that's enough. We don't treat people like that. He's been nothing but kind." Eirwyn smiled and waved goodbye to Olive.

She didn't wait or listen to Helga's whining either as she seemed to glide over to him with a smile. The sunlight fell on her face, making her seem full of life and energy.

She held a hand up to him, and he blinked as he remembered what they were doing.

He shook his head. "You're riding with Scarlet today." The less he touched her, the less haunted by her memory he'd be.

Eirwyn looked at Scarlet then she looked back at him, her smile widening. "I think I'd rather ride with you. Don't you think a strong lumberjack such as yourself is better... equipped... to protect an innocent princess such as myself?"

Scarlet snorted, and his own lips twitched at her fluttering eyelashes and hand resting on her chest. The blatant flirting wasn't something he was used to. Most humans in town avoided him. Scarlet was a Hunter and more than capable of protecting them all in town. It would be better for his sanity if she rode with Scarlet.

Eirwyn's dainty little hand touched the top of his boot, near his knee. She didn't even touch his pants. There were layers between them, but he felt her touch like a brand.

His body jumped at the chance to hold her one more time. He was the best protector in the forest too. Who was he to deny such a simple request?

"If that's what you want, princess." He moved his foot out of the stirrup and helped her up. She immediately sat astride today and wiggled against him as she found a comfortable spot.

He growled as his hand gripped her hip. "For gods' sake," he muttered.

Was that a giggle? She was definitely shaking.

"Are you laughing?" His voice was a hard whisper near her ear.

She glanced over her shoulder at him, her blue-gray eyes twinkling with mirth. "Maybe. At least both of us will have a miserable ride now."

She turned back to watch Scarlet assist Helga onto the donkey. She was miserable? He knew it. She didn't want to ride with him, and her ass was punishing him for the inconvenience.

He stiffened and turned the reins, waving at Olive as they walked slowly into the forest. "Hey, you asked for this, princess, so now you have to deal with the consequences."

"That's what they all say," she sighed, and he kept quiet since he had no idea what she was talking about.

"So, did you like the eggs this morning?" Eirwyn asked.

He frowned at the topic change. "Yes, they were good. Why?"

"Well, I made them, silly. I'm glad you like them. I like to cook."

She kept up a steady stream of one-sided conversation as she talked about the tavern at the center of town where she'd learned to cook. He'd actually visited that tavern before, long before she started attending. She also entertained the patrons with stories and light-projected puppets at the tavern.

"Do you spend a lot of time in town?" he asked.

"Oh yes, as often as I can escape, I do. Probably a few hours every other day, when I feel well enough. I like to visit the local medicine woman too. She has an apothecary shop across the square from the tavern that smells like my childhood. I was a pretty sickly child and loved when we'd come to the summer palace at Demerel."

He frowned, leaning away from her and putting a few inches between his chest and her back. He didn't want his breath to make her sick.

He asked, "How so?"

She told of how lethargic she'd always been, how her stomach was upset all the time. "But I haven't felt sick at all since I went to Glathen to negotiate peace."

He narrowed his eyes, a thought forming. "Have you been poisoned?"

She tilted her head to the side. "Poisoned?" She snorted. "Not likely. Everyone loves me, so who would even think to do it?"

She waved a dainty hand in the air as if it were the most ridiculous thing she'd ever heard. "Besides, surely Lailant would've been able to identify being poisoned by now. She's the medicine woman, but I've heard whispers of her being a witch. It's said she can cure anything for the right price. Surely, she would've identified it and exploited it for a little coin."

He didn't respond, and the forest's shadows danced around them. He wiggled his fingers on his knee, keeping Naturos magic flowing to keep them safe on the road.

Maybe he could get some information out of her about the war. The Robins would definitely ask if he'd learned anything useful.

"I heard the peace negotiations didn't go well."

She sighed, and her shoulders seemed to slump. "No, they didn't. I thought everything was going in the right direction. We were making progress. Then the Chancellor stepped in and said I actually had no authority to sign any legally binding documents for Busparia. If that was true, why did Gastone even send me in the first place?"

Her hand fisted on her knee. "He's never let me participate in politics before. Sure, I get along with everyone and have a way of setting people at ease. But I'm no diplomat, and I despise the limits of court."

He let the silence fall, listening to the birds and sounds of the forest as they found the Lone Road and turned toward Busparia.

She finally said, "Actually, I do know why I was sent. I was being punished for running away to the tavern instead of attending a ball. But it wasn't just any ball. It was a masquerade, and everyone knows those things are just fancy orgies."

He sucked in a breath, his mind rolling with images of her in a situation like that. He was both turned on and on high alert. "And you don't like participating in orgies?"

She shook her head. "That's not my cup of tea, especially when I know my brother will be in attendance. I like some kinky stuff, but I like my privacy too. At least at the tavern, I can take someone to a room instead of going down in public."

He choked, a puff of green gas escaping and slowly sinking to the forest floor. He waved a hand to disperse it, hoping she didn't see it when she turned her head to look at him.

"Are you alright?" She looked so innocent, but with that twinkle in her eye, he realized she was trying to get a rise out of him.

Well, mission completed. He gripped her hip, and she wiggled her tight little ass on his hard dick once more.

"I'm fine," he growled. "Face forward."

Her lips tilted in a sultry smile, but she obeyed. He leaned forward, moving the long black hair to fall over one shoulder. It bared the back of her neck, and his mouth went to her ear.

"You're teasing me on purpose," he said softly, so close to touching her. He wanted to nibble on her ear but was afraid it would hurt her.

She stiffened and leaned back against him. "Maybe. Is it working?"

"Depends on what you're trying to do, princess."

"Seduce you, of course. Not that we have any time to follow through with anything," she said with a sigh. He stiffened behind her, and she let his arms cocoon her in the protective shelter of his muscles.

He didn't reply, and the silence was peaceful.

"Why did you leave me flowers on the windowsill this morning?" she asked softly.

He hesitated between telling her it was just a nice thing to do or the truth. They were approaching the edge of the forest, though, and the closer they got to town, the more he wanted to hold on to her.

Desperation ate at him, demanding that he claim her. At the very least, he had to know if this was one-sided, if only to heat his dreams on the cold, lonely nights in the forest.

He dipped his head, and his breath on her neck made her nipples pucker through her dress. He wanted to reach around and cup them but didn't dare.

She closed her eyes, shuddering as his nose grazed her ear. "I wanted to tell you how I felt but didn't know how."

His heart raced as she leaned back against him. "How—how do you feel?"

He licked the shell of her ear, and the air shifted. Green gas sank to her shoulder, and he blew it away to sink to the grass. She didn't notice the gas but shivered at the wind.

He couldn't hold back the truth. He had to know if she was just flirting with him or if she truly did desire him.

"Peach roses for desire and hope that one day we can have a moment together."

She gasped, her hand reaching down and gripping his thigh. He wrapped an arm around her waist, and she grabbed his forearm with hers.

"Do you truly desire me, princess, or are you just toying with me?"

She moaned and moved his hand down to cup her mound through her dress. "How—how can you even ask that? Of course, I desire you."

"Are you sure?" he asked, licking the pulse under her neck. His fingers were on fire, so close to her heat, and he wanted more. He may not have ever been this close to a woman before, but he'd watched others. He knew how it worked.

She whimpered and wiggled on the saddle. "Hells, yes, I'm sure. If Helga and Scarlet weren't here, I'd climb off this horse and ride you now."

He kissed her neck, growling as his heart raced. "I would love that." The intensity of his desire took him by surprise. No wonder people had sex all the time. No wonder there were camp followers and brothels and...

He took a deep breath, trying to calm himself before he turned the horse off the road and ravished her, Helga and Scarlet be damned. They needed a distraction.

"White peonies are for admiration and awe at how you handled the carriage accident yesterday. You're so brave and strong, princess."

She shivered at the praise of his words. "You—you're kind to say so."

He shook his head, his nose nuzzling under her ear. She tilted her head to the side to give him greater access.

"Nothing kind about it. It's the truth."

"Not many would see it that way. I run away when things get tough. It's why I always ran to the tavern."

He gave her a soft kiss under her ear, and he opened his mouth to tell her to run to him, to run to the forest where he'd always be waiting.

But Helga looked back and frowned with a glare. "We're almost there. See?"

Knox straightened, pulling back and already missing her closeness.

She shifted on the saddle as the road widened. His cock still bit into her ass, teasing her with what wasn't meant to be.

She pointed and practically bounced on his dick, making him groan. "Look, it's Demerel. We're almost home."

He felt a pressure on his chest at her excitement. He might live most nights in Vidrland, but he didn't really have a home of his own. He'd thought of Olive's cottage as home growing up, but it hadn't been home in a long time.

This was why it didn't matter that the princess was going back to her perfect little life. He had nothing to offer her anyway.

They left the forest and onward he went. As they went through town, people stopped and pointed. Eirwyn waved the entire time. It seemed like every other person she saw she asked a personal question.

How's your wife? How are the chickens laying this year? Did you get any new books in the store? Do you have any powdered treats?

The last one had been directed to a baker, who sent a boy inside as the baker talked with Eirwyn. They went on and on about some sort of delicious fried sugary goodness? Perhaps he should've ridden at a faster pace so they wouldn't be stopped by every Tom, Dick, and Harry in town.

They were already on the next block when the boy caught up with them, handing Eirwyn a small brown bag. She thanked him and dug inside.

"Oh yes, how I have missed you, sweet olpertine." She spoke to the square confection reverently then she ate daintily. She moaned, and he took a deep breath as they turned onto the wider, cleaner side of town.

He wanted to hear her moan like that for other things. He might not have felt desire before this woman entered his life, but he'd read books. He'd watched and learned plenty at the brothels. He wanted...

It didn't matter.

"Do you want a bite?"

I want a bite of you.

She offered him a pastry, and he almost leaned forward to take it out of her hand before he remembered himself and shook his head. He wouldn't hurt her.

They approached the gates of the palace, and the guards' eyebrows rose as they opened the metal portcullis and bowed. Eirwyn wiped her mouth daintily with a kerchief and rolled the now empty bag up.

They went around the wide circular drive to the stairs that led to the front door. A servant ran forward to offer her a hand down, but Knox swung off the horse, careful to keep his hood up and his cloak covering his tail.

He blocked the servant with his body as he didn't want to watch anyone else touch her. Then he grabbed her hips and pulled her off the horse, letting her slide down his body. If this was the most he would ever feel of her, he wanted to memorize what it was like.

She gasped, her head thrown back as she stared up at

him. When her feet touched the ground, he lifted her hand and almost kissed the back of it, careful not to actually touch her.

"Take care, princess." His voice was barely a whisper, and she gripped his bicep with her other hand. Then he stepped back, taking the reins of Ryder and walking away.

After a few steps, he turned to see Eirwyn still staring at him. Helga was complaining to the servant who had moved a dismounting ladder beside the donkey.

He met Eirwyn's gaze, and for a moment, he swore his every thought, wish, and desire was reflected in her eyes.

Then Helga was tugging her up the stairs, talking about how they needed to get cleaned up as soon as possible. Knox swung back onto his horse and took the reins of the donkey from the servant.

Scarlet pulled her horse up beside him and sighed. "Well, that's one less thing to worry about now. What do you say we stop by the tavern for a drink? I need to relax after listening to that woman complain every step of the way."

Knox nodded. "Maybe we can stop at the bakery too. I have a craving for something sweet."

Scarlet snickered. "I bet you do, brother."

They rode back through the gates of the castle into the bustle of the town. He couldn't stay long, but a few hours to run errands would help take his mind off Eirwyn.

Chapter Seven

Helga followed Eirwyn through the oversized front door of the castle and into the wide foyer. The grand staircase led up the middle, then split into two more staircases, one going left and one going right.

The downstairs rooms were a flurry of activity. The butler, Hobbs, closed the door behind them.

"Welcome back, Your Highness. We have all been worried about you."

She beamed at him and nodded. "Aw, thank you, Hobbs. It's good to be home. Has the Chancellor returned yet?"

Hobbs nodded, his gaze flitting up the stairs to the west wing and her brother's rooms. A loud crash echoed, followed by a roar.

"Yes, but have you heard? There's to be a wedding, Your Highness."

Eirwyn gasped and met Helga's worried gaze. Her heart raced. No, this couldn't be. Not yet.

She sighed and bit her lip. "Hobbs, would you refrain

from telling the king that I've returned? I need to tidy up a bit."

She pulled her stained and filthy skirt, and he frowned. "Absolutely, Your Highness. Will an hour suffice?"

She nodded and turned to the stairs, racing up them as fast as she could and turning to the east wing and her rooms. Helga immediately ran a hot bath, and Eirwyn set her bag on the settee. She pulled out the peach, white, and blue blossoms and emptied her makeup cup on the vanity.

For once, she didn't care about the mess and lack of order on her desk. She went to the bathroom and filled it with water, then put the flowers in the cup and set it on her bedside table.

She took a deep breath of it as if drawing strength from the blooms to withstand the storm that was her brother. With a sigh, she turned to the bathroom and disrobed, sinking into the water with a sigh.

"Ah, and this is why I could never live in the forest." Eirwyn absently swirled the white bubbles with beams of light to form a kaleidoscope of colors.

Helga bustled behind her. "We should probably not mention sleeping overnight in the forest to his majesty."

Eirwyn sat up and began scrubbing. "Why not? It's the truth."

Helga nodded and paused, a wary expression on her face. "I know, but with his temper, I'm afraid of what he might do if he found out we stayed with the druid."

Eirwyn took out her braids. "They were nothing but hospitable. What could he possibly do?"

Helga shook her head. "I'm not sure, but you know how he feels about the forest. He blames it and the druids for your parents' deaths."

Eirwyn stepped into the tub, the warmth washing over

her. That had always confused her, as he also claimed that Glathen had assassinated their parents. It couldn't possibly be both. She'd always assumed Gastone just used it as an excuse to invade Glathen and ban people from going into the forest.

"You saw how he reacted when he found you in the tavern last month. He almost burned the place down before shipping you off to Glathen."

Eirwyn sighed. "If you think that's best, then so be it. I won't say anything. What will we say instead?"

Helga went to her walk-in closet, muttering, so Eirwyn dipped under the water. When she came up and began to lather her hair, Helga was draping a soft, silk white and red gown on the hook by the mirror.

"We'll say most of the truth. That our carriage was overrun by the forest's magic, that we were rescued by the Hunter Scarlet and her brother, and that they escorted us home."

Eirwyn hummed as she cleaned, finally feeling more at ease in her own skin now that she had scraped off all the dirt and grime. An hour later, Helga put the finishing touches on her hair. She pulled it into small braids at the back of her head.

"When you're married, you'll be able to wear your hair up." Helga's eyes met hers. They'd argued for years about the fashion and rules of society. Helga always said she was the leader of her people, and she had to present herself thus. But not even Eirwyn could change the cultural norms.

Working women could wear their hair however fit their station and job. The baker's daughter wore her hair up in a bun on top of her head. So did Bella, her friend who owned the tavern.

But unattached marriageable noble women wore tiny

braids from ear to ear, and then the braids were pulled back to the base of the skull. The long hair hung loosely down her back for everyday tasks. Those braids could be pulled up off the nape only once they were engaged or married. Hair was supposed to cover the nape as it was too sexy to leave bare.

Eirwyn sighed. It wasn't logical. If she wanted to attract a suitor, shouldn't she show more skin to entice him? In her mind's eye, she pictured Knox, with his strong protective embrace and deep green eyes with hidden depths just waiting to be explored.

It wasn't meant to be though. She shook her head, her hair flowing down her back. This was just another reason she hated all the rules that dictated her life. The rules were made up, and what was convenient didn't matter.

Eirwyn had met her gaze in the mirror defiantly.

"I don't want to get married. You know this. I don't want to be tied down or have yet another man tell me what to do, dictating my every move."

Helga had glanced over her shoulder and whispered back as if afraid even the walls of her room would hear them speaking.

"You are a princess. It's your duty to marry well, remember? This is what I've been trying to train you for your whole life. Now, you're going to go out there, hold your head up high, and listen and learn. Negotiate this to your advantage."

Eirwyn sighed and stood, straightening her spine to walk out the door. "Very well," she said as she opened it. She turned to look back at Helga. "I'll try to make you proud."

"You always do, child."

Eirwyn snorted at the bald-faced lie and shook her head as she closed it behind her. Helga was the only mother figure she'd ever had. She'd spent years nursing Eirwyn through sickness after sickness.

Eirwyn had just walked a few feet down the plush carpeted hall when her brother boomed her name.

Her heart skipped a beat as she jumped, and then she walked faster toward the stairs. Her brother was already walking quickly down the stairs to the west wing as she stopped at the top of the east wing stairs.

"Your Majesty." She dipped into a deep curtsy before standing and walking slowly down the stairs. She didn't want to trip when he was already in a mood. Heavens knew he despised how clumsy she was.

He stopped on the landing where the two stairs met and put his hands behind his back. Whereas Eirwyn used just simple gold-colored thread on her dresses, her brother used actual thread made from gold. His buttons were jewels, and his tailored blue jacket fit him like a glove. It had an intricate but subtle gold pattern that matched the gold cording on his shoulder.

A red silk cravat was tied in a fancy knot. It matched his black pants perfectly. She glanced down. Even his boots were shiny and clean, a black that rivaled his perfectly gelled hair.

He was the exact opposite of Knox. Clean, sharp cut, and expensive tastes.

Knox was more down-to-earth, dirty, and harder to understand. She'd spent two days with the man, and felt like she didn't know him at all. Yet somehow, she felt safer and trusted him more than her own brother.

"Where have you been? The Chancellor arrived back yesterday and said you refused to take the Southern Road home. Don't tell me you went through the Feral Forest."

She reached the landing and pursed her lips, nodding

demurely. He threw up his hands and turned on his heel to walk down the central staircase.

"What have I told you about that forest? It's an abomination and should be destroyed. It killed our parents, Eirwyn."

"I thought Glathen sent assassins to kill our parents? Isn't that why we've been at war for a decade?"

He glared over his shoulder, a curl of smoke blowing from his nose. "Don't sass me, sister. You know that forest is off-limits. Do not go near it again, do you understand?"

She lowered her gaze and nodded. "Yes, Your Majesty."

Gastone took a deep breath, and they continued walking down the stairs as he berated her reckless ways.

Perhaps it was because she didn't have a real voice with her brother that made her talk too much with everyone else. She followed behind him, maintaining the two-steps-behind-him rule that he insisted on.

She tuned back into his ranting and followed him down the hall to his office.

"The Chancellor says you almost brokered peace with Glathen. Not bad for your first attempt at diplomacy. I expected worse," he scoffed, a small white smoke tendril escaping his nose as a servant opened the door to the library for them.

She frowned, unsure of why they were going to the library. Every other time he'd chewed her out, it had been in his office. The change of scenery made her forget to hold her tongue.

Eirwyn felt the frustrations of his words return as they stopped outside the door. "I could've done better. It was a fool's mission that couldn't have possibly succeeded without the power to sign a legally binding document."

Gastone spun on his heel, lifting a finger to point at her

face. A small flame of fire flickered at the end, and she stepped back, immediately regretting her boldness. She knew what would happen next. If she wasn't careful, he'd throw a fireball. She went onto the balls of her feet, ready to dive for safety.

"Don't accuse me of being a fool. You're the one who has been sneaking out of the palace for gods knows how long to fraternize with the peasants. And when I organize a masquerade, hoping to shift your attention to some more acceptable dalliances, you reject the entire thing! I don't understand you, Eirwyn."

He extinguished the flame, smoke billowing from his nose as he exhaled heavily. He tugged on his jacket, stood straighter, and entered the library, walking toward the settee under the giant window. Eirwyn paused to see Bella sitting under it, lounging on a settee as she read a book in a blue silk gown.

She looked up, her familiar brown eyes shining behind her reading glasses. She stood and set the book down, opening her arms wide as she walked forward.

"Eirwyn, you're back! Welcome home," Bella enveloped her in a hug.

Eirwyn blinked, and her heart raced. Bella was her friend in town. She'd met her almost a decade ago when she'd first snuck out of the palace. She owned the tavern and learned magic from the local medicine woman. She'd taught Eirwyn to cook and bake. Hells, she'd even put Eirwyn to work cleaning the filthy rooms upstairs. What was she doing in the palace in an expensive new silk gown?

Bella broke the hug and turned to smile at Gastone. "Did you tell her?"

He stood next to the settee with a smirk. "Not yet; I was waiting for you, dear."

Eirwyn stepped back, her jaw-dropping. "Dear?" Her voice almost squeaked.

He nodded, the same expression on his face when he beat her at chess. It was like the cat who ate the canary.

Bella grabbed her hands and pulled her down to the settee. "Eirwyn, we're getting married!"

Chapter Eight

Eirwyn's brows rose at the announcement, and she looked over Bella's shoulder to her brother.

"Isn't it amazing? When the king came to the tavern to fetch you, we started talking and fell in love. We announced our engagement yesterday to the Chancellor and Council and will get married in a month. I'm just so glad you've made it back before word got around."

Eirwyn frowned, turning to Gastone. "But you just said we shouldn't fraternize with the peasants. Yet here you are, marrying Bella? Which is it?"

Bella's eyes frowned in pain and a flash of anger as she pulled back, but Gastone just rocked on his heels.

"I just did what you were doing, sister dear. Don't you like it when the shoe's on the other foot?"

Eirwyn looked at Bella, then back at Gastone, biting her tongue. She didn't want to say anything else that would upset her friend, but something wasn't right here.

"It's an ingenious plan, though, isn't it? This will endear

me to the people even more while sticking it up Glathen's backside. A marriage alliance will *never* happen now."

Eirwyn blinked. Glathen had sent a marriage alliance and peace proposal to Busparia six months ago. But Gastone had ignored it. Glathen's representatives had asked her about it at the peace talks, but she had said her brother was still considering the option. That proposal had been for Gastone and Glathen's princess though, not Eirwyn and the prince of Glathen.

Bella turned to look up at him. "But we fell in love?"

Eirwyn ached for her friend at that wounded tone of voice.

Gastone looked down at her and winked. "Of course we did, dear. Never doubt it for a minute. The rest is just icing on the cake."

Bella still looked troubled, and Eirwyn's chest felt like a lead weight settled on it. She took Bella's hand and leaned forward.

"I'm happy for you," Eirwyn said softly with a smile. "There couldn't possibly be a better queen for our people."

The small lines of worry around Bella's lips eased as she smiled and tucked a stray brown hair back into her loose braids.

"Thanks. The king has already arranged all the best tutors, so I'm finally being formally trained in magic. And the books! Eirwyn, you didn't tell me how big your library is."

Bella's eyes turned excited again as she looked around the cavernous room. Floor-to-ceiling shelves lined the wall, and it was two stories high, with a landing and more ladders and more shelves above.

Eirwyn smiled weakly. "It never came up. What's going to happen to the tavern?"

Bella waved a hand. "Oh, I've hired a manager to oversee things for Pa until he returns from the war. It's been a hard transition to living in the palace this month, but I'm adjusting alright."

Eirwyn's eyes widened. "You moved in?"

So, her brother had moved Bella in *before* they'd announced their engagement. Interesting. She wondered what the townsfolk thought about that slap in the face of propriety. Not that she was one to judge.

Bella blushed and nodded. "Yes, it was just too much going back and forth trying to plan the wedding in secret. We kept waiting and waiting for your return to announce it, but when the Chancellor returned yesterday and said you were on the way... well, we decided why wait?"

Eirwyn looked to her brother, who arched a brow as if waiting for her to challenge him. She turned back to Bella.

"And it's a good thing I'd already moved in because of the number of people who swarmed the tavern lately. Whew! No wonder the king was concerned about security. Isn't he sweet and thoughtful?"

Eirwyn's face scrunched up before she could stop herself.

Gastone stiffened and narrowed his eyes, a faint wisp of smoke coming out of his nose. "We're having an engagement dinner tonight, so your return is well-timed. Would you step into my office, please? I have something to discuss with you."

He strode out the door, and Eirwyn felt a knot of uneasiness grow in the pit of her stomach as she followed him.

Bella picked up her book and frowned as the two walked out the library door. Was Eirwyn just surprised, or did she truly not approve of the match?

So what if she doesn't approve? This is your chance to learn everything.

She breathed deeply, and her shoulders relaxed as a happy haze filled her. She looked around the library, awe filling her that she was even there.

In just a few short weeks, this would be her library. She held the book to her chest and fell back on the settee with a giggle, her mind shifting to the first time she'd come to the castle.

She'd known from the moment they met that her entire life was about to change. The king had stormed into the tavern and almost burned it down in his anger at Eirwyn sleeping around.

The next day, he'd sent workers to repair the tavern and had invited her to the castle for a private dinner. Nerves had kept her on edge all day. Even with a calming spell, she'd almost thrown up when the carriage had pulled up to the front door.

The king had set her mind at ease within just a few minutes, though. He'd made her relax with pleasant, intelligent conversation, unlike anything she'd get at the tavern. There, the talk was rough and coarse and unrefined.

With Gastone, she could discuss so much more. They'd admired the famous paintings in the parlor and his mounted hunting collection on the walls of the foyer and grand staircase. Over dinner, he'd been so kind, discussing magic and asking about her upbringing.

She squirmed under his attention, twisting her spoon nervously. "No, I didn't go to the mage school. We couldn't afford it, and there was always more work than hands available at the tavern."

The king had nodded, stroking his chin. "You're quite talented for a low magic user. If you didn't get formal training, where did you learn?"

Bella's back straightened, and she tilted her head up even as her cheeks burned. "I studied with the priests, exchanging lessons for cleaning services. When I'd read all their books, and they no longer had anything to offer, I moved on to the local healer."

"Ah, and are you still apprenticing with her?"

Bella shook her head. "No, sadly, I've also exhausted her limited resources."

The king's glittering eyes made her feel nervous, like he was about to pounce. She'd had to be firm at the tavern, quickly learning how to defend herself and keep people in line.

But this was the king. She couldn't use the same tactics as with her customers.

He pushed back his chair and stood. "In that case, come with me. I have something you'll be interested in."

She followed him out of the dining room and down the hall. A servant opened the library door, and she stepped in. Her jaw dropped. It was multiple stories of nothing but books. Rows and rows, stacks and stacks. If she read one a day, it would take years to read them all.

She walked into the center of the room, spinning a slow circle with her hands to her lips in awe.

"Do you like it?" he asked.

She nodded, clutching her hands to her stomach. "Oh gods yes, I've never seen so many books. Think of all the knowledge that can be learned just from this."

"Think of what you could do with both the books and magical lessons from the best minds in the kingdom."

She chuckled dryly, disappointment and anger flaring in her chest.

"Indeed, Your Majesty. It's too bad that I haven't even been able to afford a wand, much less lessons like those."

He'd stepped closer, invading her personal space. She froze, an intoxicating scent filling her nose. She tipped her head back and tilted it to the side. The logical side of her questioned his actions.

"What are you doing, Your Majesty?"

He'd looked down at her, his hands behind his back. "I'd think that was obvious. I'm getting close to you."

"But why?" Her heart raced, and her hands flattened on her stomach as it twisted and churned.

"I'd like to seduce you. You're fascinating, my girl."

Bella gasped, stepping away toward the fireplace. She stood straight and turned, matching his stance with her hands behind her back.

"I'm sorry, I don't think that's wise."

He arched a brow. "Why not?"

She tilted her head up. "I may be Eirwyn's friend, but I'm not like her, Your Majesty. I don't just follow every urge at the drop of a hat."

He scowled and tipped his head. "Give me a week," he said. "That's all I ask. I'd like to pry open your mind and see what all you know. You're much more than you seem."

"Pry open my mind or my legs?" She raised her brows, afraid of what the rejection would bring her. She'd heard he was so temperamental. Eirwyn was always talking about his mood swings.

She started to shake her head, then he said, "You could have full access to the library and all the tutors at my disposal."

She looked around the room, and despair clawed at her. "A tempting offer, Your Majesty. But at the end of the week? What then? I'd simply be the rejected mistress of the king. I'm sorry, but I must decline."

He arched another brow. "At the end of the week, you'll accept my proposal, my dear girl."

Bella's heart raced, and her lip beaded with sweat. "Proposal?"

He grinned slowly. "To be perfectly frank, I need a wife. I'm a reasonable man. I wouldn't expect you to agree just because I'm the king. So get to know me, give me a week to convince you, then make your choice."

Bella smiled and blinked up at the alfresco painting on the ceiling of the library. She was so glad she'd decided to take a chance. Now, she had the entire kingdom at her fingertips.

She'd learned more about magic in the past month than she had in the previous years combined. Now that she had the resources, she had learned how to make more than just using Synthara magic to create healing potions. She'd begun exploring all four forces of magic; Vitaron, Naturos, Synthara, and Nekrosan, branching out from the animation of objects and illusions.

The only other way she would've had access to or learned any of this before was if she would've sold her soul to Asmoroth. She snorted at the absurdity of it all. Once she was queen, she'd make a scholarship to send one child a year from each village to the academies.

She sat up and set her book aside. She went to the fireplace and pinched her cheeks, then tucked a stray hair behind her braid.

There is much planning to do and so much to learn. The bottom bookshelf to the right of the fireplace has an interesting section about transmutations.

Bella didn't question how she knew. She just went to the bookshelf and found the book. She opened it, but before she could get sucked in, a servant came to tell her it was time to get ready for the engagement dinner.

She sighed and looked at the mirror. "I want this mirror

in my chamber. Replace it with the one on the vanity, please."

The servant nodded succinctly. "Of course, Your Ladyship."

Bella blushed, her heart racing as she grinned. She still wasn't used to everyone obeying her the first time she said something. Normally, she had to cajole and threaten the maids to do their actual job.

She grinned and skipped out the door. By the time she reached the grand stairs, she had the book open and read as she walked, her heart light with endless possibilities.

Chapter Nine

A servant opened the door down the hall, and Gastone went to sit at his desk. Eirwyn took the seat opposite, the straight back making it impossible to be comfortable.

Not that she ever could be in his presence. He tapped on a stack of papers on his desk, his eyes dark and glittering.

"I read the Chancellor's reports and talked with the Council yesterday. I thought I gave you specific instructions on what we would and would not agree to for a peace treaty."

Eirwyn frowned and nodded. "Yes, and I followed them."

Gastone tilted his head. "And the agreement to turn Auckwald back over to them? You said the borders would go back to what they were before the war. I specifically told you we would not give up even a foot of the land we've conquered."

Eirwyn bit her lip. "Yes, but be reasonable. Think about—"

"Be reasonable?" he said softly. Too soft. The hair on the

back of her neck stood up. "I don't think you understand politics at all. Perhaps we should have more lessons."

She shook her head, her eyes wide. "No, no more lessons. I—"

A knock at the door interrupted, and Gastone said, "Enter."

The Chancellor walked in, the dark blue robes of his office stiff from a fresh pressing. His black pants, white shirt, and blue jacket were muted and in direct contrast to Gastone's brighter, vivid clothing. Perhaps it was the lack of gold thread.

His beady gaze swung to Eirwyn, and his eyes narrowed as a tight-lipped smile spread across his bony face. "Ah, welcome back, princess. I'm glad you're here. A runner has just arrived from Auckwald."

Gastone sat straighter, his gaze sharp. "What's the news?"

The Chancellor's smile widened as he shut the door behind him and brought an envelope to her brother. "Auckwald has been reclaimed."

"What?" Eirwyn gasped, her hands going to her lips. She'd just been there for the negotiations. The Buspartans had invaded and quickly overtaken Auckwald a decade ago, but the defending army had set up camp a few miles away on the bank of a river. The lines of war had changed little in the years since.

"Our darling princess boosted morale while she was there. But as soon as she left, our forces grew despondent, even worse than before. And her formal dinners with the king and queen of Glathen bolstered their resolve to end the war."

Gastone read the letter, his eyes moving swiftly back and forth as smoke shot out of his nose and grew in intensity.

Eirwyn's stomach twisted, and when the letter burst into flames, her heart raced.

He stood up so fast that his chair tipped over as he roared. "See what I mean? You can't do anything right. I sent you there to keep you out of trouble and to calm down the nobles who felt slighted. And now you've gone and ruined everything. No matter what you do, it always turns out wrong. This is why you can't be trusted with political matters."

He lifted a flaming hand, and a burst of fire flew at her head. She ducked, nearly touching her knees where she sat, as the flame hit the back of the chair behind her. It caught on fire, and she jumped up, dancing a few steps away and holding her hands up.

"I didn't mean to. I didn't know they'd react like that. I'm so sorry—"

"You're sorry?" Gastone shouted, throwing another fireball. Eirwyn dodged, and it slammed into the paneling behind her. The Chancellor grinned and crossed his arms as he watched.

"It's time to grow up, Eirwyn. You're not a child who can just say sorry and think that magically fixes things."

Eirwyn swirled the wind to put out the fire behind her, but her air magic only made it grow brighter. She shifted a few more feet away and turned back to the greater threat.

"I know, I know. But—"

"No buts, Eirwyn. You're lucky we have the ball tonight. Otherwise, you'd be confined to your room. What am I supposed to do now?"

Another burst of fire crashed into the glass window. She covered her head as shards of glass went flying.

Chancellor Howe finally stepped forward. "Just bring our troops home. Announce to the kingdom you recalled them to celebrate your nuptials. Spin it so it's not a defeat but a deliberate move."

Eirwyn stepped away from the window and burning wall, walking a wide arch around the edge of the room as far away from Gastone as possible. She had to escape, which meant talking.

"That's a great idea. Bella has always wanted her father to walk her down the aisle. This will give you a chance to find him among all the troops being recalled."

The Chancellor said, "We've had our best people looking for him, but I wasn't able to find him during our time in Auckwald. Perhaps he's deserted."

"Don't tell Bella that," Eirwyn said as she backed up. "She'll be heartbroken. She might even call off the wedding."

Gastone tipped his head back and roared, white-hot steam escaping his mouth. Eirwyn threw open the door and raced into the hall, not stopping as he began to cuss and yell for her to get back in there.

———

Eirwyn knocked on Bella's door and waited for her friend to answer, her heart still racing from running up the stairs.

"Enter," Bella said.

Eirwyn opened the door and shut it softly behind her.

"Are you sure this is a good idea?" Eirwyn asked as she bit her lip. She hadn't ever told anyone about Gastone throwing fire at her or any of the things he'd tortured her with throughout her life.

She didn't want to complain to Bella. She'd learned long ago that it was pointless. Sure, she'd joked around with Bella about her annoying brother, but she'd kept it all fun and light-hearted. Would Bella break off the engagement if she knew how twisted her brother truly was?

Bella powdered her nose.

"Yes, I'm sure. This is going to be a good thing for our country, Eirwyn. Think of all the good I'll be able to do as queen. With all the resources at my disposal, we can finally solve the things we've complained about for years."

She knew her friend was excited, but that didn't make this feeling of dread disappear. Eirwyn leaned against the bedroom door and really looked at Bella. Some of the worry lines on her face had disappeared, and a small smile hovered on her lips.

"You're truly happy about this?" Eirwyn asked, crossing the floor to where Bella fixed her hair in the mirror. The vanity was old, but the mirror itself had sat on the mantle in the library for years.

Bella nodded, not looking away from the ugly mirror.

"Are you sure he doesn't have you under a spell? You remember how we used to talk about Gastone, right?"

Bella bumped the desk as she turned and rolled her eyes, the light bouncing off the mirror at the movement. It shimmered, and the strangeness of it caught Eirwyn's eye, but Bella's words distracted her from thinking of it any further.

"Truly, there was no potion or spell involved. Look, if you don't want me to marry your brother, fine. I can live with that. But I don't understand why you're so against it. I thought we were friends."

Bella's hurt look gutted her, and Eirwyn sighed and frowned. Bella's tone was sharper than it'd ever been, and she slowly stood up, her back as straight as any noblewoman Eirwyn had ever met.

Gone was the tavern owner who had a smile for everyone. Gone was the friend who'd washed dishes while Eirwyn cooked and complained about her brother.

Bella looked exactly as a queen should, and Eirwyn shifted uncomfortably. She felt lacking. Was it any wonder her brother was constantly disappointed in her? She'd never look that regal and poised.

She was too wild and carefree, her attention span too short. She wasn't as well-read or as good at conversation as Bella was. All she had were the fantastical stories she told in the tavern with her magic, making shadows dance and act out scenes, but that was more performing than interacting.

Eirwyn finally said, "We are friends. That's why I'm worried. I don't want to see you hurt."

Bella smiled and turned back to the mirror with a glassy look in her eyes. "Oh, stop worrying so much. Gastone loves me, and all will be fine. Now go get ready for the ball. We need to shift how they think about him, and marrying a commoner might not go over well with the nobles."

Eirwyn bit her lip and forced a smile. "You're going to be a great queen, Bella, and I'll do what I can to help with the nobles."

Chapter Ten

Bella wore a beautiful yellow and red gown that hugged curves and made Eirwyn wince with jealousy. Even though Eirwyn wore a matching red, white, and blue dress, she couldn't hide her petite figure, and the feelings of inferiority plagued her mind yet again. They went down the grand staircase, Eirwyn breathing heavily with nerves.

Several dozen courtiers loitered at the bottom of the stairs with drinks in hand as they mingled. A string quartet played softly in the alcove under the stairs, but the music stopped as they paused on the landing.

Bella and Eirwyn stood shoulder to shoulder as the butler stepped forward and introduced them.

"The darling princess Eirwyn Whikin, and the future queen, the honorable and esteemed Bellatrix Bellichek."

They both curtsied and then they moved to either side of the stairs, placing a gloved hand on the railing and descending in unison. Eirwyn felt a blush stain her cheeks at the attention. She'd done this a thousand times over her life, but the nerves never quite went away.

It's just a performance, Eirwyn. Just smile and nod.

She hoped a furtive glance at Bella would reassure her she wasn't the only one feeling this way. But Bella smiled coolly and looked every bit the queen.

Eirwyn glanced at the bottom of the stairs as the crowd parted. The king strode straight for them, his hand reaching up to Bella.

His smile was easy, but when he looked at Eirwyn, a shiver went up her spine. She'd felt like this at every function. She was constantly afraid she'd mess up, trip and fall on her face, or otherwise disappoint her brother.

There was something cold and calculating in his gaze. She had the same feeling when she used to play him in chess. It was like he knew something she didn't.

"My dear Bella, you look captivating tonight," he said just a touch too loudly, as if he was speaking for the benefit of those around him. He leaned in and kissed the back of Bella's hand before tucking it into the curve of his elbow.

He offered his other elbow to Eirwyn and turned his smug smile on her. "So good to have you home, dear sister."

Eirwyn dipped another small curtsy, then took his elbow too as he continued speaking.

"Now, Bella, I understand you might be overwhelmed by your first official ball. We're going to make the announcement to the commoners, then we'll mingle with the nobles before going into dinner, alright? Smile and nod. Just smile and nod. That's it. Well done. See? I told you that you could do this," he said to Bella.

Bella chuckled. "I suppose you were right after all."

Eirwyn's brows rose. Bella must be feeling more insecure than she thought, if she'd confided to Gastone. As a real smile flitted on his face at the sight and sound of Bella's laugh, Eirwyn's brows rose even higher.

"You'll learn in time that I am right on nearly everything." He grinned wider, and Bella laughed again.

Eirwyn began to relax at their easy, flirtatious banter. It was like the tavern, just with fancier words. Perhaps their marriage wouldn't be a disaster after all. Perhaps she could survive this ball without making him angry.

He led them through the glass doors to the wide balcony that overlooked the courtyard below. He'd opened the courtyard up for the ball, which was a rare event. People shopped at the carts along the castle walls. In the center of the courtyard, people danced to the musicians that played on a raised dais.

At the sight of them on the balcony, the music died. The dancing stopped and everyone looked up at where the three of them stood.

Bella looked at Eirwyn and said softly, "Step back. Give him his moment."

Eirwyn frowned but did as she wished. She didn't want to make Gastone mad and ruin Bella's big night stepping into the upper crust society. Had she been driving the tension between them all these years by standing just behind his shoulder? Did he feel like she was smothering him with her closeness?

Gastone stepped forward and lifted his hand as all noise quieted. "Esteemed guests, thank you for being here tonight to help me celebrate."

Eirwyn's brows rose. Esteemed guests? He'd never called anyone that before, much less regular people from town. Perhaps Bella was having a good influence on him after all.

"As you know, Glathen had requested a marriage alliance. However, I couldn't bring myself to agree. Since meeting this woman at my side, now I know why. I was simply waiting for her." He took Bella's hand and kissed the back of it, leading her forward.

Bella's eyes softened, and Eirwyn stood to the side taking it all in. She never in a million years thought she'd hear her brother talk like that. It was disconcerting. Was she the only one who could hear the faint mockery in his voice?

She watched Bella, but her eyes just shone with excitement and happiness. Gastone held up her hand, showing their hands joined.

"It is with great pride that I announce my engagement to one of your very own, the beautiful and talented Bellatrix Bellichek."

He lowered his voice and smiled at Bella. "Smile and wave, my dear."

When the applause quieted, he turned and led them back into the ballroom. They walked around the outskirts of the room as people mingled. The dancing wouldn't start until after dinner. This was the part that turned Eirwyn's stomach into knots.

One on one conversation was so much harder than putting on a show for an audience. He led them both around the room, Bella's hand on his elbow, and Eirwyn slightly behind and to the side of them.

Gastone turned to Eirwyn and smiled tightly.

"I see Chancellor Howe in the corner. Why don't you go say hello, sister?"

Eirwyn's face froze, and she stiffened. "I'd rather not. He's very handsy."

"But everyone in the kingdom knows how free with your affections you are, and the chancellor is in his prime. Perhaps with some encouragement from you, he can get some laws passed about the sky high taxes."

Eirwyn took a deep breath and frowned. This was why she didn't want to sleep with any nobles. It was too complicated, too political.

"I will not be used for your political gain, brother, not even to help lower the taxes and win you favor with the people."

He narrowed his eyes as Bella gasped again. Eirwyn felt a prickle of fear and awareness race up her spine at Gastone's flashing eyes. A small curl of white smoke drifted from his nose.

"Eirwyn, that's enough. You're going to ruin everything," Bella whispered.

Eirwyn took a deep breath and stepped back even further. She curtsied deeply, and as she rose, she said, "Pardon me, your highness. I meant no offense. I'm going to mingle before the dinner bell if you don't mind, perhaps even make my way to Chancellor Howe. Please excuse me."

She didn't wait on the king's reply and dismissal, but she figured she had already made him mad. All she could do was hope for escape and that he'd forget. She turned and walked to the edge of the room, hugging the shadows and avoiding the Chancellor. Once there, she could breathe much deeper.

It seemed like she only took two breaths before the dinner bell sounded. Chancellor Howe appeared in front of her. He was older than her by twenty years. The silver streaks in his hair should have made him appear distinguished, but the arrogant smile made her skin crawl every time. He was almost as power-hungry as her brother.

He held out a hand. "May I escort you into dinner, Your Highness?"

"Ah, yes, thank you," she said, taking his hand and

raising her head. It was pointless to argue, as the dinner processional was very strict about who sat next to whom. It was all about ranking, and since he was the highest-ranking member of the Council, she was used to dinners with him.

The man's nose twitched as he leered slightly. "I've been looking forward to your return, Your Highness. I was worried about you going through the forest home."

"Not worried enough to accompany me, though," she said with an overly bright, false smile.

He shook his head. "You couldn't pay me enough to step foot in those accursed woods. Truly, I thought you would perish on the road."

She shrugged as he seated her at one end of the table. He took the seat directly on the end, opposite of Gastone, down the long table. To her left sat a foppish, young noble.

He grinned and took her hand. "Your highness, what an honor to sit next to you tonight. I've been wanting to meet you ever since my cousin, the Duke of Edgemere, told me of your beauty."

Eirwyn smiled coyly, but inside, she cringed. The duke had chased her for years, but the man was old enough to be her grandfather. This young one must be his heir to have earned a seat at the engagement ball dinner.

She only hoped he'd get too tipsy at dinner and would be too far drunk to proposition her. There was nothing like nobles trying to outdo one another and get under her skirts. She sighed, already bored with the evening.

Perhaps she could sneak out to the tavern in a few days and get a real feel for the rumor mill about this whirlwind engagement. At the very least, she'd be able to breathe.

She sat at the table, her dress too tight, and barely leaving her room to eat. All the forks, all the place settings, the rules, and social etiquette... it was so very overwhelming.

After a nice, relaxing, simple meal in Olive's cottage, she felt the weight of her role as princess press on her that much more. She smiled at the nobles across the table and tried to bring them into conversation, the easier to manage the advances of the duke's heir and the Chancellor.

Chapter Eleven

Bella smiled, her cheeks stiff from the forced politeness of the evening. It was her engagement ball, something she'd never thought she'd experience. So why was she so on edge?

Her gaze landed on Eirwyn on the edge of the dance floor. She'd always been jealous of Eirwyn's beauty ever since she'd first stumbled into the tavern as a child.

Pa had given her everything she wanted: food, drink, clothing. He'd even made Bella share her only doll, not that she'd played with it in a while at that point. She'd been twenty, and Eirwyn only ten. Pa had given her a lot of attention, then he'd gone off to war only a few months later. No matter how much Bella resented Eirwyn taking that time with Pa before he left, Bella hadn't had the heart to ask the princess not to return once he was gone. She'd needed all the help she could get to keep the tavern running by herself.

At the memory of Pa, the pressure on her chest increased, and she looked across the dance floor.

Eirwyn had quietly held court through dinner at the opposite end of the table, everyone hanging on her every word. Those around her had laughed as she spun light and shadow figures across the table. The more they'd laughed and paid attention to Eirwyn, the more Gastone had stiffened and grown moody.

She'd seen the way he glared at Eirwyn and could feel the emotions rolling off him. It was so like the night he'd come to the tavern and turned her world upside down. Was it any wonder that she was on edge?

When the king and his guards had swept inside demanding to know where Eirwyn was, Bella knew her world was about to change yet again. She'd sent a maid upstairs to pull Eirwyn from the bed of whatever man she'd found.

The door burst open, and the king strode inside. His masquerade suit highlighted his hair as black as midnight. The starkness of his white cravat and shirt stood out against his tan skin.

The stringed lute twanged to a stop, the wounded soldier by the hearth gasping. Their other bar maids froze, and bowls of steaming stew clattered to the tables. The patrons lowered their ale, and Bella saw a few reach for their weapons. The guards at the door settled their hands on their swords, eyes ranging over the crowd.

She wiggled her fingers, weaving magic to straighten her dress and smooth her thick brown hair as she walked around the edge of the bar to the middle of the room. She dipped a low curtsy, quickly wiping her hands on the apron around her waist.

"Your majesty, to what do we owe the honor of this visit?" Bella asked.

The king looked her up and down, and she recognized the interested gaze. But his words had been cold when he'd demanded, "My sister is here instead of at the masquerade."

Bella nodded and held out a hand, palm up as she waved to the back. "We have a private room, Your Majesty. If you'd care to wait there, we'll fetch her."

Everyone in the tavern had been frozen in fear, no one moving or daring to even breathe. Even the guards that had accompanied the king stood silently at attention beside the door.

The king threw his hands wide, white smoke rising from his nose as he breathed shallowly, his eyes dilated. "My sister should be in the private room, not smashing with a dirty—"

Eirwyn had come down the stairs, her dress slightly twisted and her hair wilder than normal. She'd locked eyes with the king, and he'd lifted his hands, a fireball flickering in his palm.

Eirwyn had lurched forward, her hands up as she yelled, "No, Gastone, don't—"

But it was too late. He hurled the fireball at Eirwyn, hitting the door frame above her head. The wood crashed on top of her even as she dove to the side near the bar. She hit the bar, and Bella jumped in front of Eirwyn, her hands wide in supplication.

"Your Majesty—"

Another fireball flew toward the bar, and Bella panicked. She threw her hands up, deflecting the fireball as her heart raced. Heat slammed into her palms, and she shoved, sending it to the fireplace where it exploded.

Ashes flew over the room. Some maids screamed and others jumped under the tables to hide. Those closest to the door sprinted for the exit, the guards not stopping them.

Bella felt Eirwyn's hand on her arm, and then a gust of wind swept the ashes into a small black tornado and back into the fireplace where it collapsed.

Now that the air was clear, Bella took a deep breath, shifting on her toes as she watched the king warily. He panted, fire still in his palms as he glared at Eirwyn and lifted a hand.

She had to stop him before he burned down the entire tavern. She couldn't let him destroy it when it was all she had.

"Enough," Bella shouted, drawing his gaze. "She shouldn't have missed the masquerade. Eirwyn, apologize. Now."

Bella's tone brooked no argument, the same tone she'd used on ruffians who refused to cooperate.

"I'm sorry, Gastone. I didn't mean to offend," Eirwyn said softly, her forehead creased in a frown.

The king narrowed his eyes, and his flaming hands burned brighter. "You think an apology is all it takes? You flaunt yourself around town with no regard to who you are or what you represent."

Bella waved her wrists in circles, sending a pulse of Synthara into the stools and chairs around them.

They shifted, animating into a grotesque type of soldier. Two gathered around her and the rest formed a wall between the king and those still huddling under the tables.

Bella's temper flared. "Without her calming influence, the people would've revolted years ago. She's not flaunting herself. She's setting worried minds at ease, something you should learn to do."

His eyes flashed. "How dare you speak to me like that."

Bella twisted her wrists, growing the stool soldiers and chairmen in size. She narrowed her eyes as his hands flared brighter, readying to release another fireball.

"By Borga's blade, if you throw another fireball in this tavern, you will lose your crown so help me gods." She widened her feet, prepared to die defending her father's tavern, her home, her refuge.

The king's brows rose as he paused, so Bella pushed her luck.

She said, "You've already destroyed the sigil of Jurus over the door frame. Do you really want to tempt the gods tonight?"

The king jerked slightly and glanced over. The top of the sigil could still be seen at the base of the stairs. He glanced back at Bella, looked at Eirwyn, then back again.

"The guards will escort you home, dear sister. Go now before I change my mind," he said as the fire in his hands faded.

Eirwyn looked at Bella, but Bella didn't dare take her eyes off the king.

"Go on," Bella said softly. "We'll be alright."

She only hoped it was true.

Eirwyn whispered, "Honifery protect you."

Bella nodded, noting the way Gastone watched Eirwyn walk slowly across the floor like a hawk eying its prey. The gods would see justice served, but she just hoped it wasn't justice for her death or the destruction of her father's tavern.

She swallowed hard and lifted her voice. "The same goes for all of you. Get out."

The wall of chairs shifted, allowing the patrons to mass rush the door. Two of the guards left with Eirwyn, but two more remained, one on either side of the door.

The king released his magic, the white smoke drifting from his hands. Bella returned the chairs to their tables, but the barstools remained protectively behind her.

"You worship the old gods?" he asked.

She nodded slowly. "I find their ways make more sense than what the new religion spouts. The popular opinion isn't always the right one."

Gastone snorted, a white tendril of smoke curling from his nose as he smiled. "How clever. Jurus, Borga, and now you quote Honifery? How curious..." He paused, and she shifted on her feet as he stared at her.

"Do you follow all of Borga's teachings?" he asked.

She held her hands together in front of her, portraying an air of confidence even though her stomach was in knots. "While Borga is popular today among those who wish for more freedoms, I follow Borga

*because she ensures the ale and wine are safe and brings more travelers.
Without Borga, I'd have no business."*

*The king's eyes glittered, sending a spark of awareness through her.
She was walking a fine line and couldn't let her guard down. He
nodded regally as if deciding something and pleased with his decision.*

"You mentioned a private room? I'd like to see it now."

*Bella tilted her head, not trusting him for a second, no matter how
drawn to him she was. "Certainly, Your Highness. Would you like a
pint of ale as well?"*

*He nodded, and the light from the fireplace illuminated his high
cheekbones, straight nose, and perfectly styled hair pulled back at the
nape of his neck in elaborate braids.*

*"I would, thank you. I apologize for the mess. I will, of course,
have it fixed tomorrow."*

*Bella nodded and waved to the narrow hallway that led to the
room, her stomach twisting in knots as nerves assailed her.*

Just like her stomach did now, she hadn't been able to that
night in the private dining room with the king nor tonight at
the ball. When the king had asked her to sit with him in the
parlor that night, she'd retreated to the kitchen for a tray. It
had given her a precious few moments to prepare a calming
spell, pray to the gods for the words to say to him, and beg
their protection for herself and the tavern. Then she'd
served him the stew Eirwyn had made earlier that night
before sitting down.

She had kept their conversation on safer topics than his
sister. They'd discussed religion, books, music, and art. He'd
been attentive, and she'd slowly relaxed around him. The
next day, word arrived that Eirwyn was going to Glathen to
negotiate a peace treaty. Then, the workers had shown up to
fix the tavern along with an invitation to a private dinner at

the castle. That was when he'd propositioned her for a week-long dalliance that had morphed into so much more.

Her mind wandered as she twirled and met her dance partner in the middle. He was some random duke that she couldn't remember the name of who only danced with her for political favor.

She'd learned a lot over the past few weeks living in the palace, most of it regarding her position. She was the gateway to the king, and he asked questions about the political pulse of the people in town.

During their first week together, he had wooed her with flowery words, bringing her books she'd never heard of and asking about the rumors in town. He had been invested in her opinion.

He had declared his love and proposed exactly one week after they'd met, had promised her all the books, tutors, and magic school she could ever want... if she would help him learn to be a better king to the peasants.

How could she not love him with that noble goal? How could she not when he had given her the world? But her stomach twisted every time he said something derogatory toward the commoners, folk just like her.

She felt Gastone's gaze on her, ever watching, ever appraising. She'd come to crave his approval in such a short time.

Lailant said it was because her father had been gone to war for so long. Only those who were too old or too young came to the tavern anymore. And the injured, shady characters, and draft dodgers.

She went to the next partner, the dance blurring together along with the passing evening. She finally bowed low and begged for a reprieve. She went up to her room to use the facilities, not wanting to chit-chat with any of the noblewomen in the large bathroom on the main floor.

She sat in front of her vanity and powdered her nose.

Gastone is going to lose the throne if you don't do something about it.

She sighed, not sure what she was supposed to do. She'd spent weeks coaching him on how to reshape his image with the people. He was too temperamental, too volatile, too passionate.

It's not his fault, though. He needs a strong woman at his side, and Eirwyn's been dragging him down for years.

She touched up her lips, her mind wandering in a haze. They had compromised to have the wedding here in her hometown; then they were going to take a wide honeymoon tour of the nation before going to the capitol.

Eirwyn should stay at the summer palace. She's less likely to make Gastone mad if she's out of sight.

Bella nodded at her reflection as it shimmered. Gastone had been strict but pleasant in the past few weeks as they'd gotten to know each other. She knew they could have a great marriage, but more than that, she could change the kingdom for the better.

Maybe even bring Pa home and end the blasted war. She stood, going back downstairs to continue working on the nobles. It wasn't only the commoners who needed to think differently about the king.

When Eirwyn awoke the next morning, she was in her large bedchamber with plush sheets and giant pillows. She snuggled in deeper, turning onto her side with a sigh. She winced at the pain in her stomach, and soft footsteps approached the bed.

"Are you awake?" Bella whispered.

Eirwyn hummed and rubbed her face against the clean sheets. With a start, she sat bolt upright, her gaze swinging around the room to find Bella standing next to her bed.

She wore a gold and red brocade gown, the corset laced tight. The silk sleeves shimmered in the soft afternoon sunlight that spilled into the room from floor-to-ceiling windows.

A bell tolled outside, and she knew she was back in Demerel in the palace. Her dreams had been full of Knox and the forest and flying over the trees.

She took a deep breath, calming her racing heart. Bella clasped her hands in front of her. Not a strand of hair was out of place, and her brown eyes were concerned but curious. All of their friendship, Eirwyn had felt like Bella watched her like a science experiment.

She looked around and held her stomach. "What—what are you doing here?" she asked.

Bella smiled tightly. "I wanted to check on you. You disappeared last night."

Eirwyn groaned and laid back down, rolling over and pulling the covers back up. "I just don't feel well."

"Aw, I'm so sorry," Bella said woodenly. Eirwyn looked up at her, blinking and trying to think. It was too early for her brain to make sense of why Bella was acting slightly off.

Bella went to the window and stared out. "I wanted to talk with you about your behavior last night at the ball. You shouldn't talk to your brother like that. He's trying his best, and ruling the kingdom is a difficult thing to do."

Eirwyn slowly sat up, frowning. A month ago, Bella

would've been complaining about Gastone with her over a pint of ale at the tavern.

Eirwyn breathed deeply and closed her eyes, tears threatening. "You're right, I'm sorry. I'm not trying to cause problems between you two."

Bella turned from the window, her back straight and her eyes cold. Her expression made Eirwyn freeze on the bed, reminding her of Gastone. She'd seen that same stone-cold expression as a child, and it always led to pain.

Her stomach twisted in worry, confusion, and fear.

"I know, but with that being said, I want you to consider staying here at the summer palace after the wedding. We'll be touring the nation before going to the capitol for the winter."

Eirwyn nodded, breathing through her nose and trying to control her roiling stomach. Sweat beaded her upper lip.

"I'm happy to give you two space. I know I set the worst off in Gastone. I don't know why he hates me so, but if it will help you start your marriage right without me underfoot, I understand."

"And the rest of the engagement dinners and balls. You should take a step back and let your brother have his moment in the spotlight."

Eirwyn's stomach rebelled, and she raced to the bathroom and retched. Bella's voice came through the open door. "Are you pregnant?"

Eirwyn groaned and heaved. "No," she croaked. She took the potion from Lailant every month, disgusting though it tasted. She'd last taken the potion just before she left for Glathen a month ago, and she hadn't been with anyone since.

Bella's voice came echoed in the room. "I'll tell your maid you're awake. She'll be right in to help you."

Eirwyn heaved, and tears pricked her eyes. It was the same feeling she'd had her whole life. She was weak, nauseous, and shaky. Why did this always happen to her? Why was she constantly sick? Was it the castle that made her so anxious?

Or was it just always walking on eggshells around her brother?

Perhaps she'd visit Lailant and see if she could help. She didn't have time to be sick, not with the wedding coming up so quickly. She had to help Bella prepare while staying out of her brother's way.

Chapter Twelve

Knox heaved his heavy axe and grunted, the metal slamming into the wood with a satisfying crack. Now back in Vidrland, he'd been out of sorts since taking Eirwyn into town. He itched for activity, for something that he couldn't quite identify, and hadn't been able to sit still for long since letting her go.

"It's time to ramp up our efforts with the Robins. The timing is right, what with the king getting married in a month. It's time for phase two."

The small band of former soldiers, rangers, and convicts sat on their horses, but Ashur leaned on his pommel. They were the highest-ranking Robins, other than John and the druids, having earned the trust of the inner circle. Yet Knox still kept his face and tail hidden from them as much as possible, even while he swung the axe again, splitting another log in two.

Will shifted on his saddle. "Are we finally going to make a bigger push to rob more than just the tax collectors? What about the rich snobs?"

Knox lifted another log onto the stump. "You're already doing that, Will..."

Ashur flushed and clenched his jaw, glancing away from Knox's heavy stare. He hadn't been as involved as he could have been, and Ashur had stepped up the past few months. Knox had given him the lead and watched and waited.

Anger burned in his chest, and he leaned on his axe handle as he glared beneath his hood. "Phase one was to follow the tax collectors and steal the money back from the king. Phase two of the plan was to slowly work our way around the kingdom, robbing the rich. You jumped into phase two without permission or voting on the matter. My reports say you're doing well organizing the attacks and have stuck to our rules of only robbing the king's men or rich men, so that's good."

Knox turned his eye back to Ashur. "However, you should've come to me first. We should've put it to a vote before taking action. Jumping to phase two without the consent of the people is a violation of what we stand for. Am I clear?"

His voice was soft, but none of them could mistake the steel undertones. Ashur's jaw clenched, and his back straightened. "Aye, Master Warden."

Knox sighed and hefted his axe to his shoulder. "We're not simply thieves. We're here to chip away at the king's power so we can protect and provide for the people. We don't rob just anyone, regardless of what some of our people's former professions might've been. We have to be strategic. Don't forget the Robin's oath."

They all nodded, several putting their fist to their chest and bowing their head slightly. When they'd recovered enough from their wounds and had decided to stay, he'd made them all take the oath.

Knox sighed and rubbed his head under the hood with his free hand. "Have you been turning the money over to John for inventory so he can ensure it gets to the right people in the local communities?"

Ashur spat on the ground and nodded. "Hells, Knox, you know we have. We gave our word."

Knox stroked his jaw, his five o'clock shadow already prominent even in the mid-morning sun. He wasn't sure how trustworthy the promises of criminals and deserters were, which was why he made sure upstanding soldiers always accompanied them.

Although he did trust them with his life. He wouldn't have let them join the Robins if he hadn't spent time with each and every one of them, learning their personalities, goals, dreams, and fears. This part of gentle reprimand went a long way to keeping order in Vidrland with so many types of people.

Will murmured softly. "I'm sorry we started phase two without express permission, but the wedding will have a lot of wealthy nobles going to and from the summer palace. Robbing from the rich would then put pressure on the king to end the war, right? Isn't that our entire end goal?"

Others nodded, and Knox looked at him thoughtfully. He never wanted them to see him as a tyrant, so he said, "I see what you're saying, but it should be put to a vote for our people to decide. Let's vote tomorrow night. In the meantime, do you have a plan or an idea to pitch at the meeting?"

Will nodded and spoke softly and slowly. Knox stroked his chin as he listened, nodding and asking questions here and there.

Knox had returned from Demerel with a cart and the

donkey. He'd loaded up Olive's supplies, but he'd also worked to get three more prisoners out of the dungeons.

They had families and had simply been in the wrong place at the wrong time. Some noble had accused the three of robbing him simply because the noble didn't want to pay for the new clothing and shoes that he'd ordered.

He'd snuck them out of town on the cart, too. They were busy repairing the clothing, shoes, and tents in Vidrland but had begged him to go back to town and bring their families to the safety the forest provided.

He shook his head at the irony of the forest providing safety, careful to keep his hood up.

Knox sighed, "You're right. Officially launching phase two and robbing the rich will help force the king's hand. With all the foreign dignitaries from neighboring nations and the nobles from the capitol coming for the wedding... it presents a great opportunity to rob the rich on the roads within Busparia."

"What about robbing the wedding reception ball itself?" Will asked. Knox looked around and tried to get a feel for how the others felt about it.

Ashur said, "It will take stealth and a lot of planning. Several of us will need to dress as servants or nobles to get in. Others will need to stand guard. Those who go inside will need to make sure no harm befalls anyone."

Will asked, "Not even the king? It'll be a good opportunity to assassinate him."

Knox shook his head. "Other than being annoying by passing overbearing taxation on the people without their consent and prolonging a war no one wants, he hasn't done anything outright illegal. So no killing the king."

"He's killed plenty by sending them to a pointless war. And now he's throwing people into prison for the most minor of offenses, some of them dying too. This might be our best chance," Ashur said.

Knox held up a hand. "I said no. We will not vote on murder. However, I might have a better idea for the king that I think you'll like, but let me think on it first. We will present it to the Robins tomorrow night and vote as a group. Then we'll need to prepare to be in Demerel at least the day before the wedding, prepare and plan. I'd like everyone to have their eyes and ears open. No getting drunk from the festivities leading up to the wedding."

More groans from his men, but he knew they'd obey.

He paid his men well, but it wasn't bought loyalty that kept them with him and silent. Only these half-dozen men even knew he was the one behind the Robins at all. Them, the dwarf John, and the two old druids, that is.

These had been with him the longest and were the ones he trusted. And they trusted him in return.

John was their steward. Every week, he did a random check of the records and the distribution of their contraband, reviewed the sales of goods, and sent spies to confirm bits and pieces. It was part of the system he'd woven to check and make sure no one was stealing or doing something illegal. Not many realized their little band of outlaws had a very strict code of honor and rules, all created and enforced by the big man in the black hood and cloak.

Everyone else in camp saw a man in all black. It was as the Robin, the druid Master Warden protector of the forest, that he led them with speeches and worked alongside them to fell trees and even eat. The hood provided anonymity and gave the people someone to look up to without focusing on the flaws of humanity.

"Alright, Will, take your goods to John for inventory and eat a good meal. Relax for the day and gather provisions.

Then I'm going to send each of you on another mission before the wedding. You can cast your vote before you leave on whether we're going to rob the rich on the roads or rob the wedding. Will, you'll stay until after the vote is counted and discuss the results with Ashur and I."

They all nodded and straightened on their horses, so Knox continued. "Sharo, go west and report back on Glathen. There are a few liars in the town outside the Lone Road who are telling travelers they are the ones to pay for protection through the forest. Stop them, then set up in the town as the toll taker and guide."

Sharo nodded, and Knox continued. "Also, find out what they're going to do about the wedding. I want to know what they think about the king marrying a commoner instead of their princess. They might be offended."

Sharo nodded and turned his horse, then he and Will disappeared into the encampment, riding straight for the large, long wooden building that John used as their storehouse.

"Nineel, go back to the tavern in Demerel and keep your ears peeled. I want to know everything about the future queen or anything else to do with the king. Are they staying at the summer palace during their honeymoon or leaving for the capitol? We need to know."

Nineel turned and followed Sharo into the encampment. Knox watched as Sharo swung off his horse and began to unload his saddlebags.

"Zomoya, go east into Busparia, then circle onto the Southern Road. See if any of our people need help on their way back home into Busparia. If we need to send food to the soldiers, let me know. No one should starve this winter, but we need to be prepared to help."

Zomoya disappeared, joining the others in front of the lodge.

"Pari, Simta, I want you both far away from the Growlers while they're in mating season. You can help us with the wedding reception plan, but the next day, go north and patrol the borders. One of you go northeast, and one go northwest. Let me know if either kingdom is pushing into the mountains."

Pari and Simta nodded, and they turned and disappeared, their long hair in a solid braid down their backs.

When it was only him and Ashur, he sighed and turned to grab the reins of his horse grazing nearby.

He swung up onto Ryder and turned to stare at the encampment.

Ashur had been with him from the beginning of the war. He'd been bloodied and scarred and had been discharged to go home. But the kingdom had not protected the Lone Road from the Growlers. Knox had found him closer to death than life in the forest, an assassin vine wrapped around his neck.

Knox had saved him and taken him to a safer part of the forest. Using the skills he'd learned from Olive, he'd patched Ashur up and listened to his delirious talks of the war. As he'd healed, Ashur had the idea to build up Vidrland and form the Robins.

They would help his fellow veterans trying to make it home. They could provide an escort service through the forest, a protection detail for those who wanted to go between Glathen and Busparia without being detected or dying in the Feral Forest.

That had led to talk about taxes and the war, and a plan had begun to form.

When Little John had stumbled into the forest, then

another soldier, then another, the plan took on a life of its own. The Robins were born and had worked all these years to end the war.

"I was waiting on your reports, but as soon as the vote is over tomorrow night, I need to go north to the dwarves. They have been working on a device that will aid us in bringing the king to his knees. Then I need to see Olive and deliver her supplies. Will you stay here, watch over Vidrland, and see to the preparations for the wedding reception? It seems like every week, this place grows bigger. We need to start building permanent structures for those still in tents."

Ashur nodded, still leaning on his pommel. "Aye, I'll see that it's done. Did you meet the newbies? Lots of women." Ashur nodded to Vidrland.

Knox sighed and rubbed the sides of his head. "Not this again, Ash. We're not heathens."

Ashur shrugged. "They're camp followers, mate. Sex work is their bread and butter, and if you don't put out, someone else will. You might as well get yours."

Knox snorted. He might consider Ashur a friend, but he wasn't about to explain how complicated his love life was. Or the lack thereof. It would mean exposing his face and abilities, and that couldn't happen.

"Don't worry about me, Ash."

Ashur wiggled his eyebrows. "Speaking of, I'm going to go debrief Little John and see who's available for some roughhousing."

Knox wrinkled his nose in disgust. "First, don't call him that. You know he hates that. Second, don't call sex rough-housing. That's just—"

"The fun way to do it?" Ashur grinned and kicked his horse, setting off into the slowly growing village at the northern center of the forest.

He wasn't really attracted to any of the camp followers and had felt no attraction before meeting Eirwyn, but Ashur didn't need to know that. Sure, he had itches to scratch, but it wasn't anything his hand couldn't handle.

Except now he dreamed of fucking Eirwyn every night. Every morning, he woke up harder than when he'd gone to bed. Even his hand was getting tired now, and it'd only been a few days since he'd said goodbye in Demerel.

He turned Ryder into the forest and rode north to the dwarves. Perhaps he'd get to see her in Demerel when they infiltrated the wedding reception. He was fairly sure the people would vote for that option, and he smiled as he imagined her dressed in her royal finery.

Even if he wanted to throw Eirwyn over his shoulder and ride into the forest to fuck her for days, he couldn't escape the responsibilities of leadership. The people in the forest counted on him.

Knox sighed and rode into Vidrland.

Chapter Thirteen

"And that's how the king fell in love with our very own tavern mistress," Eirwyn said with a flourish, swirling her hands and making the dancing light projections dissipate around the tavern. A burst of colors exploded on the ceiling, raining down on the patrons.

It distracted everyone, but also distracted herself from her not having a special someone like the story. Her mind went to Knox, but she probably wouldn't ever see him again. She looked over the crowd, but none of them appealed to her. Ever since she'd come back from Glathen, she'd had no interest in taking anyone upstairs.

Applause broke out, and the new manager nodded his head approvingly. He'd been hesitant to let Eirwyn into the tavern tonight, but after a few days cooped up in the castle, she'd needed to escape.

First, there'd been the engagement ball. The courtiers had fawned over Bella, which Eirwyn was happy to see. She wanted her friend to be accepted as queen, and if Eirwyn were being honest, she'd been worried the rich lords and ladies weren't going to welcome her.

She shouldn't have worried, though. Bella was very well-read and could always find a topic of common interest, unlike Eirwyn's own conversations with them. All she could do was flirt, and it often sent the wrong message.

But then there'd been the dress fittings and organizing Bella's lessons. Eirwyn had interviewed all the people Gastone had hired for Bella. The history tutors, etiquette teachers, dance instructors, and magic professors all met her approval as well.

Then, she'd scheduled daily classes with her soon-to-be sister-in-law in the management of the castle. It was the one job that Gastone actually gave her any power to perform. And now it was being turned over to Bella.

Eirwyn grew more worried about her future in Busparia with every passing day. Gastone paraded young and old men alike in front of her. The pressure to make a match, get married, and move out made her skin itch. She'd not found any of them attractive at all, and most were boring, stuffy old men or practically little puppies for as young as they were.

None of them held a candle to Knox's outdoor manliness.

Eirwyn also found Bella growing more and more frazzled as the days passed, especially when the visiting dignitaries from the other countries and continents began to arrive for the wedding.

Bella had never met elves before and had been worried about making a fool of herself. Then there had been the dignitaries from the fae kingdom and even a representative from the newly reclaimed mermaid kingdom. The man and wife's tentacles for hair had been unexpected. Eirwyn had put on her happy face and charmed them like always, but it had just added to the stress for all of them.

She could play the adorable princess role, but it was exhausting to always be *on*. After yet another ball to celebrate the visiting dignitaries, Eirwyn had snuck out to the tavern.

Willis set a mug of ale on the table. "Here you go, Your Highness."

She grinned and reached into her pocket for some coin. "Thank you, sir, for letting me entertain tonight. I needed that bright spot of fun."

He waved away her coin. "No, you've earned the ale at the least. You've a knack for storytelling, and I'm mighty proud to have heard you. Sorry about hesitating to let you in earlier."

His cheeks reddened as he scratched the back of his neck.

She smiled and waved a hand. "Don't worry about it. Bella and I had an arrangement, which I'm happy to continue. But if it'll make you feel more comfortable to talk to her first, I understand."

He nodded. "I'll do that. And thank you. Let me know if you need anything else, Your Highness."

She nodded, and he walked away. She sat back and nursed her ale, enjoying her corner seat. It gave her the best view of the entire room, and she loved people-watching.

She wrapped the shadows slowly around her and sipped. Soon enough, most of the people in the tavern forgot she was even there. She frowned as she listened to the gossip.

The people were excited about the wedding and all the soldiers returning home from war. They were due home within the next week, as the Southern Road was a longer route.

Some grumbled about the king chopping down trees to the south of town.

"He tried it a few years ago, do you remember?"

"I'm not sure what he hopes to do. No one can get through the forest without the Robins' help."

Eirwyn's ears perked up, and she turned slightly to better hear the dirty chimney sweeps two tables over.

"The Robins will stop him, don't worry," the tall one said.

"Bless them. Did you hear they got Matt and Bob out of the stocks?"

The tall one raised his mug and made eye contact with the bartender. "Really? I wondered where they'd gone. The missus is already grumbling about having to do more work. She's taking in more darning since the tailor's been gone."

"The Robins got their families out, too. They're tucked away safe and sound in the forest, I bet."

"I'm telling you, there's no such safety in the forest. It's all haunted and will kill you if you even go near it."

The other chimney sweep leaned forward and lowered his voice, but Eirwyn pushed a small gust of wind to make his voice flow directly to her. "I heard there's a secret town in the forest where we can escape the mad king."

"Psh, I'm sure Matt and Bob have just gone to start shops in a new town, one that the king doesn't frequent as often."

Eirwyn's stomach knotted. It wasn't her first time hearing about the Robins' work, but it was the first time she'd heard of a town in the forest. In her absence last month, the townsfolk had started calling her brother mad? That was new too and sent a shiver of fear down her spine.

She finished her ale, but her stomach kept rolling. It was probably stress-related. Heavens knew her brother could make a saint sick from stress.

She pulled her hood up and stood, her legs shaky. She frowned as her stomach cramped. Then she ducked through the hallway to the kitchens. Her shadows wrapped around her and prevented the staff and patrons from seeing her as she found the privy attached to the back wall of the tavern.

She shut the door just in time to retch. Her forehead beaded with sweat, and she took a deep breath when she was done. She picked up her cloak and wiped her mouth with the inside hem.

When she stepped out, she could barely see the stars in the darkness, but at least her stomach wasn't aching. She went to the water spigot by the stables and rinsed her mouth out before starting the walk back to the palace.

It'd be faster to go through town instead of through the secret entrance. The way she felt right now, she wanted to be home as quickly as possible. Helga had long tried to talk her out of walking, especially at night. But with her shadowy Nekros magic and the birds' help, she could avoid most unsavory people.

She strode swiftly through the dim alleyways, wrapping her shadows around her like a second cloak to obscure her features. If anyone saw her, they'd blink and question their eyesight. It was how she'd been sneaking in and out of town for years.

Helga had no reason to worry. Despite her fancy dress and obviously expensive cloak, she had no fear as she walked through the narrow streets.

Eirwyn passed a beggar in a narrow passageway whom the birds weren't worried about.

"Spare some coin for an old man?"

Eirwyn danced out of his reach, picking up her smooth silk gown to avoid having it touch him even as she dug in her pocket.

She handed him three coins. "Here you go." Then she turned and continued on her way.

Her stomach twisted and the ache returned as she turned onto an even narrower alley. When she went up the steps to the next street, she tried to distract herself from her stomach by thinking of what changes this wedding would bring.

Some birds cawed overhead, and she looked up. A lone man stood waiting at the top of the stairs. She frowned, but at the birds' message, she spun on her heels. Her heart raced at their warning. Two men in shadows stood at the bottom of the alley.

She paused, her breath catching in her lungs as they began to walk up the steps. She looked behind her to the man at the top. He too was walking down toward her. They were going to box her in, and the birds were not happy as they began to circle above her.

She wrapped the shadows around her tighter and pressed herself to the wall, head whipping side to side to watch both angles. The lone man at the top paused when her shadows obscured her, but then the two men at the bottom of the stairs were jerked back. A huge, hulking figure moved with such speed that even she couldn't see in the shadows. The two men crumpled in a heap at his feet, then he stepped over them and came up the stairs two at a time.

"Duck," the man hissed.

She squatted, and a loud thud hit above her. She turned to see the lone figure grasping his arm as he turned and fled back up the stairs.

She breathed heavily and looked up at the looming figure now only a few steps below her. He tipped his head back, and brilliant green eyes met her own in the dim light.

He held out a hand. "Are you alright, Eirwyn?"

She took it, her mind splintering. "Knox? What are you doing here?"

He shrugged. "I placed an order for some supplies for Olive and was told to come back in a few days to pick them up. What are you doing here?"

Her stomach twisted, and she put a hand on it, breathing deeply until the spasm passed. Then she said, "I went to the tavern. I just needed to escape all the wedding preparations, the fanfare of the diplomats, and court."

"You shouldn't be out alone and unescorted."

She sighed. "I've gone back and forth to the tavern for years, Knox, and was perfectly fine. Besides, it was worth the risk. I needed a break, a fun night to just relax. Do you ever feel like that? Like the world is just pressing down on you, and you need to fly free, or you'll burst?"

He rubbed his chin and leaned closer, one palm on the wall above her. Her breath caught in her throat as she stared up at him.

"I feel like that all the bloody time, princess." His voice was deep and sent a shiver up her spine. She tipped her head back and swayed closer to him, her shadows wrapping around him too.

But he stepped back, waving in front of him. "Let me escort you the rest of the way."

She nodded, disappointment twisting her stomach, and turned to walk up the steps. She lifted her skirt and stepped over the dark liquid from the attack.

"Thank you for taking care of those men. I've walked all

over this town for years, and I've never been attacked like that. Look at me, I'm shaking."

She held out her hands and laughed from nerves.

He stopped at the end of another alley and hesitated before pulling her into a hug. His strong biceps wrapped around her, and she melted into his arms. It was the first time anyone had touched her since he'd dropped her off weeks ago.

"You're safe now, princess. As long as I'm around, you'll always be safe."

A delicious honey scent filled her nostrils, mixing with his woodsy musk and the city around them. It made her mad with desire, her core aching. Her desire mixed with the protection of his arms was heady feeling and made her dizzy. She didn't want to let him go.

She sighed, her shoulders relaxing for the first time in weeks. She'd felt like she was walking on pins and needles since she'd gotten home. Gastone kept staring at her over the dinner table, and the look in his eye gave her pause.

It wasn't new. She'd seen that look on his face a lot over the years. But the intensity had shifted, and now he'd added a little smirk to it like he knew something she didn't.

Knox pulled back and looked down. Eirwyn sent a gust of wind flowing up to push his hood back and look him in the eyes, but he quickly caught the edge, holding it in place before it fell back. It was enough so that she could see his emerald eyes though, and they shone with concern. "Is there something else going on? You seem tense."

She bit her lip, then smiled as she stepped away from him. His arms dropped to his sides, and they began walking once more.

"No, nothing else. Just stressed about the wedding, tired and hungry, I suppose."

She felt empty as she walked, and she had an over-whelming need to touch him. They reached the wider streets of the wealthier side of town, and she took Knox's arm. He gave a look down at the contact but crooked his arm like a gentleman and walked next to her.

"Do you come into town often?" she asked. Gods, there she went, asking stupid questions again.

"Rarely, although I've found myself in town more and more the past weeks."

She wanted to ask what he normally did when he wasn't in town. Did he just chop down trees? Did he work with the king's forces to the south to create a new road? Somehow, she doubted it.

She cleared her throat to ask, "How are Olive and Scarlet?"

He nodded, his head turning side to side and scanning the deserted streets for trouble. "They're doing well. I took Olive some of her supplies last week and told her about the wedding. We're all eager to see how this will impact the kingdom."

She snorted as the palace loomed ahead. "You and me both. But Bella is a good woman, and she'll make a great queen. Not sure that even she has the power to temper my brother's unique nature, though."

"That's a very tactful way of saying he's a pain in the ass. And you don't consider yourself a diplomat?"

She laughed as they finally walked along the palace wall to the back gatehouse. She waved to the portcullis.

"This is where I'll leave you if you don't mind. But I really would like to see you at the tavern the next time you're in town?"

"I'll be back for the wedding, but you'll probably be busy

with royal duties. Are you leaving for the capitol now that summer is almost over?"

She grinned, leaning forward to stroke his forearm. "I'll actually be staying in Demerel while they take their honeymoon tour, which will be a relief. The best party in town after the wedding will be at the tavern. I'm hoping to sneak away by midnight when Bella and Gastone retire from the ball and go to their room. Then I can escape to the tavern and really let my hair down. Will I see you there?"

He nodded, the faint lights from inside the archway illuminating the lower half of his face. "Sounds like a date."

Her heart fluttered at his deep voice and beautiful smile. She wanted to see more of him, and her fingers itched to push his hood back.

But she didn't want to jeopardize her chances of seeing him again. She would wait till they got to the tavern, a neutral place where the fear of her brother seeing them wouldn't loom over her head, where he'd feel comfortable removing more clothing than just his cloak and hood.

She'd need to talk to the new tavern manager about renting her usual room, cleaned to her specifications.

She smiled and caught herself from leaning in closer. She squeezed his forearm and dropped her hand.

"Thanks for seeing me safely home."

He stiffened and nodded, his lips still smiling softly. "I'll see you around, princess."

Then he turned and strode away. She slipped through the gatehouse, hugging the shadows and avoiding the guards who were already dozing. She didn't want them to say anything about a man walking her home.

But now that she had a plan to meet up with Knox after the wedding, she wasn't dreading it so much.

Chapter Fourteen

Eirwyn sat on her own pew to the side of the raised dais in front of the cathedral and watched Bella marry the king.

She never thought in all her wildest dreams that her friend would become queen. Or that her friend, her smart and talented friend, would fall for her arrogant brother.

The few weeks since she'd last seen Knox had flown by. She'd been cooped up at the palace for days now, helping Bella put the finishing touches on the wedding.

She was happy for her friend whose fortune had changed drastically, but it put Eirwyn on high alert. Every day, she woke with dread as she panicked about her own future. It was like she couldn't catch her breath unless she thought about Knox, which was more often than was probably healthy.

She'd stolen a few precious moments on the roof, feeling the wind in her hair and listening to the birds chirp. Yesterday morning, she'd snuck out before the rest of the castle had awoken and ridden to the edge of the forest near the road.

She didn't go in, and she didn't see Knox. But just being closer to him, feeling the energy from the forest, helped settle her nerves. With all the chaos of the wedding, thoughts of Knox still took up most of her brain.

The priest rang a bell, and Eirwyn blinked. The wedding was over, and Bella and the Gastone turned and faced the crowd. Her brother stood tall, strong, and proud as he stared icily at the crowd.

His eyes stopped briefly on Eirwyn, and he gave a small twitch of his lips. Every time they'd spoken this week, she felt a slimy feeling down her spine, like when they'd been children and something bad was about to happen.

Bella knelt in her pale yellow lace gown, and the priest said some boring, monotone words before placing a crown on her head. The king offered her a hand, and she stood as the priest introduced her as Queen Bella. The crowd clapped and cheered as the two walked down the stairs and aisle to the end of the giant cathedral in the middle of town.

She and Bella had snuck out in the middle of the night and woven a spell, making the entire cathedral shine like new. It had been nice to have the old Bella back. They'd talked like the good old days at the tavern before going back to the castle.

The illusion on the cathedral would wear off in a few days. Less if it rained. Bella's magic had been something they had bonded over all those years ago. Eirwyn had taught Bella all the things she'd learned in school and had snuck her a few books here and there. But Bella said Eirwyn never paid enough attention to the details, which frustrated the knowledge-obsessed Bella.

Eirwyn hung back, clinging to the few shadows in the church and waiting for the rest of the cathedral to empty out. There was to be a celebration at the summer palace tonight, and then the King and Queen were going to take an extended honeymoon and tour the kingdom, eventually landing at the capitol just in time for the seasons to change.

Eirwyn would be staying in Demerel at the summer palace, so that was a blessing, at least. She was looking forward to having the run of the palace without her arrogant, condescending brother breathing down her neck. Then there was the possibility of seeing more of Knox.

The townspeople had mostly forgotten about the war in their excitement about the wedding of one of their own beloved to the king. Even the Robins had quieted in town. Although she'd heard they were robbing the nobles and dignitaries traveling throughout the country for the wedding.

She'd listened to more gossip from the servants, but they rarely discussed the Robins or the war. Helga waited at the back of the church, and Eirwyn stood and shook out her blue silk dress.

With head held high, she followed her brother and now sister-in-law down the aisle. Helga stepped into the aisle and helped her put on her red cloak before falling into step behind her. Together, they walked to the enclosed carriage on the left while the crowd gathered around the open-air carriage to the right.

Gastone and Bella were stepping into it, waving to the peasants and nobles who lined the streets. Guards stood shoulder to shoulder to keep them from pressing too close.

The carriage door shut, and Eirwyn tipped her head back with a sigh. Her stomach still twisted and turned, and she couldn't wait until tomorrow when this nightmare week would be finished.

"How's your stomach?" Helga asked.

Eirwyn sighed. "It'll all be better tomorrow. Just a few more hours, then I'll be free."

The swaying of the carriage almost lulled her to sleep. She jerked when the carriage rolled to a halt in front of the palace. The footman opened the door, and Eirwyn waited until her brother and friend ascended the stairs before she stepped down.

Gastone had been very clear on his instructions. He didn't want anyone looking at Eirwyn. He wanted all eyes on him and his beautiful, loving bride.

Eirwyn didn't mind, and she wasn't going to do anything that might make him angry on his big day. She hoped Bella would be a calming influence on him. Maybe they could be a real family now.

She snorted at the absurdity of that idea and went up the steps, dread sinking into her stomach like a brick. She glanced over her shoulder at Helga and said softly, "I need to go to my room before the reception."

Helga frowned and nodded. "I'll inform the butler, then I'll be right up to help."

Eirwyn waved at her. "No, I'm just going to lie down for an hour. I think it'll help settle my stomach. See if anything else needs done, if the housekeeper needs anything for the reception."

Helga nodded as they walked through the doors, and Eirwyn went to her room. She pulled her dress over her head and laid it on the back of a chair so it wouldn't wrinkle. Then she crawled between her cool silk sheets with a sigh.

When Eirwyn woke up, the reception ball was in full swing downstairs. She needed air, though. A weight was pressing on her, threatening to suffocate her. She stretched, grateful that at least her stomach felt better, and went to the window to let in fresh air. The always present birds tweeted on the sill, gossiping about what had happened so far in the gardens and reception while she got dressed, washed her face, and reapplied her rouge.

She stared at her wedding slippers where she'd kicked them off by the settee, but went to her closet for the walking boots. She wanted to wear them to the tavern later, so she might as well put them on now.

With a smile and deep, calming breath, she waved the birds goodbye as she closed the window. Just a few hours of schmoozing with the court, and then she'd be able to see Knox. Her smile turned into a grin as she thought about the dainty, red lace underwear she'd specifically worn today for him.

She just hoped she'd finally have time to show him. She turned to walk to the door, but a bird at the window made her pause. What was happening in the gazebo that she needed to see? The bird wasn't specific. Just overall impressions of danger.

She couldn't let anything ruin Bella's big night. If all went according to plan, Bella and Gastone would be leaving in the morning for their honeymoon, and for a few precious months Eirwyn would be free to spend time with Knox. Whatever was happening at the gazebo had to be taken care of.

She grabbed her red cloak and went down the servants back stairs and outside. She wandered the gardens, following the bird's suggestion and turning toward the gazebo as voices echoed softly.

Quickly, she ducked onto a side path with tall hedges as a pair of guests walked past, looking for a place to kiss. Their voices faded, but other whispers came from the other side of the hedge. Eirwyn thanked the bird, even though she wasn't sure what she was thanking him for yet.

But she had to find the danger and fix it. Most likely, it was some clandestine meeting of passion. In a few hours, maybe she'd be able to convince Knox to give in to his feelings and explore passion with her. She continued on the path through the now dark gardens, hoping for more than a one-night stand with him. With a few months away from her brother, she might be able to have her first actual, stable relationship.

She stared up at the giant castle, the peaks looming into the sky and shining with a thousand lanterns on the parapets. Pigeons chattered with excitement for the party, but the crow that squawked nearby led her to be cautious.

She walked around the blooming rose bushes that edged the pond in the center of the gardens. The hedge wall on the other side muffled the voices, and she rounded the bend and spied the gazebo. She subtly shifted the wind to carry their voices to her.

"She doesn't know a thing, but I need you to take care of it tonight," a familiar deep voice echoed from inside the gazebo.

Eirwyn's footsteps slowed as she listened, and she wrapped the shadows around her more, snuffing out the light. This was one reason she loved going to the tavern. She liked to see and hear all the juicy gossip and know who was doing what. It led to fewer surprises and being more prepared when everything went to shit.

That was why it'd been so stressful and such a shock when Gastone had shown up at the tavern that night to drag her back home. She'd not seen it coming. And now it had led to a chain reaction of the wedding.

"Are you sure this is necessary?" a soft, feminine voice asked.

"Yes, absolutely. It's long overdue. The kingdom depends on this, do you understand?"

Eirwyn frowned. What was Gastone doing out here? He should be inside with his guests.

"No, but you're the king. Your word is my command."

Eirwyn's eyebrows rose. It was her brother! And he was meeting with this woman on his wedding night during his wedding reception? What was he up to?

"Your wife won't be happy," the woman said.

Eirwyn's rage began to boil. Was the king already cheating on Bella too? It definitely wasn't true love. Bella deserved better.

The king snorted. "She won't be that torn up about it. Trust me. I know my wife. Now, will you do it or not?"

Eirwyn frowned. How could he know Bella when they'd only met two months ago? What could her strict, tyrannical brother be planning that her friend would approve of?

The woman said, "Aye, but half now and half when I bring back the heart."

There was a pause, then a soft clinking sound echoed.

"We're done here. I'll send a note to the guild master when you return with a meeting place for the other half and the heart."

Boots slid on the floor of the gazebo. Eirwyn dipped in between two big rose bushes as her heart raced, not even caring if her new gown became torn. There was no telling what her brother would do if he found her eavesdropping.

She watched through the leaves as he walked out of the gazebo and down the straightest path to the veranda. She could barely hear the faint music through the open doors. The night was muggy but much cooler than it'd been in the day.

She stepped out of the bushes on silent feet, intent on sliding past the gazebo while trying to glimpse this mystery woman. Whoever she was, Eirwyn wanted to find out what she was getting paid to do and how it could hurt Bella or the kingdom.

She turned to the gazebo but hadn't taken even two steps when a hooded figure appeared in the doorway. Eirwyn frowned.

She'd heard a woman, but this was a small man wearing dark pants, boots, and a cloak. A hood obscured his face, but then he lifted small gloved hands and blew sparkling dust in her direction.

Eirwyn coughed and jerked to the side to avoid it, but it was too late. Her vision swam, and she fell, inky blackness welcoming her with open arms.

Chapter Fifteen

Scarlet scarfed down a bowl of meat and potatoes. She'd just raced back from a job in the north so she could attend the wedding festivities. She hadn't made it in time for the ceremony, but she could still relax with the other Hunters before they dispersed into the crowd, each going about their business as mercenaries. Tonight would be a big night for them, with all the extra visitors in town.

Some were using the revelry in the streets to complete jobs undetected, but those who were still at the guild hall were already well into their cups and gambling. Scarlet hurried to eat, keeping a clear head so she could fleece the drunks of their coin in an honest game of chance.

The guild master of the Demerel branch came into the common room with a letter. He looked over the lot of them and pointed a bony finger at Scarlet.

"You. Come." He jerked his thumb and spun on his heels. She sighed, resigning herself to another job. So much for winning more coin tonight and relaxing with her coworkers. She followed him to the office, where he waved to a chair. He tapped on an open letter on his desk.

"The king was pleased that you brought the princess safely home last month. I'm not surprised you found her first. We lost another Hunter to the forest, even though we warned him that you were the only one who could go in and out of there."

He shook his head in disappointment and sank to his chair, pushing an unopened letter across the desk. "The king included a bonus in the fee along with another request. He insists no one but you read it. I wouldn't put it past him to have enchanted it to make sure no one reads it."

Scarlet's brows rose as she read the letter, and then the guild master leaned forward to demand, "Well? What's he want?"

After she read it twice, it burst into flames. She jumped up, and ash fell to the floor.

The guild master peered over his desk to make sure the rug didn't catch fire.

She looked up at him as dread settled like a knot in her stomach. "He has another job but only wants me to do it."

She had to play this off as no big deal. If the guild master or anyone else in the Hunters found out how much the king was offering for this job, they'd jump into action. Money was king for the Hunters. A Hunter would kill his own mother for the right price.

The guild master eyed her, making the hair on the back of her neck stand. "It's a great honor, but you know what happens when people get repeat business from the king."

She nodded, swallowing hard as her spine tingled. "I need to go prepare. It will take a few days, but I'll check in when I get back," she said.

He nodded, then slumped in his chair and propped his

feet up on his desk. "May Fysica protect you because you're the best Hunter I've got. Don't go getting yourself killed. You're the best Hunter I've got."

She nodded and opened the door. "And you."

What could this be about? The letter was cryptic.

Five times the standard fee if you meet me in the castle's gazebo tonight at eleven for another job.

She repacked her bags and re-saddled her horse before riding through the noble district. The houses were large, with walled gardens and narrow alleys between them, but she barely noticed as she tried to think of what job the king could possibly want on his wedding night. Surely he wasn't going to murder the queen so soon?

She rounded the edge of the palace wall and followed it to the small gatehouse in the back behind the gardens. She checked her father's pocket watch, then snapped it shut. The noise of the revelry in the front courtyard drowned out her footsteps as she left her horse in the alley. He was a swift-footed gelding she'd had specifically trained. He wouldn't wander off, and anyone who tried to lead him away would have their hand bitten.

She peered around the gatehouse. The portcullis was open, but guards stood under the archway. Two cheered and chugged ale, a small crowd of guards egging them on. The one who finished first lifted his mug, and the crowd cheered. Money was exchanged as she slipped unnoticed behind them and into the garden.

Getting in and out of places came easy to her, which is why joining the Hunters had been a simple choice to make.

Her senses sharpened as she hunted for her target. Where would the gazebo be? She stalked on silent feet over the grass, avoiding the pebbled garden paths. Several nobles were on the back terrace, some smoking roots and talking quietly.

She reached out with her senses, somehow feeling where people were in the garden. Someone was in the gazebo, but it wasn't a couple seeking privacy. She moved closer, listening to every sound, watching for every aura.

Her grandmother and mother had hoped she'd be a druid. She'd trained until she'd reached ten, but her druidic magic had never come in, perhaps the divine blood was too diluted. All she had were a hunter's instincts and aura readings from her father.

Her mother had died thirty years ago when Scarlet was five. She'd lived with her grandmother and Knox until she'd been old enough to join her father on the road. He'd been a fighter, a ranger paid by the crown to do a circuit through his territory and solve problems for the people.

Then he went to war and died.

Scarlet had been filled with anger for a long time after that, and the Hunters had provided a way to channel that into an income. She listened behind the gazebo and looked at the moon.

There were no others around, so she slipped inside. The king paced in the middle, and when he turned around, he sucked in a breath and froze in his tracks.

He scowled, "Don't sneak up on me like that. You're the Hunter that brought Eirwyn home?"

She nodded, her hood hiding her face and keeping herself in the shadows.

"You're going to take her into the forest and cut out her heart. Bring it back to me. The official story is that Eirwyn's going to run off to the tavern again. But she gets lost in the dark and killed."

Scarlet's stomach clenched, and her blood went cold. She blinked in surprise. "You want me to kill the princess?"

He nodded. Scarlet's body remained frozen as she tried to find a solution. She couldn't turn him down; he'd just kill her and find someone else to take her place. She'd heard of it happening before. Her mind raced as she breathed through her surprise. She didn't move, just focused on breathing and watching him.

His aura was steady. He wouldn't attack her. Not yet, not unless she refused. A small curl of smoke rose from his nose, his hands behind his back as he stared with those cold, emotionless eyes.

She couldn't question him too much, or he'd see it as a challenge of his authority. A Hunter took a job and did it, regardless of the personal feelings on the matter.

They talked more, but Scarlet sensed another aura. She hurried him along by asking for half the payment. When he left, she'd turned to sense the aura on the other side of the gazebo wall.

She felt it was Eirwyn, recognizing her aura from before. She pulled out the sleep powder and stepped into the garden. It had to look like she was doing what the king wanted.

Scarlet slung the princess over her shoulder before she hit the ground and grunted. She was heavier than she'd thought a petite little woman like her would be. It didn't matter, though.

She turned to go through the back gate of the gardens, juggling the princess on her shoulder.

The guards were now passed out drunk on the ground outside the gatehouse. Scarlet clung to the shadows and slipped past them.

She tossed Eirwyn over the front of the horse, wincing

as she flopped. Knox would not be happy about this. He'd clearly been smitten with Eirwyn, and there was no way she could go through with the king's request.

But she couldn't let anyone else go through with it, either. Eirwyn had been nothing but kind to her. When Scarlet had first seen Eirwyn in the tavern years ago, she'd been telling the most fascinating story with bursts of light figures dancing on the ceiling. Scarlet had kept to herself and ignored most of the patrons, but she liked to keep her ears and eyes on gossip in town, especially when the royals were in residence.

It was always best to be prepared.

She swung into the saddle behind Eirwyn and led them through the back alleys toward the edge of town. Then she turned to the Lone Road and pursed her lips.

It was a full moon, and the fear and adrenaline from the king's words had grown within her chest, threatening to drown her. She focused on her breathing even as fear licked at her heels. Fear of the king, fear of the Growlers, fear of the forest itself… it spread through her body like ice.

She kicked the horse into a gallop. They had to reach Grandmother's house before the Growlers caught their scent.

Ashur eyed the cylindrical tube warily as they crept down the hallway of the castle. "Are you sure that's going to work?"

The rambunctious crowd in the courtyard had provided good cover to get into the castle. They'd easily picked the lock and knocked a guard out, entering through a parlor of some sort.

Knox shook his head and peered around the corner. "We've tested it for weeks, Ashur. It'll work."

Ashur sighed and muttered a common prayer to Borga, but Knox didn't look at him as they continued to the servant's stairs. They went up to the main floor. At the top of the stairs was a door that led to the kitchens.

They walked toward the door, his heart racing. If the king captured any of them, it would be the end of all their hard work. Fear beat at him, but he couldn't stop now.

The king's forces were still pushing into the forest. Will hadn't been able to stop them, and the king didn't respond to their letters in the newspapers.

With Auckwald reclaimed, it was time to lower the taxes and stop the war. Then Knox could send all the bedraggled and weary villagers in Vidrland back home. That was the only way to get peace in the forest.

But first, they had to rob the palace and show the king they meant business.

Knox took a deep breath and opened the door. There was a bustle of activity, and no one paid him any attention. Until he lifted the magical tube, pressed the three gems on the side, and blew a concentrated toxin into one end.

His green gas mixed with the magic in the tube, changing the gas from a deadly poison to nothing more than a sleeping gas before it was expelled at the other end of the tube. John had gone back to his brothers, the dwarves, to perfect the invention.

They'd tested it on almost every person in Vidrland, including the magic users. The sorcerers in the forest weren't as well-taught or magically gifted as the nobles or king. Knox just hoped it was powerful enough to last the thirty minutes it was supposed to.

The green gas sank to the floor, mixing with the feet of

the kitchen staff. No one noticed it billowing up around them. Several yawned. When the green reached their knees, they began to slump over where they stood. The cook laid her top half on the table, falling on the jam-covered pastries.

When they were all put to sleep, he walked through the kitchen toward another door, swiping an olpertine pastry as he went. He put it in his pocket to give to Eirwyn later, and a rush of anticipation shot through him.

The door opened onto another small hallway. Several nobles were going into a few doors on the side, and Knox stepped into each one, even the ladies' facilities room. When he'd walked through all the surrounding rooms, he stepped into the back of the ballroom.

Ashur and the other Robins had taken a preventative elixir to counteract the effects of the sleeping gas. Knox took a deep breath, growing dizzy from the deep breathing. The green and white smoke began to fill the room, sinking to the ground as nobles danced. Knox breathed out, his eyes scanning the crowd as he looked for a black-haired beauty.

The dancers slowed, and the music faded as everyone sank to the floor and curled into sleeping positions. Within seconds, snores were heard throughout the room. The Robins moved in, picking pockets and shoving gems and jewelry into bags.

Knox walked the perimeter before going onto the outdoor terrace and putting more people to sleep. Ashur disappeared up the grand staircase to finish his part of the mission. They'd spent weeks meticulously planning this heist.

He blew more gas into the ballroom, watching it roll across the floor. He walked up to the king and queen, both slumped in their throne chairs on the raised dais on one end of the room.

He stared at the king. Eirwyn had grown up with this man, this selfish tyrant who couldn't decide whether the forest killed his parents or the Glathens. Knox knew the truth, though.

Or rather, he suspected the truth since he'd been there when their parents had died. Perhaps he could tell Eirwyn about it soon. Not tonight, though, since they had plans.

He smiled and walked away from the sleeping drakin king, blowing more sleeping gas through the crowd. The external rooms would be waking soon, and he wanted to give them one more pass.

Two shots each. Less than an hour to get in, put them to sleep, and get out. The plan was working well, yet the more he walked around, the more his stomach tightened. Eirwyn was nowhere to be found; she was supposed to be here at the reception ball celebrating with her brother and the new queen. Perhaps she was upstairs in her room.

Knox shook his head. If she were, Archer would see her when he completed his mission on the floors above. Ashur was going to use sleep darts on anyone he met, though. Knox looked around, calming himself.

She wasn't the type to hide in her room during a party. She was vivacious and full of life.

No, the more logical explanation was that she wasn't in the palace at all. Perhaps she was already on her way to the tavern.

He smiled, anticipation building within him even as his hands began to shake and his eyes blurred from using so much magic. It was time to wrap this robbery up and get out of there. He had a princess to woo.

Chapter Sixteen

Knox sat in the corner of the tavern and watched the rest of the patrons get drunk. He nursed the same mug of ale that he'd gotten over two hours ago when he'd arrived.

Ashur nuzzled up with a barmaid on his lap, and her giggling was bloody annoying. He was anxious.

Eirwyn hadn't been waiting for him at the tavern and Ashur hadn't seen her in any of the rooms above stairs. She had said midnight, so she should be here soon. Unless their little infiltration and drugging of the entire castle caused a bigger problem than he thought. Unless she hadn't been in the castle at all, and if she hadn't, where had she been?

Why hadn't he gone upstairs to search for her himself? He'd searched the ground floors and the main reception floor and ballroom.

When they'd left the back gate guards still passed out, they'd all split up into pairs. They were to rendezvous at the tavern at two in the morning. Knox and Ashur had arrived hours ago.

Knox finally rubbed his temples and accepted that she

wasn't going to show. The drunken revelry just grew louder and louder, so Knox checked the clock above the bar and went outside. He had a few minutes before the rest of the crew showed up, and he needed some air.

He wasn't used to the tight spaces of town. Even after years of going in and out, he still didn't feel comfortable with so many people around. If someone saw his head, they'd panic and run him out of town. It'd happened before when he was younger. Different time, different town, but still painful.

He'd been careful to stay cloaked in public ever since. Only three people knew what he looked like without the hood, and that was fine by him. He frowned and stared up at the stars. Well, four now, if he included Eirwyn's maid.

He walked around the tavern, checking on the horses in the stable. He tried to work out the tension and worry about Eirwyn's absence, but something about it made his stomach twist. With time to spare and unable to sit still, he walked around the square.

An old woman sat rocking in front of the apothecary shop. He walked a wide arc around her on his way back to the tavern, but his feet grew heavy.

He turned to look at the woman as if pulled like a puppet on a string.

She looked up at him with her rheumy eyes as she stopped rocking. She stared into his eyes, and he felt uneasy as she didn't blink.

"I know you," she said softly.

He looked behind him. Perhaps she meant someone else.

"Yes, you. Knox. You're Olive's boy. Except you're no boy, are you? I met you when you were just a few days old. Olive sent for me. My, how you've grown."

His mind spun. Why would Olive send for this old woman?

She turned her head as if peering through him. "Do you know who I am?"

He shook his head, his feet heavy and rooting him to the ground even as he wanted to leave her presence.

"They call me Lailant here, but I've gone by many names in the past."

His eyes widened. "I've heard you can cure any curse."

She cackled a laugh, her head thrown back and revealing a missing tooth. "For most, yes. For you? No."

He frowned, his spine straightening. "What does that mean?"

She shrugged and started to rock again. "It means you're not cursed like you think you are. But if you want more information, you'll need to give me some of your venom."

He clenched his fists at his side. "No," he said. Who knew what kind of deadly magic could be used from the venom? No, it was safer to keep him far away from others who could die from it.

"Don't you want to know about the princess?" Her voice was smooth and hypnotizing.

He swayed on his feet, feeling the pull of compulsion magic.

"What about the princess?"

She held out a small vial. Where it came from, he had no idea. "Hand over the venom."

He wrapped his hand around his tail, shifting it into a barbed deadly weapon. It was shaped like a dagger tip with notches on the sharp edge. It didn't hurt him, though, as he squeezed the tip and dripped the gooey green liquid into the vial.

He frowned at the old woman and held it up just out of her grasp. "Swear an oath that it will not be used to harm, hurt, or kill anyone."

She sighed and shook her head. "I can't do that, but I'll swear that it will only fight against evil in the realm."

A hot wind swirled around them, and then she said. "There. Are you happy now? Come on, you don't have all night. It's already past the witching hour."

He handed it over, and she slipped it into a knitting bag at her feet. When she just started rocking again, he rubbed his temples and scratched his scales, careful to keep his hood up.

"Well?"

She chuckled. "Still impatient, I see. At least that hasn't changed. I knew you had the venom just as I know you. It's time for you to go to the heart of the forest and find your destiny."

He nodded, picturing the blank spot on the map. "Hartsgrove?"

"Exactly."

"But not even the druids go there. It's forbidden." Olive had warned him away from that place for years. He'd tried a few times, decades ago when he'd been a rash youth. But the forest had stopped obeying his command, and he'd been forced to give up.

She pointed the vial at him. "Are you going to let that stop you?" She snorted. "I thought you would have more backbone than that."

"Hey, I tried years ago, and it didn't work out."

"Yet you're stronger now, especially since you've met her."

The old woman's cryptic words sent his mind reeling.

Since he'd met *who*? She didn't give him time to process as she continued.

"The protections that have been in place for hundreds of years are no match for you. Once you reach Hartsgrove, you will find your home. There, you will find love. There, you will break what you think is a curse."

He blinked and rubbed his chin. "What will I find when I get there?"

She arched a brow. "Answers. Eat the golden apple and find answers. Come see me when you're done. I will tell you more after your blinders have been removed."

He frowned, feeling his feet loosen. "You—I," He pinched the bridge of his nose. "You mean to tell me that I could've broken this curse years ago if I'd only gone into the most dangerous part of the forest and eaten a snack?"

She threw her head back and cackled a laugh. His hands fisted at his sides, and he spun on his heel, stumbling the first step.

When the laughter died after only a few steps, she said, "Oh, and one more thing. Ask Olive about fated mates among dragons, will you?"

His spine straightened, and pressure built on his chest. His mind swirled. Why would she have him ask Olive about dragons when they'd been hunted down and driven from the land hundreds of years ago?

He raked a hand along the side of his head. The memories and stories of his birth made his gaze shoot to the old woman with raised brows. He'd hatched from an egg, but only Olive and Scarlet knew that. Olive had always told him he was a drakin, and he needed to avoid the royal family.

Hells, he needed to avoid regular people, too, as they'd force him into politics or try to take out their anger at the king on him.

He'd always been so careful to keep his head covered with the hood and cloak. For years, he'd thought about what kind of being he was. The scales on his head and back, the poisonous breath, the venom-barbed tail. He'd tried to learn all about the drakin royal families of Glathen and Busparia and had read all the books he could find in the nearby villages and towns. He hadn't had the money to search the magic school's libraries further into either country, but there had been no records of anyone with similar magic and abilities to his. But if he was a dragon, not a drakin...

"Is it—am I..."

She chuckled again. "Talk to Olive. Tell her I said hello and the time is right. Now run along back to the tavern. Your men are there, and they need you to save the princess."

She held up the vial and waved it at him. "The men that attacked her a few weeks ago? The one that was hit with your venom is dead, and the other two are running for their lives, not from you but from the man who hired them. The attack wasn't random. You must protect her."

Knox's heart jumped at the mention of the princess. What did the princess need saving from? Who was behind the attack? He strode away, his mind reeling between the princess and dragons.

Only the royal bloodlines were descended from dragons, from both Glathen and Busparia. Eirwyn was one of them, the darling drakin princess whom everyone loved.

Drakins were supposedly weaker than actual dragons. Yet the king was one of the most powerful sorcerers in the land. All drakins were. It was why they ruled.

What would they do if they realized he was one of them, too? Would Eirwyn accept him, scales and all? Would her brother try to assassinate him?

No, first things first. He had to find answers, and that included finally identifying what fucking species he was.

His head began to hurt as the questions and possibilities went through his mind. He walked into the tavern, several people singing a bawdy ballad by the hearth, and strode straight to the stairs.

Chapter Seventeen

Ashur stood near the stairs with a grim expression, leaning against the wall with a foot propped up behind him. He spied Knox and straightened.

Knox strode through the crowd and past the sleeping patrons who still held cups in their hands. If Ashur was wide awake, sober, and without a woman, then it was time to work.

He reached the top of the stairs and strode down the hall, following Ashur into the last room on the left. He closed the door behind him to find several of his most trusted men sitting around the room.

The old woman had said his men needed him to save the princess, but he couldn't come right out and ask about her.

As soon as the door closed, his eyes narrowed on them. "Everyone is back from the wedding reception? How did it go?"

Nineel's eyes glinted, and he grinned, revealing one tooth missing. "Aye, well, that was a great plan, Master

Warden. It worked! Every single piece of it. Your spell put the entire castle to sleep, even the magic users. Then we lifted every jewel off those rich bastards."

"Only two people were coming awake as the last of us left, so the sleep darts took care of them," another said.

Several of the men chuckled, and Knox sighed in relief. He'd left the stealing to the men as he'd overseen the perimeter and made sure no one sounded the alarm.

"Excellent. Tomorrow, go to Vidrland and turn everything over to John. He'll see that it can't be traced back to us, sell it, and send the money to those who need it most. "

The man nodded. "Great. We circled around the city a few times to make sure no one was following us. All good, though." The man kicked his saddlebags on the floor.

Knox sighed in relief. "Excellent."

"Well, not quite," Ashur said. "Tell him what else you heard while patrolling."

Knox's heart skipped a beat.

Several of them looked at each other, and then Nineel continued. "The princess might've been kidnapped."

Knox felt his breath still, then he snorted. A green vapor escaped, sinking to the floor. He took a deep breath and controlled his racing emotions. The old woman was right. Eirwyn was in trouble.

He stood still, motionless, as he tried to process. He growled, "Explain."

They all began speaking in rapid succession.

"Exactly what I said. She's missing. No one knows where she went, but the king doesn't seem too concerned about it."

"Not true, the king sent his men to fetch her from the tavern tonight. They searched every room for her, but she's not here."

Knox frowned, thinking of a way to explain his deep

interest in the princess. "It's probably too early for a reward for her safe return?"

One man shook his head. "There's a rumor going around that she's run off to stop the war and intercede with the Glathens. They will be mad about the marriage. The king was apparently angry about that rumor and burned a chair."

"I heard that she has left for the winter palace already and just wanted to give the newlyweds some space."

A few chuckled at that, but Knox began to pace.

"That's not like her at all," he murmured. Some of the men's chatter died down at his comment. A few glanced at each other, but he ignored them. She had promised to meet him tonight, and if she had planned on going away, she would have sent word.

Nineel said, "Those are just rumors, but that's not *our* theory, Master Warden."

Ashur sighed and nodded. "After you went outside the tavern and the guards came to search, a bloodied soldier came in, desperate for shelter and a drink. He'd been chased by the Growlers, then they pinned him down. They were about to rip him apart when they caught a scent. The wolves had howled and bounded away on the hunt."

Nineel nodded. "And earlier, before we robbed the palace, I overheard some guards talk about a woman who was thrown over the shoulder of a cloaked figure. They took off toward the woods on horseback."

His heart raced, and green gas escaped his nose again. He waved it away, the men backing away from him and their chairs grating on the wooden floor.

Knox scowled, ignoring their wary expressions. "And the guards didn't stop it? This is why the monarchy needs to change. The king doesn't even care that his sister is missing."

"He'll care about being robbed in his own castle," Ashur said confidently.

Knox rubbed his head. "But will he care enough to stop damaging the forest and chopping down trees with no regard for balance? Will he stop bleeding us dry with taxes? Will he stop the god-forsaken war? Or will he get angry and push back now that this wedding is over with?"

Knox straightened and turned to pace in front of the door as he thought. The men shifted in their seats but didn't interrupt or respond to his rant.

They had debated whether to go through with the robbery or not for days. Everyone knew he doubted the wisdom of it, but ultimately, they had voted to go through with it. So Knox had led them anyway.

None of that mattered now, though, because something had happened to Eirwyn, and he hadn't been there to stop it. If she was in the forest at night during Growler mating season...

He squeezed his eyes shut, turning and reaching for the door.

"If the princess was taken into the forest, we must find her before the Growlers do. Ashur, ride with me. The rest of you stay the night here and listen. Try to find out which rumor is the largest and who's saying what. Send three of you back to Vidrland tomorrow with the goods and the refugees. Two of you stay here in Demerel and keep watch."

He stared at each of them. Now, he could add protecting the princess to his list of responsibilities. A wave of apprehension washed over him.

"The princess is my priority. If anyone finds her, send

word to me as soon as possible. She might be the key to the king's downfall."

He threw open the door and strode down the stairs, out the door, and to the stable. Ashur quickly saddled his own horse, and as they mounted, he murmured softly, "About the king..."

Ashur trailed off, and Knox turned their horse to take the most direct route back to the Lone Road. His back straightened as he glanced around, but the streets were empty except for the occasional drunk sleeping in a doorway.

Ashur leaned close and said softly, "I still don't understand why we didn't just gut him. We had the opportunity. He was passed out with the rest of the lot."

Knox frowned and sighed. "I still think we can end this war peacefully. We know he's gathering Buspartan forces to try to retake Auckwald. Did you leave the message for him?"

Ashur nodded and spoke more freely as they exited the town and entered the empty field that separated it from the forest. The moonlight shone above, almost full but not quite.

"I did. I took the queen's lipstick and wrote it on the mirror in the king's bed chamber. *Heavy is the head that wears the crown, but it severs just as easily. End the war or lose yours.* Word for word, just like you said."

Knox placed a hand on the side of his horse, softly petting it. "Wonderful. We never heard from the king about the olive branch petition. This message might get the point across more effectively."

Ashur's horse shifted as he replied. "Perhaps. I still think we should've just killed him tonight. If it had been Will instead of me, the king would've already been dead. But you're the boss, mate."

Heavy is the crown, indeed. He just led the rebels, but the responsibilities were endless. At least he'd been able to convince Will that the wedding was the perfect distraction to finally stop the king's progress on the new road.

Knox sighed and rolled his eyes, making Ashur grin as they entered the forest. "Right, let's hunt a princess."

They turned their horses along the Lone Road, listening for the Growlers and watching for signs of passage. Sure enough, they found horse tracks.

Knox swung down to inspect them. The back left shoe had an arrow print on it. His blood ran cold, and he strode back to Ryder.

"It's Red," he said curtly as he swung onto his horse. "I'll take it from here, Ashur. Go check on Will and see if he's been able to stop the king's men from trying to build that fucking road."

He kicked his horse's sides just as a howl echoed through the forest.

Dear gods, don't let him be too late.

Chapter Eighteen

Eirwyn slowly awoke to a jostling, rhythmic movement. She blinked her eyes, but all she saw was brown. She lifted her head. Grass and shrubs passed in front of her, and her jaw dropped open in surprise.

She was thrown over the side of a horse, her face in its side with her hands tied behind her back. The pommel of the saddle dug into her ribs, and the rest of her was pressed against the body of her captor.

She began to struggle, but the fiend spanked her.

"Quiet. The forest is dangerous, especially at night. It would bring you a swift death, but I need you alive."

The voice was the woman's from the gazebo and somehow familiar. Eirwyn's memories came slamming back at the voice, and she turned to hiss, "Scarlet, is that you? What are you doing? Let me go."

The woman leaned down, her hood still obscuring her face. "Sorry, I can't do that. We have to get to Grandma's house."

"Let me ride like normal, and it'll go faster," Eirwyn's

words were rushed as the sense of impending doom and dread welled within her.

A howl echoed in the distance, and the horse skittered on the well-worn path.

"Shit," Scarlet said, regaining control of the horse. Eirwyn felt something cold on her wrists, then the bindings fell free. Scarlet shoved her, and Eirwyn went sprawling back into the dirt.

She landed on her backside with a grunt. "What the—"

"Listen, we need to get out of here. The Growlers are coming, and it won't be pretty if they catch us. It's mating season, and we're fertile females." Scarlet held a hand down to her, and Eirwyn hesitated.

Another howl sent her into motion. She grabbed Scarlet's hand and put her boot in the stirrup. She swung up awkwardly behind Scarlet, still in her ball gown and red cloak.

Before she'd gotten settled, the woman kicked the horse's sides. They lurched forward, and Eirwyn grabbed her waist. Her teeth jarred, and she bit into her own lip at the bruising pace. The metallic taste of blood made her wince, but she used her magic to blow their scent up into the trees as they passed. The air grew colder as the night went on.

It might've been hours later, Eirwyn wasn't sure, but eventually they slowed. It was the wee hours of the morning, and the sun would be rising soon. She could feel it in her bones.

Scarlet stopped the horse at a small stream to drink. Eirwyn slid from the back, falling to her knees and taking a drink herself. The water was refreshing, but her body still felt the jostling motion of the hard ride.

She looked up at Scarlet. She'd been so wrapped up

with escaping the cloying responsibilities of the court that she'd gotten herself kidnapped. As much as she listened to gossip and flirted with everyone, why hadn't she heard anything about her brother wanting to kill her before now?

"Are you going to kill me?" Eirwyn asked as she scooped more water to drink. "Oh gods, I can't believe he wants me dead. No, not just dead. He wants proof with my heart? What kind of sick, twisted bastard—"

"Fuck, stop panicking, I'm not going to kill you, and we can figure out why later."

Eirwyn looked around. "But why are we here? Why your grandma's house? Olive's house, right? Is that where we're going?"

Scarlet stared down at her. Eirwyn couldn't see her eyes, but she felt the weight of the stare bore into her. Then Scarlet pulled a knife from her belt. It gleamed off the light of the half-moon.

"Because she'll help us think up a solution, princess, now hold still."

"A solution to what problem?" Eirwyn asked as she looked up, searching the shadows and faint light to see her expression.

Scarlet sighed and waved the knife. "The king demands your heart."

Eirwyn gasped, scrambling back and falling into the water. The cold jump-started her into action, and she quickly got to her feet.

"You can't take my heart. You just said you wouldn't kill me, and why does he want my heart anyway? He just married Bella, so I'm less of a threat to him than ever before."

The woman shrugged and threw the dagger at the

ground. It stuck, point up and gleaming, in the light of the moon. "Apparently, he thinks you are. That's not for me to decide. I'm giving you my dagger to show I'm not going to hurt you, alright? I'm just taking you to Grandma and Knox."

"Knox?" Eirwyn gasped.

"Yes, Knox. You're the only woman he's ever wanted, and if I let anything happen to you, he'd have my head. Now will you stop talking and get back on the horse already? We're not safe yet."

Eirwyn's heart raced for a different reason now. She'd thought of him for the past few weeks so much, had dreamed of him every night. What was it about that giant, growling lumberjack that made her want to rip his hood off and ride him into oblivion?

Another howl echoed, and they both froze. Scarlet whispered, "They're never this far north. Shit, shit, shit."

She glanced at Eirwyn and back toward the howl. "Grab the dagger, and let's go. Hurry."

Another howl echoed nearer this time. Scarlet swung the horse around and offered her hand, her hood falling back to reveal her massive curly messy bun on top of her head.

"Look, I promise not to kill you, alright? But if we stay here, we'll both be dead."

Eirwyn ran, grabbed the dagger, and reached for Scarlet's hand. She put her foot in the stirrup and hiked her dress up to sit astride on the horse, then tucked the dagger into her boot.

Scarlet kicked the horse into another gallop. They raced further into the woods, and Eirwyn pushed more shadows around them, funneled the moonlight to show the path better, and pushed their scent into the treetops. It was only a little magic for each, but the steady drain of it over the course of the next few hours made her so tired. Eventually, she fell asleep on Scarlet's back.

When Eirwyn awoke, it was to arguing voices. The biting hunger that clawed at her made her stomach growl. She licked her lips, the faint taste of dust making her yawn.

If you're hungry, get up and eat something. You're not in the castle anymore, princess. If you're going to be at the tavern so much, go get your own food.

Bella's voice echoed in her head, and she felt tears threaten. Her friend was married to a monster who had tried to have her killed. And that monster was her own brother.

Eirwyn's heart raced. Why was her brother so evil? Tears pricked her eyes, but she refused to just lay there.

She had to get up and figure this problem out. She opened her eyes slightly, just enough to see into the barn. At the end of the aisle stood Scarlet. She blinked, the memories of the previous night flooding her. Fear licked her spine, making goosebumps dance on her skin.

Scarlet argued with a giant of a man.

Knox.

Her heart leaped, but her body wouldn't respond. She just laid there, staring at them in the aisle of the barn as her body slowly came awake. She had fallen into the Edge yet again, but somehow her body had brought her back. She was desperately hungry and thirsty, and her magic reserve was depleted for the time being.

It was fully dark outside the open barn door and a storm

brewed outside. She could see the faint light of the cottage, the back door nestled beside the tree. Only a lone lantern by the barn door illuminated Scarlet and Knox.

Eirwyn finally found the strength to sit up, the shadows hiding her movements. Scarlet threw her hands up and stomped outside. Knox followed her, and Eirwyn stumbled to her feet.

She crouched along the wall of the stalls to the lantern and pushed with her hand, making the shadows and wind blow it out when she got close enough. Then she peered into the darkness outside the barn.

Their voices carried now, brought to her on the wind.

"I can't believe you did this, Red. You've put us all in danger."

Scarlet shook her head, her cloak closed at the neck and her hair askew as the wind blew harder. She stared up at the man.

"I had no choice. When the king summons you, you go."

He straightened and glared. "Why you? How am I supposed to protect you if you're taking such high-profile contracts?"

She shrugged. "I stopped needing you to protect me a long time ago, Knox. As for why he picked me? That's easy. He wanted the best Hunter."

Eirwyn's jaw dropped. She was a *Hunter*? How had she not known that? She'd assumed she just worked with Knox in the forest.

"Is he mad? Last month he wanted her rescued from the forest. Today, he wants her dead."

Scarlet crossed her arms and cocked a hip. "He said that's why I was the perfect person for the job. I'm supposed to make it look like she ran off into the woods, and I just went to fetch her again. Only this time, I wasn't able to find her and escort her safely back to the palace."

He jerked his thumb toward the barn. "Are you going to go through with it? Because I can't let you do that."

Eirwyn's stomach twisted at his words. She was both excited that he would keep her safe and afraid of what her brother would do now.

Oh hells, her brother was trying to kill her. Panic clawed her throat, and she breathed shallowly.

"Of course, I'm not going to go through with it. I know what she means to you, Knox, which is another reason I took the job and why I brought her here."

Wait, what did Eirwyn mean to Knox? They'd only met twice. How could she mean anything to him? What had Scarlet said last night about it?

Knox rubbed his head. "Alright, we'll come up with a plan to see you both safe from the king. The rumors were already flying around the tavern. He had the place searched for her, probably to help shake suspicion off himself."

"He seemed cold and calculating when I talked to him. Face to face with the king, Knox. Can you believe it? He said he didn't want any witnesses and didn't want her body turning up in town."

Eirwyn was cold, but she barely felt it. Rage and hurt boiled in her chest at his treachery. How could he order his own sister's death?

The back door of the cottage opened, and Olive pointed to the sky.

"Alright, we can figure this out," Knox asked.

Scarlet turned and waved to Olive, then glared at him. "It better; otherwise, I'll be next on his kill list. I'm hoping Grandma will have an idea. Bring Eirwyn inside when she wakes, will you? She was so exhausted and will probably sleep a little longer."

She spun on her heels to go to the cottage.

Knox watched her walk away as thunder boomed, rubbing his temples under his hood. Scarlet was almost to the cottage when the man turned back to the barn and walked to the door, leaving Eirwyn alone with him.

Chapter Nineteen

Eirwyn stood just inside, cloaked in shadows as the wind whipped up around Knox, anticipation at being closer to him rising within her. The storm was moving closer. The wind tore his hood from his face just as lightning shot across the sky.

She gasped, her eyes widening. He glanced up at the sound, his green eyes meeting hers even as he reached for his hood and pulled it back up.

His expression was serious and resolute as he strode forward into the barn and out of the wind. She waited, but as soon as he relit the lantern, she sent a small gust of wind to pull his hood back again.

Her jaw dropped as she stepped closer, her hand reaching up.

"What are those?" Her voice was breathless, but she didn't care.

He scowled, backing away and pulling his hood over his head. "Nothing. Are you steady? We can make a run for the cottage before the storm breaks."

She seized the edge of his hood and tried to tug it away. "Let me see," she said in the commanding voice of a princess.

He ducked out of her reach, grabbing her hands and turning them both. He pressed her against the side of the stall, his body trapping hers.

She gasped, the lantern now falling directly on his face. He froze, his body going absolutely still.

"Don't order me around, princess. I'm not one of your servants."

No, he definitely wasn't, not the way he practically dwarfed her frame against the stall.

He had a strong jaw with a cleft in the chin, pouty lips that should be outlawed on a man, and freckles everywhere. His jaw was covered in short brown stubble, and his nose looked like it'd been broken a few times.

He was a hooded, mysterious, outdoorsy type who would fit in at the tavern. Except for the rest of his head, that is. He was the exact opposite of the pompous dandies at court.

And yet, there was something about him that drew her to the edge of insanity. He made her want to throw all her cautions in the wind and jump into his arms.

How many times over the past few weeks had she wanted to sneak into the forest and find him? She licked her lips, and his eyes drifted down to watch the movement.

"Please? Let me see," she asked softly.

Something flickered in his eyes that made her want to hold him and tell him it would be alright. A flash of vulnerability crossed his face, and a small, green tendril of gassy smoke came out of his nose.

Her eyes widened, and he stepped back. Her heart raced as she froze. If he was anything like her brother, that smoke meant anger, and who knew what would happen next?

She waited with bated breath for Knox to freak out, but he just waved the air and forced the gas to sink to the ground. He pursed his lips and held his hands behind his back as he watched her warily.

Maybe it didn't mean anger and pain.

She held her hands out, but he didn't attack. Slowly, palms up, she reached for his hood. He didn't step away, just stood there rooted in place as he watched her. The hood fell back, and she sucked in a breath.

The hundreds of freckles that dotted his face faded into larger spots past his temples. The spots grew larger and larger, some with bumps and ridges and even points. Most were the same brown color as his freckles, but the skin from his temples back was tinged green in some places.

She blinked, running her fingers lightly over the bumpy knots. His eyes fluttered at the touch, but it almost appeared as though he'd stopped breathing.

She traced the two larger pieces, triangular like a cat's ears but hard like horns where they jutted out from the skin on the sides. He shuddered, his eyes flickering at the touch.

He had long brown hair at the top of his head that was pulled back in a tight braid down his back. She ran her fingers over the braid, then moved both hands back to his...

"What do you call these?"

His eyes opened, and he seemed to snap out of a spell. He stepped back, his spine straightening and his chin going up in defiance.

"Horns and scales."

Her eyes widened. "Scales like a snake or a lizard? Are you a lizard man?"

He pursed his lips and scowled, stepping back from her

and walking to the door of the barn. "No, I'm not a lizard man. If—if it bothers you, I'll put the hood back up."

He stared out at the darkness, the storm still building and his body stiff as if waiting for her ridicule or judgment.

She stepped up beside him and slid her hand into his big, calloused one. She linked their fingers together and stared out into the night with him. He froze at her touch as if afraid to breathe.

Her voice was soft and low, the way she'd talk to a bird she didn't want to startle. "It doesn't bother me."

"Are you sure?" Uncertainty clung to his tone like a cape, the shadows rolling around them both now.

She stepped in front of him, her hand trailing up his bicep and across his chest. "I'm sure. In fact, it turns me on. What else are you hiding under all these clothes?"

A flash of lightning lit his face, brows high in surprise. Then he grinned and leaned a hand on the frame of the door, caging her in. Her core clenched, and she licked her lips.

"Would you really like to know?" He practically purred, and she breathed deeply of the woodsy aroma that was him. His scent had haunted her dreams, and she'd leaned close to one too many nobles over the past few weeks just trying to find someone similar.

No one smelled like Knox, though. No one—what would he taste like? She licked her lips and hooked her fingers into his pants, popping a button off.

"I really would," she said softly. "You're not a lizard man, then. What do I call you? Are you a monster that prowls the forest?"

His eyes turned wary but were still glazed with desire. "I'll show you my monster," he gritted between clenched teeth, popping another button on his pants.

She flicked the next one open, then he undid the last one. It was more erotic than any dance she'd ever participated in before, like they were daring each other to keep going. Her heart raced, and her body was on fire.

She sank to her knees and gripped his dick through his pants. He didn't move, didn't even breathe, as she stared up at him. "Can I play with your monster, Knox?"

He groaned, and a green curl of smoke sank out of his nose and onto her head. Her body flashed with heat. She needed him. It was like a clawing hunger, and she pulled his monster out.

It stared at her, larger than any she'd seen before. She blinked up at him, suddenly worried as she bit her lip. "I–I've done a lot, but I've never done this. Tell me if I do it right?"

Before she could second guess herself, she wrapped her lips around the head. He groaned, his hips thrusting slightly as he held himself up against the door frame with one hand.

The other settled on the back of her head, and she sank down on him. Her mouth wrapped around him in a hot, wet slide, and her eyes fluttered. Every movement of her mouth, every swirl of her tongue sent a shiver of pleasure straight to her clit.

She began to throb, and her hand cupped her mound over her dress. He gripped her hair, pulling her forward and back faster and faster. She rocked on her knees as he began to thrust into her face.

She moaned as the honey taste of him burst on her tongue. It was sweet and salty, the perfect combination. Why hadn't she ever done this before?

Oh yeah, because she was the princess. She didn't want to bow to any man, but Knox made her forget all of her preconceived ideas about it.

The sweet nectar pulsed into her mouth, and the hunger between her legs made her quiver with anticipation. She needed more than just this teasing taste. She needed all of him, filling her again and again.

Her eyes fluttered open as he twitched, his head leaning on the back of his hand on the door frame. His breathing was labored, and a rush of joy spread through her. She'd brought this great hulking brute to this mindless moment. She paused, rubbing herself as she thought through what this meant.

He was different. She didn't mind kneeling for him. There was a certain rush of power that came to her from doing this.

His green eyes opened, practically glowing in the dim light. "That was—incredible," he panted. "But now it's my turn."

He cradled her head, his hand tangling in her wild, black hair. He lifted her by her hair, and she gasped at the sharp stab of pain as she stumbled to her feet.

It made her core ache. Then he released her, caressing the back of her head and pressing her against the door frame. He buried his head in her neck and sucked on a sensitive spot at the base of her neck.

She gasped and arched her back. "Knox, what are you doing?"

"If you can talk, then I must not be doing it right," he growled out. He picked her up by the ass and tossed her onto the pile of hay by the door.

She bounced, the scent of grass surrounding her before he caged her in between his arms. Hay and dirt flew into her mouth, and she laughed as a rush of liquid need flowed through her veins.

"Oh gods," she chuckled, arching and trying to bring her mouth up to connect with any part of his body.

"No, not gods. Just me. Just Knox." Another flash of vulnerability in his voice left her opening her eyes. She reached up and caressed the scales on the side of his head.

He growled, and his hands grabbed her wrists, holding them by her head. "Now, now, don't start that again, or this will lead to more than heavy petting."

She whimpered. "I want more than heavy petting. Please, Knox, I need you."

She turned and bit into his arm. Her hips thrust up as she moaned.

By the gods, he felt amazing. None of her partners had held her down like this before. She hated the idea of being weak and vulnerable. She felt like that enough in her everyday life.

But this man, this brick house lumberjack with tree trunks for legs, tossed her around like she was nothing. She wasn't treated like a fragile princess but like a virile woman, a heavily desired woman. In his arms, she felt safer than she ever had at the castle.

He held her wrists in a vice-like grip that made a tingle run down her spine.

"Oh yes, how I like to see you squirm, feel your body wiggle under mine."

His voice was mesmerizing, and she thrust her hips, flattening her feet on the dirt floor to get more traction.

Chapter Twenty

Knox's body shifted on top of hers, his legs pressing into the vee of her body that ached so much. It was a lust unlike any she'd ever experienced, a hundred times worse than ever before.

The man groaned and ground his hips down even as he cursed.

Clothes separated them, and her dress hiked in the scuffle around her knees to give him enough room to straddle one of her legs. His other hand roved over her breasts, then dove lower to her mound.

It wasn't enough. She rocked her hips on his leg as he inched her dress up. His big hands on her wrists made her crave skin-to-skin contact.

"More," she groaned, tilting her neck so he could take all he wanted. He nipped at her neck as his fingers found the slit in her undergarments.

His fingers raked up and down as he whispered in her ear. "Dripping wet, I see. And the smell–Eirwyn, you're intoxicating. I need to taste you, princess. I'm going to release your hands, but leave them there, alright? Just let me feast."

She whimpered at his words, but then he slid down her body and pressed her knees wide. His face was so close to her, and she bit her lip.

She'd never done this either. Her partners had always gone in and let her call the shots. Now, the tables were turned, and she was panting like a dog in heat.

His tongue licked up her slit, and her hips thrust as her eyes fluttered. It was like a spell washing over her, sending a jolt of energy and magic through her, her previous exhaustion forgotten. Only there was no magic. It was just pure desire.

His tongue circled her clit, then he began to suck. A finger slid inside, and she gasped. A second finger slid in, then a third.

She was stretched wider than ever before, and it felt so good. She gripped her own wrists above her head and pushed her hips up into his mouth.

His free arm wrapped around her thigh and pressed down with his palm on her lower stomach, holding her in place. Then he feasted. The swirl of his tongue drove her higher and higher.

She felt like she was standing on the roof of the castle, the wind blowing through her hair. She drew ever closer to the edge, like a runaway horse racing to the cliff.

Then she broke apart in his hands with a scream. Stars burst behind her eyelids, and her magic flared. She imagined herself diving off the cliff and flying. His tongue slowed, and his fingers slowly slid from her body.

He licked her clit, making her legs twitch beneath him.

Then he sat back on his haunches and stared down at her with a small smile.

"How was that?" he growled, stalking his way up her body and pinning her in place. He dipped his head, kissing her softly on the jaw and back to her ear.

"Divine," she panted. "Transcendent. Unparalleled."

He chuckled, the deep sound vibrating through them both where their torsos touched. She thrust her hips up and ground on his dick, somehow now locked safely in his pants.

"I'm glad I could return the favor, princess. But the storm is about to break, and we should get you inside. Don't want you to escape your brother only to fall prey to a common cold."

He backed away and offered her a hand. Shakily, she stood and brushed her skirt out. The aching need was no longer a raging inferno but only a steady fire now. Her entire body was inflamed, but she forced herself to take a deep breath and turn with him toward the door.

His hand on her elbow kept her grounded as he asked, "You sure you're not bothered by the horns?"

She leaned her head on his arm and linked their fingers. "I'm definitely hot and bothered by the horns and scales, Knox, but not in the way you keep asking about. I can't explain what came over me just now. I may sleep around, but I–I've really never done that before. I didn't know it was possible."

He chuckled and stopped in the doorway once more, his face relaxed. "I'm happy to have expanded your horizons, princess. I–I've never done that before either, so I'm glad I could satisfy you."

She grinned and tipped her head back, pulling their bodies closer. "Well, it was a great appetizer, but I'd still like to explore the main course soon if you don't mind."

He laughed and wrapped an arm around her waist, tucking her to his side as they walked to the cottage. "It's a deal, as long as my features don't bother you."

He waved a hand to his head, and Eirwyn shook her head, breathing in the deeply refreshing scent of him.

"What bothers me is that my brother tried to have me killed. Considering that, your scales and horns are simply fascinating."

He turned to look down at her, a faint flash of disbelief in his eyes. "Truly?"

She just nodded and reached up a hand to trace the scales. "Truly, I want to explore them, touch them. I could spend hours exploring you and still not get enough."

The words hung in the air between them, and she held her breath. They had just come out of her mouth, but the truth of them settled in her soul.

What was she doing? She couldn't explore him. Who cared if he had horns and scales? It didn't matter when she was stuck in limbo.

She couldn't go back to Demerel, not until she figured out what was going on. She drew strength from his solid, stoic presence.

He might be a lumberjack, but he was a great oak, standing tall and unwavering as the storm of life tried to sweep her away.

His green eyes held so many promises, and she leaned closer, her hand on his scales dropping to cup his cheek.

She felt as if a spell was weaving between them, the tendrils tightening around them like a drawstring. She wanted to step into his embrace and kiss him on those beautiful pouty lips while she rode him until they both burst.

He didn't pull away, and she considered that a huge win from their previous encounters. This night hadn't ended up in a small room above the tavern with a fantastic but quick orgasm.

It was so much more than she'd ever expected. As she held his hand, touched him, tasted him, and finally saw him for who he really was... it was like a missing puzzle piece had finally found its way home.

Lightning flashed, and thunder boomed, scaring her into jumping away. Her hands dropped to her sides, and she gave a self-conscious laugh as rain drops began to fall.

"Ah, the storm. Scarlet—she's not going to kill me, right? I mean, she said she wouldn't, but she's a Hunter..."

Eirwyn hated that her voice came out small and breathy. She wanted to be strong and independent, be someone Knox could be proud of. She wriggled her fingers, sending a small disc of wind over their heads to hold the storm at bay for a few more minutes. She was relieved that her magic was already coming back.

He shook his head. "No, I won't let her, and she knows that."

Silence settled between them, and he reached for her hand again to walk toward the cottage. The warmth from his hand helped settle her nerves. There was something in his gaze that made her want to dive deeper.

"Why won't you let her?" she whispered.

His green eyes sparkled like the clearest emeralds. "That's another question that I haven't been able to answer yet."

He finally broke his stare and looked into the darkness around them. "Scarlet's in quite a bind now, but we'll make a plan that will keep both of you alive."

There was a steely undertone to her words that made her feel safe.

"Are you hungry?" He waved with his other hand at the cottage.

"Food would be great, Although..." She trailed off as they approached the back door of the cottage.

"Although?"

She shrugged, a sly grin slowly spreading over her cheeks as they stopped and faced each other.

"I'm not just hungry for food. I wouldn't mind a snack of one big, burly lumberjack. Not going to lie. I was looking forward to meeting you at the tavern tonight for a long night of fun."

His brows shot up, then he grinned down at her, the light from the lantern illuminating him.

"I have a big body to explore. Depending on our plans to keep you safe, maybe we can do some exploring together soon?"

She threw her head back and laughed. "We'll see just how good you are with your wood?"

He wiggled his eyebrows, and she laughed again, putting her other hand on his arm and leaning against him.

"That's right, princess. I'll show you how I can wield my axe. Just wait and see."

Last month, he had been closed off, stern and gruff, but now, he was different. He seemed to have a softer side, now that the protective barrier of his hood and secret scales had come down. Or maybe it was the explosive orgasm.

She grinned, her hand caressing his forearm as she leaned closer to him, rubbing her breast against his bicep.

"Oh, so you've graduated from a knife, have you?"

He grinned and nodded. "I figure I need a heftier weapon to handle you, princess."

She giggled as he reached for the door handle. Perhaps

when they'd first met, he'd been too nervous flirt. Either way, she was loving this more relaxed version of himself.

"Ready to talk this out and find answers?"

Eirwyn took a deep breath as Knox pushed it open. The lights were bright, and she blinked several times before her eyes adjusted. She released the soft breeze and let the storm crash on the cottage. Then she stepped inside the hallway as a flash of lightning ripped the sky behind them.

Chapter Twenty-One

Knox met Scarlet's gaze as he hung his cloak by the door. He turned to do the same for Eirwyn, taking her bright red cloak, now dirty from the ride, and hanging it next to his.

Eirwyn eyed Scarlet carefully as Olive peeked around the kitchen wall, still in her nightgown and robe.

"There you are! Scarlet was just filling me in on all that's happened tonight. Are you alright, dear?"

Olive pulled her into a warm embrace, and he let her hand go, stepping over to the fireplace and warming his hands.

He couldn't take his eyes off her. A tightness settled on his chest at the tear that fell down Eirwyn's cheek.

"I'm sure I'll be fine, but I don't know why he wants to kill me."

Olive pulled back and held the princess' cheeks. "You poor child. I've put on a fresh pot of coffee and some scones. Are you hungry?"

"I am rather hungry, yes. I missed dinner at the wedding

reception, then used so much magic on the ride, I fell asleep."

Knox's back stiffened as his heart leaped in worry. "Did you enter the Edge? Do you need a tonic?"

Eirwyn shook her head and smiled at him. "No, I think just regular food and drink will do the trick."

Scarlet frowned and kept picking at her nails with her dagger, her leg thrown over the armrest of the other stuffed chair by the fire. She looked relaxed, but Knox knew she was ready to spring into action at a moment's notice.

"Well, let's fix that right away. Tell me about the wedding, dear." Olive bustled over to the kitchen and poured Eirwyn a cup of coffee. He pulled the bench seat out for Eirwyn, then sat at the head of the table.

Eirwyn chatted about all the details that had gone into the wedding and how the past month had flown by.

His body turned to her. He wasn't a Hunter, but she had triggered a hunting instinct. He wanted to chase her down and devour her, but he would bide his time and make sure it was safe to do so first.

The old woman in Demerel gave him hope that maybe there would be a way to be with Eirwyn without killing her.

Olive pulled the scones out of the oven and set them in the center of the table. "And is the new queen as beautiful as they say?"

Eirwyn's spine stiffened, and she nodded with a frown as she stood and washed her hands at the sink. "Yes, she has the ageless beauty befitting a queen. It's probably why the king decided to marry her instead of the princess of Glathen."

"Do you think the king ordering your death is political?" Scarlet asked.

Eirwyn's face crumpled, and she blinked rapidly as she shook her head. Olive wrapped an arm around her shoulder, helping Eirwyn sit on the bench again.

Knox couldn't keep from reaching for her, too. His chest had grown tight as the emotions flew across her face. His hand settled on her knee under the table, and he felt her body relax at the touch. He wanted to comfort her and protect her from her stupid brother.

Olive said, "There, there, child. It's going to be alright."

"How can it be alright when my brother wants me dead?" Eirwyn choked with a gasp.

Scarlet sat up and leaned forward, propping her elbows on her knees as the dagger hung between her legs. "The bigger question is why, like you tried to talk about on the ride. Does he just want you dead, or does he want your heart specifically?"

Eirwyn sat up a little straighter, her hands dropping to her lap as she frowned. "What do you mean?"

Olive released Eirwyn and glared at Scarlet. "Did you really accept the job without knowing?"

Scarlet shrugged. "Coin is coin, grandma. And I needed to get her away from him and back to Knox- as quickly as possible."

Eirwyn's eyes widened, and her mouth opened, but Knox shushed them with his words as he traced his thumb back and forth on her skirt. "The only way to find out for sure if he wanted her heart or just wanted her dead is to ask. He's already expecting Scarlet's return, so you're going to have to go back to the king with a heart."

Eirwyn gasped and jerked out of his hand. He turned to look at her, reaching under the table for her knee again.

"A heart, not your heart. I can hunt an animal down–a

deer, a boar—it doesn't matter. Then Scarlet will take that heart to the king and ask some questions, observe, and listen to how he reacts. His motivation will determine our next steps in keeping you safe."

Scarlet snorted. "And it could just be that the king doesn't want a threat to the crown. Maybe that's why he sent those three men to jump you a few weeks ago."

Eirwyn's eyes widened. "Wha—what do you mean? The attack in the alley?"

Scarlet nodded her head. "Yeah, the king sent them to kill you. When I approached the gazebo, he was complaining about needing to hire a Hunter because the cheap thugs failed. He specifically said *everything has failed. No more fake accidents.* "

Knox felt his rage simmer at the king's blatant disregard for Eirwyn. A king was supposed to protect his people, not murder them. Not destroy the forest. Not tax the people into losing their homes and businesses.

"Gods, he's the worst," he murmured. He wanted to pull her onto his lap and just hold her.

Her hand found his under the table, and her fingers linked with his. Some of his anger eased, and he took a deep breath as the knot in his stomach lessened with it.

Eirwyn's big blue-gray eyes looked at Scarlet, a frown marring her smooth forehead. "No more fake accidents? What does that mean? Has he tried to kill me before?"

Her voice grew higher and higher, and he squeezed her hand and tugged. She turned to look at him, her eyes wild in panic.

"Breathe with me, princess. That's it. Nice and easy," Knox said softly, stroking the back of her hand with his thumb. "We're going to talk about this calmly and rationally.

It's going to be alright because you're safe now. Nothing to worry about, alright? Now, you need to eat. Do you like scones?"

She took a deep breath and nodded, her shoulders relaxing.

He smiled. "Good, you should try Olive's. They're the best in the land. Go on."

He pushed the plate to her, and she bit into it. Her eyes fluttered as her body relaxed. Her moan filled the room. Scarlet smirked and Olive beamed, but Knox felt his pants grow painfully tight. Eirwyn chewed, and Knox cleared his throat, trying to stay on topic.

"About him trying to kill you before... Didn't you say you were sickly as a child? Are you only sick around your brother? I still think we should consider the possibility of being poisoned."

She frowned, nodding slowly. "Sort of. I mean, I've been sick for so long, I don't know that he's ever had direct access to my food. So at least one servant would have to be involved, and I just can't believe that's possible."

"Were you sick while you were in Glathen?"

Eirwyn took another bite and chewed slowly, her face scrunched up as she thought. Finally, she said, "No, I wasn't, but I've been sick pretty much every day since I've been home. Lailant verified that it's not a disease or pregnancy, so maybe you're right. I don't know how to test for poisoning though. Does that exist?"

Olive said, "There's a spell for it, yes, but it's not the most accurate. How do you feel after eating the scones?"

"I feel fine now. Tired but not exhausted."

Scarlet pointed her dagger at them. "Then yeah, he was probably poisoning you for years."

Knox ran a hand over the side of his head, jerking

slightly in surprise. He'd forgotten that he wasn't wearing his hood. It was amazing that Eirwyn hadn't run screaming into the night.

He looked at her, no doubt that hope shone in his eyes. If she could handle him like this, perhaps she could handle all of him. He needed to ask Olive about fated mates, but first, they needed a plan.

Knox turned back to Scarlet, his mind working furiously as he thought through the possibilities.

"Red, if the king finds out you didn't kill her, find the Robins in the taverns."

She sat up in her chair. "The Robins? Are you fucking serious?"

He nodded. "I know your work is mostly against them, but if he turns on you, the Robins will get you safely out of town."

She sighed dramatically and threw herself back against the chair, pulling one leg up to dangle on the armrest and ignoring him yet again.

Eirwyn yawned. "So that's the plan? Scarlet will take an animal heart to my brother, and we'll see what happens?"

Knox nodded and released her hand. "Why don't you go upstairs? You've had an exhausting day and should get some rest."

She blushed furiously and leaned closer. "Will you be sleeping there?"

He leaned closer to her, drawn like a moth to a flame, as his heart raced at her nearness. "Do you want me to?"

Scarlet gagged from across the room. "Ugh, barf. I know you've waited for this your entire life, but I veto any sex happening in this house while I'm here."

Olive gasped, her eyes widening. "Yes, I agree. My house, my rules. No sex tonight for any of you."

Eirwyn giggled, and her eyes twinkled. "That might be a greater tragedy than my brother trying to kill me."

Knox chuckled and leaned back, crossing his arms. Eirwyn's gaze slid over him, making the hair on the back of his hands stand up. She stared at him the way a fox stared at a chicken.

He licked his lips and grinned. "I might have to agree with you on that one."

Scarlet's brows rose. "Nice to see you learning to flirt, brother, but this is the princess you're talking to."

Eirwyn shrugged her delicate shoulder and stood. "Even princesses have needs, Scarlet. But all this talk of sex has me suddenly realizing how filthy I am. Does anyone have anything else I can wear? Something clean?"

Olive nodded, "Scarlet, take her upstairs and get her some of your old clothes. They should fit well enough. And run her a bath while you're at it. Heavens knows she might not get one up with the dwarves."

"Dwarves?" Eirwyn asked, her eyes going to Knox for answers.

He was secretly pleased about that. "Yes, I think it's safer for you to stay with the dwarves up north. Your brother has no reach in the Feral Forest and even less in the dwarves' camp."

Scarlet's boots landed on the wooden floor as she stood, stretched, and walked to the stairs. Eirwyn's bright eyes caught Knox's before she walked around his chair. Her fingers trailed from his shoulder, up his neck, and over his scales and horns.

"Will you be escorting me there, Knox?"

It surprised him yet again that he was just sitting in the same room as her with his head bare. At her touch, a shiver of ecstasy swept him like a flash flood.

"Absolutely," he grinned. She winked and walked away, her hips shaking in her ripped and dirty silk blue, white, and red dress. It reminded him of her station, and some of his hope dimmed. He wasn't sure what their future held, but hopefully it was more time with the princess.

Chapter Twenty-Two

As Scarlet and Eirwyn's footsteps echoed up the stairs, Olive moved to her chair by the fire and frowned at him.

"Have you decided to take a chance on love?" Olive asked, her face guarded with an emotion he couldn't identify.

He nodded and moved to sit in the other chair by the fire. "I don't know about love, but I have a message for you from Lailant."

Olive's eyes widened at the name, and he continued.

"She says I need to go to the Hartsgrove to step into my destiny. She says to tell you it's time, and something about dragon mates?"

He didn't want to hope, but he couldn't stop himself. If he could identify what he was, maybe he could convince Eirwyn to accept all of him.

Olive sat up straighter and grinned. "I knew it."

His brows rose. "Knew what?"

"When I saw the way you looked at her last month, I knew she was your mate."

He shook his head and leaned back on the chair. "Mates aren't real, Olive."

"But you don't deny that you're attracted to Eirwyn, right? Well, it's a start."

"Can you just tell me what Lailant meant?" He shifted on the chair, trying to distract himself from wanting to go upstairs and help Eirwyn with her bath.

Olive reached for her knitting basket. "Do you remember what I told you when you were a child?"

Knox nodded. "You said to keep hatching from an egg a secret. You said to never reveal all my powers to anyone, only the plant manipulation, which was a normal druidic ability. Lailant said she came to see me as a baby? Is that how she knew about the venom?"

Olive leaned her head back and sighed. "Yes, we thought it'd be best to wait to tell you the truth. You know how innocent kids are. We didn't want you wandering into town and telling the entire kingdom that you..."

She trailed off, and Knox sat forward on the edge of his feet. "That I'm what?" He rested his elbows on his knees and waited, his heart pounding.

She sighed and shifted, pulling her knitting basket from beside the chair to in between them. She rummaged around to the bottom, then pulled out three pieces of broken egg.

She fit the pieces together. It was the size of Knox's two fists put together. Once it was back together, she held it up to the light. It glittered green and brown with streaks of gold here and there.

"You weren't born, Knox. You hatched."

He blinked. "Yes, you've said that."

She sighed, "Knox, think about it. When was the last time there was a hatchling? Do you think Eirwyn was hatched? Or the king? No, they were born like normal humans with inherent magic from their drakin bloodline. But you..."

She turned the egg, both of them staring at how the light reflected off its surface. "You're not just a drakin. You're a dragon."

Knox blinked and took a deep breath. All this time, and she'd known he was a dragon? Why hadn't she just told him? His chest tightened, and he leaned back, crossing his arms as he waited for Olive to continue.

"Three hundred years ago, the continent was ruled by one powerful dragon king. He had four children. When they reached maturity, he divided the kingdom into four. Busparia, the Feral Forest, Glathen, and the mountains to the north."

Knox frowned, reaching out to take the egg, carefully making sure it didn't break apart again. The pieces were incredibly tough, though, and it took both hands to hold it together.

"The druids of the forest served the Feral King. But the in-fighting among the other dragon siblings brought devastation to every corner of the continent. Whole cities were razed to the ground, which caused the people to rebel. The Hunters were created to kill the dragons, eliminating them from the land."

Knox shook his head, leaning back in the chair and staring at the egg. "That doesn't make any sense. The royal families still claim to have draconic heritage. They're drakin."

Olive nodded. "The original Hunters were drakin, the failed offspring of the dragons, according to legend. They fed into the humans' fear and assimilated into human culture, hiding their dragon abilities, or at least disguising them to be more acceptable."

"But they ultimately used their drakin magic to seize power and rule?" Knox said.

Olive nodded again. "Exactly, with the Hunters backing them, they've been ruling both nations ever since."

Except the Hunters were just a mercenary guild now. They didn't work only for the ruling families anymore. The Robins had grown in just a decade to rival them as one of the leading guilds in the kingdom, and the only guild not aligned with any crown, but their missions were completely different. The Robins were about freedom and protection; whereas, the Hunters were for hire to the highest bidder.

Silence settled, the crackling fire and the thunder booming outside the only interruptions. After Knox thought through the importance of it, he asked, "What's all that have to do with me?"

Olive leaned back in her chair and closed her eyes. She wasn't used to the late nights, or rather the early mornings. It was now past sunrise.

"When the Feral King was hunted down, he enchanted the forest to protect his home. And his faithful druids swore to watch over his heir."

She pointed to the egg in his lap. "Honestly, most of us assumed it was an old wives' tale. The egg sat on a custom made egg cup on my parents' mantle while I was growing up. They used to tell me bedtime stories about the dragons and our duty to protect the egg."

She chuckled. "I think I actually slept with your egg in my arms when I was about six. I held you like a stuffed doll and even put the egg in a tiny dress."

Knox smiled. "And then one day, I just hatched?" It boggled the mind. It didn't make sense. "After hundreds of years of not being nested, I just decided to break free? Wait, I'm not thirty? I'm hundreds of years old?"

She wrinkled her nose. "I don't think dragons start counting their years until they actually hatch. Your hatching was triggered by the attack on the cottage by the Growlers."

"The one that killed Scarlet's mother?"

Olive nodded. "Everything was busted up, and your eggcup fell off the mantle. The egg rolled near the fireplace. It was several days of cleaning before I found you. By then, the first crack had appeared. Lailant thinks there was a spell on the egg to protect you."

The fire had kept him warm enough to make him want to hatch. He nodded, trying to process.

"So that makes me... a dragon?"

Olive stared at him, her lips thinning. "A dragon king," she corrected.

Knox scowled. "I'm no king."

Olive stood, taking the egg gently from his hands and putting the pieces on top of her knitting in the basket. "Not yet, but you will be if Lailant's prophecies are to be believed. It's why I've hidden you in the forest, why I wouldn't let you go off with Scarlet and her father as they ranged Busparia, encouraged the other druids to turn over the Master Warden job to you. What else did Lailant say?"

Knox rubbed his head, scratching at his scales. "Go to the heart of the forest, eat the golden apple, and find answers. Then go back and see her."

Olive nodded. "Then it's a plan. Scarlet will go to the king tomorrow with a heart. You will go to the heart of the forest and find your destiny."

Knox stood and stretched, yawning as he finally grew tired. "After I take Eirwyn to the dwarves, I will. But for tonight, I'm going to see if I can find an animal and get Scarlet the heart she needs before turning in. The storm will make it extra challenging."

Olive rolled her eyes as she stood, saying, "Typical man. You just love the hunt, don't you?"

He shrugged sheepishly, but before he could answer, she wrapped him in a hug. He froze. It'd been a while since she'd hugged him, not since he'd almost accidentally killed her when he was a teenager. It was what had triggered him to go train with the other two druids at what was now Vidrland.

She was the only mother he'd ever known, but he'd been on high alert his whole life. He was always afraid that he was going to make a wrong move or hurt someone.

But there might be answers at Hartsgrove. He wrapped his arms around her small frame and took a deep, calming breath, careful to exhale away from her.

Perhaps it was alright to hope for a better tomorrow. Eirwyn was safe upstairs, and he might break his curse after all. He might find a home and family of his own.

He kissed the top of Olive's head and cleared his throat, stepped back, and grabbed his cloak from beside the door.

"I don't want you to catch a chill, so don't stay out all night," Olive said.

He turned, pulling his hood up once more. He couldn't leave without asking one more question.

"What about fated mates among dragons?"

Olive's brow arched. "You want to know even though you don't believe in them?"

He shrugged, not meeting her gaze. Finally, she said, "The stories passed down generation after generation might be wrong, Knox."

He adjusted his cloak and kept waiting. Finally, she sighed and looked into the fire.

"Like I said when you were entering your teens, you can have sex with anyone, but for dragons, it's often violent.

Sometimes, their partners do not survive. When a fated mate is found... it changes both partners. The stories don't say how."

Knox's heart raced. "So—I could've had sex before now?"

Olive blushed and scowled, waving her hand. "Well, maybe, but with your tail?" She shook her head. "When you were a kid, it was hard for you to control it. If you got worked up during sex, there's no telling what your tail will do. We've talked about this, remember?"

He nodded slowly. There was no forgetting their birds and bees talk years ago. It involved actual birds and bees in the forest and had occurred after he'd had a particularly hormonal outburst and almost stabbed Olive with his tail. He should've been paying more attention to his surroundings instead of playing with his dick. Maybe then he wouldn't have bee surprised.

Then she'd reminded him that being intimate with someone could see them poisoned or stabbed with his venom. Their talk had been purely academic, though. He'd only had passing feelings of arousal throughout the years, even during puberty. Sporadic but intense, often when he was alone with his own thoughts and imagination.

He'd never felt attracted to an actual person, though. Not face to face. Only when he closed his eyes and pictured a shadowy figure was he able to take himself in hand and find relief.

He'd tried, though. He'd gone to the brothels and watched some activities, intending to join in. But the urge to participate had never come.

Until now. Until Eirwyn.

He narrowed his eyes at Olive's comment. "My tail isn't

a separate being, Olive. It's part of me, and I have control now. I'm not a child."

She nodded, crossing her arms. "I know, I know. You're thirty years old. Trust me, I know." She put her hand on her back and stretched.

Guilt stabbed his gut, and he walked over to her. He put his hands on her shoulders and looked down.

"I'm sorry I was such a pain in the ass growing up, but *if* she's my fated mate... if we can be safe..."

Olive pulled back with a scowl. "I'm very excited that you've found her—"

"Maybe. We don't know for sure." He was so conflicted about it. He wanted to go upstairs and be with her but also wanted to run away, just to protect her from himself.

"I don't want to witness dragon mating rituals. So go distract yourself and kill something." She shooed her hands, and he grinned. On impulse, he leaned down and kissed her cheek.

She blushed but relaxed as she smiled, so he strode to the door, pulling his hood up.

She called out before he could reach the door handle. "I'm serious about no sex under my roof. We don't know how violent it might be. Wait and find the answers at the heart of the forest. Better safe than sorry, right?"

He paused, turning to meet her gaze, but he didn't reply as he pushed open the door and closed it behind him. The stinging rain hit his face. It was a welcome reprieve from information overload and raging hormones.

He'd had a rough few years when he'd hit puberty. Controlling his emotions had been one of the hardest lessons he'd had to learn. His tail barbs had almost hit Olive more than once.

Perhaps that's why he'd never felt the urge to mate with

someone before. His body had been too busy trying to control his tail, venom, and poison.

But it'd been years since he'd gone out of control. Maybe his tail wasn't as big of a deal as he thought. As long as he didn't stab her with it, she'd be alright if they had sex. As long as he didn't breathe on her, they should be fine.

He grinned and strode into the forest on silent feet, letting his mind wander to all the possibilities with Eirwyn. He wanted to try so many things.

His thoughts shifted to dragon sex. What dragon mating rituals were there? Would he know what to do, and it'd just come to him, or was there a book out there somewhere on it?

Stalking and finally hunting his prey far into the woods, he smiled again. He was so excited—about Eirwyn, about finally finding answers—and just needed to be patient a little longer.

Now that he knew what he probably was, he had a starting point. He could ask the right questions, research, and find the answers.

A stag walked slowly through the trees ahead of him, making his smile widen. He was a dragon, and dragon's hunted to kill. He closed in on the massive stag, the rush of adrenaline flowing through him.

Chapter Twenty-Three

"No, you cannot go to Demerel and snoop around. You're the princess. Everyone knows you, Eirwyn," Scarlet said, shaking her head as she paused eating, her spoon halfway to her mouth.

Eirwyn sighed, disappointed but not too much, since that meant she'd spend more time with Knox. Last night, she'd dug in a trunk of clothes and talked with Scarlet about Knox's childhood and growing up in the forest. Scarlet had told her to be careful as Knox had never been with a woman before, but Eirwyn didn't believe her. Scarlet probably just didn't know all of Knox's business, which was as it should be.

She certainly wished her own brother kept out of her business, that's for sure. They'd talked about him, too. It was well past dawn when she'd finally fallen asleep, the storm still raging outside and her thoughts and memories just as tumultuous.

Sadly, alone. She'd taken a bird bath in the wash basin by the window and had changed into Scarlet's black breeches and green shirt. Thank the gods she'd worn her walking boots to the reception.

Eirwyn leaned forward onto the table, imitating some people she'd met at the tavern over the years. "I have to warn Bella and make sure she doesn't get caught up in Gastone's web of treachery. She's still my friend, even if he has completely brain washed her."

Scarlet glared at her sternly. "You forget that she's a queen now."

Eirwyn shook her head, frowning. "No, I haven't. They'll be leaving on their honeymoon tour today, but if I can just get a message to her before she leaves, maybe she'll begin to see through his deception. Surely she'll stop by the tavern to check on the place one more time before she leaves. It's been her home for twenty-five years."

Olive set a bowl in front of Eirwyn, and she thanked her. Then Olive said, "I agree with Scarlet. There's no way you can go into Demerel. It's too risky. Besides, it's already afternoon, and she's probably already left."

The door opened, and Knox stepped inside, taking her breath away. His eyes swept over them, and as he stopped to stare at her, he deliberately pushed his hood back.

His eyes were defiant and wary, like he was afraid that she had changed her mind overnight. So she smiled and winked for good measure.

His eyes widened, and his posture seemed to relax. Then, he held up a small wooden box. "Got the heart of a stag. The meat's in the cellar waiting to be dried or cooked. The pelt is stretched and drying in the sun, but you'll need to move it by the fire if it starts raining again."

Olive beamed. "Thank you, dear. I appreciate it. Will you please tell Eirwyn she's not going to Demerel to warn the queen what her brother is up to?"

Knox glowered, and Eirwyn shrunk in on herself a little. He stood tall, fierce, and proud as he said, "You're not going to Demerel."

His tone brooked no argument, and her jaw dropped. She wasn't used to people talking to her like that. Only Gastone.

Olive raised her brows at Eirwyn. "See? It's too risky, like we said."

He set the box on the table then washed his hands at the sink. "Actually, you'll be going with me today."

He turned and fixed a plate of breakfast Eirwyn had helped Olive prepare. He sat, and she leaned closer to him, propping her head on her hand.

"Are we going to the dwarves?"

He glanced up at her, then back down to his food as he stabbed a potato. "Yeah, I'll leave you there while I go to the most dangerous part of the forest, then I'll come back for you."

She frowned, not liking that plan. "How long will it take to get to the dwarves? Why are we going there when I can just stay with Olive?"

He waved his fork, chewing. Eirwyn sat back in impatience, but Olive said, "I'm just me, princess. If something happens, I can't protect you as well as the dwarves can, even though the Growlers wouldn't dare come here again. But the dwarves are fierce fighters and have defenses beyond our understanding."

Eirwyn frowned. "I've never even heard of them."

Scarlet said, "You'll get there in a few days." She grabbed the small box from the table and opened it, nodding grimly. "This will work, I hope. I'll meet with him today and hopefully meet you at the dwarves' place later this week. Assuming he hasn't left on his honeymoon already, in which case I'll have to track him down."

Eirwyn frowned. "I still don't know why I have to go hang out with the dwarves."

Knox finished eating and took his plate to the sink. "We can talk about it on the ride. Are you ready?"

She shrugged. "It's not like I have any bags to bring with me."

He turned and strode to the door, but Olive stopped him and gave him a hug. Eirwyn watched him stiffen, then relax. She took her own plate to the sink and then turned to the door. Olive held her now cleaned red cloak up and smiled.

Eirwyn put it on and said, "Oh you didn't have to clean it, but thank you so much. I hate being dirty."

"You're very welcome," Olive said as she hugged her. "Take care of my boy, princess. Don't give up on him."

Eirwyn frowned, but simply said, "Thank you so much for having me again."

Scarlet grabbed her own cloak and strode out the door. It was a gloomy day, so they both pulled their hoods up as they stepped outside. She had ripped three fingers of her gloves, which were now stained with dirt. But at least they were cleaner, thanks to Olive.

She walked to Knox and his horse, his hood back up. He didn't say anything, but she felt a heaviness between them. Like they were both about to cross a threshold of no return. He'd been so stiff and abrupt at breakfast. She should be more worried about her friend, stressed about her brother... but no. She was nervous and excited to take this adventure with Knox.

What was wrong with her? She'd never felt like this before.

She took his hand and climbed up in front of him, riding astride like before. She waved to Olive and saw Scarlet ride away in the other direction.

When the woods closed behind them, and there were only the sounds of animals, she wiggled on the saddle. His hand gripped her hip again, and she smiled.

It was like all those weeks ago when they'd first met. Had it only been a month? But there were so many more layers to their relationship now.

"Careful, princess. Don't wiggle too much, or this will be a painful ride."

She grinned and leaned back into the safety of his arms. "Maybe it already is," she said. "I believe you promised me a good time last night, yet here I am, still wanting."

He growled, wrapping his arm around her stomach and settling her deeper on his lap. She practically wasn't even on the saddle anymore.

She gasped at his length, and her mind splintered with need. She hadn't been with anyone else in weeks either, not since they'd met.

He said, "We have a long way to go, princess. We both know this is going to get physical between us, and we need to talk first."

She gripped his arm. He held her tight, and she felt safe and protected as the horse walked through this magical forest.

Her stomach flipped in anticipation, and she marveled that she didn't feel sick like she had for the past few weeks. "About what?"

His breath tickled under her ear. "About us. If we're going to do this, there will be no kissing. If I say stop, we need to stop, alright?"

She nodded, biting her lip. He was so bossy, and she was surprised by how much she liked it. "But why?"

"Safety. If I am what I think I am, I need to keep you safe."

"How can having sex be unsafe?" A gentle drizzle began to fall around them, and he wrapped his arms protectively around her.

"I have poison breath, for starters. Don't want to poison you, princess, as we're currently trying to keep you alive."

She snorted, and then her eyes went wide as she processed. She twisted to stare at him. "Wait, you're serious? How is that possible? I've never heard of that type of magic before."

The line between his forehead appeared worried. "I know, which is why I need to go to the center of the forest and find out what I am."

She frowned and turned back to the front as she thought, wiping away the mist that gathered on her face. She held up her hands, ticking off on her fingers as she talked.

"Poison breath. Scales. Horns... but you're not a lizard? What about a horny toad? Or a poison frog?"

He snorted. "What's with you and amphibians?"

"Me? You're the tough nut to crack, with your magic, that's literally the most amazing I've ever seen." She waved her hands wide. "I mean, look. You can control the forest itself. Don't think I haven't noticed how you've been keeping the brush and vines away with just a wave of your hand."

He shrugged. "I've lived the past thirty years in these woods. You have to stay on your toes around here and develop some defenses."

She shook her head. "You must be pretty powerful. Most magical people have to use a focus object until they master at least one specific magic type. Some magical people even go their whole lives needing their wands. I know of several high-ranking nobles who *still* need help focusing, although they've moved to more easily hidden items like hair pins and brooches. Others at court talk about them behind their backs all the time, of course."

He asked dryly, "Your point?"

She stroked his forearm where it still loosely held her, his hand settled easily on the pommel. "Have you always been able to control the forest? What else can you do? How does your poison breath work? Have you ever killed anyone?"

He shook his head and sighed dramatically. Hours passed as they talked, and Eirwyn knew she was annoying him with the incessant chatter. Yet she couldn't help herself. She wanted to know everything about him.

Eirwyn started to ask another question when she saw something land on his hand. She looked down and screamed, leaning back to smack at it with her other hand.

"Spider!" she yelled, swatting at his arm. Knox jerked on the reins, making the horse dance a few steps to shift off the faint path. Another spider landed on her and another.

The ground around them seemed to roll as black spiders ran toward them. More fell from the trees above, and Eirwyn screamed.

"Shit," Knox growled, then reached into his saddle bags and pulled out a stick with a gem on the end. He pulled out his axe and hit the gem, cracking it.

A bright, red glow swept over them and the horse as the spider swarm fled from the light.

Eirwyn's heart raced as she looked around, checking her body for the dreadful things, but none remained.

He brushed a hand along her back and shoulders. "Are you alright? Did you get bit?"

She shook her hands with a shaky breath, so grateful for her dirty gloves now. "No, I think I have enough layers that they couldn't penetrate them. Did you?"

He flicked a spider away with a wince. "Yeah, damn thing got my hand. The one place that's not covered."

She wiped her hands on her pants, trying to wipe off the creepy crawling feeling that left her on edge. Worry made her frown. "What kind were they? Are they dangerous? Are you going to be alright?"

He grunted and began to list to one side. "Annoying kind," he slurred.

She jerked his arm around her stomach, trying to get him to stay upright. "Stay with me, Knox."

He slumped against her back, wrapping his arm tightly around her. "Darkling spiders. Doesn't help to control the forest when I can't keep the spiders away. Take the stick before I drop it."

She reached for the reins and the glowing red stick, easily taking them from his limp fingers. "Knox? Tell me you're going to be alright."

Her heart raced more from the fear of losing him than the fear from the spiders. She couldn't lose him, not when she was just getting to know him.

She grabbed the stick, holding it out with a death grip to keep the tiny little creatures away.

"I'll be alright. It's happened before, and I'll be fine. Humans die from them, but I just—might pass out. If I do," he paused, his words slurring as he began to wheeze. "Just head for the creek. Ryder will take you to the water, don't worry."

She held him with her hand on his, gripping his arm tight as he slumped over on her. The pommel dug into her pelvis, making her wince.

She grunted as the rain began to grow steadier. "You great ox. Is that why they call you Knox? You weigh enough to be an ox. Maybe that's the type of shifter you are."

He grunted, not moving on her back. She winced at the weight and looked around, holding the red glow stick up.

She was alone in the Feral Forest with spiders and crawly things, and who knew what else would try to kill her. That wasn't even mentioning the gloomy sky that seemed to open up like turning a faucet or the vines that were now silently stalking toward them.

And her only help was now passed out behind her. His control on the forest slipped away, and the vines began to reach toward her.

She gritted her teeth and nudged the horse with her heels, reaching out to the birds nearby to find a path to the creek. She tried using wind to blow them away, and shadow magic didn't affect them, but the spiders' grip was too strong to dislodge them, and they seemed to only be afraid of the red glow stick. Still, she kept her magic flowing to combat her fears of the dark forest.

She swallowed hard as the horse began to follow the path, praying to the gods that she was going in the right direction.

Chapter Twenty-Four

When Knox woke up, his entire head, shoulders, and neck felt like they were on fire. He blinked and looked around. Ryder drank from the stream, and he lay on his back in the soft grass.

Eirwyn cursed as she stabbed down into the earth with a bloody dagger. Birds of all kinds swarmed around her head, randomly diving to the ground. His heart raced, and he jumped up, preparing to lunge at whatever she was fighting.

But she looked over, straightening onto her knees as a look of annoyance flashed on her delicate face. Blood stained her pants and shirt.

Her hood was thrown back, and her gloves protected her hands. She didn't look to be in any more danger as she scowled at him. "You're finally awake, I see. Just in the nick of time, too."

She stood, kicking at the dirt in anger before striding to the stream to wash her blade. Some birds followed her, and some pecked at the ground.

He stood on wobbly legs as dizziness washed over him.

He stumbled a few steps to where she'd been, and his eyes widened as he looked back to her.

"Gods, Eirwyn, that's a bloody adder," he said. "It must be six feet long."

She wiped the now clean blade on the hem of her cloak. "Well, it's dead now, no thanks to you."

He frowned and strode to her, gripping her arms in fear. "Did it bite you? Are you alright?"

She frowned up at him, her small hands with bloody gloves fisting on his chest. "I'm fine, but it almost got you. What would I have done if you'd gotten bit and died? You can't do this to me. I need you to—"

She gripped his shirt and shook, and he pulled her into his arms, hugging her tight. "Shh, it's alright. I'm alright. We're both alright."

She breathed heavily, but eventually she began to relax in his arms. His hands ran up and down her back.

"If you're sure," she said softly into his chest. He let his hands drop and stepped away, rubbing at his eyes. His head was still fuzzy from the spider bite, but his heart was over-joyed that she'd sought solace in his arms.

"You protected me," he said softly as he walked to Ryder to get his canteen from the saddle bag. No one had protected him in a while.

"Of course, did you think I was some spoiled princess who couldn't fend for herself?"

At her tone of voice, he glanced at her as he sank to his knees to fill his canteen in the stream. "Have people made that assumption before?"

She shrugged and sat cross-legged on the ground. "All the time, especially with how sick I was as a child."

He then drank almost all of the water before filling it

again. "I saw you after the carriage accident, remember? You have a good head on your shoulders in a crisis."

Her mouth opened in surprise, then she blushed. Interesting that she blushed at the compliment. He'd have assumed a princess would be used to compliments and would even expect them.

"Where are we?" He held out the canteen to her and looked around, not recognizing this part of the forest.

She took it and shook her head. "I don't know. I followed the path until I couldn't see it anymore. Then I asked the birds for directions to the creek."

She took a drink and dabbed at her lips, distracting him. But finally he asked, "The birds?"

The forest was calm here. Normal sounds of the plants and animals faintly echoed over the swift-flowing stream that led to the river in the south. A few birds settled on the branches above Eirwyn, multiple types all tweeting excitedly.

She glanced up and shrugged. "I can feel things from birds. Sort of like talking with them, but it's more impressions than anything."

His brows rose. "That's pretty amazing. How many others have an ability like that?"

She frowned and shook her head. "I'm not sure. I've never met anyone who can do it who wasn't a bird shifter. Helga told me when I was a kid not to talk about it."

She shrugged, taking another drink and kneeling to refill the canteen.

"But you feel comfortable talking to me about it?"

She handed him the canteen and he refilled it as she said, "I figure you keep your horns a secret, so you might as well know mine. Plus… I trust you."

He met her gray-blue eyes gaze, and time seemed to

still. The creek, the birds, all sounds faded away as he stared into her eyes.

"I'm honored," he said softly.

She glanced away, blushing once more and looking around. "I take it this isn't the part of the creek you were talking about. Have you been here before? Are we lost?"

The tinge of fear sent him into action. "No, we're not lost. We'll just look at the map and be fine."

Ryder now stood beneath a tree in the shade near the bank. Knox went to his saddlebag and pulled out a palm-sized disc about two inches thick. He sat beside Eirwyn next to a tree along the bank and pressed the gems on the side, making the glass top light up with a red dot. He pinched the red dot and zoomed out with his fingers. Eirwyn stepped closer and looked at the device in his hands.

"Is *that* the map? I've never seen anything like that before."

He tilted it to show her. "A type of map, yes. It's called a wayfinder. The dwarves made it for me so I could always find my way in the woods."

Her jaw dropped as he pointed and continued. "This dot is where we are. And this is the heart of the forest, better known as Hartsgrove."

"And you've never been there?"

He shook his head. "No, too dangerous and not worth it until now. There are assassin vines, helroses, and flytraps that don't obey my magic at all."

She snorted. "Is that all?"

He shook his head again and rubbed the back of his neck. "Nope, there's also a cursed oak grove, which I've only ever heard about from stories from the druids. And the giant eagles—I've never been able to get past them before."

He trailed off and sighed as his arm dropped, and he stared at the wayfinder.

"And you have to face all of that alone?" she snorted. "Sounds impossible."

"It may be, but I have to get to the center to find some answers. Lailant said so."

His tone was resigned, but he was afraid to hope that this would end his curse. He used to lie awake at night and dream of what he'd do if he could get close to someone.

"Lailant! When did you talk to her? If she said something so cryptic… Knox, do you know what she is? She's a witch who speaks in prophecies, and if she told you to go to this dangerous place—oh, there must be some great destiny awaiting you. Who *are* you?" she asked softly.

He looked at her, the soft light playing with the shadows and light swirls that always surrounded her. He took a deep breath and nodded slowly. He reached up with one hand and scratched at the side of his head.

"I don't know, but I grew up thinking I'm a drakin."

Her eyes widened, and she blinked. "Oh, that makes so much sense. Why didn't I realize?"

His brows rose. "Realize?"

"The scales, horns, poison breath. My great-great-grandfather had a tail, according to the royal portraits. I should have known. What else can you do?"

His tail flicked up, pushing the side of his cloak away. It came even with his head, curving out with the barb pointing down. Carefully, he kept it from pointing at her.

Her jaw dropped. "By the light, his tail wasn't like *that.*"

He pursed his lips. He was going to be stuck with her for several days alone in the forest. They'd flirted at the cottage, but he wanted to be clear on how dangerous this could be for her.

"A venom barbed tail."

She frowned. "It looks like a broom handle, not a barbed anything."

He arched a brow and his vision sharpened as he concentrated. Then a green sap began to secrete from the tip. Barbs shifted between the scales, extending about an inch on three sides.

He tightened his stomach and grunted. The rounded tip grew a sharp dagger-like point as long as a pine needle.

Two green drops fell to the ground. She reached out a hand as if to touch the tail, and he grabbed her wrist, keeping her hand away.

"No, you can't touch it. It's dangerous, and I won't have you getting hurt or worse."

Her eyes softened, and she smiled softly. "You won't hurt me, Knox."

"Not on purpose, but who knows what dragons are capable of anymore?"

She frowned, glancing from his face to his tail. "Dragon? You said drakin."

He kissed the back of her hand, and his stomach knotted with worry that she'd reject him. This was why he never wanted to show his face or features to anyone.

He took a deep breath and powered through. "Lailant and Olive think I'm a dragon, and Hartsgrove holds the truth."

She shook her head, pulling her hand back into her lap. "Dragons have died out. Drakins are much tamer and that's how they've survived."

He felt the loss of her touch as she pulled away. "Have you ever met anyone like me?"

She cupped her chin in her hand and whispered, "There's no way."

He glanced at the creek, unable to watch her rejection. "I hatched out of an egg. Do any of the royal drakin's hatch out of eggs?"

Eirwyn's eyebrows rose in surprise, and she tapped her chin with one delicate finger as she thought. "Well, drakin's manifest all kinds of things. I specialize in shadow and wind magic, bending light, making illusions and things. My brother has destructive fire magic. The Glathen royal family has ice, fire, and water. I can believe you're drakin, but no one has ever hatched. We're all born like normal."

He winced, raking a hand over the scales on the side of his head. "This is why I never want to show my face to anyone. There are too many questions without answers. All I know for certain is I'm not normal and never will be."

She tilted her head and leaned closer. He kept one hand on his tail to keep it as far away from her as possible. It seemed to have a mind of its own around Eirwyn, despite what he'd told Olive. But the way she kept looking at him made him start to crave more of her attention, more of her acceptance, love, and desire.

His voice dropped to a low growl. "It's why I've never been with a woman before or gotten close enough to people. I'm dangerous, Eirwyn, and will never lead a normal life like everyone else."

He wanted everything from her, but she couldn't accept him like this. Would she want to make a home with him? Would Eirwyn live in the wild, waiting for him to come home from protecting the forest? He'd never thought having kids was an option since he might kill anyone he tried to—

Her small hand on his arm brought him back from his fears and worries. She was now kneeling directly in front of him, and his tail nearly vibrated in his hand. She looked up at him with those gorgeous eyes that shone in the shadows of the gloomy, misty day.

"Being normal is overrated," she said softly.

He shuddered a breath, holding it as he clung to hope. He was prepared to have all his hopes and dreams dashed on the rocks.

She reached up a hand and cupped his cheek. "If you're a dragon, you're not cursed, Knox. I think there's more to this than either of us knows, and it could be a blessing from the gods. There are books in the palace that date back to our dragon ancestors. Surely one of them has something in it on how to live with your tail and breath."

Her fingers trailed softly over his scales to trace the tip of one of the small, triangular horns. A soft smile played on her lips. "The poison breath, the tail, we can work with all of it and still be safe. As for the scales and horns... well, those are sexy as hell."

His brows rose, and he released his breath. "Truly? You—you still want to be with me after all this?"

She nodded and ran both hands over his head, a soft caress that he never thought he'd feel. He growled, his eyes fluttering in ecstasy.

She'd said the same last night, but he was hesitant to trust her words. Words could change. But the way her hands felt on his body made him hope.

She pulled him down closer to her face, and his heart raced. Her lips tempted him like a shiny, red apple. He licked his own and tucked his chin to his chest as he breathed in the honeysuckle and jasmine that clung to her.

A faint line of green gas curled away from his nose and sank toward the ground, and he thanked the gods that he'd not blown it directly into her face.

His chest tightened, and he closed his eyes. He couldn't

do this. It would hurt her or kill her. She could be poisoned so easily, and his tail ached at her touch.

Then she kissed his temple where the scales began, startling him. He froze in her hands.

"Truly, you are one sexy dragon that I can't wait to ride," she whispered, her breath warm on the scales.

His heart raced, and adrenaline began to snake through his stomach, twisting and turning as his dick grew to painful proportions. He licked his lips, keeping his head down, his eyes closed to focus on her hands, lips, breath, and words.

"Do you want that?" she asked.

He grunted. "Damn right, I do."

"You don't have to go to Hartsgrove if you don't want to. We can look for answers at the palace after my brother leaves on his honeymoon. Assuming we make it out of the forest alive."

His free hand found its way to her hip, unsure of what to do as he opened his eyes and stared at her. On her knees in front of him, between his legs stretched out, he wanted to drag her down on top of him as he fell back onto the grass.

"We'll make it. I'll protect you, princess, and keep you safe."

Her eyes softened, and her hands fell to rest on his shoulders, her thumbs stroking the side of his neck and sending a sizzle down his spine.

She wiggled her brows and winked. "Well, when we do, I'm going to take you up on that offer of mutual exploration. You owe me a ride."

He snorted a laugh, thankfully with no gas, and she grinned. Her face was in shadow, but he could see the twinkle in her eye. The heat from her hands sent awareness down his chest and straight to his dick.

He wanted her hands on him everywhere. He ached for

her, this princess who was the exact opposite of every expectation.

She wasn't some cold, calculating princess out of reach of mere peasants like him.

No, she was alive and very real, warm and welcoming. Her eyes widened as his hands slid down to cup her juicy derrière. Then she grinned and tilted her head, arching her back and wiggling closer as he squeezed.

"Ah, are you an ass man?"

He shrugged. "I don't know, but I'd love to find out."

She grasped his shirt and grinned, her eyes glittering in anticipation and desire. Her hands on his chest were so small it made him feel like he needed to be gentle with her.

But she was no damsel in distress.

He grinned down at her. "We could do that right now if you like?"

Her brows rose, and her arms slid up around his neck. He wanted to kiss her ripe lips. They called to him, and his own tingled.

"Outside? In the dirt and grass like animals? How uncivilized," she said, the puff of her breath soft against his skin.

"I think you might like to be a bit uncivilized. Maybe we can explore now and still keep you safe," he whispered, afraid to hope as his heart raced.

He dipped his head, sliding his mouth along her jaw to her ear. "What do you say, princess?"

"I—I've never done anything outside before. How do you want to do things? What things do you want to explore? Where— oh," she broke off on a moan as his lips latched onto her ear lobe.

He sucked softly, and her hands clenched on his shirt. He pressed her closer, desperate to feel more of her. He licked his way down her neck, her pulse drawing him closer.

He flattened his tongue and licked up to the spot under her ear. "Hm, you taste so good, princess. Will you give me more?"

He straightened, still holding onto her, their bodies pressed so close yet not nearly close enough. He wanted to feel her naked against him.

But this wasn't the time or the place. Hells, for his first time, he probably wouldn't last long at all, even after the release last night in the barn. He needed her, though.

Her blue-gray eyes blinked up at him, her gaze hazy with desire.

Chapter Twenty-Five

Eirwyn tilted her head slightly, her heart racing. "I'll give you my everything, Knox, my body, the world. You name it, and it's yours."

Her eyes widened at her words in surprise. Did she really mean that? She'd only known him a few days, so why was she making dangerous promises?

If she'd learned anything from growing up at court, it was to keep your dreams and hopes a secret. She might be a bright, bubbly, sunshine smiling her way through a cruel society, but she never let anyone get too close emotionally.

What was she doing?

She needed to distract herself from the promises his eyes gave. She pushed forward to kiss his neck. He'd said no kissing, but she could kiss his neck like he'd done her. Lick him. Suck him.

He shivered in her arms as she straddled him. Her eyes closed as she brushed her lips over the salty, raspy skin.

"Oh, Eirwyn, you have no idea what you do to me," his voice was low and deep. His hand squeezed her ass and pressed her against him. The other hand stroked up her back to bury into the hair at the base of her neck. He turned her so that his lips feasted on her neck, too.

She gasped at his nipping, fisting his shirt as her eyes fluttered closed.

It was completely different from what she'd experienced in her short life. The men she'd been with had been practically spellbound over the fact she was a princess. They did whatever she wanted, and she'd gone in, gotten hers, and left. They'd left sated, and she'd gotten a few hours of relaxation in. Kisses hadn't been the priority since she'd first started exploring sex.

She wanted to kiss Knox, but there was so much more to explore than just his mouth.

His cock seemed to jump where it pressed against her mound, making her gasp. His lips on her neck shifted, turning harder and more desperate. It was a different desperation than anything before.

With the others, it had been more curious, laughing fun, but with Knox, the intensity shocked her. His lips on her neck turned almost feral, making her legs shake.

He thrust up, their clothes barring them from finding that sweet release. Dusk was near, and she flared light to cocoon them. She moaned, gripping his shirt.

His hand shifted to her shirt and slid along her stomach up to her breast. She gasped, her head falling back and turning to the side.

His mouth pushed all the chaos of the past few days from her mind. The only thing that took up her brain space was the ever-growing pulsing need in her body. It was every-where, threatening to consume her. Between her legs. On her tongue. In her heart.

She pushed the last thought away. It was too soon to

open her heart, but her body, that she could share. She gripped his shirt in her fists and rocked her hips with a moan.

"More, princess?" he murmured.

She pushed her hands up, her fingers raking along the scales on his head. He closed his eyes, his body shaking.

She gasped, "Please."

He kissed over her jaw back to her neck, making her whimper.

"I like the sound of that. You beg so prettily."

Her heart raced in anticipation, and then he latched onto her jugular, making her go limp in his arms. She didn't know that a mouth could feel this good on her neck. He sucked, not breaking the skin, but still, the sensation made her grip on his head tighten.

"You'll be my cum princess, yes?" he whispered, moving his mouth down her neck and sucking again.

She squirmed in his arms, the need building as she nodded and whimpered. "Yes, gods, yes."

He swiftly set her on her feet and stepped away as he reached for the button on his pants. "I don't want to rip your only pair of clothes, princess, so strip."

She giggled and looked around, self-conscious about being naked outside, but there was nothing to fear and no one to see. She pulled the shirt out of her pants and tossed it to the ground. Her breasts were unbound and jiggled with the movement, making Knox freeze. She giggled again as his eyes dilated and his mouth opened, green gas escaping and sinking to the ground.

She unbuttoned her pants and shimmied them down her hips. "Your pants, Knox. I want to ride you."

He grinned as she kicked her boots off and stood naked

as the day she was born. "Actually, I have another plan in mind, if that's alright?"

She shrugged and ran her hands over her breasts, pinching her nipples. "It's your first time, big guy. I'll do whatever you want to make it special for you."

His eyes softened as they met her gaze, and she felt the emotions rolling off him. "I just want to keep you safe," he said softly. "So turn around and put your hands on the tree." His voice was a pleading command, but she did as he requested, shaking her ass as she did so.

"Like this?" she asked, thrusting her ass back and looking over her shoulder, her long, black hair falling down her back. His barbed tail sank into the bark above her head with a thump, making her jump.

"Gods, yes. I'm so excited and don't want to risk hurting you, so give me a moment to calm down."

"I don't want you to calm down. I want you to fuck me like an animal." She moaned at her own words. By the light, what had gotten into her?

His hands slid up the outside of her thighs, and she groaned, her head falling forward as she spread her legs wide.

"Very well, I'm going to fuck you now. It's going to be hard and fast because night is falling and I won't last long, but one of these days, I'm going to get you in a bed and fuck you for days. Do you hear me, princess?"

She nodded, licking her lips, her spine-tingling and goosebumps slithering over her skin. His hands slid around to the front, one skimming along her torso and one diving to cup her mound. He touched her clit, and she jerked in his arms.

He circled the little nub then slid his finger down her clit to her pussy. His head rested between her shoulder blades.

"Gods, you're so wet. I have dreamed of sinking into your warmth."

His hand on her torso slid away, but she didn't care. She was too focused on the smooth slide of his finger in and out, each time coming up to circle her clit before diving back in. He set up a steady rhythm, then she felt a probing behind her.

She pushed back, arching her back and throbbing for more. His finger settled on her clit, and she felt the wide head of his dick push slowly inside. Inch by inch, his erection filled her, stripping away everything but her need for more.

He pressed her shoulder into the tree, seating himself into the heated core of her body. Then he stepped back and adjusted them, moving her down the tree until she was almost bent at the waist. One hand settled on her hip even as his fingers played her clit like a lute.

Vines came up to give her a handhold, cradling her upper body. They wrapped around her ankles and calves, forming a sort of bench for each knee to rest on. Flowers bloomed, cushioning her body and flooding her senses with the sweet smell and bright colors. Her feet left the ground, and she was held in position by vines and his hand on her hip.

"Gods, princess, I never dreamed you'd be so tight," he groaned before plunging back into her wet heat. The scalding hotness of him seared into her like a brand. She gasped, throwing her head back as her eyes widened.

Light and shadows surrounded them, blinding her to anything but the tree in front of her and his tail buried in the bark. A green ooze dripped down the tree, and the strangeness of it all made her want even more.

"Knox," she moaned.

He was impossibly huge, and it hurt so good when he wiggled his hips as if feeling around inside her. Her pussy tightened around his shaft, and he groaned. "Eirwyn, I–I'm not going to last very long. I–"

She shook her head. "Please, Knox, just move."

His hand on her hip tightened, and she felt his nails sting as they bit into her skin. "Gladly," he groaned, setting up a slow but deep rhythm as old as time.

She was stretched, filled by his manhood, as she squeezed down on him. Deep, steady strokes shook her. Every inch brought her closer and closer to the edge, making her tighten.

She couldn't believe how wide he was. It was like she'd never been with anyone else before. He put them all to shame.

With a gasp, she lost herself in the wild, wet hunger that grew inside with each hard thrust. Too soon, the rhythm changed, the plant like bench changed angles, and he hit deeper. He stopped going slow, savoring the moment, and became a wild animal bent on making her scream.

It was inevitable. She couldn't hold back and her body flirted along the edge of orgasm. Pleasure racked her body as he pistoned harder, and she tried to hold off her orgasm. His shaft slicked in and out, the sounds melding with the forest noises around them.

He hammered into her, a hot rush of pure need racing up her spine. The fast fury of his deep thrusts filled her, and white spots began to form behind her closed eyelids. Her body raced along the edge, the fire burning brighter until it flashed like lightning in the sky.

Mindless ecstasy gripped her as a wild orgasm sent her voice screaming into the night. Her eyes shot open, and a rainbow of color burst around them, sparks of light shattering the air.

Her mind splintered, shrinking into primitive passion. Pleasure short-circuited her brain, shocked her body, and made her bones go liquid.

He grunted, his hand on her hip tight as his finger flicked her clit furiously. Then he stilled as he thrust and moaned. She felt him tense as he came with a hot and violent release. His body jerked with every spasm as she milked him. The hot spray of his seed was like lightning inside her as he exploded, coating her core.

She shivered and spasmed, and his finger finally released her clit to hold her torso. Thank the gods for the vines because her legs felt like she would fall into the dirt without them. For once, she didn't even care if she got dirty.

He slid out slowly, and the light magic faded. The plants receded until she was lying on a bed of blue and red flowers, her face still near the base of the tree. Adrenaline began to slow through her veins, but the scent of the venom mixed with the flowers made her sniff.

The honey sweet smell drew her in, and she wanted to lick it. It was like a haze, her mind wrapped in desire and need, and she couldn't think straight.

She leaned closer to where the barbed tail dripped the green syrup down the bark. He wrapped his hands around the tail and pulled it out of the tree.

The sharp movement made her blink and pull back. What was she doing again? She looked around, fingering the flowers around her.

"These are beautiful," she said softly as she sat up.

He bent at the waist and took her chin in his fingers, tilting her face up to meet his glittering green gaze.

"They're nothing compared to you, love."

She gasped, her heart melting at his words. He ran his hand over her cheek, pushing her wild hair away from her face. She nuzzled into his palm, then he stepped away. She sighed and reached for her pants.

She stood on shaky legs, carefully avoiding the venom still dripping and she tugged on her shirt.

Knox lifted her like a bride, making her gasp and hold his neck tight. Then he laid her reverently on a soft plant bed, stems woven together into a hammock.

He brushed the hair away from her face again and smiled. "Are you alright? How was it?"

She nodded, more relaxed than she'd ever been before. She blushed at his attention. "I feel amazing. We should definitely do that again."

He grinned with pride and stood straighter. "Gladly, princess. The light show took me by surprise."

She chuckled, her eyes growing heavy as he set the hammock to rocking. "Yeah, me too. It's never happened before."

She yawned, not wanting to think about why her magic had slipped her control.

Knox then reached over her to wipe the venom on the grass. "We might as well camp here for the night. Get some rest while I check on Ryder and make sure he's safe. I'll be right back."

Eirwyn laid on the gently rocking hammock and smelled the sweet flowers on the ground below. She was barely drifting to sleep when the hammock dipped, and she rolled into Knox's arms.

Her head fit perfectly against his chest, and she hummed. "This is nice," she said softly, her hand coming up to rest on him.

He took her hand and kissed the palm, her bloodied

gloves somewhere on the ground below. Then he turned his head and kissed her hair. "Sleep well, princess."

Her eyes fluttered open to see the hammock growing a type of shell over the top of them. She felt like they were sleeping inside a giant acorn or something, but the gentle sway of the hammock pushed her into a deep sleep.

Hours later, the hammock dipped as Knox pulled away from her. She groaned, "Just five more minutes."

He stood, stopping the hammock from rocking too much as he chuckled. "Dawn is here. We need to get a move on if we're going to make it to the halfway point to the dwarves."

She groaned as he walked away. The vines no longer covered over them like a shell, and the misty morning held a slight chill in the air. She blinked, the faint lightening of the sky the only sign that day was coming.

Knox walked back toward her, looking up and tucking his shirt into his pants. At his worried frown, she sat up and listened to the birds.

He frowned and whispered, "The eagles are coming. Are you awake? We need to go before they find us."

She stretched and swung her feet over the side of the hammock. Knox gently grabbed her arm, pulling her to her feet. Once she was standing, he let her go and then turned to look up, scanning the trees.

She blinked, her mind still asleep, but tension grew between her shoulder blades. Something was wrong. She stepped around the tree and took care of her morning business before kneeling at the creek and washing her hands.

When she turned back, Knox stood tense, a frown on

his face as he stared overhead. She wiped her eyes and yawned. "Is there food?"

An owl hooted nearby, and the wind began to blow through the trees in strange patterns.

Knox walked to her but didn't look at her. He reached out a hand, and she linked their fingers. "Yeah, in the saddlebags. We'll have some jerky in the saddle once we're safe from the eagles."

"What eagles?" she asked, tilting her head. She didn't hear any eagles. She tried to clear the confusion and wake up, but she just wanted to curl up next to him some more.

The owl hooted again, and her eyes widened.

Knox pushed her behind him and backed up slowly toward the horse, his eyes never leaving the treetops above them. "The eagles that terrorize the edge of the Hartsgrove land. I didn't think we were that close to the center."

The owl hooted. She gasped, "We have to go." The fear from the owl tinged her own words. "The owl says danger is coming."

He frowned and grabbed her hand as they reached the horse, who now stood frozen, his eyes wide with fear. Knox helped her swing into the saddle, the soreness between her legs still pulsing so good from the feel of him.

He sat behind her and gathered the reins. "We can't outrun them to the dwarves. They're too fast. We're going to have to head into Hartsgrove and hope they won't go near the place."

They waded into the stream, leaping on the bank on the other side. "I hear a but in your tone," Eirwyn said, gritting her teeth and holding onto the pommel at the rough jump.

"But I don't want to take you to Hartsgrove," he growled as the horse plunged between the trees. "It's too dangerous, princess."

"If we have to get a few scratches to get to safety, it'll be worth it. The owl—we have to get to safety, Knox. Now."

An ear-piercing screech made her gasp and wince. The horse reared up on his back legs. Fear licked at her stomach, twisting it in knots.

Knox cursed, his arm holding her tight around the stomach as he crooned to the horse. "Hells, we have no choice. I'll protect you, princess. Don't worry."

They plunged into the forest, the underbrush growing thicker. The eagle screeched overhead, and she held on tight. How could she not worry or be afraid?

Yet somehow, with Knox wrapped around her like a cloak, she knew she'd be alright as long as they stayed together.

Chapter Twenty-Six

Knox heard the crashing in the underbrush, and his heart raced. He turned Ryder deeper into the forest, going north-east toward Hartsgrove. A shadow passed overhead.

"How big are the eagles?" she gasped, looking over their shoulder.

He grunted, "They're big enough to cart off a horse."

And princesses. He clenched his jaw and pulled her back against his chest as he wove Ryder back and forth around trees, no path in sight.

He had to get them to safety but still avoid the beasts. Assassin vines descended from the trees ahead, and he cursed. He took his axe from its strap on Ryder's side, swinging deftly as the vines tried to grab both of them out of the saddle.

They'd reached the part of the forest where his magic didn't work to control it.

Eirwyn gripped the horse's mane and held on for dear life as he tried to protect her. A whoosh sounded overhead, and he ducked to the left, barely avoiding a crash with a tree and the assassin vine.

He looked back to see a giant talon jerking out of the vines, it's shriek deafening. He turned Ryder and went deeper into the forest. After a few moments, he looked back. The vines and giant birds battled each other as they escaped.

Eirwyn looked around his shoulder, her voice gasping. "Did we make it?"

He grunted and pointed his axe. "Yeah, but the flytraps are ahead. Do you still have that little stiletto dagger of Scarlet's?"

She nodded, pulling it out from her sleeve. "Yes, but I'm not sure I can do this."

He gave her a quick hug from behind. "Of course you can. I believe in you. You killed the adder, right? And got us out of the spider swarm. Here, the flytraps come. Can you take our left flank, and I'll take the right? Aim for the stalk, not the head with all the teeth. Sever it if you can."

She nodded, her body rigid as she scanned the area around them and took a deep breath. "Don't you have more of the glowing sticks? Do they work on flytraps?"

He shook his head. "No, they don't. It just works on insects, not plants or wildlife."

She shivered as the giant flytraps rose in front of them, half as tall as the trees, the bell shaped bulb opening and closing with long rows of tiny, jagged plant teeth. He wrapped his left arm around her waist in front of him. He leaned forward and kissed her cheek. "You're doing so good, princess. Keep fighting."

She shivered again and leaned back, twisting her neck and nuzzling into his neck. He barely dipped his head and hugged her tight when the ground began to slope slightly downward. He could feel her fear, but he couldn't–no, he wouldn't–let anything happen to her.

He pulled back, tightening on the reins.

They were going in the right direction and almost there. The first flytrap latched onto her leg like a dog, and she screamed. He tensed, ready to turn to cut it and free her. But she sliced it off under the head, and it rolled to the forest floor.

He grunted approvingly and turned back to the right, swinging his axe repeatedly. He felt one bite his left boot, but she shifted in the saddle, swiped, and it fell off with a thud.

The axe split the hard stalks relentlessly. He wrenched it from the side of one with just enough time to strike at another. Over and over, the axe became an extension of his arm, and he lost himself in the battle.

Thankfully, Ryder barreled ahead, used to the terrors of the forest, and they eventually made it to the other side. As the last of the flytraps fell away, he panted and looked around, petting Ryder's side.

"Good boy," he murmured.

Eirwyn panted. "Good boy? What about me?"

He chuckled and kissed her hair. "Good girl, princess. You fought like a true warrior."

She sighed and leaned back against him. "Gods, I'm shaking. That was intense."

He wrapped her in his arms and reached for his wayfinder, turning Ryder to circle the ever descending basin. "I'm proud of you though. See? I told you you're good in a crisis. Were you hurt?"

She wiped the juice from the flytraps off on her cloak and took a deep breath. "Just a few bites here and there, but I can't tell how bad they are. What's next? Is there any break in all this to heal, or is it this constant battle into the center the entire way?"

He showed her the wayfinder. "The helroses are next, then there is an abandoned ruin where we can stop for a few hours rest. It's haunted, so I'm not sure how safe it is, but it should be better than the forest."

Her lips thinned, and then she sighed. "Great. That's just what we need. Ghosts."

He grinned and felt her ass pressed against his groin. His hunger for her had only grown since he'd been with her yesterday. He'd woken up this morning with a huge hard-on, but there had been no time to remedy it. The movement of the ride and pressure from her body was growing increasingly difficult, especially in these moments of calm.

Now that it was fully light, she'd thrown her hood back. He leaned forward and kissed under her ear, feeling her shudder and whimper as he whispered, "It could be worse."

He pulled her back against his chest and wrapped his arm up to cup her breast. "I didn't get to play with these earlier, but next time..."

He trailed off as she moaned and arched her back. Some flying creatures swooped down toward them, and she waved a hand in annoyance.

"Shoo," she said, and the bats flew away. He blinked, sitting up and looking around. Now wasn't the time to be fooling around. They had to stay alert.

He let his hand drop, but it fell against her pussy, making her gasp, so he pressed his fingers to her clit and then moved his hand to her thigh.

He cleared his throat. "So you shooed away bats. The owl warned you of danger. But the giant eagles hunted you anyway?"

She shrugged. "Most flying creatures like me, but I felt

nothing from that giant eagle. I'm not sure why not. I've always assumed it was something to do with being drakin. I can feel things from them."

He nodded. "That's pretty convenient."

"The birds and the shadows help me sneak in and out of the palace."

"Tell me about your escapades, and I'll tell you about mine," he said, kissing under her ear again.

She chuckled, relaxing slightly against him as she explained how she would escape the palace through the cellar and entertain the tavern folk. He handed her some jerky to eat when she finished.

He was just beginning to tell her about the time he took down a rogue lion when the helroses appeared in front of them. A solid wall of thorny rose bushes stopped them in their tracks.

She leaned forward as if peering into the bushes but said, "I can't see a thing. They're as tall as the trees."

He glanced down at the wayfinder, the faint moonlight barely helping. "If the map is accurate, it's only a hundred feet thick."

She snorted. "Only. How do we get through?"

He turned the horse and lifted his axe, slicing down and cutting neatly through several vines. Immediately, the vines regenerated, producing two more for each one severed, along with making the thorns lengthen to the size of a forearm.

Ryder danced back away from the growing wall of bushes. After a few seconds, it stopped. The helroses themselves were bright spots of blood red bulbs the size of a human head.

Knox rubbed his hand on the back of his neck as he

thought. Finally, he sighed and pulled a glow stick from his bag.

Eirwyn watched him and said, "I thought those wouldn't work on plants?"

He nodded, his lips pursed. "Regular glow sticks won't. This one is a flame blade. It only burns what it touches. We don't need fire to spread into the forest."

"So it's relatively safe?"

He nodded. "But the problem is it's only supposed to last a few minutes."

"Supposed to? Haven't you tried it before?"

He shook his head. "No, it's a prototype. But it has to work well enough, or the dwarves wouldn't have sold it to me."

He took a deep breath. "If we get trapped inside the helroses—"

"We'll figure it out as we go," she smiled tightly at him, then leaned over and kissed his cheek. He blinked in surprise, forcing himself to stay still and not turn his head to meet her lips.

He blinked down at her. "What was that for?"

She smiled. "For luck."

His chest swelled with pride to know that he'd not scared her off yet. Another part of him swelled to think of her soft lips on something other than his cheek.

She turned back to face the hedge, and he clenched his jaw in determination. He clicked the small gem on the side, and the large gem on the top produced a small, thin blade of fire the size of a full-length sword.

He took the reins, turned the horse, swung the blade, and cut neatly through the hedge. The vines and thorns sizzled as they were severed, but they didn't grow back. He hacked with a fury, fighting against time more than the vines, and nudged the horse into the hedge.

He was a lumberjack. He was used to working days at a time to fell timber, hauling whole logs by hand, stripping the bark, and dragging wagons to the edge of the forest to sell.

Yet, all too soon, even his arms started to shake. He glanced back, the end of the now tunnel of roses showing him the starting point. The blade began to flicker, and he redoubled his efforts.

He swung in savage fury, cutting a path through with his blade. He grunted with every swing, and the blade began to flicker again. He slid off the back of the horse and went around to lead them, swinging with a ferocity that wouldn't stop. He couldn't stop.

If they got stuck in the helroses, Eirwyn would die, and he couldn't let that happen.

His muscles burned. Sweat dripped into his eyes. And still, he kept chopping at the blasted helroses. The cloyingly sweet scent of roses threatened his nose, making him sneeze.

It was like the roses were alive and attuned to his weakness. The scent hit him again, and he sneezed and swung even as the blade flickered. He felt Eirwyn's hand on his back, and she slid her hand down his arm to the blade.

"Let me," she said softly.

He showed her the blade with shaking hands. "Keep the gem pressed down. Don't let up on it until we're through."

She nodded, biting her lip as she took the flame blade and began to hack and chip away at the helroses with both hands wrapped around the flame blade handle. The scent became so cloyingly sweet a haze lingered in the air as he grabbed Ryder's reins and followed Eirwyn.

He covered his nose with his elbow, trying to keep from

breathing in the too sweet smell. It didn't seem to bother her though, as she didn't sneeze even once. She swung in an arc, her small frame belying her strength.

He'd thought she was delicate before, but she was no wilting long-lost princess. She was Eirwyn, his drakin warrior who refused to back down in the face of danger. She pressed forward, never giving up, and a small part of him felt guilty.

He'd given up on his foolish quest to break the curse long ago. If their places had been reversed, Eirwyn wouldn't have given up. She would've figured it out long before now. He wanted to be worthy of her, but she was a damn princess.

He'd never be worthy of her.

But maybe he could try. His eyes refocused as he peered in front of them. The roses were thinning out.

She grunted and swung, finally breaking free as the flame flickered and died. They had to squeeze Ryder through the end, but they finally made it.

She leaned on her knees, panting from the effort like she'd run a marathon. He held his axe, prepared to defend them if something else jumped out.

He looked at the overgrown rows of flowers. There were barely discernible paths through them. One led to a gazebo, and one led to a bench under a tree. Another led to a group of small stone buildings that were almost too dangerous to go into. They looked like they would fall down at any moment.

He straightened with a frown.

"What the hells is this?"

She stood and shook her hair behind her, the thin braids looking like a halo as the sunlight landed on her head. He looked back around them as she said, "I think we're in a garden."

Yet another path, the one they were closest to, led to a sprawling castle. He'd never seen one up close before. He'd only seen the one in Demerel when he'd escorted Eirwyn to the front steps and when they'd robbed it.

This mansion rivaled the palace in style but was on a smaller scale than the one in Demerel. Narrower but perhaps taller. He craned his neck. Its peaks swirled into the afternoon sky. He saw clouds circling the spires, and in some of them he couldn't even see the tops.

"Dear gods, it goes up to the heavens," Eirwyn said in awe. If she was awed—someone who'd grown up in palaces—he knew it was something to behold.

"Is this the ruins on the map?" she asked.

He pulled out the wayfinder and checked, then looked back up. "Yes, it is. It doesn't look to be too ruined though."

She sighed and put her hands on her hips. "Right, let's find a safe place for the night." And off she strode toward the mansion.

He smiled and dropped Ryder's reins as he began to munch on the tall grass by the hedge. He followed her through the overgrown path. She had cried that first night when she'd been kidnapped by Scarlet, but since then, she'd grown stronger. Had it really only been a month ago that he'd met her?

He shook his head, hoping she was right about the safe place. He wanted more time with her. More time to talk with her to hear her hopes and dreams and stories. And maybe even her cries of passion.

This haunted mansion might not be so bad after all.

Chapter Twenty-Seven

Eirwyn approached the side of the castle and stepped onto a tiled deck covered in grass, leaves, and weeds between the cracks. Floor to ceiling windows were so dirty, she couldn't see inside, but when she came to the double doors, she paused.

She glanced at Knox and he nodded behind her. "Go ahead. I'm right here if anything tries to attack."

She smiled, warmth filling her at his steady, reliable presence. She'd not had anyone to rely on before, and it made her feel cherished and protected.

She checked the handle on the glass door. Her brows rose in surprise as it creaked open. "Not locked."

Knox snorted behind her. "Who would dare to rob this place? No one even knows it's here, and I doubt anyone's been here in centuries by the looks of it."

She shrugged, looking around the dark room. Sheets covered the furniture, but it appeared to be a sitting room. The curtains were nothing but a pile of dust on the floor, and when she touched a sheet to remove it from the couch, it too turned to dust and disintegrated into pieces.

He coughed, waving his hand in front of his face. "Darkling hells, this place is old."

"Excuse me?" a voice screeched. "How dare you say it's old. I'll have you know this is the finest castle in all the land."

A flash of light filled the room, and Eirwyn covered her eyes as Knox jumped in front of her, hiding her behind him as he held up his axe.

"Who are you? Show yourself," Knox demanded.

The light faded, but an ethereal figure remained floating above the dusty floor. A man, almost as big and broad as Knox, jumped at them, his hands open as he screamed and tackled them.

Except he fell through them. Eirwyn felt the cold and shivered, Knox spinning them so he was facing the figure.

"Who am I? Who are you, and why are you here? Get out, get out, get out," the figure yelled, trying to punch Knox.

Knox looked at him incredulously and said, "Sorry to disturb you. We just need to fetch a magic apple, and then we'll be on our way."

The figure stopped and stood tall, his brow furrowed. He raked his hand through his long hair and looked around in confusion. Then he looked at his hands.

"What—alright, there has to be some logical explanation for this," the figure mumbled, turning to pace in front of the glass doors.

Eirwyn peeked from behind Knox's shoulder, her hand gripping his bicep, and said, "Um, do you not know that you're a ghost?"

The figure whirled on her, his square jaw dropping in

surprise. He glanced between the two of them, then back to his hands before striding to the dirty mirror above the fireplace.

He seemed to startle as he looked into the mirror, then peered closer, turning this way and that. A shadow of confusion flickered in his expression—like he didn't quite recognize the man staring back at him.

"You're a nobleman, aren't you?" Eirwyn asked. His clothing shimmered, and she could see through him as if he were a haze of smoke. It was obviously well-cut fabric and the only thing in the room that appeared in good condition, even if it was a bit old-fashioned.

The figure turned, his face grave as he looked down his nose at them. He snorted, "A noble? My dear girl, I am the cousin to the king of this forest. It was decreed by his father, the great Xander the Red and my uncle, that I would protect his favorite son, Feralt."

Knox stiffened. "Never heard of them," he said.

Eirwyn looked at him in surprise. "Are you serious? Didn't you read the great historical records?"

Knox shrugged. "My access to books has been limited, and I didn't have all the best teachers and schools, princess."

The figure's brows pinched slightly, a flicker of doubt crossing his face. "Strange... I thought—" He stopped himself, shaking his head sharply. "No, never mind. It doesn't matter."

The figure drew himself up to his full height and demanded, "Excuse me, but did you say princess?"

Eirwyn stepped around Knox to face the ghost and dipped her deepest curtsy. "Yes, sir. I'm Princess Eirwyn of Busparia."

The man sniffed, his head tilting up before he gave a formal bow. "I am Leopol. It's a pleasure to make your acquaintance, princess. However, this is all superfluous. It has no bearing on the fact that *I'm a bloody ghost*."

He yelled the last part, and the chandelier overhead rattled, making them all jump. Knox held out his hands in a placating gesture.

"Well, I wouldn't say bloody," Eirwyn said.

Knox's lips twitched as he tried to take control of the situation. "Alright, alright. Take it easy, and we'll figure this out."

The figure whipped around, his face a mask of fury that made his features sharper. "Take it easy? What the hells does that mean?"

He began to pace, waving his hands as he continued, "My cousin was under attack from some group calling themselves the Hunters. His weak-watered cousins, the drakins, were in the middle of a coup. I was tasked with protecting Hartsgrove. King Feralt cast a spell over the place to protect it, leaving me in charge of protecting the queen and heir. I–I don't remember anything after watching him ride away, the helroses closing the path behind him."

Eirwyn tilted her head. "The drakins were his cousins and you were his cousin. Does that mean you were a drakin?"

The man turned on her, his hands out wide. He was so threatening, Knox protectively stepped back in front of Eirwyn.

"I beg your pardon, but do I look like a dirty drakin?"

Eirwyn crossed her arms and glared at him from behind Knox. "Hey, I'm a drakin, so none of that name-calling, ghosty boy."

The man blinked then burst out laughing. His long hair shimmered around his shoulders as his eyes crinkled.

"Ghosty boy? Oh by the gods, you're a delight, Your Highness."

She bobbed a little curtsy. "Happy to entertain, my lord, but if you're not a drakin, what are you?"

Leopol waved a hand, a ring glowing faintly on his finger. "Oh a dragon, of course. The drakins were from the other side of the family, I assure you. Xander the Red's step-brother's line, I'm afraid."

Eirwyn perked up. "Would that have been Sir Gavin? That's my ancestor."

Leopol pursed his lips and sniffed. "Indeed, sneaky little man who was always jealous of Xander. My own father was Xander's little brother, Pirames."

Leopol stared out the window as his voice faded. Eirwyn looked at Knox with a frown, but he just shrugged. Apparently they were painful memories.

Knox slowly lowered his axe and relaxed. "So this is your first time—uh, awake?"

Leopol nodded and turned to face them, his face troubled with worry as he held his hands behind his back and stood as straight and proud as any noble she'd ever met. "Yes, I believe so, but why now? I assume from the state of the parlor that quite some time has passed."

Knox took a deep breath and shook his head, but Eirwyn slipped her hand into his.

"The dragons have been gone for hundreds of years now, including Feralt," Eirwyn said softly. The poor man had lost everything.

Somehow, he blanched whiter. "What happened? Did the drakins win then?"

Eirwyn nodded. "They did, yes. The drakins seized power in Busparia and Glathen and have reigned ever since.

No one knows what happened in the North as no one ever goes there and returns. Same with the forest we're in."

Leopol rubbed the back of his neck and felt his hair with a sigh. "Then I have failed. We've all lost, and the king is dead. They're all dead."

Knox shifted on his feet and gave Eirwyn a quick, worried glance. Then he turned back to Leopol.

"Not all of them," he said, pushing back his hood and revealing the scales on his head.

Leopol gasped and stepped closer. "By the gods, you're a dragon."

Knox nodded slowly. "I believe so, but that's why we're here. To find answers of who I am."

Leopol walked around him slowly, and his ghostly hand hovered over Knox's head.

"This changes everything," Leopol said softly. His brow furrowed, and he added, almost to himself, *"But... that form. It's not quite right. Like something interrupted the becoming..."*

Then he turned on his heel and ran out the door, shouting, "The egg."

Eirwyn looked at Knox, who frowned. "We have to follow him, but stay on guard." Then Knox ran after Leopol into the hallway.

Knox's stomach flipped as they turned and followed the ghost up the marble stairs. Dust swirled at their feet, and he sneezed. Eirwyn stumbled, and he grabbed her elbow. Together, they went round and round up the stairs, barely able to see the ghost's glow ahead.

"Where are we?" he finally asked as Leopol stopped at a closed door at the very top of the castle. Both he and

Eirwyn panted. A glance out of the small, narrow window showed nothing but blackness. No trees, clouds, nothing.

Leopol waved to the door impatiently. "The nursery. Quick, open it."

Knox turned the latch, but it didn't budge. Then he leaned his shoulder on the heavy oak door and shoved. Finally, it opened with a long creak.

Leopol went inside, a soft light emanating from around him. In the middle of the room was a round, open firepit about two feet off the stone floor. Above it hung a hammock of vines, each end tied to a living tree that grew out of the walls. Knox stared at it, surprised to see the same type of bed he made for himself wherever he was in the forest.

Leopol searched the room, pointing and demanding, "Open the drawers. Move the bookshelf. What about here?"

Knox did as he asked, curious about what they were looking for. Eirwyn and Knox moved furniture around, but much of it was either too heavy or too fragile with age to handle.

Finally, Leopol was on his hands and knees, searching each crack and brick on the fireplace. His hands moved through the items, but then he'd take a deep breath, a brick would vibrate, and then he'd move to the next one.

"There," he said, moving back. "This brick is different. Move it."

Knox pulled the brick out, and a small ring with a green emerald rolled onto the floor. He picked it up, turning it over in his hand.

"Put it on, dragon," Leopol said softly.

Knox frowned, the emerald and gold shining in the faint light. It was too small to fit his giant, calloused hands, but he did as instructed anyway. He slid the ring down his third finger, and it somehow grew to fit him.

"Tap the gem three times," Leopol said.

Knox tapped, and a brilliant flash of green light filled the room. Knox closed his eyes, and when he opened them, more ghosts were striding through the room, except it looked different. The furniture wasn't broken and decayed but new and shining. It was as if they had been transported back in time.

Eirwyn's hand found his, and she held him tightly as they watched.

"We don't have time. We have to go now," a young woman in a druid's cloak said, holding his egg in her hands and rocking it gently. "We have to protect the heir."

A beautiful woman with long, thick brown hair spun on her heels, her full green silk skirt billowing around her ankles. "I will not abandon my home. I am duty bound to protect it while he's gone. Feralt said he'll return, and so I will wait for him."

"But the heir—"

"Take him with you. It'll be safer that way."

"But my queen—"

"Do as I say," the woman's green eyes shone with unshed tears as she took the egg into her arms. She leaned close to it and murmured, "I'm sorry, my love. But I might not be there when you come into this world. Your papa is off fighting for our people, and I might need to protect the forest while he's gone. Grow strong and brave, my son."

Her voice broke on a sob, and she thrust the egg to the old druid woman in the shadows while the young woman packed a cloth bag. The figures sped up, and another flash of brilliant green filled the room.

Knox's stomach twisted as he closed his eyes and his

entire world seemed to spin on its head. When he opened them again, they all stood in the garden in front of the mansion.

The beautiful woman stood with hands on her mouth, her eyes wide as she stared up at the sky. Flying figures fought above, swooping and dodging each other. Dragons the size of horses ridden by humans carrying spears and magic fireballs swarmed around a brilliant green dragon four times bigger than the others.

One spear struck through the throat of the big green dragon, narrowly avoiding a gold necklace with a single emerald in the center. The dragon roared and fell to the ground as the woman screamed. The ground shook as he landed, and the woman rushed over to his side, tears streaming down her face.

The smaller dragons dove at them both, but the woman stood over the green dragon and lifted her hands. Her cry of grief sent a green shock wave through the ground and sky. Magic wrapped around her and shot through the forest.

Knox felt the magic of it, and his eyes misted. It was the source of the magical protection that had created all the dangers in the forest, a familiar presence that he'd felt his entire life.

Her magic hit some eagles that had been nesting nearby, and their chicks grew to as large as the small dragons with riders above. The eagles attacked the riders, easily maneuvering to avoid the spears.

The ground began to shake again, and lightning ripped through the sky. Trees around the castle grew twice as tall. Servants ran out of the castle and down the road, the thorns of the helroses closing the gap and tearing their clothing. The last of them were the pair of druid women. They both stopped to stare at the woman and dragon.

The old druid woman clutched the egg to her chest, then they both turned and raced down the road and into the forest. The helroses closed the gap behind them, then grew up, up, up to encircle the entire castle. The ground formed roots, and vines, and they wrapped around the woman and the dragon, creating a cocoon of oaks.

Another flash of light left Knox blinking, grasping Eirwyn's hand tightly just to have something to anchor to. When he looked around, he was outside the mansion near the front stairs. There was a circular drive that led to a road and the helrose hedge. In the center of the drive was an oak grove.

The largest oak in the middle of the circular grove stood over a massive boulder, the gold and emerald necklace embedded within it. The certainty of who and what he was settled on him like a cloak, weighted with the mantle of responsibility. He stared as he came to terms with the truth.

It could've been minutes later when Leopol floated over from around the corner of the mansion.

"Those are my parents. The egg that the old druid took away... that was me," Knox said, his throat closing with emotion.

"You really *are* a dragon," Eirwyn said in awe.

He nodded, his eyes taking in the oak grove. This was where he came from. This was his home.

Leopol said, "Those were drakes, and their drakin riders, the Hunters. I saw—well, my story isn't important right now." His voice was shaky and upset as he stared back to the side of the house. Knox hadn't seen that part of the vision, but maybe it only showed him what he was supposed to see.

Knox tensed at the mention of the Hunters, his mind going to Scarlet. He worried whether she was safe or if the king realized the heart was the wrong one.

"Your father was a great man and fiercely protective of what he considered his, whether that be this castle or the forest or his family and friends. And he was a great friend, the best friend anyone could ask for," Leopol said softly, his voice choked with emotion. Silence settled between them as they tried to process their grief. Ryder chewed grass nearby, and birds trilled somewhere above. But it was Eirwyn's steady presence that grounded him in the moment.

Knox finally cleared his throat and asked gruffly, "And my mother? Who was she?"

"Your mother was a rare gem. Analise grew up in the village near the hot springs. The old druid was her mother, you know, and had a gift for healing and sustaining life, but it was Analise who brought life and vitality everywhere she went. She was funny, brave, kind, and fiercely loyal to those she loved." Leopol's voice had grown stronger and warmer the more he talked, but then he sighed the weary sigh of someone used to loss. "King Feralt kept meticulous records in his office. When you're ready, find me there, Your Majesty."

Knox blinked, and Eirwyn gasped as Leopol floated up the stairs and through the front door behind them. Knox sank to the stone steps heavily and held his head in his hands, elbows on his knees.

Eirwyn sat beside him and rubbed soft circles on his back. "Are you alright?" she asked softly.

He nodded slowly. "I will be once I get used to the idea of it all. I mean, I was just a lumberjack a week ago, and now there's a ghost calling me a king?"

"There could be worse kings," she said, and he knew she was thinking of her brother.

Knox groaned and shook his head, scratching at his scales. "I'm no king, and the forest doesn't need one. It only needs a protector, which I'm already doing as the Master Warden."

He shook his head and sighed as he sat up. Her hand fell away, and he took it in his, linking their fingers. "Thanks for being here," he said, staring at the oak grove. "Not sure I would've wanted to find out all this alone."

She leaned her head on his shoulder and hugged his bicep. "I'm glad I'm here too, Knox, even if we did have to fight our way in."

She chuckled and the sound dislodged some of the pain and heartache in his soul. It bolstered him enough to stand, keeping their hands together as she followed him. He smiled and kissed her forehead, careful not to expel any gas.

"You're more than a princess. You're a diamond among thorns."

Her eyes misted as she smiled. "Big guy, if you keep saying things like that, I'm not going to want to leave your side."

He grinned and shrugged. "That's alright with me."

She rolled her eyes, and he tugged her up the stairs of the castle. His mind wandered back to Leopol's words. Olive had been right, but there was no need for a king of the forest. It'd just cause more political upheaval when the forest lay directly in between two warring countries. Sure, the soldiers were returning and the king said it was due to his nuptials, but Knox knew it was only a matter of time before the mad king retaliated on Glathen.

Knox pushed the door open, creaking as he went.

Eirwyn followed him down the hall to where a faint light shone under a door.

He pushed it open, and Leopol was leaning over a desk, reading an open book. He took a deep breath when Eirwyn's hand on his back gave him pause.

She smiled up at him and looked at Leopol. "I'm going to go explore the kitchens and check on Ryder. Yell if you need me, alright?"

He nodded and frowned. "Same, if you see some beast that I need to slay, yell for me."

Her eyes twinkled as she tilted her head. "Like an adder? Will do, big guy."

Some of the tension in his shoulders eased at her teasing tone. If she wasn't panicking over all this information, then he wouldn't either. He went through the door to dig through the king's records.

He paused just inside. His *father's* records. He shook his head in disbelief.

Chapter Twenty-Eight

Eirwyn hummed as she found the kitchen. A thick layer of dust covered the petrified wooden table in the center of the room. One wall had nothing but a giant fireplace and wall had an outside door.

She found the empty pantry and sighed in relief. After a few hundred years, there were no more bugs feasting on rotten food. Even the shelves were nothing but dust.

She went outside and called to the birds to get a lay of the land around the castle as her stomach growled. The front of the castle held the oak grove and old road that led into the helroses. The side where they'd entered had the flower garden. The back of the house opened onto a beautiful but overgrown pond. The side where she'd exited the kitchen held what used to be the herb and vegetable garden.

The birds directed her to the pond, and several swooped down to hunt fish. A chirp led her to the back corner of the vegetable garden near the helrose hedge. She followed the bird and found a blackberry thicket.

With her cloak held by the bottom corners, she made a

type of bag and loaded all the ripe berries she could find. They were delicious, and she might have eaten one for every two she put in her cloak.

When she turned, two bluebirds were dancing near the wall of the castle. She walked over and found a few carrots and potatoes. She added those to her cloak and went back to the kitchen, leaving the door open to help get rid of the dust.

She took off her cloak and set it on the table, careful not to let any berries fall. Then she rolled up her sleeves and got to work. A few hours had passed when Knox walked in with a handful of flowers.

He handed them to her, his cheeks tinging with color. "I brought you flowers."

She inhaled the beautiful scent and looked up at him. "What do these mean?" she asked softly.

He raked a hand on the side of his head and looked away. "I've been thinking about how my parents died, and I understand why my mother didn't want to live without my father. The red carnations are for my devotion to you. The pink roses are to show how grateful I am to be in your life right now. And the white peonies—"

"I remember that one! They're for admiration, right? What about these blue ones?" she asked, sniffing in the intoxicating aromas.

He lowered his hand and swallowed hard. He raked a hand down the side of his head, but when he opened his mouth to answer, he asked, "What in the world? Did you do all this?"

She beamed at him and nodded. "Not too bad for a princess, eh?" The floor was now swept and mopped, and the table and counter wiped down. She'd found a curtain that was salvageable and turned it into a cleaning rag. The broom she'd used to clean out the chimney, what she could reach of it anyway.

It was enough to get a fire started in the fireplace. She'd filled a few pots from the spigot off the back door and had fish from the birds in a skillet with the vegetables.

She put the flowers in a cup of water then went back to cooking. She leaned over the skillet and tested it with a fork she'd cleaned to a shine.

"There are no spices other than the rosemary and basil I found outside. There's no oil, so I'm afraid it's sticking to the bottom of the pan a bit, but it should be edible."

Knox sat with a dumbfounded look and laid a leather-bound book on the table. "I had no idea you were so industrious. I know you made eggs at Olive's, but when you said you cooked at the tavern occasionally, I–"

His cheeks tinged pink, and he shrugged. "I didn't really believe you."

She shrugged. "I don't blame you. Helga doesn't believe I can do any of it, either, but that's one thing I loved about visiting Bella at the tavern. She didn't treat me like a princess. She put me to work right alongside the rest of the barmaids. I learned every job in that place, from changing the beds and cleaning to cooking and helping in the stables."

He smiled, crossing his arms, and a look of pride shining in his eyes. "I had no idea. But you actually like doing all of it?"

She flipped the potatoes and looked at him from the stool beside the fire. "What do you mean?"

"A lot of people grumble and complain when they have to do work of any kind, but you seem happy about going to work at the tavern."

She shrugged again, letting the scent of a good meal fill

her. "It's peaceful, for starters. But since I was such a sickly child, I didn't have the chance to do a lot of things other kids did. I was in a protective cage, unable to do anything that might make me run a fever or vomit."

She stared into the flames. She'd need to find some better wood. This had been a broken table in another room that she'd pried apart with her dagger.

"I'm glad you're not sick anymore," Knox said softly.

She sighed. "Me too, although it bothers me to realize that it was probably my brother poisoning me this entire time."

"I can't imagine doing something like that to Scarlet. Brothers are supposed to protect their sisters."

She shook her head. "I mean, we're not certain, but I've been thinking about all the times I haven't been sick, when I was away from him."

Knox sat at the table and thumbed through the book while she cooked. "Is that why you first ran away to the tavern?"

"Partly, yes. I felt smothered, suffocated by all the rules and being told what to do and when to do it. I was worried about how he'd react, but I just had to get out of there. I was lost little girl, hungry, tired, and dirty in a back alley of Demerel. Somehow, I found myself at the square. Lailant took me into her shop and cleaned me up. She said that I was stronger than I knew and to start acting like it instead of a shrinking violet."

Eirwyn smiled, poking at the food. "She took me across the street to the tavern. Bella wasn't so sure about me being there, but her father welcomed me with open arms, and slowly we've become friends. She's the only friend I've ever had, if I don't count Helga, which I don't. She's more of a mother to me than friend."

She wrapped the rags around the handle and carried it to the table. She set it in the center and handed him a fork.

"I couldn't find any plates, so we'll have to eat out of the pan. Would you like some water? I checked on Ryder and unloaded the saddlebags for the night."

She handed him the canteen, and he took a drink. Then she turned back to the brick stove and pulled another pan closer to the flames before turning to sit across from him at the table. It was an ancient stove but leaked about the same amount of heat as those she'd used at the tavern.

He stabbed the fork into the food and took a bite. She bit her lip and waited, nerves making her tap her chin. "Well? How is it? Don't leave me in suspense here."

His brows rose, and he moaned. "This is delicious, Eirwyn. Thank you."

She sat taller, beaming as she picked up her own fork. They made short work of the meal, both of them too hungry for conversation. When it was almost picked clean, she turned back to the fire and brought the other pan to the table.

"What's this?" he asked. "It smells delicious. Are those blackberries?"

She nodded. "With honey and some seeds and nuts. I hope you like it. I only got stung twice to get that honey." She took a bite, not waiting for him this time, and showed him her other hand. The sweet burst of flavor made her sigh.

"Darkling hells, Eirwyn, are you sure you're not a hedge witch? You whip up this fantastic meal out of practically nothing with only two little bee stings to show for it?"

He took her hand and kissed her twin spots as she chuckled, her cheeks heating. "Well, I have a few more cuts and scrapes, if you want to kiss those too."

He laced their fingers together across the table and grabbed his fork with the other hand. "I will add that to my to do list before bed, but first, I want more of this sweet, sticky goodness. It's delicious, and I want to compare it to the sweet, sticky goodness between your thighs later."

Eirwyn choked on her bite as she snorted a laugh. She let go of his hand to grab the canteen and wash it down, choking and sputtering as tears pricked her eyes.

Finally, she gasped, "Gods, warn a girl next time. I'm not used to such language at the dinner table."

Knox looked sheepish and glanced away, so she reached back for his hand and said, "But it's sweet and unexpected, and I love it."

The word love caught her off guard, and she leaned back and let go of his hand. It was way too soon to be throwing that word around. She had to change the subject.

"So you're a lumberjack, but I don't know much else about you."

"What do you want to know?"

She shrugged and took another bite. "I have a lot of hobbies and interests. The cook let me help at the castle when I was a child, but they kept me away from the stove. That was another reason I started to run off into town. By the time I was ten, I'd already tried all the hobbies around the castle. I was very bored by then."

He licked his fork. "I guess that means you've read all the books in your massive library then, huh?"

She winced. "Not quite. I might've read the first few pages of every book, but my attention span is rarely held to finish a book in its entirety."

He tapped on the book on the table. "Speaking of, I found this interesting in..." He paused, frowning. Then he said slowly, "My father's things."

She took another bite and waited as he flipped to a page.

"Apparently, dragons with my abilities can do things I never even imagined. Like with my tail? Apparently, it can be used during sex."

Eirwyn's spine straightened. "Really?" she asked breathlessly. "Care to test it out?"

His eyes glittered from the firelight as he grinned. "Most definitely. Do you want me to tell you the rest or show you?"

Her stomach twisted, and she licked the fork slowly. He watched, his eyes glittering. Then she reached over and grabbed his fork and put them into the now empty pan. She took them to the pail of water to soak.

"Eirwyn?" His voice was soft and sent a shiver up her spine.

She turned to face him, her hands resting on the counter behind her. "Show me. Always show me," she whispered.

She tugged on her shirt, pulling it out of her pants and over her head. She dropped it onto her chair, then walked around the table to where he sat. She hopped up on the table and spread her legs, holding up one foot near him.

"Can you help me take off my boots, please?" She batted her eyelashes at him, and he licked his lips.

Then he reached up with shaking hands and began to unlace her boots. They fell to the ground with a thud, one after the other. His hands slid up her legs to the buttons on the front.

His hands hovered over them, lightly caressing under her belly button. "Do you want me to help you take off your pants too?"

She nodded, leaning back on her hands and pushing her breasts and hips up. His eyes flared, and she reveled in the power she had over him. A tail during sex? Who would've thought of such a thing? It was new, exciting, and dangerous.

But the way he looked at her like she was the most important thing in his life right now is what made her racing heart melt. After years of being ridiculed, looked down on, and ignored by her brother, having all of Knox's attention was like the sweetest ambrosia on her lips.

He flipped the buttons and slid her pants down her hips, every trace of his fingers on her skin lighting a fire that couldn't be quenched. She sat back down on the table as he tossed them onto the chair.

Then he stepped back, his eyes growing heavy-lidded with desire. "You're so beautiful, Eirwyn," he said softly, reaching up to caress her cheek. "Sex with dragons can turn violent, and I don't want to hurt you."

She laid back on the table, now naked, and set her feet on the chairs. Her legs spread, and she traced her fingers up her sides to cup her breasts.

"You could never hurt me, Knox," she whispered, arching her back. There was no doubt in her mind that he would protect her no matter what. It was just one of the things she loved about him.

Her mind stuttered to a stop. She wasn't some innocent miss who fell in love with every guy she slept with. She'd protected her heart all this time, yet she'd been powerless to resist Knox.

She bit her lip and pinched her nipples as he undressed, not sure if she was trying to distract him or herself. He reached up and unclasped his cloak, dropping it to the floor.

She lay naked in front of him, her heart open and vulnerable. A tiny sliver of fear snaked up her spine. She barely knew him, had only spent a few days with him. She'd only learned he was a dragon yesterday. What else did she not know?

What if he turned out like her brother? What if he put on a good show, said all the right words, but then poisoned her?

He pulled his shirt over his head, and a tiny tendril of green gas snaked out of his nose, sinking to the floor. Her heart raced, and she froze, waiting for the panic to recede.

He kicked off his boots and stepped out of his pants as she sat up and closed her legs. His eyes never left her, but she couldn't meet his gaze anymore.

"What's wrong, princess?" he asked softly as he fisted himself.

She stared as her mouth went dry. "I don't know. I'm just suddenly nervous."

He gathered her into his arms, and she rested her head on his shoulder. Her feet were on the chairs and his hips were cradled against her, teasing her with his nearness. His hand stroked down her back slowly and green gas began to surround them.

She wiggled her fingers and created a gust of wind to disperse it. "Careful, Knox. Your poison is showing."

He leaned back and grinned wide, making her heart trip again. "Maybe you should get closer. Give it a real sniff."

Desire and curiosity warred within her as she arched a brow. "You've been adamant that I stay away from the gas, but now you want me to get closer? What exactly did that book say?"

He looked down and his eyes grew brighter with desire. "It said that the gas might be poisonous to others, but to my mate and my children, it's harmless."

"Really?"

His hands came up to caress her breasts, his eyes

focused on them as he said, "Actually, it said my mate would find the gas irresistible. Same thing with the poison on my tail. It's supposed to be an aphrodisiac and lube."

"Lube?" she gasped as he rolled her nipples between his thumbs and finger.

He nodded and hummed. "Oh yes, I even had an interesting and somewhat embarrassing conversation with Leopol about it. Are you up for testing the theory?"

She bit her lip, and one hand came up to caress her cheek. Finally, she met his gaze.

"You know I'd never do anything to hurt you, princess. I'm not your brother."

She took a deep breath and nodded. "I know, I trust you. It's just…"

"What?" he asked. "Tell me. I'll give you anything, do anything you want. Just name it, love."

His words were like honey to her soul, and his eyes held so much love it scared her. The way he fisted his cock and his tail curved up to hover next to his head was what made her push away the fear and overwhelming thoughts of love and cling to the excitement of the unknown.

It was covered in brown and green scales, the ridges like plate armor. Bright green pooled on the tip, dripping down the side. She slowly reached up, never taking her eyes off his tail as she touched the thicker middle and ran her fingers up to the tip. She paused just before touching the green wetness and excitement raced up her spine. This man, this *dragon*, was more powerful than even her brother. Fear of the future warred with excitement for the moment within her.

She bit her lip and touched the liquid, pulling her forefinger away and rubbing it with her thumb. "Hm, feels like honey."

It was warm, sticky, and smelled of all her favorite

things mixed together. He watched like a starving man as she brought the finger to her lips and licked. His nostrils flared as she moaned and her eyes fluttered.

An explosion of taste danced across her tongue, slightly salty like his eruption in her mouth in the barn, but completely unique and somehow sweeter. Her eyes opened and she grinned. "Well, not dead yet, so maybe the book and Leopol are right."

He snorted and fisted his cock, bringing it closer to just where she wanted it. "Ready for me to show you more?" His voice was low, making her shiver as she put a hand on his chest and slowly pushed him back.

"Wait, you said it could turn violent? How violent are we talking?"

His eyes began to glow and his tail shook behind his head, more of the ooze dripping down it. "I don't know, but if I hurt you, princess, I will never forgive myself."

She bit her lip, but excitement won as she stood up and danced out of his reach. He frowned as she turned at the still open door.

"Yesterday it was rather animalistic, and I very much enjoyed it. Think we'll enjoy it if you chase me down and stab me with that big cock of yours?"

His brows rose as he growled, "I thought you weren't used to such language."

She grinned and leaned against the open door, nipples pebbled and core aching. "Doesn't mean I haven't heard it in the tavern or around town while I slink in the shadows. What do you say?"

He grinned and fisted his cock. "I'll give you a three second head start. One, two—"

She giggled and took off into the garden. When she

glanced over her shoulder, he stood at the doorway with a grin and said, "Three." Then he leaped after her.

She turned and ran barefoot into the overgrown garden toward the front of the house, her laughter echoing on the wind.

It was dark now, and the moon wasn't quite high enough to be seen over the treetops. The pounding of her feet on the grass made a roaring in her ears. She glanced over her shoulder to find Knox just a few paces behind her, a wide grin on his face.

Without thought, she ran to the oak grove. Surely he wouldn't try anything in front of his parents, the giant tree, and the boulder.

She reached the center, and the ground began to shake. Vines shot up from earth, and she tripped. She screamed but didn't hit the ground. A sharp sting pierced her ass, and she jerked at the prick of pain. It was like a bee sting, uncomfortable but fleeting. The plant ropes wrapped around her ankles and wrists, and her ass throbbed as they spread her legs and arms wide.

They held her as she squirmed and gasped, her heart racing as she stared up at the dirt beneath her cheek. Anticipation built as the pulsing need for him flowed through her.

Chapter Twenty-Nine

Knox panted, staring at the barb that stuck on her skin like a thorn. The green venom dripped down her ass, and his chest tightened. "By the light, are you alright, love?"

It went against everything he'd been taught growing up, but the books and Leopol had been clear. Dragons only lusted for their mates, and there were requirements to finish the mating process.

"What the hells was that?" she gasped and wiggled on the vines.

He chuckled. "You didn't say I couldn't use my abilities to catch you, princess." He reached forward, running his hands up and down her soft back before pulling the barb out swiftly.

She sucked in a breath. "Ouch, what was that? Was it another bee?"

He palmed her ass, rubbing the sore spot and soaking the venom into her skin as he snorted. "No, it wasn't a bee. It was a barb from my tail. How do you feel? Are you alright?"

Her skin was warm to his touch, and he reached up with his other hand to squeeze more liquid from his tail. His heart raced, hoping desperately that the books and Leopol were right. He massaged it into the round globes, and she moaned, pushing her ass up into his hands.

"Do you like it? Do you want me to stop?"

Her breathing was rapid and shallow, and she shook her head. He slowly traced his way between her legs, sliding the gooey liquid of venom over her cleft to her clit. He shifted back and removed his hands.

"Gods, don't stop," she gasped, wiggling her ass.

He slowly made the vines turn her facing up, still spread and at his mercy. "Don't worry, princess. I'm just honoring my word. I told you I was going to worship your breasts next time, yes?"

"Gods, yes," she said, throwing her head back.

Her breasts rose and fell with her breathing, and he dipped his head and took one pebbled nipple into his mouth. She moaned as he sucked and nipped, getting a feel for what she liked and what made her wince. He slowed and shifted position.

She threw her head back and arched, pushing her breasts to him. "Damn it, don't stop."

That was all he needed to hear. He knelt between her legs and rubbed her clit in circles until she was moaning, thankful for all the observing he'd done at the brothel. She thrust her hips but couldn't move with the vines holding her.

He shifted the vines, wrapping them around her thighs and stretching her wider until her legs shook. Then he took his cock and rubbed it up and down her slit, coating it in the green venom.

Her eyes shot open wide as she stared at the sky blankly. "Gods, yes," she gasped.

The pressure at the base of his spine was already building as he slid slowly inside. Her tight, wet pussy wrapped around him, squeezing like a glove. His vision swam, stars blinking behind his eyes.

Once he was seated all the way inside, he wrapped his hand around her waist and switched to her other breast. He set up a steady, slow rhythm. He wanted this one to last. He wanted this one to be a mate claiming.

Only then could he truly protect her.

He shifted, nuzzling her neck as his tail wrapped around them to slide up and down her spine. "Be my mate, Eirwyn."

Her head fell back, her mouth open with a gasp. "What does that even mean?"

He kissed her neck. "It means you'll be mine forever. Say yes, so we can do this every day."

She gasped as his tail teased down the crack of her ass, a trail of green left in its wake. He kept the tip of it smooth, the barb now expelled and the tip rounded like a smaller version of his cock. He grabbed her ass and pulled her cheeks apart.

She squirmed and gasped. "Knox? What—what are you, oh gods."

The tip of his tail teased her asshole, and she clenched, keeping him out. "That's it, princess. I'm going to fill every hole. I'm going to make you scream in pleasure. Do you want to try it?"

She tossed her head side to side. "I—gods, I can't think with you inside me, Knox."

"The aphrodisiac is working for you, my mate," he said, pressing his lubed-up tail into her hidden depths, slowly at first, just teasing. His rhythm never let up, his cock moving in and out alongside his tail in her ass. The slicking noises of sex mixed with the crickets and sounds of night in the forest.

"I—I need more" she demanded, thrusting her hips as she tried to wiggle closer.

He kissed the side of her neck, then took her ear lobe between his teeth. "Whatever you desire, Eirwyn. I will protect you to my dying breath and give you all that's within my power to give."

He knew it was true, had known it on some level since the day he'd seen her looking up at him from the wrecked carriage.

"You're mine," he growled, his tail finally pushing into glory as far as he dared. She tensed, and he eased back out, shallowly thrusting his tail in time with his hips.

She grunted as he began to thrust deeper and deeper. "Yours," she said.

"My mate."

"Mate," she gasped.

"Forever," he demanded. He needed her to know that she was it for him. There would be no others.

"Forever," she groaned, her head falling onto his shoulder.

He dipped his head and sucked on her neck, tasting the metallic tang of blood as he thrust as deep as he could go. There were no more words, both of them beyond the ability to speak. They panted in pleasure, lost in a mad embrace. She moaned, gasped, and writhed in the vines, wild in his arms.

And still, he wanted more. The air around him shifted, whipping leaves and grass around them as he stretched her. Her damp heat held him prisoner, but he never wanted to escape.

He rammed himself home, his body hard and primal

against her as he rode her with rough strokes. The feel of her slick heat wrapped around him. Hips bucking, shaft and tail throbbing, he plundered her, ever trying to go deeper, closer.

He groaned and pulled out a little, then drove back in with sure, possessive thrusts. She writhed against the vines, her mouth falling open as she panted. Her moans went higher and higher.

She was close, and he wanted to soar with her.

Her body went taut, and she screamed. Her back arched, and pleasure rippled through her like a blast of magical energy. Her body convulsed, and spasms wracked her as she milked him.

He couldn't hold back anymore, needing to join her in a hot release. The explosion rocked his core as he continued to pound home. He grabbed her hips, pulling her hard into his final thrust. His pulsing cock gushed into her in time with the pumping of his tail. He roared his release, burying his head in her neck. The hot spray of his seed erupted from him, and he melted into her heat.

He stayed inside, just holding her as her body pulled more from him, demanding every drop as hers. Every muscle was tight as he poured into her. Together, they shuddered, bowing into each other's bodies as if neither of them could get enough of the other.

The vines disentangled from her body as he slid out of her holes. She curled into his arms, and he slid them both down to the soft grass under the oak grove. He held her, cradling her head on his chest as his arms protected her. Hard loving had become the heavy breathing of afterglow, peace swirling around them like a gentle summer breeze.

Exhausted, she fell asleep in his arms. His half-lidded

eyes slid closed as he breathed her name, her body sprawled limply half on him.

Chapter Thirty

The next morning, a rustling sound made Knox open his eyes. He glanced over to see Ryder munching grass near the oak grove as the faint light of dawn spread across the sky. A soft dew covered them along with a grass blanket.

He frowned in confusion. He was decent with magic manipulation of trees and shrubs but a master with vines. They were easy and took very little magic, but grass had long given him trouble. How had he formed a blanket? He turned his head, Eirwyn's warm body curled into his side. Perhaps it was the mate bond making his control better.

He reached down and traced her cheek with his finger, shifting to lay more on his side as his tail had fallen asleep in the night. It tingled with awareness, and his cock throbbed at the feel of her pressed against him.

He kissed the top of her head, and she hummed in her sleep, rolling onto her back. Her black hair fanned out around them, and he pushed the grass blanket off them both. It absorbed back into the ground, but he didn't pay attention.

He couldn't get enough of Eirwyn. He sat up on one elbow and traced a finger down her breasts to her navel, then on down to the cleft between her legs. She gave a soft hum and rolled onto her side.

Knox got on his knees and caressed her ass before dipping his hand around her hip to cup her mound. She sighed and rolled onto her back again, this time her legs falling apart. He grinned at the sweet smell of victory.

Desire and honey, venom and earth swarmed his senses. Heat settled in his groin. White hot animal longing drew him down, close enough to part her pussy and set his mouth to her clit.

She gasped, her back arching as her feet settled flat on the ground. "Wha– Knox?" she asked sleepily.

He slid two fingers inside her as his tongue kept her prisoner to desire. He teased her open, questing, conquering as he worked his strong fingers into her. She writhed against his hand, already lost to pleasure. She was slippery as his tongue circled her tight bud. He drank from her, ate her, never stopped working his mouth on her hot clit. He found her trigger and fired off short little licks and sucks, all the while pumping his fingers.

Her breathing turned ragged as he adored her. Her hands settled on the sides of his head, her fingers raking along his scales and making him moan into her pussy.

"Gods yes," she gasped. "Knox, please, I need you."

He pumped harder, wanting her to cum for him first. She panted, her breathing turning ragged as her hips lifted in time with his fingers. Then her body was shaking, and she thrust up, grabbing his horns and holding him close.

Her body went taut, every secret part of her crying out his name. She made guttural sounds that spoke to his beastly nature. Her pussy clenched on his fingers, pulsing as she shuddered in ecstasy.

When her legs went limp, he released his hold of her clit and pulled his fingers from her. He slid up her body and grabbed his throbbing cock, teasing her folds. She looked up at him with heavy-lidded eyes, her chest rising in shallow breaths.

Then he slid home in one deep thrust. Her mouth fell open as she moaned, her back arching and her nails digging into his biceps. He pressed harder, shifting his hips to start a driving rhythm. Beat for beat, she met him thrust for thrust, arching her hips and clawing at him.

His fingers dug into the dirt next to her head. His cock seared into her, burning like a brand. His tail buried into the ground above her head. She was deliciously tight as she quaked and trembled around him.

She locked her legs around his hips, and he pounded her into the ground. The ground rolled beneath them, and her pussy squeezed down, trapping him inside.

He buried his head in her neck with a groan as her muscles gripped him tighter. Still, he rammed into her with relentless thrusts. He drove into her with an animal fierceness, and they moved as one.

Her inner walls rippled against him as she gasped, "Yes, gods, yes, Knox. Please, Knox."

He hammered into her, a hot rush of pure need. Hunger matched hunger as their bodies slammed together. She was wet, wild, and all his. Forever.

She thrashed and moaned, her body spasming around his cock as she thrust her hips up and screamed. Birds flew from the trees overhead, and the wind swirled around them.

He thrust deeper, faster. His balls tensed up, but something drove him to keep going. He couldn't stop, not yet. He had to get deeper. He clenched his jaw, and it felt like his balls exploded into his cock.

His shaft swelled, making Eirwyn scream and buck with every ripple and movement. She thrashed under him uncontrollably, her moans and groans not even words as she shook her head, her hair lifting and twirling with the wind. Light swirled around them in bursts.

He plunged into her hidden depths, then went absolutely still, paralyzed by pleasure. His release was hot and violent, like a geyser that was long overdue for eruption. He stiffened and convulsed inside, a roar of satisfaction upon his lips. His body jerked, every muscle tight as he poured himself into her.

The heat spread from their joining as they climaxed. They came hard, each fueling the other's release. Their bodies fused into one shared hot, sticky orgasm.

The ground continued to rumble underneath them, shaking softly as they both went limp. He gathered her into his arms and turned onto his side, wrapping her in a cocoon of protection. Together, they watched the light grow brighter as the sun rose until Knox's stomach rumbled.

Eirwyn chuckled, her hand slowly tracing up and down his bicep.

"Is that your stomach or the ground?"

He lifted his head up and pushed her wild, black hair out of her face. He kissed the tip of her nose and smiled. "Definitely hunger. I'm going to take a dip in the pond. Do you want to join me?"

She wrinkled her nose and shook her head. "No, thank you. There's no telling what kind of slime is on the bottom. I'm not a fan of being dirty."

His brows rose, and he pushed himself onto all fours to offer her a hand. He helped her up as he replied, "There's the princess side of you. After last night, I was wondering where she'd gone."

Eirwyn rolled her eyes and walked back to the house through the garden. He followed her, loving the sway of her hips in the morning light. She walked with a straight back, her head held high like the princess she was, regardless of her lack of clothing.

She ducked into the kitchen, and he continued on to the pond. He strode straight into the frigid water, the sun not yet heating it. He ducked under the surface, washing quickly before swimming across to the other side.

It was deep for a pond and wide enough to get his blood pumping from the swim. Then he waded into the shallows and saw several small fish. An idea formed, and he held his tail poised over the water with barb ready. A large fish swam lazily by, and Knox speared it. He flicked his tail, sending it to the bank, where it flopped.

He turned his attention back to the water. After a second one joined the first, he strode out of the water and gathered them both, hooking a thumb into their mouths. He carried one in each hand to the kitchen door.

He paused, dripping water on the threshold. Eirwyn was dressed, her hair braided in one big braid down her back as she talked with the ghost, Leopol.

She turned from the skillet over the fire in the hearth and looked him up and down. Her eyes glazed over, and he grinned as she stared at his cock.

He held up the fish. "I caught lunch," he said. "Where do I put them?"

She waved to another skillet on the counter, now cleaned from last night's dinner. "In that one. Breakfast is ready if you'd like more berries and nuts."

He set the fish down, then turned to dunk his hands into

a pail of water, rinsing them off. "I'll eat your berries if you'll eat my nuts," he said.

Leopol snickered, and Eirwyn laughed.

"Well, it's been lovely, Your Highness, but duty calls. I'll be in the office," Leopol said, a grin on his face as he floated through the kitchen door into the house.

Eirwyn watched him dress out of the corner of her eye. He left his cloak on the back of a chair, for the first time in years, not automatically putting it on. He loved the feeling of freedom this place brought him.

She set the bowl of berries in front of him and turned to walk away. He reached out a hand and pulled her close, nuzzling her breasts through her shirt. Her hands landed on the sides of his head with a gasp, and he moaned.

"Your fingers on my scales are heaven, Eirwyn," he sighed, his shoulders lowering. She kissed one side of his head, her breasts nearly suffocating him. Not that he was complaining, not at all.

"I love touching you, so I'm glad you like it," she said before twisting out of his arms and going back to the counter. She hummed a soft tune as she took her dagger and skinned the fish.

"We need to leave after lunch today if we're going to get to the dwarves before dark," he said.

She nodded and kept singing softly under her breath as she worked. He wanted to just sit in the kitchen and listen, watch her, be in her presence. But if he was going to learn all he could about who he was, he had to get back to the office.

He grabbed the bowl of berries and nuts and walked silently out of the room.

A few hours later, he rubbed the sides of his head and

sighed. Leopol and he had gone through book after book, and his head was aching.

"Do you really think it'll break the spell of protection on the forest, though? I don't want to undo my mother's spell. She gave her life for it," Knox said, flipping through yet another book in his father's office.

Leopol shook his head. "I don't know. There are so many unknowns, including how I died, where my body is, and why I'm even here."

Knox raked a hand down his face. They'd been digging through the books for hours, but every answer led to even more questions.

Eirwyn's singing had echoed through the halls, making him smile. He glanced outside and noticed the sun was overhead. He closed the book and slid it into his saddle bag.

"I'm going to take this one with me too."

Leopol frowned and followed him through the door and down the hall to the kitchen. "Do you have to leave today? Can't you stay another night?"

"We need to get to the dwarves by nightfall. Eirwyn will be safe with them for a few days, but I'm worried about Scarlet."

He'd explained to Leopol about his upbringing. It'd been a touchy subject at first, with Scarlet being a Hunter, and Hunters of old being the drakin that had destroyed the dragons. But Leopol didn't say a word at the mention of her name now.

Knox went through the kitchen and breathed deeply, peace filling him. The smell of simmering fish and vegetables filled the air, but Eirwyn wasn't there.

He went out the open door to see her carrying a cloak full of berries, her hand stretched out to feed some to Ryder.

The horse followed along beside her like a puppy, and Knox didn't blame him at all.

He felt like that too. He adored her and wanted to spend every moment with her. He'd follow her into the depths of hell if he needed to.

She turned and smiled. The sun peeked behind a cloud, lighting her like a halo, and he sighed. She was his mate. He still couldn't believe fated mates were real or that *she* was his.

Chapter Thirty-One

Eirwyn smiled wide as she walked to the kitchen door. "Knox, there you are! Just in time for lunch too."

Knox carefully adjusted the saddlebags on Ryder, ensuring they were securely fastened. The movement of his muscles was noticeable, but it was the calm expression on his face that made Eirwyn's heart flutter. It was reassuring to observe him so at ease in this environment. Notably, he had not worn his hood today, and his posture remained relaxed.

"Leopol doesn't want us to leave," he said.

Eirwyn sighed and went into the kitchen, spying Leopol leaning against the table. "I don't want to leave either, Leopol. I like it here."

"You do?" Knox sounded so vulnerable as he came inside behind her, and her heart melted.

She nodded, washing the berries and then adding them to a pan to boil. "I do. It's peaceful here, and the company's pretty good."

She winked at them both, and Leopol grinned. It made

him appear less the stuffy noble and more the noble rake. He'd been very vague about his background, and she had a feeling there was more to him than met the eye.

But she hadn't wanted to pry too much. Most of his time was spent talking with Knox and searching for answers. So she'd cooked, cleaned, and explored one room at a time. After she'd tidied the kitchen, she'd gone to work on the parlor and then the foyer.

Leopol crossed his arms and stroked his chin thoughtfully. "I like the company too. Now that I'm awake, do you think once you leave, I'll go back to sleep? Or will I just be wandering around this old place alone until you come back?"

Eirwyn frowned and shook her head. "I don't know. I didn't pay attention to the nekromancy classes. My brother spent a lot of time in them, and I preferred avoiding him. You're the only ghost I've ever seen, actually, but I don't like the idea of you being alone."

Leopol snorted. "Me neither. Maybe I can go with you?"

"We'd love that," Eirwyn said with a smile. "But first, let's eat."

They sat down, the conversation flowing smoothly between the three of them. Eirwyn had just served the berries and honey for dessert when the ground rumbled. The table and chairs began to shake, the rumbling increasing the until the pan on the counter crashed to the floor.

"Oh gods!" Eirwyn said, leaping up and heart racing. Knox stood, his feet widening as the ground continued to shake.

"What's happening?" Leopol asked, a frown marring his ethereal face.

271

A crash sounded in the foyer, and Knox walked unsteadily to the kitchen door. Eirwyn followed close behind, her hand on the small of his back.

When they left the hall and rounded the stairs, Eirwyn gasped. Knox's spine tensed under her hand. A complete and animated dragon skeleton now stood in the foyer, a cloud of dust and debris settling around him. Eirwyn recognized the necklace around its neck.

She shook her head. "By the gods, the necklace. It's Feralt!"

Terror shot through her spine, and she stepped closer to Knox's back.

She wasn't a weak, helpless princess anymore, but this dragon was huge. It stood tall, its head barely grazing the two-story ceiling. Its head bent, and Eirwyn shivered as it looked at them through empty eye sockets. One wrong move, and it would rip her in two. A wave of apprehension washed over her, twisting in her gut.

Leopol whispered in awe, "The king."

Knox's head dipped down as he glanced around the foyer. The front door had been ripped off its hinges. It was a skeleton, yet the chandeliers and walls rattled as it breathed. Knox kept Eirwyn behind him and inched back toward the kitchen. She hoped it hadn't seen them and wasn't sure how skeletons could see without eyes, but she held her breath anyway as she stepped back.

The great dragon's head lowered, and it opened its mouth. A red glowing flame where the heart should be began to glow brighter as it inexplicably drew air inside, pulling energy into its core. Eirwyn felt the air sweep toward it as it breathed in, and her body froze.

She was all too familiar with that type of energy core, the flaming orb, the sudden rush of air toward it.

Eirwyn screamed, "Run! Fire!"

The air shimmered like a wave, and a stream of fire slammed into them. They hit the wall of the hallway. Eirwyn fell to her backside, and she cried out as the back of her shirt caught fire. Flashbacks of her brother's temper tantrums from when she was a child threatened to choke her.

Terror came gasping up her throat in a cold, panting fear. She fought against it, but it seemed hopeless. Still, she rolled to put out the fire just like she'd done all her life.

Knox stumbled and grabbed her hand, pulling her up and shielding her from the dragon. She took a deep breath, finding strength in his arms to battle the fear. If she gave into it, who would help Knox, who would defeat her brother?

She choked as smoke filled the air, the old tapestries blazing on the wall.

"Come on," Knox gasped, turning to look behind them.

The dragon's jaw unhinged wider, sucking in the air with a monstrous growl. Eirwyn's heart slammed against her ribs as Knox seized her hand and yanked her down the hall.

She reached for the currents in the walls, pulling the stagnant air into motion, and whipped it backward, snuffing out fire in pockets behind them. The flames hissed and recoiled, but even as she fed her will into the wind, the heat clawed closer.

The hallway trembled. Knox ripped at a door handle— only for it to snap off in his grip.

"Damn it," he spat, slamming his shoulder against the frame.

Eirwyn's breath hitched. She hadn't come this far down the hall before. Panic clawed through her spine like talons.

Around her, shadows bled from the corners, curling like frightened fingers, reacting to her fear.

"What now?" she gasped, spinning, trying to orient herself. The shadows dragged behind her, sluggish from the weight of her exhaustion.

"It's not budging. Back to the kitchen, move!"

They bolted. The roar of fire thundered behind them. A chandelier crashed to the floor with a blast of air and crystal, blocking the hallway ahead. Knox veered hard and dragged her left—through a tall glass door.

It exploded around them. Eirwyn threw a wind barrier around her body, cushioning her fall, but the effort came too late for finesse. Glass sliced across her arms and shoulders. She hit the floor with a choked cry, magic stuttering.

She gasped, her breath shallow. Her vision spun. She could feel the dragon's malice pressing down like a weight on her chest. This wasn't like the spiders or the adder. This was a living storm of death, and it wanted her.

Knox pulled her upright. "You alright? There's a door, go!"

She nodded stiffly, legs trembling beneath her. The shadows around her twitched and flickered, attempting to shield her from the encroaching heat.

They bolted across the ballroom. One wall shimmered with floor-to-ceiling windows. She could see the faint outline of night outside but it felt impossibly far.

Then the ceiling groaned and another chandelier dropped.

Knox threw himself sideways, dragging her down.

Her shoulder hit the floor with a sickening crack. Her head snapped back, stars exploding behind her eyes. Pain raced down her collarbone, just like the old break Gastone had given her.

No.

No!

She clenched her fists and pulled the darkness toward her, wrapping her body in a cocoon of swirling black. The shadows kissed her skin like armor, drawn not just from the room but from inside her; where her terror churned with raw, desperate fury.

Her voice broke as she whispered, "Not this time."

In the center of the marble floor stood a massive tree blooming with pink and white flowers, their petals luminous in the dark. Nestled in the heart of each blossom was a golden apple—radiant, pulsing faintly with magic.

Eirwyn's legs wobbled beneath her, the weight of overused magic clawing at her limbs. Her shoulder throbbed where it had been injured, and her breath came in ragged gasps. Still, when she spotted the apples, her hand tightened around Knox's.

"There," she rasped, pointing with her good hand. "The apple—it's here! You need it!"

They sprinted toward the tree, but the lowest branches were just out of reach.

"We can't grab it and outrun the dragon," Knox panted, gaze flicking to the shattered wall.

A thunderous crash echoed through the chamber as the skeletal beast tore through the wall, bones splintering stone like brittle parchment. The floor trembled beneath their feet, and Eirwyn's balance faltered. She grabbed Knox's tunic.

"We'll come back for it," he said, urgency in his voice. "We need to fall back, regroup—"

"No." She shook her head, sweat slicking her brow. "Boost me. While he's recharging. We don't get another shot."

Knox hesitated only a moment before locking his fingers and bracing himself. "Hold steady."

She stepped into his hands and let him lift her. Her injured arm throbbed as she stretched upward, gripping a flowering branch for balance.

Her fingertips brushed a golden apple, and a hum passed through her—a deep, resonant thrum that pulled at her blood. A voice, not her own, echoed faintly inside her thoughts. *Feed the spirit. Restore the balance.*

Her fingers closed around the fruit, and just as she yanked it free, a subtle ripple of magic twisted the air around her.

Knox jolted beneath her. She felt it too—an unnatural pulse, like a tug deep inside her chest. Her eyes briefly caught a flicker in a nearby mirror—a distorted shimmer, like a shadowed face whispering from glass.

A whisper that never reached her ears.

Something unseen brushed her mind. And then—craving. Not hunger, not need. *Compulsion.*

Her breath caught. Her body obeyed the pull even as her mind tried to resist.

She stared at the apple. Its glow turned soft, inviting. Her mouth watered. Logic dissolved. Nothing else mattered —not Knox, not the dragon, not the war. Just the bite.

She brought it to her lips and bit.

The juice exploded across her tongue, sharp and wild, pure Vitas magic flooding her mouth—and colliding violently with the Nekros essence bound to her soul.

The scream tore out of her, more magic than breath. Knox shouted her name below, but the ground heaved. The dragon roared. Her body convulsed as the apple tumbled from her hand. The floor rushed up to meet her. She struck hard—her shoulder blazed white with pain, and her head cracked against marble.

The pain, the pleasure, the pull—they all crashed into her like a tidal wave. Magic flared from within her, but it was too much. Too much too fast. She slipped past the Edge and into the Beyond.

Everything went dark.

Chapter Thirty-Two

Knox's heart stopped cold.

One moment, Eirwyn had been radiant—full of magic, fierce and alive in his arms—and now she lay sprawled across the marble floor, her limbs tangled in a graceless heap, the bitten apple rolling from her open fingers.

"No. No no no no—"

He was on his knees before he realized he'd moved, his hands trembling as they skimmed over her body. The bump on her head pulsed a deep purple, and her skin had gone deathly pale. Her chest rose—barely—and her pulse fluttered against his fingers like the wings of a dying moth.

She was alive. But only just.

He exhaled shakily, already shifting his weight to scoop her up when the world shattered.

The skeletal dragon burst through the glass doors with a scream that pierced through his bones. Flames licked across the floor in jagged arcs, carving lines of fire between them. Shards of windowpane rained down, glinting in the light of the inferno.

Knox didn't hesitate. He grabbed Eirwyn's limp body, tucked the cursed golden apple into the crook of her arm, and ran.

The world blurred. Smoke, fire, and fear chased him through the ballroom. He burst through the scorched doorway and sprinted toward the remnants of the old garden gazebo—half-buried in ash and overgrowth but still intact enough to shield her, at least for now.

He crouched low, cradling her in what little shadow clung to her in the shade of the gazebo. She was still breathing. Still with him.

"You're alright," he whispered, brushing damp hair from her forehead. "We're fine. Just stay with me."

But he was lying. He wasn't fine. The shaking in his hands betrayed him.

He stood and turned, eyes locking on the skeletal horror emerging from the ruins of the mansion. The dragon was wrong—its bones burned from within with crimson light, and its skull turned unnaturally, as though guided by a puppeteer's hand. A tether of some kind flickered at the base of its spine—Nekrosan, but not the normal kind.

Knox's gut twisted. This thing wasn't just reanimated—it was being driven.

His eyes snapped to the orb glowing in its ribcage. A magic core, a nexus of cursed flame and rage. That was the key.

He needed a weapon. He needed to move.

"Ryder!" he roared.

The white warhorse shrieked from near the helrose hedge, pacing frantically. Knox didn't wait—he sprinted toward him, his chest tight at leaving Eirwyn unconscious, the earth shaking beneath every step of the dragon. Fire lashed out. Knox dove, rolling through gravel and scorched weeds, the edge of the blast peeling back skin along his side.

Pain screamed up his ribs. He ignored it.

He tore the axe from Ryder's saddle and slapped the horse's flank. "Go! Get clear!"

The horse bolted into the overgrowth as Knox turned back, axe in hand. The dragon's eye sockets blazed.

He planted his feet between the dragon and the gazebo, one hand steadying his weapon, the other fisted at his side. His chest rose and fell like a war drum.

"You're not taking her from me."

The dragon lunged.

Knox ran forward to meet it.

He met the beast with everything he had.

Knox ducked under its swiping claws, its bones groaning like rusted iron as it twisted to snap at him. He flung himself to the side, rolled, and came up swinging. His axe caught one of the dragon's ribs and splintered it with a resounding crack. Bone dust filled the air, but the dragon barely faltered.

It snarled, the core in its chest pulsing brighter, and Knox felt the hairs on his arms rise as it began to suck in breath.

Too late.

A blast of liquid fire screamed toward him.

Knox dove behind a chunk of fallen marble, his back howling as the flames licked across it again. The heat was unbearable, but he clenched his jaw and forced himself upright. Every breath was a labor, every heartbeat too loud in his ears. He had to end this.

He sprinted low, zigzagging through scorched hedges and ruined topiaries as the dragon turned its massive skull to follow. It lashed out with its tail, cracking through the fountain like thunder. Knox ducked under it and slid into the shadows of the skeletal belly.

One shot. One chance.

He grabbed the axe with both hands, called vines up through the cracked garden floor, and launched himself into the ribs again. He climbed—fast and messy—hauling himself higher as the dragon thrashed, trying to throw him off.

He hooked one foot over a jutting spine and swung the axe downward. The orb pulsed inches from his face, burning his eyes with its corrupted glow.

"For Eirwyn," he snarled, and slammed the axe home.

The impact was like the birth of a star.

The orb shattered in a shockwave of light and flame, hurling him backward with the force of a cannon. He hit the ground hard, rolling across broken stone and tangled vines, the world a blur of fire and pain.

His skin burned. Not just from the blast—but from something deeper. Something inside him pulling too hard, pushing too far.

He coughed, every breath a knife. Smoke filled his lungs. His vision swam.

The dragon gave one final, shuddering screech and collapsed in a shower of bones and ash. The magic core was gone. Only dust remained.

Knox tried to stand. His legs buckled, but he caught himself against a splintered beam.

Eirwyn.

He staggered toward the gazebo, his boots crunching through scorched flowers and shattered glass. She hadn't moved.

"Princess," he rasped, dropping beside her.

She was too pale. The wound on her head had bled down her cheek, and her magic reserve—he couldn't feel it anymore. Not the wild hum of wind and shadow he'd come to recognize. Just silence.

Panic clawed at him.

"No, no, come on, you don't get to leave me now," Knox whispered, his voice cracking.

He pressed his forehead to hers for a breath, then pulled back and whistled—low, hoarse, desperate.

The sound barely made it through the smoke, but Ryder emerged from the swirling ash like a specter, hooves pounding softly over the scorched earth.

Behind him, a faint shimmer in the air caught Knox's attention.

Leopol.

The ghost stood near the gazebo's edge, half-transparent and flickering in and out like candlelight in the wind. His expression was strained, and his form seemed... frayed.

"Knox," Leopol said quietly, eyes fixed on Eirwyn's still body. "You must go. Now."

"She's not waking up," Knox said, voice shaking. "What the hells is happening to her? What *was* that thing?"

Leopol stepped closer, his voice thin but urgent. "What-ever power touched that apple—it didn't come from this realm. That was your father, but it wasn't, there's no time to explain. Grab that necklace and go, it will help you focus your new powers."

Knox nodded, gripping her tighter. "Come with us."

Leopol glanced toward the broken bones of the dragon, the scorched ground, the shattered windows of Hartsgrove. His form flickered again.

"I can't leave. Hartsgrove's bound to me. And something —something else stirs beneath the roots."

Knox's stomach dropped, but he didn't have time to ask more. Not now.

"Stay safe, Leopol."

Leopol offered a faint smile. "I'll try."

Then he vanished.

He pressed the apple into his saddlebag, already stuffed with books from the manor, then bent to gently gather Eirwyn into his arms, the weight of her limp body grounding him even as the world threatened to spin apart.

The wind howled through the wreckage as the first rain-drops fell.

He didn't look back.

Knox winced as her head lolled against his chest.

"Stay with me," he whispered. "Just stay."

He mounted Ryder one-handed, shielding Eirwyn's body from the wind. His shirt was in tatters, his skin raw and oozing, but he didn't feel the pain. Only the weight of her.

And the fear.

He could go back to the druid hut, but no, it was too far. What about the dwarves? Surely they had something that might save her. Yes, they could help, they always had some new amazing magical device.

He had to get her to the dwarves.

The wind picked up as they raced through the hedge and into the forest. A storm churned overhead, wind lashing through the trees like fury unspent. The forest mourned, not even the eagles threatening them. The earth pulsed faintly beneath him—like something had shifted, something ancient disturbed.

He didn't care.
Not yet.
Only her.
He whispered her name again and again as they rode into the night, the storm closing in around them.

Chapter Thirty-Three

When Knox finally rode into the dwarven little stronghold, it was well past dark, and the rain had turned to a steady, freezing downpour. He'd cursed himself for racing out of Hartsgrove and forgetting both their cloaks in the kitchen.

He stopped his horse at the large, long wooden building, eight small cottages stretching around it in a semi-circle with four on each side. He knew from past visits that they were connected through tunnels below.

He slid from Ryder's back and fell to his knees with a grunt, juggling Eirwyn in his arms to keep her from hitting the ground. His legs felt like he'd run the entire way himself, and he was drained. His body shook from the cold front, his clothes wet, his skin tingling. The front door opened, and a short man half his size frowned into the rain.

"Knox, is that you?"

Knox grunted an answer and slowly stood. He carried Eirwyn to the front door to stoop inside. Thankfully, the dwarven homes had taller ceilings in the main lodge.

Krys waved him over to the fire and shut the door

behind him. "Set her by the fire before she catches a cold. What seems to be the problem? Who is she?"

Knox laid her down on the dirty, threadbare rug. "Hit her head," he grunted, kneeling on his feet and brushing the hair gently from her forehead. He winced at the knot at her hairline. "She's my mate," he said softly.

"Bloody hells, did you say mate?" Ashur said, standing in a doorway.

Knox blinked, trying to make sense of his friend. "Ashur? What are you doing here?"

Then Ashur's eyes narrowed on his head. "Fysica protect us," he whispered.

Knox shook his head, turning away from him. He couldn't deal with him right now, not when he was so close to saving Eirwyn. "Help her," he asked Krys.

Krys strode to the hallway to the left and yelled, "Flint, Jasper, Mica, get in here."

Footsteps came swiftly, and three more dwarves came into view. They wore various shades of brown pants, green and red shirts, and sturdy but dirty leather boots. When they saw Knox's head without the hood, they began to whisper to each other, but Knox didn't care. He just wanted them to save Eirwyn.

"She should've woken up by now," he said, turning to stare up at Krys. "She hit her head just after lunch. It's been hours. Why isn't she waking up?"

Krys was the oldest, with white hair that stuck in every direction and a full white beard.

He looped his thumbs in his suspenders and shook his head. "I don't know, but we'll figure it out. Flint, bring Knox's horse to the stable and see he's tended to. Jasper, get the medicine kit. Mica, do you have any of the pain cream left?"

The three nodded and turned to run down the hall while Krys knelt and began to inspect Eirwyn for more injuries. From the other hall came three more dwarves. The youngest, Copper, gasped when he saw Knox's head. He appeared around Knox's age, but Knox knew they were actually much, much older.

Copper rubbed his eyes and yawned as he walked over. "What's wrong with your head?"

The twins, Stone and Slate followed him, tucking in their shirts. Krys looked at them and frowned. "No time for questions. Fetch the bone stick, just to be certain."

The twins turned and went down the third hall toward their workshop just as Jasper came back with the red medical bag.

Ashur sank onto a human sized chair around the fire. "What happened?"

Knox filled them in as they assessed Eirwyn's injuries. Krys waved the bone stick wand over her body, lights dancing along the gems on one side. He was thawing out from the fire, but inside, he was still cold with worry. His voice was monotonous as he told them of Hartsgrove.

Krys finally said, "Her arm's broken, but it's not a terrible break. I'm more concerned about the bump on the head combined with her entering the Beyond from overusing magic."

Knox's blood ran cold at the mention of the Beyond. He looked at Eirwyn, swallowing hard past the knot in his throat as he realized he could lose her. The chances of coming out of the Beyond decreased with every passing hour, and she's been in it for half a day already.

Krys pulled a potion out of his tool belt and opened her mouth. Knox recognized the smell, but it usually only worked on someone who was entering the Edge, not the

Beyond. Some dribbled down her cheek, and Knox gently wiped it away.

Krys put his tools back into his bag and sighed. "Let's put her in the stasis chamber."

The other dwarves looked at Krys then Ashur in concern, then began to talk over each other.

"Are you certain?"

"Shh, that's a trade secret. What about the Robin?"

"He's kept his head a secret for years, and now we're sharing our secrets with him?"

"Why can't we just let her wake up on her own?"

"No, he's right. It will give her the best chance at survival."

Knox looked around as they argued, his eyes fighting against exhaustion, burning, and tearing up.

"Please," he croaked, swallowing and trying to get convince them.

None of them even looked at him, though, as Krys stood and made a chopping motion with his hand. "Enough. I've decided, and that's that. Are we clear?"

"Yes, Captain," the rest mumbled in unison.

Krys frowned at Knox. "Think you can carry her again?"

Knox nodded, scooping her gently into his arms. He pushed to his feet with a grunt and followed them down the third hallway into the workshop. She looked so delicate and fragile in his arms.

He winced at the dirty, disheveled state of her clothes and hair. She would not be happy about that when she woke.

If she woke.

No, *when*.

He argued with himself, fear and hope two sides of a

coin that kept flipping back and forth. They entered the back of the workshop. Set into the side of the mountain, it opened into a mining shaft. To the right was the stable with several mounts of reindeer inside.

Krys went to the fireplace on the left and pulled on a candelabra. The wall behind the fireplace shifted, and he waved to Knox. "Watch your head. This is meant for only dwarves."

Knox cradled Eirwyn closer and turned sideways to squeeze into the narrow passageway. His heart was heavy and tight with emotion. They walked, the floor sloping downward until Knox's legs began to cramp from the half-squatting position.

His legs burned and shook, and finally, they came to a door. Krys pushed a series of runes on the door, and it slid open as if by magic to disappear into the wall. He stepped inside a cave with metal walls. Eight coffins were laid in a circle, connected by metal tubes to a giant, glowing crystal.

Krys walked to the nearest one and pushed several gems on the side. The glass top flipped up, and he stepped back with a wave. "Set her inside."

Knox held her closer, loathe to let her go. But the dwarves had never treated him wrong. He trusted them, but theirs had always been a business arrangement. He didn't know what this was going to cost him, but he didn't really care.

He couldn't lose her. He looked down at Eirwyn. Was she growing colder? Her lips were definitely blue.

His chest ached, and he set her in the glass and metal coffin. Krys pushed buttons on the side, and the glass closed over her. A pale blue fog filled the coffin, and Knox put his hand on it with a gasp.

"Don't worry. It won't harm her." Krys began to ramble

on about the technical details, but Knox was too exhausted to care.

Finally, Krys said, "I've set it for twelve hours. We'll reassess and will know more then. That might be all she needs. Come on, Knox. You look like you could use some rest too."

Krys' voice rang with false hope, and Knox's stomach twisted. He shook his head and sat on the floor, his hand never leaving the coffin as he leaned against it. "I can't leave her," he whispered. "Can you fetch me a healing potion and a salve for my back?"

His vision blurred, and his hands shook. This was as close to the Edge as he'd ever gotten, too cautious as a child to overuse his magic.

Krys' voice echoed as if from far away. "Alright, but the salve isn't going to help your back. Not with all the scales."

His chest ached, and he ignored Krys. There were no scales on his back, but the crazy old dwarf didn't matter.

He never should've taken her into the heart of the forest. He should've left her at Olive's. She would've been safer there instead of with him. How could he have been so selfish? He'd failed to protect her.

He'd seen dozens of wounded soldiers stumble into the forest with head injuries, but not even half of those survived their wounds. If something happened to Eirwyn before he could tell her how he felt—

He frowned, his eyes growing heavy. Had he really not told her how much he loved her? How much he admired that she never gave up? She was strong, capable, and no wilting wallflower like those in his books or those he saw strolling through town.

He wanted to know everything about her, and it felt like time was slipping through his hands. If she survived, would she stay with him? He'd begged her to agree to the mate bond, but he hadn't explained what that was or what he'd learned in the books in his father's office.

Krys returned with the bottle and ointment then walked away. Knox took both and tossed his head back, the bitter taste making him wince as he chugged it. It burned going down almost as much as the fire on his skin earlier.

She might want to return to Demerel and her life there. If she left him behind in the Feral Forest, alone, yet again... He wouldn't survive without her. She was like air and water, and he needed her to live now.

Despair swept over him, pressing on his chest and making him slump.

He unscrewed the lid on the salve and dipped his fingers into the gel, then reached behind his neck. He smoothed it over and frowned. His scales, which had previously just wrapped around the back of his head, now extended down his neck and over his shoulders.

He shivered as the gel turned cold on his skin, and he peeled the remnants of his shirt off. He felt his back, unable to reach between his shoulder blades to see how far they extended.

Was it the mating bond that was changing him? Did that mean that Eirwyn might live? Surely he wouldn't change if the mating rituals hadn't been completed, and according to the books he'd found, they still had a few more things to do.

He shook his head and dipped his fingers into the ointment, rubbing it around and under the bumps and ridges of his back.

Chapter Thirty-Four

Knox jerked awake to the sound of beeps. Krys stood over him, pushing gems on the side of Eirwyn's glass coffin.

Knox pushed to his knees, every muscle screaming at him as he grunted. Krys didn't take his eyes off his work, his fingers flying as he said, "Something's wrong. She's not coming out of the Beyond."

Knox's chest burned, his hand—now covered in small scales—on the glass. "What can we do?" His voice was raspy, and he needed a drink of water.

"I want to make sure we're not missing something, so we're going to hack into your mind to see if we can replay the memories."

Knox looked at him dumbfounded and blinked. "What the hells does that mean?"

Behind him, a scraping sound came from the open door. Ashur carried a mirror that was nearly four feet tall and barely fit in the corridor. He stood it up against the metal wall as Flint came in behind them.

Slate and Stone connected metal tubes to either side

of the mirror's frame then connected it to a cylindrical metal stick similar in size to the glow sticks and flame blade.

Then they handed him the stick. "Hold this," one of them said.

Knox wrapped his hand around the rod, and Krys immediately began pressing the hidden rune-stones along the side of the polished Synthara cylinder. The smooth stick grew warm in Knox's grip as the dual gems at either end lit up—one a soft silver, the other a pulsing red.

Light bled into the etched lines of the mirror's frame, cascading like living script. The silver surface shimmered, then activated with a flash of pale blue that swept across its face.

Ashur's brows lifted. "That's not one of the king's spy mirrors, is it? The ones that eavesdrop?"

Krys snorted. "Hardly. The king's toys are bastardized copies. This is original tech—ours. Memory mirror. Untampered. Protected."

The image on the mirror came to life.

Knox flinched as he saw himself—shirt scorched and skin blistering—as he ran through the ballroom with Eirwyn in his arms. The scene replayed in eerie silence: glass shattering, magic flaring, her scream cut off by the dragon's roar.

Krys muttered something about rewinding and narrowing the focus as he touched the device. The image swirled and they watched silently, eyes narrowed.

Eirwyn rose into frame again, balanced in Knox's raised hands, as she reached for the apple.

Krys exhaled quietly. Ashur grinned and gave a soft whistle. "Now that's trust."

Knox didn't smile. He watched, jaw tight, as the next

moment played—Eirwyn reaching, struggling, hand closing around the apple just before the shimmer hit her.

Eirwyn bit the apple.

The mirror pulsed violently. A shock of energy flashed through the frame. The image jumped and slowed. Krys growled and jabbed more runes, isolating the flicker in time.

"Something hit her," Krys muttered.

The image zoomed in on the ballroom wall—just behind the apple tree.

A tapestry shimmered.

No, not a tapestry.

A mirror.

The dwarves leaned in as the mirror's surface warbled with hidden magic. And inside it—a face.

Not a reflection. A man.

Robes of opulent, old-world design. His hand was outstretched toward the skeletal dragon, fingers glowing with unholy green fire.

"Gods," Ashur breathed. "Is that—?"

Krys froze the image. "That's Gastone!"

Knox's pulse pounded in his ears. "He was in the mirror the whole time."

"He's not just in it," Krys said, voice low. "He was casting through it. That apple? That wasn't just a coincidence. He *pushed* her to eat it."

The dwarves exchanged uneasy glances. A hush fell over the room.

Krys advanced the image again.

As Eirwyn's teeth broke the apple's skin, the mirror *glowed*—not just the one in the room, but the one in the ballroom too. A flare of corruptive magic surged across the tether between them. The same green light seen in the dragon's core.

Krys cursed. "By the beards of Avalon!"

Ashur rubbed the back of his neck. "That wasn't an illusion. That was coordinated."

"She wasn't just poisoned," Krys said grimly. "She was targeted, and he used magic to do it. Vitaron against Nekrosan. It was meant to unmake her."

Knox's gut twisted. "But why didn't it kill her?"

Krys shook his head. "Because she's already bound. You sealed the mate bond. That apple should've unspooled her life thread—if she were alone. But the bond might've redirected the backlash."

Ashur added, "Or delayed it."

Knox leaned against the wall, his breath shallow. "So what do we do?"

Krys stepped back from the mirror, eyes stormy. "We stabilize her, keep her from crossing the Edge, and pray to the gods the bond is strong enough."

Krys stepped away from the mirror and back to the coffin. Knox frowned in worry. If Krys' plan was to just hope and pray, then they were well and truly doomed. The dwarf always had an answer to any problem.

He turned the stick over to one twin while the other powered it off.

"Why does he want to kill her so badly?" Knox asked, rubbing his forehead. His hands were clammy, and his body shivered in the cold, metal room as he stood in pants and boots.

"Maybe you should ask him. My guess is jealousy. For now, we need to keep her in stasis to see if she'll heal. It will also help hide her from the king."

Knox shook his head, his thoughts fuzzy. "If he knows Eirwyn is alive, that means Scarlet is in danger. She might've failed in her mission to give him a false heart."

Ashur sighed and stepped toward the coffin. "Actually, that's why I'm here. I came looking for you because Scarlet has been captured."

Knox's blood ran cold even as his rage began to simmer. He'd failed Eirwyn and now Scarlet too. Was there anyone he could protect? Some king of the forest when he couldn't even protect two little women.

The words overwhelmed him as he stared down at Eirwyn. The pressure on his chest increased, threatening to bury him in an avalanche of emotions. It wasn't fair. If they couldn't bring her back from the Beyond, then she would die.

It was his job to protect her, love her, mate her.

A ringing in his head began to grow. It was a feeling, a pressure, an idea that wouldn't let go. It sank into his mind and before he could think about it too much, he leaned over and kissed her ruby red lips.

Green swirls of light mixed with blue. A jolt of energy shot through him like lightning, then he slumped into darkness.

Knox drifted through the clouds and blinked rapidly. His eyesight was better than it'd ever been. He could see for miles. Hells, he could even see the deer in the field below him as it frolicked with its mother.

He took a deep breath of the crisp, clean mountain air.

He looked down, his eyes widening as his breathing turned shallow. He glanced to the side. He had wings, great, giant wings. They shone iridescent green and brown in the sunlight.

A slow pump of his glorious wings, and the wind sliced around him, almost causing him to fall. He turned this way and that, slowly writhing through the air and learning how to maneuver this huge body.

A glance down, and he saw his hands and feet were now four sharp scaly claws. He snorted, and green gas shot out of his nostrils, sinking through the air and dissipating in the clouds.

He circled the mountains, dipping low and learning how to shoot high in the air. The freedom and joy that came from flying was unlike anything he'd ever felt before.

No, that wasn't true.

He'd felt this same intense feeling when he was with Eirwyn.

He sucked in a quick breath, his heart racing with a stab of worry. Where was Eirwyn?

At the thought, his head turned to the north to the foot of the mountains. It was like she was a beacon of light. He knew exactly where she was as if he were staring at the wayfinder and zooming in on her location.

He flew over the forest, his mind racing as he saw the dwarves' lodge. His body twisted, and pain shot through his side. He was being ripped in two. His claws spasmed, and he screamed as he fell.

Water went up his nose, making him jerk. A hand shoved his head into a horse trough. His tail went up, but something grabbed it.

The hand on the back of his head lifted, and he came up for air, gasping. He blinked and looked around. Several dwarves held tightly to his tail, sitting on it to keep it from stabbing someone.

Ashur backed away, his hands raised and water dripping down his forearms. He frowned, but there was relief in his eyes.

"Easy, mate. We figured it was worth a shot," he said.

Knox sat back on his haunches, and the dwarves scrambled off of him. He looked around. He wasn't in the metal cave anymore. Now he was in the stables area of the workshop.

"Eirwyn–" His voice was hoarse as he stood, shaking his head.

Ashur and Krys exchanged a look, and it made Knox's heart race. He stumbled through the still-open door and down the narrow hallway. He found Eirwyn still in the coffin, the glass covering her now and the blue mist surrounding her inside.

He laid his hands on the glass. "Eirwyn," he whispered.

Krys' voice sounded far away even though he stood at Knox's elbow. "We've done all we can. Your kiss changed her vitals, though."

"For the worse?" Knox croaked, afraid that his poisonous breath would kill her faster. It felt like a knife was stabbing him in the stomach over and over.

Krys shook his head. "No, they stabilized. Her body is trying to fight the Beyond now."

"She–she's alive?" Knox asked, the pressure on his chest tightening.

Krys nodded. "For now, yes."

"How long can she stay in here and fight the Beyond? Has anyone ever come out of it safely?" he asked, afraid to hear the answer.

He'd heard the warnings all his life from Olive. The Beyond was dangerous, more so than even the deadliest parts of the forest.

Krys paused, then rubbed his large stomach and sighed. "The stasis chamber was made for dwarves. With the different biology and cell structure–"

"How long?" Knox demanded. The tone was sharp, the one he used with the Robins when they were training in how to survive in the forest.

The silence in the room was heavy, and it pressed on him. His eyes stung, and he felt like he couldn't breathe.

"Three days," Krys said softly. "If she's not awake in three days..."

Knox leaned his head on the coffin and closed his eyes. He'd failed her. They wouldn't have the chance to argue over where to live or for him to convince her to stay by his side forever.

A single tear rolled onto the coffin, the blue smoke inside following the liquid as it slid down the side.

"Open the coffin," his voice was rough with emotion.

The dwarves murmured behind him that it was a stasis chamber, not a coffin, but Knox ignored them as Krys pressed gems on the side. The glass slid over, and the blue gas dissipated.

Knox brushed her hair back from her face, the knot in his throat making him swallow hard. He leaned closer and whispered, "I'm sorry, Eirwyn."

Then he pressed his lips to hers once more. Her lips were soft, and he wondered how they'd mated multiple times but had never kissed before arriving at the dwarves' stronghold. Tears and water from the trough dripped onto her, and he pulled away.

She wouldn't like the dirty horse water. He cleaned her face as the pressure built, his eyes blurring.

Pain seared through his chest, and he wanted to scream.

He held it in and let the pressure build. His hands lengthened, aching. He straightened and turned away, tilting his head up high. He didn't meet the gaze of anyone as he walked out of the passageway, out of the lodge, and into the forest.

It took all night for him to regain control of his emotions. His body burned in pain, his skin and scales shifting. He grew massive claws, then they went back to hands, then claws again.

He hunted deer and rabbits, bringing each carcass back to the lodge before going back out. He took his axe and chopped down dead trees.

But he couldn't bring himself to start another sapling in its place this time. All he saw was death and destruction, not new life. The shadows enveloped him in the night, reminding him of Eirwyn. His cheeks turned cold in the frigid night air, the storm bringing a cold front that suited his icy, empty heart.

Chapter Thirty-Five

When dawn broke, Knox strode through the clearing to the front door of the lodge. His eyes were red-rimmed, and he avoided eye contact when he sat at the kitchen table. The dwarves spoke in hushed tones, avoiding him.

But Ashur sat directly across from him and cleared his throat. He ate a bite of porridge, but Knox looked up at him and then back down at his own bowl.

"Out with it," he told Ashur, his voice hoarse and scratchy.

Ashur paused, eyeing him warily, then said, "What's your plan for Scarlet?"

Knox took a deep breath. "Rescue her."

Ashur nodded. "In that case, you should know that she's in the dungeons, safe for now, but there are dozens of others down there with her, including a few Robins."

Knox lifted his chin and met Ashur's wary gaze. Knox sat up slowly, his spine stiffening as he waited for more details. "Dozens?"

Ashur nodded. "The king has gotten worse since the

wedding. That next day, he set fire to one of his guard houses because they didn't protect the reception and stop the robbery. Each day since we robbed the nobles, he's done something new. First, it was increasing the watch on the town and surrounding areas, adding more spy mirrors on every corner, and publicly arresting anyone who might be withholding information about the robbery."

Ashur took a drink before continuing. "Then he started arresting dozens of people, families even, burning down their houses and claiming they were in league with the Robins or the Glathens. Innocent people with no shred of evidence against them. Now the whole kingdom is under martial law. The returning soldiers are now guards and jailers for their own families."

Knox's eyes narrowed. "Why?"

Ashur rubbed his chin. "He's using them to interrogate the people for information on the Robins, even kids and women. He—he might have found the magical runes that we used to get through the forest with relative safety."

"What?" Knox released a sharp curl of smoke from his nose.

"Some of the stronger men he's arresting and using as forced slave labor to chop down the trees to make the new road. Will stopped the work crew with a stomach bug, but he can't keep them all sick for much longer. He had to infiltrate the camp and pretend to be one of them for a day and saw two with similar rune tattoos to ours on their wrists. That's how they're keeping the forest's magic from retaliating while they strip the trees. With the runes, he's going to launch an attack directly into the forest."

Knox wiped his mouth and sighed. Eirwyn would be gone in three days, but he couldn't sit here doing nothing.

He had to protect the forest. Rescue Scarlet. And her people. Eirwyn would expect no less.

He took a slow breath, letting the anger solidify into cold resolve. He couldn't hide forever. At least now he knew who he was.

Ashur waved a hand and added casually, "Also, the king had an interesting chat with the General and the Chancellor. He's recalling his troops under the guise of a wedding celebration, but it's not a honeymoon. He's planning to invade Glathen—with a skeletal army. Raising the dead from both Glathen and Busparia battlefields. But to strike from an unexpected direction, he needs that road."

Krys sat down across from him and stirred his bowl. "Just like when he tried to kill Eirwyn with that dragon skeleton. That wasn't desperation—that was a test run. He's pulled most of his Spell Corps and dreadknights to the road's entrance."

Knox narrowed his eyes. "How do you know where they are?"

Krys blew on his porridge. "We analyzed Eirwyn's memories while you were out. She saw him use nekromancy before —he's not new to it. Plus, she overheard a hushed conversation between him and the General a few months ago. She may not have realized what she heard, but it was buried in there."

Knox rubbed his temples, the headache flaring behind his eyes. "So... he's building a nekromantic army, protected by rune-casters, backed by dreadknights, and moving through the forest under our noses."

Krys gave a slow nod. "And don't forget voidstalkers. Will swears he saw one near the camp. Shadowy. Fast. Too coordinated to be anything else."

Krys looked at him over the rim of his glasses. "You

have to stop him, Knox. That poor girl has been hurt by him for a long time. Just watching what he's done to her in the past few months made me want to go fight him myself."

"Was he poisoning her? Did you find any evidence of it in her system or in her memories?" Knox asked softly.

Krys paused, then nodded once. Knox's hand fisted on the table, and he took a deep breath to try to calm the rage.

Knox took a deep breath, some of his anger turning to cold resolve in his stomach. He'd known he couldn't keep who he was hidden forever. Hell, at least he knew who he was now.

Ashur held up a hand. "How do we stop him without killing him?"

"I have tried to stay out of the bastard's way. All I wanted was to protect the forest and it's people." Knox's jaw clenched, and he slammed a fist on the table. "But he's gone too far. The king will die for what he's done to Eirwyn."

Knox's chest tightened, and a snort of green gas escaped his nose, and sank to the table.

Ashur seemed to relax in his seat at the outburst, even as he leaned away from the table. "He's not going to rest until she's dead. She's a threat to his power as the only other familial drakin in the kingdom."

Silence descended around them, all eyes turning on him.

"She's not the only threat to him," Krys said. "I'm not sure any of us are strong enough to take him on, but you might survive if you're a drakin."

Knox sat back, the weight of responsibility heavy on his shoulders. He tried to ignore them, but he'd been doing that his entire life. He couldn't just ignore who he was anymore. There were people to save and a forest to protect, but he had to stop hiding in the shadows to get the job done.

He took a drink of his water and forced the last bite of breakfast down. It all tasted like ash in his mouth. Without Eirwyn, everything had lost its luster. Eirwyn was all but dead already, and there wasn't a damn thing he could do to stop it. Pressure built in his chest, and his stomach clenched.

But he could stop the king and save the people. He pushed his bowl away and growled.

Ashur said. "The king might know you're a drakin. He saw you both in the mirror when he was controlling the dragon, so he might know your weaknesses too. We can't just go in blind."

Krys cleared his throat, his cheeks reddening more. "Uh, I might've gone through your saddlebags and read your books. *Are* you a drakin?"

Ashur waved his hand and frowned. "Come on, Krys, what else could he be?"

Knox crossed his arms and leaned back. "I'm a dragon, not a drakin."

Silence settled on the table, then Ashur scowled and reached into his pocket. He handed a few coins to Krys, who was grinning widely.

Knox's brows rose, and Ashur shrugged.

"They said you were, but dragons died out ages ago. Who would've thought you were a full dragon? Sorry, mate, but not I."

Knox snorted a laugh and shook his head, rubbing his temple. "It's fine. It *is* rather hard to believe."

"What can you do? Can you turn into a big, hulking dragon like that skeleton in your memory?"

Knox winced and stood, picking up his bowl and tankard. "That dragon skeleton was my father, so maybe. I haven't tried, although, in the past few days, I seem to have grown more scales and can shift my hands into claws."

Knox took a deep breath as memories flitted through his mind. If Eirwyn were here, she'd be humming while she cooked and cleaned the kitchen. What he wouldn't give to hear her voice again, see her smile, watch the way she danced with the birds in the grass outside Hartsgrove.

The pressure on his chest increased, and the emotions threatened to drown him once more.

Knox cleared his throat and turned away from the sink. "We need a plan. We'll ride to Vidrland to rally the troops after you're finished eating."

Ashur arched a brow and waved to Knox's head. "The Glathens might help with the rebellion if it means ending the war."

Knox pursed his lips and nodded. "We can at least send a runner to Glathen to warn them of the skeletal army, but I don't want them to warn the king of Busparia we're coming."

Krys stood, gathering his own bowl. "I can help plan the rebellion. When going through Eirwyn's memories, we saw how she could sneak in and out of the palace so often."

Ashur nodded, and Knox swallowed past the lump in his throat. He wanted to go through all of her memories, see everything she'd ever seen in her too-short life.

He turned to face Krys, blinking rapidly as a thought made his heart race. "Do not bury her," he said. "I'm going to go take care of this drakin king and save her people, and then I'll be back. Leave her in there until I return?"

Krys nodded and frowned as he put his bowl in the sink, but he didn't argue. "We'll keep her alive and in stasis, but whether she wakes up from the Beyond or not is up to the gods."

Knox turned to walk to the stables, his legs shaking from emotion and leaving Krys and Ashur talking in the kitchen.

He leaned on the workshop table, his thoughts racing and his heart aching. Somehow he had to find the strength to leave her here, even though his entire being was telling him to stay by her side.

He didn't want to leave Eirwyn, but he couldn't just stand by while the people suffered. They were counting on him. His saddlebags lay on the work table, and he dumped everything out.

His father's necklace shone bright, cleaned of dirt. The emerald brought a sense of peace, and he slipped it over his neck. His mother's ring began to heat on his finger, and he pulled it off and placed it on top of the book.

He'd barely read half of one book while at Hartsgrove, but there was no need to read anything else. A book wouldn't bring Eirwyn back, and that was all that mattered.

He picked up the golden apple, a single bite marring its side. His heart skipped a beat, and he caught his breath. What if the answers to save Eirwyn were in the apple, too? He threw all caution to the wind as a flare of hope drove him to desperation. He sniffed it, then took a bite too.

"What the hell are you doing?" Krys asked.

Knox chewed as the flavors burst on his tongue. It tasted nothing like a regular apple, but all the flavors in the world wouldn't bring him a measure of joy in the delicious fruit.

He shrugged. "I'm doing the only thing I can do. I'm sticking to the original plan. Eat the golden apple and get fucking answers."

He took another bite, but nothing happened. The pressure in his chest burned, and he screamed and threw the apple at the wall. It broke into multiple pieces.

"Fucking thing isn't working." He rubbed his temples, his breathing labored as he tried to calm down. His tail wavered behind him, shaking slightly at his heightened emotions.

Krys' stare bored into him from across the room, but Knox refused to meet his gaze as he walked to the pieces and picked them up, placing them on the table next to his books and the ring. He didn't want to face anyone but Eirwyn's smiling face, and now she was going to die. He couldn't do anything to stop it.

Well, he could do one thing.

He turned to Ryder and led him out the side door of the workshop stables. It was time to kill a king.

Chapter Thirty-Six

Little John stabbed a pudgy finger to the map. "This is the layout of the castle that we mined from Eirwyn's memories."

Knox forced himself to breathe evenly and deeply, but even then, green gas curled around his nose and sank to the wooden floor of the meeting house in Vidrland. He sat in a chair at the end of the oval table while half a dozen men and women stood around it staring at the large map.

He'd ridden into Vidrland next to Ashur as dusk fell. For the first time, he rode without his hood up, and he didn't even care. The feel of the wind on his scales and horns had even helped settle some of his churning emotions.

Ashur had asked him on the ride what to tell everyone about his head, but Knox had just shrugged and said, "Tell them the truth."

When they'd ridden in, he'd seen the raised eyebrows and heard the whispers. He just didn't give a fuck who stared at him or what they said. Ashur had ridden beside him and loudly proclaimed him as king of the forest.

So now the entire camp was abuzz with the news that he was the son of a dragon and the heir to the forest king. Ashur had even started telling them he had come to stop the tyranny of the Buspartan king once and for all.

People kept a wide berth from him and his tail. It'd barely been a few hours, and already people in camp were bowing to him. He didn't stop them, though. He just didn't care anymore, too numb to anything but the pain of losing Eirwyn. He's brought the plan from Krys to his brother, Little John, along with some supplies and magic items. Little John had jumped into action, gathering more resources and making the entire camp jump at his every command.

Little John continued. "The prisoners are held here. Scarlet and others will be executed in two days. Tomorrow night, we will break into the dungeon and rescue everyone."

"Everyone?" Will asked, his brows raised. He'd arrived in camp just before they did to report on the push into the forest.

Little John nodded. "Everyone. Half are in there for simply not paying taxes."

"And the other half?" Ashur asked.

John shrugged his dwarven shoulders. "Stealing because they used all their money to pay the taxes. Or they're suspected Robins. Or they're the slaves Will made sick, whom the king then threw in the dungeons for not working. Or the king took offense at mud hitting his carriage as a street urchin ran through a puddle. Or–"

Ashur held up a hand. "We get it. The king's becoming more and more unstable."

Will rubbed his hands together and grinned. "We'll need a distraction. Knox can't blow a sleep spell into the dungeon like he did at the castle robbery. We need the prisoners to walk out on their own two feet."

A slow smile spread across John's face. "Ah, as for that, I have just the thing." He flipped open the leather satchel that sat on the table next to him and pulled out a glass jar and a bundle of sticks. Inside the jar were three bees.

Ashur crossed his arms. "How are bees supposed to help distract an entire castle."

John shook his head and pushed his glasses up on his nose, reminding Knox of his brother Krys.

"The distraction is from these." John held up the sticks. "We'll light one end and toss them at the wall of the palace. It'll make a loud pop and create a lot of smoke but won't do much damage."

John pointed to the map. "As for the bees, they're not real. They're mechanical. They can get into the castle and inject sleep dust with their stinger on anyone in our path. I can send them in first, then the rescue team can follow while the distraction team works here."

Knox frowned, leaning back in his chair and listening as his people formed a plan. They were wasting daylight, and his skin itched. It had taken them the rest of the day to ride from the dwarves to Vidrland. The need to move clawed at his stomach, twisting and turning ever since he'd left Eirwyn's side.

His leg bounced under the table, and most of the Robins ignored him. He thought of nothing but Eirwyn and killing the king. Vidrland, the Robins, Scarlet, everything else was all irrelevant.

When their plans were made, Knox stood slowly. All eyes turned to him.

"We created this place as a haven, a safe, peaceful place of freedom and equality. The king threatens the forest, he robs from his people, and when we do something about it, he retaliates tenfold. Not only that, but he's killed the princess."

Gasps echoed through the wooden lodge. Knox's jaw clenched as his stomach spasmed.

"In the past, we've tried to reason with him. We sent the petition to him, pleaded in the newspapers. Hells, we even sent letters to the Council. His reign of tyranny ends tomorrow night. If given the chance, I will kill him. This isn't just a rescue mission for our people. It's a full out rebellion, and we will succeed. The first step is the rescue. Second step, rebellion. Third step, peace and freedom."

No one breathed as his voice went louder and louder. A soft breeze blew through the room, and he got goosebumps remembering how Eirwyn used to shape wind. Green smoke curled around his nose and sank to the ground. Those closest to him shuffled a few steps away, then Ashur slapped one of them on the back and grinned.

"Aye, well said, Your Highness. We ride at dawn if we're going to reach Demerel before dark. Tonight, we feast. Tomorrow... To the rebellion!" Ashur said, raising a fist in the air. Everyone joined in and began to chant and laugh as they walked out the door.

Little John remained behind, staring over the map and tapping his chin.

"Do you really think it'll work?" Knox asked the dwarf. He'd left his seven brothers in the north for adventure years ago, and Knox wasn't sure what he'd do without him.

John frowned and nodded. "I do, with a little luck and ingenuity, we can save them all."

Knox sank heavily back in his chair. He didn't feel like joining the feast outside. He just wanted to curl up on his bed and dream about Eirwyn. Instead, he walked to the old druid circle past the hot springs and prayed to Gaiana until he fell asleep.

The next morning, they rode into Demerel two at a time, the distraction team staggering arrival times and from which direction they entered.

Knox rode along the edge of the forest away from Demerel and then turned to lead the rescue team.

He walked with Ashur, Will, John, and a few others into the forest until he couldn't see the edge of it anymore. Then he closed his eyes and called on the vines. A bird tweeted to his left, and he turned, somehow pulled to follow it.

The bird danced on a branch, and Knox looked down. At the base of the tree was a metal grate. He smiled and pulled on the metal, grunting with effort. Will dropped in first and lit a torch, then Ashur said a prayer and joined him. Another made a protection sigil, a shape of a magic rune in the air that quickly dissipated, and dropped in.

One other stood guarding their horses while John pulled out a metal, hand-sized box. He pushed gems on the side and they lit up. John nodded, ready to control the wasps.

Knox went down the metal ladder into the darkness below. A few seconds later, his eyes adjusted and the dizziness of the tight space passed. They were in a short hallway, the walls cold and wet stone. The hallway steadily went down deeper into the earth.

How had Eirwyn used this path to escape the castle time and time again, coming into the forest before turning to go back into Demerel? How had she done this multiple times, and he never knew or met her before? How had she never been attacked by the forest? Even just a walk in the first fifty feet in the trees should have claimed her.

Would their story be different if he had met her in the woods here? Would they have spent years as mates? Would he have recognized her as the other half of his heart and swept her into the forest to live happily ever after?

He took a shuddering breath, green smoke curling out and sinking to the ground. Will waved to them, and they came to a stop in front of a wooden door. He handed the torch to Knox, and then knelt and pulled out two small metal pins from his pocket.

Knox arched a brow and reached for the handle, opening it with a loud creak. Will's brows rose, and he looked at Knox in surprise.

Knox grinned, and Ashur struggled to muffle a snort laugh. Knox pushed past Will and took the lead into a large room stacked with boxes.

They had found the cellar. Rows and rows of wine lined walls and shelves, and they walked past.

According to the map they'd memorized, there were two more doors. One led up to the kitchens. The other led down to the dungeon. They turned and went deeper, leaving one of them to guard the cellar.

When they reached the bottom of the stairs, another wooden door stood in their way. Knox reached for the handle, but found it locked. A small crack was in the peep window, but he couldn't see anything.

He stepped back and waved for Will and Ashur, wiping sweat from his brow. Ashur opened the jar and released the bees. They wiggled through the crack and into the next room. He had no idea how John was controlling them with the little box, but he didn't care, as long as it worked. Will dropped to his knees and picked the lock.

Knox stood in the stillness, his stomach twisting and his forehead beading with more sweat. They were now deep underground, and he couldn't feel the forest. It was like the air had grown still and damp with death. His breathing turned shallow before Will pushed the door open.

Ashur slipped in first, then opened the door wider. There was a small room with seven guards sleeping around a card table. The mechanical bees flew down a hall, and Knox followed them carefully.

Cells lined both sides of the hallway, many filled with too many people. Ashur brought the keys from the guard and unlocked the doors while Will stood guard. Knox strode down the hall, peering into each cell to find Scarlet.

The stench of unwashed bodies made his stomach churn. He wanted to vomit, but he had to find her. Only one more cell remained. He looked through the small square window bars on the wooden door.

"Red," he whispered, barely heard over the hushed shuffling of feet behind him as the others led the freed prisoners out.

A wave of dizziness washed over him. He'd found her. Chained to the wall, dirty and beaten, but alive.

Ashur opened the door, and she lifted her head. Her arms were in chains attached to the wall above her head. She wobbled as she rose to her feet, blinking furiously.

Her red hair was matted to one side of her head, and her shirt was ripped down one shoulder, hanging loosely. "Knox?" she whispered.

He nodded, his chest tight with emotion. "What are you doing hanging around? Let's get you out of here, Red."

She snorted a laugh that ended with a sob as Ashur unlocked the metal at her wrists. "Don't fucking call me that," she cried, hitting him on the arm weakly.

She fell into his arms, and he pulled her into a hug. "Shh, it's alright. You're going to be alright. Are you ready? Can you walk?"

She nodded, trying to compose herself even as tears continued to stream down her face. Ashur led them down the hall back the way they'd come. Will kept watch over the guards until they were all out, then he followed Ashur and shut the door softly behind them. Knox and Scarlet were the last ones out, following Ashur as they left the guards behind.

In the cellar, Ashur stood at the bottom of the stairs to the kitchens with a frown. He waved them quickly, holding his finger to his lips then pointing above.

Knox's adrenaline pumped at the worried look on his face, and he nodded. Scarlet's legs gave out, and she stumbled. Knox picked her up, and Ashur closed the wooden door to the tunnel behind them, careful to be as quiet as possible.

Knox strode a few feet and turned at the first corner, but the tunnel was crowded with escaping prisoners. There was nowhere to go. The crowd had come to a halt as they had to go up the ladder one by one.

The wooden door behind them banged open. The prisoners cowered and whimpered. Scarlet gasped, and Ashur and Will swung around, his stance wide and hands held out ready to attack.

Chapter Thirty-Seven

Eirwyn blinked awake to a steady beeping noise. Her stomach rolled, and she felt like she might be sick. She turned on her side and looked around. She was inside some kind of glass case.

She pressed on it, grunting as she tried to lift it. She knocked, then paused before banging on it with a fist.

"Hello? Is anyone there?"

Only the beeping kept her company. She looked down. She now lay somewhat on her side. The shirt and pants she'd borrowed from Scarlet were now stained, ripped, burned, and stiff with dirt. She wrinkled her nose at the smell of body odor that filled the tiny chamber.

She frowned as her stomach rolled and cramped. She slid her hands down, feeling the bulge, and her eyes widened. She jerked the shirt up, twisting to get a better view.

Darkling hells, her stomach looked like she'd shoved a pine cone under the skin. She touched it, and the hardness of it surprised her, the ridges on it reminding her of Knox.

She frowned, her stomach rolling as she was both hungry and sick at the same time.

A noise drew her attention, and she put her shirt down, turning and banging on the glass. "Hello? Let me out!"

A man stared down at her with white hair that went every which way and glasses on the tip of his red nose. He leaned back and more beeps echoed, then the glass slid to the side.

She sat up with a deep breath of fresh air. A few small men stood around her, and she yawned.

The oldest one looked through his glasses at her, holding a strange metal wand over her face. It lit up in colorful patterns as he said, "You—you're alive!"

She scowled and swung her legs over the side of the... "Is this a coffin? Did I die?"

The old man sputtered, "Nearly so, yes. You got a bump on the head and entered the Beyond."

She frowned and hopped to the ground, her legs wobbling under her. Her dirty boots left dirt on the shiny metal floor. She winced at the mess and looked around.

"The Beyond? How did I come back? Where's Knox? Who are you—wait, are you the dwarves?" "

The dwarves nodded their heads and talked over themselves to answer her.

"Duh."

"Silly humans."

"This planet sucks. There's no logic."

"Of course, we look like dwarves, don't we?"

They all nodded, and she yawned again. "Well, it's nice to meet you. Do you have a facility I can use?"

She clenched her legs together, and the old man blushed and nodded.

"Absolutely, follow me."

"Where's Knox?" she asked as they walked.

"He—uh, had some errands to run," the old dwarf said.

Eirwyn had to use the restroom so bad, she didn't pry for details. He led her through a narrow hallway and to a small bathroom off a giant workshop and stable.

"Let me see about getting you some fresh clothes, dear."

He closed the door behind him. It barely clicked shut before Eirwyn was shoving her pants down and using the toilet. She sighed and glanced around.

Her eyes widened at the tub. It had nozzles, and when she was done, she reached over and turned one. Hot water shot into the bottom, and she grinned.

A knock sounded on the door, then a muffled, "I found you some clothes, princess, if you'd like to change."

She opened the door and smiled, taking the stack of neatly folded clothes from the old man. "Thank you so much. May I wash in your tub? I'll just be a few minutes."

"Take your time. We'll have supper ready. It's just through the workshop in the lodge." He pointed, and she nodded before closing the door behind him.

She had so many questions, but as she sank her tired body into the water, she frowned. The first question was where was Knox. The second, what the hell was going on with her stomach?

She soaped her body, paying attention to the bulge. She poked it, but it was hard under her skin. She frowned, sweat from the hot water beading on her skin. It was the fastest bath she'd ever had, even with soaping herself three times.

Helga would be proud. A stab of worry over her maid led to more questions. She brushed and braided her wet hair while she dried in the humid room. Then she put on a red shirt, but the dwarves pants were two sizes too big around the waist. She ripped what was left of Scarlet's shirt and tied it into a belt around the pants.

As she dressed, her worry mounted. Pain kept shooting through her body, and her anxiety went through the roof. Something was wrong. Where was Knox?

She felt in her soul that he was in trouble or hurt. She scrubbed her boots to a shine and rinsed out her mouth as she tried to think through her feelings and identify the problem.

Was it less than a week ago that she'd put on these boots for a walk in the gardens before the wedding reception? She sighed, her body brimming with energy as if preparing for a race. She couldn't sit still, her mind and hands flying as she tidied up the bathroom and opened the door.

She stepped out of the short hall into the workshop.

The smell of manure assaulted her nose, and she gagged, pushing a soft gust of wind to clear the air. She wanted to retch, but choked it down, the wave passing as quickly as it came. A twinkle on the workshop table caught her eye, and she walked toward it.

It was the ring they'd found in the tower. The emerald reminded her of Knox's eyes, and she slid it on her finger, tears pricking at her eyes. She'd thought it'd be too big, but somehow it fit exactly right. The gem sparkled in the light.

A flash of pain left her bending over. She clutched her stomach at the stabbing in her ribs. *Knox*. Where was he? Was he hurt?

Her mind knew nothing was wrong with her body. She was perfectly fine, if hungry. But on some level, she knew the pain was tied to Knox. She had to get to him, but she'd be no use without some food first.

Her hands shook as she looked at the ring, hunger clawing at her from the inside out. The golden apple lay in pieces on the table beside the stack of books. Her stomach growled, deep and hollow, and she instinctively picked up a piece.

Juice dribbled down her wrist as she chewed, her eyes drifting to the book on top. She brushed away a thin layer of dust, revealing an embossed emblem: a stylized spiral dragon curled around a sun.

A dragonology encyclopedia.

Eirwyn flipped it open, scanning sketched anatomy diagrams and sprawling descriptions of ancient wyrms. The pages detailed various aspects of dragons, including mating and reproduction. There were annotations, too, scribbled in the margins in a tight, old-fashioned hand, the scrawl reminding her of some of the ancient books she'd studied in school. There were theories about how dragons almost exclusively birthed male offspring on Celawynn, and how their kind had dwindled, relying on other races to bear their children in the desperate hope of producing a rare female.

The word *Drakin* appeared over and over—underlined, circled, occasionally followed by scrawled frustration.

"Not failed dragons. Not broken. Just... something else."

Her eyes widened and her jaw dropped as she read.

"It's very rare but some dragons have just one fated mate. These dragons have no sexual desire at all until they meet their fated mate, and then their bodies will only sing for their one true love."

He loved her? That's what he'd meant by asking her to be his mate? Mating meant love to dragons, not just having sex.

Her chest tightened, and a small smile played on her lips. A stab of pain came out of nowhere and wiped the smile off her face, making her gasp. She flipped the page, seeking answers on how to help Knox, how to find out what was wrong with him.

"Fated mates must complete the rituals to seal their destiny. The male dragon must penetrate all female holes, building from one to two to three. There must be an exchange of multiple body fluids. They must seal their love three times in three days."

Eirwyn's lips twisted wryly. They'd definitely done all that. She turned her head to read the handwriting.

"Venomous tails do not harm the fated mate. Actually, the venom barb acts like an aphrodisiac combined with a psychedelic and paralytic. The venom itself can be used as a lube and likewise, with poisonous breath. The breath draws the mate closer."

She tapped her chin and flipped the page.

"Fated mates almost always reproduce during the mating ritual. After the mating ritual is complete, the egg will grow for different time frames for different dragon types. Some types only grow the egg a week before being delivered but others take up to six months. If the egg is not fertilized, one or both will die (mother and child.) Almost all the time, losing the fated mate also brings the death of the remaining mate."

She turned to another section and paused.

A detailed drawing filled the page—six dragon scale palettes arranged around a central sigil, a spiral sun wrapped in a serpentine wing. White, black, red, yellow, green, and blue—each aligned with different magical forces. The notes beside each palette read like half-warnings, half-prayers.

"White dragons: light, ice, water, stasis."
"Red: fire, heat, destruction—volatile."
"Green: poison, plant, decay. Beware the slow killer."
"Yellow: storm, sand, lightning—untamable."
"Black: shadow, Nekros, rage—unknown."
"Blue: change, sea, illusion. The trickster's blood."

Another scribbled note curved around the margin: *"True dragons sense each other on sight—not by color, but by resonance. It's how they know who belongs. If one is unknown… they are feared."*

She blinked, heart fluttering.

A newer, messier line had been added just below: *"He is not green, not fully. Poison, yes, but… the resonance is wrong. There's something older inside him. Vitas? Divinity? He is not known."*

Her eyes lingered on that phrase. Not known.

She flipped again and landed on a sketched dragon— half-transformed, scales curling around humanoid limbs, its wings not fully formed.

"Too long in the egg. Magic saturated. Divine death altered the ley. Emerged a hinge. Not beast. Not man. Not like the others. A key?"

Eirwyn's heart raced. She looked up at the echo of foot- steps to see the old dwarf watching her warily.

She set the book down. "Where's Knox? When will he be back?"

The dwarf took his glasses off and cleaned them with a sigh. "He went to Vidrland, the village a day's ride south in the forest."

She frowned. "Vidrland?"

He shifted and avoided her eyes. "Between us and the Lone Road. It's the ancient druid ruins that the Robins have turned into a village."

Eirwyn sucked in a breath. "There really is a village in the forest, then? Led by rebels?"

He nodded, pursing his lips and putting his glasses back on. "Knox leads the Robins from Vidrland."

Eirwyn's jaw dropped. "He does what?"

The old man stepped to the side and held out a hand. "Let me explain over dinner. Are you hungry?"

She nodded and set the book down before following him. Every step brought more clawing fear and worry into her stomach. She wasn't sure that she'd be able to swallow past the knot in her throat, but she practically inhaled the stew as he talked.

The more he explained, the more worried she grew. A harder stab of pain made her gasp. Then she pushed her bowl away and stood. "Thank you so much for your hospitality and for helping me return from the Beyond."

Guilt weighed on her for not cleaning her bowl, but the dwarf didn't seem to mind. The pain subsided into a pulsing ache between her ribs as she stood.

He shook his head, taking the bowl to the sink. "I wouldn't have believed it if I hadn't seen it with my own eyes. I don't know how you came back, but I suspect it has something to do with that dragon of yours."

She bit her lip and looked outside. There was a wind blowing through the trees, and it called to her. That was the answer, the way to find him.

"I need to find Knox," she said, something shifting in her chest. "I need to find him *now*."

It wasn't this growing worry anymore. It was immediate, and she had to take action. There was no more time to waste seeking answers.

The old dwarf shook his head. "No, we told Knox we'd keep you safe. He'll come back for you."

She spun on her heels, her hands going wide. "No, he won't. You don't understand. Something's wrong, and I need to find him. He's in danger."

The dwarf shook his head and opened his mouth, but Eirwyn threw the door open and ran into the clearing. He shouted behind her, but the wind whipped through her hair, and she threw her head back.

Pain shot through her again, like someone was punching her in the side. It had nothing to do with her stomach and felt nothing like being poisoned, but the driving need to find Knox battled with the pain.

She spread her arms, letting the wind and shadows surround her as she tried to stretch her sides from the pinch in her ribs. The surge of magic was stronger than ever before, flowing through her at lightning speed.

When she opened her eyes, she blinked. Surrounded by clear blue sky, she looked down. There were several dwarves outside the lodge now, pointing and staring up.

Her heart raced. *What was going on?* She turned to see her hands still outstretched, shadows wrapping around them to form wings. The mate bond had changed her somehow. It was so much more than the old stories had said.

The wind shifted, and she began to fall. She pushed more wind into her wings, flapping and turning her body by instinct. Now parallel with the treetops, she looked over the forest below.

She had to find Knox. With a flap of her magical wings, she looked to the southeast. It was like a beacon filled her mind. It called to her to hurry. Find Knox before it's too late.

She shot through the air, the wind flowing over her face and making her eyes sting at first. Then she blinked and her vision shifted, growing sharper. The wind was cold, but she didn't feel a chill. It welcomed her like a long-lost friend as she finally soared through the air like a bird.

Chapter Thirty-Eight

"Come out, come out, wherever you are," came a playful and insidious deep voice around the corner of the tunnel.

Scarlet trembled in his arms and gasped, gripping his shirt tightly. "The king."

Panic shot through him at her fear but rage overcame it, and Knox passed her into Ashur's arms. "Take her. Get them to safety."

"What are you going to do? You can't face him alone."

"I'll help," Will said, cracking his knuckles.

"No, the people are the priority. We have to stick to the plan." Knox turned to go back toward the cellar, righteous anger burning in his chest. "I'll buy you some time. Go, get them safe, then initiate step two of the rebellion."

Ashur nodded and faced the crowd, Scarlet tucked under one arm with his hand around her waist. Knox strode with purpose, unlocking the hatchet that hung from his belt. He wiped his forehead and stepped into the cellar, his rage morphing into determination to teach this drakin a lesson.

The king stood with his legs spread wide and hands behind his back. "Ah, there you are. I've found you."

Knox's brow rose. "Were you looking for me?"

The king's jovial smile turned down, his face reddening in the soft light from the lantern. "I was actually. A little birdie says you're the leader of the Robins. Would you care to join me upstairs? These cellars are such dreary places."

Knox's eyes narrowed, and he widened his stance. "I'd rather not."

The king shook his head. "Tsk, tsk, tsk. No manners. You will address me as Your Majesty."

Knox snorted. "You're no king of mine."

The king's hands glowed orange as he gathered energy. "I guess I'll just have to teach you etiquette myself."

The king's smile turned into a wide grin, and Knox's heart raced with adrenaline. He widened his stance. The king threw a fireball, and it exploded above Knox's head, making boxes fall from the shelves.

Knox jumped out of the way, but more boxes rained down on his head. He lifted his tail and arms as they crashed down on him, his hands shifting and his arms growing scales. The wood splintered, and Knox heaved, throwing them off with massive claws.

The king raised a hand and a fireball exploded to the left then another to the right. Knox was thrown to the floor, trapped between burning boxes. Smoke began to fill the room.

He coughed and beat at the flames as he struggled to his feet. There was a soft pop and a fine, black dust settled over the room. A shot of pain ripped through Knox's head, making him groan as he came to his knees.

A coil of rope lashed around his upper arms, binding

his tail and arms to his sides. The rope burned, and he roared. It turned into a cough as blood filled his mouth.

The cellar floor was filthy beneath his knees, but it was the pain that made him groan. The pulsing magical rope was made of white hot fire.

He flexed his shoulders, stumbling to his feet as he pushed against the bonds. They squeezed tighter, the air rushing out of him in its ruthless grip. His shirt began to smolder at the hot coil of fire. He panted with shallow breaths, grunting as he strained.

The king laughed.

Knox froze, then looked over to the stairs.

The boxes that had fallen all around were now burned to ash, and the smell of smoke lingered in the air and on his clothes. Eirwyn wouldn't like all the dirt and grime.

His chest burned as he coughed through the smoke, his own green gas sinking to the floor to mix with the smoke.

"Ah, there you are. I had wondered if you were the type of drakin who was resistant to fire, but it seems like you're just tougher than the average human like Eirwyn."

Knox spit, the metallic taste of blood making him want to gag. His blood boiled in rage. "You've been throwing fireballs at Eirwyn?" The terror had to stop.

The king chuckled. "Why of course. How else was she to learn her lesson."

"And what lesson would that be?" Knox said as he spit blood onto the floor.

The king sniffed. "Why, that she doesn't stand a chance against me. She has to be kept in her proper place, the weakling that she is, her useless shadows and parlor tricks are nothing compared to my power."

"You've been hurting her all this time, poisoning your own sister. You're no king. You're a monster," Knox said, struggling against his bonds and lurching awkwardly to his feet, his arms still lashed to his sides.

The king stepped back, a snarl of disgust on his face. The king shook his head and spread his hands wide, fire glowing from his palms.

"Monster? No, you're the hideous, scaly monster, you low-life, no good bastard."

Gastone threw another fireball, and Knox jumped to the side, straining against the rope as it tightened and jerked taut. He crashed to the soot covered floor, and pain raced up his side, grunting as he saw spots.

Gastone continued with no change in his tone from the exertion of magic. "Imagine my surprise when I realized that not only was Eirwyn alive but she was slumming it with the leader of the Robins. Who—by the by—was a drakin too."

The king kicked him in the ribs. Pain exploded in his other side, the kick driving the fiery rope into his skin and burning through his clothes.

"No one threatens my crown, do you understand me? No one."

Knox grunted and curled up on the floor, the stinging bite of pain making his vision swim. Dizziness and nausea flooded him, and he groaned, tucking his head into his chest.

"Have you learned your lesson yet?"

"Go to hell," Knox said.

Gastone just laughed and kicked him again. Knox lost track of how many kicks, the time, and everything outside of the cellar. His core began to go numb from the pain as he disassociated. When his grunts of pain stopped, Gastone stepped back, tugged on his cuffs and straightened his jacket. "Now that you've learned that lesson, we're going upstairs. There's something I want to show you before you die."

Knox's heart raced as he coughed, smoke filling his nose. A small fire burned along one wall.

The king crooked his fingers, and the magical bands around Knox's arms and tail grew tighter. They burned into him, a slow burn that made his teeth clench.

"Why don't you just kill me now?" he gasped, struggling against his bonds.

The king jerked, wrapping the end of the rope around his fist and dragging him to his knees. "Like I said, I have a surprise for you. Then I'm going to teach you another lesson in manners before I kill you."

Knox stumbled to his feet, and Gastone grinned, a cruel light in his eyes as he began to walk up the stairs, jerking on the rope with every step and keeping one beady eye on Knox.

"Come along now. How my dear sister could traipse around the forest with a mongrel like you is beyond me. Too bad that bitch, Scarlet, failed to kill her. If I'd known she had a connection to the Robins, I never would've sent her after Eirwyn."

His tone was conversational as they walked up the stairs, but the rope threatened to choke him. Knox couldn't respond, all his energy was going to staying upright and breathing. He might have some broken ribs, based on the sharp pain in his side.

"I finally caught a few of the Robins behind the robbery of the palace. Quite high-handed of you to steal right from under my nose. Why you thought that was a logical way to negotiate is beyond me."

Knox couldn't breathe; the burning rope was too tight around his arms and chest and his shirt smoked.

He gasped, "You ignored our petitions about the taxes. You pushed into the forest and ignored us. You burned houses and villages and robbed from us all."

The king raised his brows and pushed open the cellar door at the top of the stairs. "The entire kingdom belongs to me. I can't rob from myself."

Gastone snorted and shook his head as they entered a small hallway. To the right were sounds of the kitchen. Knox didn't cry out. He didn't want any of the servants to get hurt, and there was no telling what the king would do. The wild look in his eyes had Knox gritting his teeth more.

It contradicted the logical, even tone of voice he used. They could've had this same conversation at the pub or over a cup of tea, instead of trussed up and being led around like a dog on a leash.

"You don't own the kingdom. We're a free people. Your right to rule depends on us agreeing to be ruled. And we only agree in exchange for protection." Knox said as Gastone tugged him to the narrow stairs on the left.

The king snorted again. "Protection? Ha! They'll obey what I say or they'll suffer the consequences. As for free-dom... it's overrated. It's so much easier when one person organizes everything into neat order."

They continued up the stairs.

The king waved his free hand, the other fisting the burning coil of rope. "The Robins think they want freedom, but what they really need is a strong leader."

He arched a brow and looked Knox up and down as they walked up the stairs. "They made a terrible choice in their current leader. Sure, you might be a drakin, but you brought the full wrath of the king down on not just their heads but everyone in the city. That bitch Hunter was captured, some of the Robins were captured, and where's Eirwyn?"

Gastone stopped, his eyes glinting as Knox looked up at him on the stair above. Knox swallowed hard, and Gastone's smile widened.

"That's right. Her heart is no longer beating, so she's finally dead. Quite a relief, that one, as she's been a thorn in my side for so long. Now to just get rid of you, and I'll have secured my rule over the land."

Knox's body went numb. He told himself Eirwyn was still in the stasis chamber and the dwarves would keep her alive. He told himself to not lose hope.

But Gastone was right. He'd failed them all, and Eirwyn was probably dead already. What magic did he have that he could see her heart?

"At least Red is free now. They've all been rescued from the dungeons," Knox mumbled.

The king laughed maniacally and jerked the rope up the stairs. The burning of the fire along his skin no longer bothered him.

"Oh, that? I put the spell on the cell doors to alert me when someone opened it. I knew you'd come after the last few people went missing from the dungeons. You took away all my fun, but that's the last time–"

"You call this fun?" Knox grunted through gritted teeth.

The king looked over his shoulder and grinned like a maniac. He tugged on the rope, and Knox stumbled onto the next step. His knee landed on the cold marble, and Gastone's fist landed in his ribs, Knox's own gravity driving the punch deeper.

Knox grunted and bent double. He would've fallen on his face if not for the burning sting of the rope biting into him. His stomach twisted from the pain and the smell of burning flesh, and he gagged.

"This is definitely fun," the king laughed.

Crunch. Knox gasped at another punch, the pain blinding him as he felt another rib shift. He blinked, shaking his head and sending blood flying.

The king jumped back, stepping up on the stairs and out of reach. "You filthy animal. How dare you? Keep your secretions to yourself."

The king narrowed his eyes and tugged hard on the rope. Knox stepped forward, barely keeping upright as he followed the king once more up the stairs.

"No wonder Eirwyn is so obsessed with being clean. You probably beat it into her head, didn't you?" Knox growled.

"I tried, but if she slept with you, the lesson obviously didn't stick. Did she spread her legs for you like she did for every other commoner in the city? Too bad she's finally dead. I would've preferred one more chance to teach her that particular lesson," Gastone said coldly.

Anger burned in his chest, the hot flash of emotion rivaling the rope. Eirwyn might be dead, but Knox wouldn't let him besmirch her memory. He wiggled his fingers at his sides, straining to call forth vines from outside.

"Don't talk about her like that," Knox growled, his fingers lengthening into claws at his sides. Knox straightened slightly as they reached a landing, trying to relieve the pressure on his rib.

The king held the rope in one fist and let the dangling end lengthen into a whip. He grabbed it with his other hand and swung it slowly in a circle as he talked.

"You think you're special?" Gastone snorted. "You're a piss poor leader of a ragtag band of rebels. You may claim to be a drakin, but I can see why you'd wear a hood in town. You're quite the ugliest thing I've ever seen."

"Shows just how much you know." Knox wiggled his fingers, pulling the vines toward the narrow window of the landing. The king turned to face him and with a flash of excitement across his face, the rope flashed through the air.

Crack. The dangling part of the rope whipped across his thighs, making him jerk.

"I know everything I need to. I'm the most powerful and well-trained sorcerer in the land. I'm the Buspartan drakin king. You're nothing but a commoner, a filthy peasant who likes to sleep in the mud, dirt, and filth like a disgusting pig."

Knox gritted his teeth, determined not to give the bastard the satisfaction of a response.

"You're pathetic, attacking me unarmed," Knox spit blood on the floor and stepped back from the king. The rope pulled taut, and then the burning rope tip slapped across his cheek, making his teeth rattle.

"I believe you have it backward. You're the pathetic sorry excuse for a drakin. Just look at you. Where did you even come from? You can't possibly be related to the Glathen drakins. Are you from some barbarian clan in the north?"

Knox tried to ignore his words, but they cut deep. This was why he'd hidden himself in the forest all these years, only coming into the city with his features heavily cloaked.

"Whatever does Eirwyn see in you? It must be the appeal of the savage."

The king swung the rope again, the burning coil lashing across his chest. Knox hissed and stiffened in pain, and then the king followed with a solid punch to the gut.

Knox bent over, wheezing. He crept the vines over the windowsill and slowly along the wall toward the king's back.

"Pathetic indeed. You're nothing but a weakling. I can't believe you actually pose a threat, but the mirror's never been wrong before."

He couldn't give in. He had to take care of Eirwyn, even if it was just her empty shell of a body. He had to protect the forest, save the people from this madman, and make Eirwyn proud.

Shouting and clanging echoed through the stairs, and Knox smiled. "Ah, phase two. The people are tired of your tyranny."

Gastone's eyes widened, and his lips went tight with anger. Knox wiggled his fingers at his side, and the vines wrapped around the king's ankles, pulling his feet out from under him. He slammed into the floor and dropped the magical rope, and Knox strained once more with a roar of pain.

The burning rope unraveled and disappeared in a puff of smoke. Knox dove at the king just as a fireball engulfed the vines. They rolled on the landing in a flashing ball, flames shooting from the king with every punch Knox delivered.

Knox grunted, breathing out poisonous gas and letting it sink into the king's face. What would normally make a human grow limp in seconds made the king's eyes water and glow red. His nose began to run, and he choked, blowing white smoke up at Knox as he screamed.

A hot fiery blast of steam flew from the king's mouth into Knox's face, knocking him onto his back from the intense heat. Thumbs dug into his windpipe, choking the green gas and air from his lungs.

The king straddled his stomach, dripping snot and mucus as Knox twisted, his clawed hands wrapping around the king's forearms as he bucked. The choke hold sent him spinning into darkness, and he called for the vines.

The king rasped, "You son of a bitch. You brought those dirty maggots into my castle to take my crown! Die, demon spawn, die like my bitch sister."

Knox blinked past the pain and roared, bucking and moving his claws to the inside of the king's arms. He hit the inside of the elbows, dislodging the king's straight arm attack.

Knox seized the advantage, rolling them as he said, "No one threatened you."

The king shot another fireball at close quarters, screaming, "They won't take my crown. Not now, not ever!"

The shock wave blew him along the floor, slamming into the wall of the landing under the window.

Knox choked on the smoke as the tapestry on the wall caught fire. When he looked up, the king's boots were disappearing into the ballroom. He followed, hissing poisonous gas through the large space and trying to hit the king in the back.

"Eirwyn didn't want your crown," Knox yelled as he ran into the ballroom. The light of the sun through the floor to ceiling windows on one side of the ballroom blinded him, and he skidded to a halt.

Chapter Thirty-Nine

The king rounded on Knox, his hands wide at his sides with balls of flame in one palm and the fiery rope whip swinging in the other.

"The hell she didn't. The darling princess of the nation? Everyone loved her. They'd have rejoiced to see her on the throne instead of me."

"Was that why you've poisoned her for so long?" Knox asked, careful to stay just out of reach of the rope. His hatchet was long gone, lost in the cellar.

Knox slowly circled the king, but at his words, the king went mad. His face reddened, and he swung the end of the rope again. It lashed out like lightning, and Knox dove.

But he wasn't quick enough, the pain and weakness slowing him down. Knox grunted, his body falling, the rope wrapped around him once more. The stabbing pain in his ribs made him choke down bile.

"She has undermined me her entire life. Trying to make her death look like an accident has been the hardest thing I've had to do as king. She was supposed to die in that carriage accident twenty years ago with our stupid parents, but some sad fool brought her home."

The king took a step with every word, dragging Knox on his back toward the balcony. He released the whip, and Knox gasped a full breath of pure pain.

Blood dripped down his chin as he pushed onto his knees. "Ah, that would be me."

The king's boots turned in the middle of the balcony. "What?"

Knox looked up, coming up on one foot and using his knee to push the rest of the way to standing. He breathed shallowly through his mouth against the wave of pain in his ribs.

"*I* found the carriage on the Lone Road and pulled the baby princess from the wreckage. *I* saw the vampire assassin finish the job."

The king's face turned almost purple in rage, and he raised the rope whip. Knox lunged at him, hoping the offensive attack would throw the king off.

They exchanged blows, swift and sure crunches of pain. Knox landed a solid punch to the king's jaw, which just made him more angry. He pounded the hell out of Knox with both rope and fists until Knox's mind began to wander. It was the only way to detach himself from the constant biting pain.

His vision spun as blood dripped into his eyes. The king shot red-hot knives of pain into him, each one burning. Knox yelled, jumping to the side and hitting the wall behind him. Darkness clouded his eyes, and he fell to his knees.

The wind whispered to him through the open air. It caressed him like Eirwyn's fingers playing over his scales and horns. He groaned, the pain trying to drag him into the darkness.

"Why did you have to save her? This all would've been so much easier if she would've died with our parents like planned," Gastone grunted with every slash of the rope and punch of his fist.

Knox blinked and fell to his back, dipping his head to wipe his eyes on his shoulder. He heaved a deep breath, the wind soothing him. He rolled onto his side and stumbled to his feet, using the little alcove of the door to stop the blows of the rope whip.

"Eirwyn doesn't matter anymore. You're still going to lose the kingdom. Look, the rebellion is here."

The king turned from Knox and peered over the balcony, giving him a precious second to breathe.

Below, battle cries and metal clanged—a cacophony swallowed by Gastone's roar of fury.

Then came fire.

Flames erupted from the king's outstretched hands, twin infernos that surged past the castle walls, swallowing nearby buildings in a wave of searing heat. Knox ducked behind the balcony door just in time, shielding himself as the air turned molten.

When the blaze finally died down, he coughed against the smoke curling through the doorway, blinking away the brightness seared into his vision. The clouds above drifted on, serene and oblivious, while the horizon shimmered with heat. Sunset kissed the sky with gold and red, its light tangled with the king's flames, casting a surreal, hellish glow across the city.

Knox pressed a hand to his ribs and stepped into the scorched air. Beyond the castle, he saw the edge of the city—and beyond that, the forest. But something was wrong.

Now that Knox was standing, hand on his side, he could

barely see the trees in the distance, the glow of magic turning them yellow.

The edge of the city lay between them and the trees, and everything burst into flames as the king's roar turned into a shrieking laugh. Buildings that were in the path of destruction went up in a blaze. People began to scream as they ran for safety as the fighting in the courtyard began again.

Knox's heart stopped, his entire body freezing in awareness. The blast of heat from the king dwindled to a stop, but the glow on the forest remained.

"You see that, Robin? I'm flushing out all of those precious people you just rescued. Soon they will come screaming from the burning inferno of the forest and running into town where my guards will capture them all."

Knox shuffled forward, a knot of dread settling in his stomach. His heart began to race. "The forest—"

"Is on fire, yes. Beautiful, isn't it?" Gastone turned to the railing, a smile on his face.

"You've set the forest on fire."

"Yes, so nice of you to catch up on your surprise, Robin. Now, let's teach you those etiquette lessons, so I can kill you before dinner. I'm getting a little peckish, and there seems to be a little rebellion downstairs that I need to attend to."

Knox took a shallow breath, the sharp stab of pain in his ribs still present. Not as bad as before, but they were definitely broken.

"My name is Knox, not Robin. You're burning *my* forest, robbing from *my* people."

He couldn't quite bring himself to claim a kingship. It was too soon, too strange, too anathema of the freedom he spouted. Knox widened his feet and squared off to the king, his hands shifting into fierce claws. His tail waved behind his head, preparing to strike.

Gastone smiled, the cruel tilt of it matching his wild eyes. "Yours? I think not. You're nothing but a mongrel, a disgusting sad excuse for a drakin. You can't be allowed to live. I'm putting you out of your misery, actually. And putting others out of the misery of having to look at you."

"Are you feeling threatened?" Knox taunted, his fingers lengthening into sharp claws.

They circled each other, Gastone gathering more flickering flames into his palms. "You will die today, you ugly demon spawn. I can't let another drakin live. I'm the only one who will rule this kingdom."

Knox swallowed hard, his hands fisting at his sides as he wove vines up the side of the castle. "Is that why you went to war with Glathen? Because they're ruled by drakin too?"

Gastone threw a blast of hot flame from one palm to the other, catching it like a ball as he watched Knox advance. "Glathen's a spoiled little kingdom just waiting for me to conquer."

A gust of wind snuffed out the flames. Gastone shook his hands, sparks lighting them up again as he frowned. "If I'm going to be the only drakin, I have to purge world of the rotten, dirty mongrels like you. It's my divine destiny."

Knox breathed harshly, the smoke filling his nose but the wind bringing a calmness before the storm of battle. Hope warred in his chest to see Gastone's flames growing weaker. He was overextending. If Knox could just wear him down and last longer...

Green tendrils of gas sank to the stone at his feet as his emotions heightened and vines stretched over the railing and across the tile floor. His body began to shake from the effort to grow so many vines so fast.

"You're no king. You're a savage mockery of what a leader should be. Killing your sister and parents? Bleeding the people dry with taxes to pay for your selfish war?"

His heart hammered in his chest, and his stomach twisted. Anger threatened to choke him with smoke, but he breathed in the crisp air of peace and out a steady stream of green poisonous gas.

It sank to the stone, billowing up around their heads, growing in intensity. His nose began to bleed at the use of too much magic. This was more than even blasting the entire castle with the sleeping gas during the robbery.

The drakin king was tougher than most humans, but he wasn't immune. He began to choke, his eyes and nose dripping and his flickering hands burning brighter, a beacon for Knox to attack.

Knox launched himself at the king's legs, tackling him to the ground. They rolled with grunts, and Knox straddled his torso. He landed a blow to Gastone's head, making it snap to the side. Wet-hot drops of crimson splattered across the stone.

"Burning down the forest? Blowing up homes and half the city? Those people have done nothing to you but obey unjust laws that benefit *you*. They've bled and died on a battlefield for a pointless war for *you*. No more," Knox ground out as he rained down a flurry of blows with claws as sharp as any dagger. Skin ripped beneath him and blood flew.

The king roared, a burst of flame shooting out from him as he bucked. Knox fell back, his stomach twisting and his eyes growing heavy at the sharp pain in his side.

The king whipped an elbow up and drove the point into his jaw, his red-shot eyes wild with madness. Knox bit his tongue, and the taste of copper flooding his mouth. Pain pulsed through his head, making him see stars, but he couldn't stop.

Knox grunted and kicked, his tail whipping out to seek its target. Gastone rolled out of the way, the venom landing uselessly on the ground. He had to stab the king through the heart and inject his venom. The poison breath wasn't working fast enough. The venom barb was his strongest weapon, and the king had to die.

Knox's stomach twisted with guilt at what Eirwyn would say about his death, but the king was mad with power. Knox scrambled to his hands and knees and dove at Gastone again just as he began to gather more magic. The two tumbled, exchanging blows and kicks with merciless force.

Knox's tail wrapped around the king, trying to hold his arms down and block punches. The king twisted a wrist and another flaming rope wrapped around Knox's tail, jerking it back as the king landed a blow to Knox's temple.

Blood stung his eye. His breathing became labored and still he pushed more gas into Gastone's face. The king choked, and the flickering flames on his hands shifted from red and white to blue.

His claws raked through the king's jacket, shredding it and drawing blood. Gastone's hands burned Knox where they hit, the sharp sting of pain in his ribs making it harder to breathe.

The magical rope tossed him back, dragging him by the tail. A mixture of red blue flames shot at Knox, but he rolled just in time. The flame hit the stone, melting the wall. Knox's heart stopped and his eyes widened. The king's arms shook, but he didn't stop.

Knox blew green gas at the king and roared, launching to his feet and picking his opponent up around the waist to slam him onto the stone tile.

His tail struck down at the king's face. Gastone's red-rimmed eyes widened, and he bucked. The barb punctured through the jacket, and the king jerked, bucking Knox off again and throwing a blast of sputtering blue heat.

The heat didn't hurt Knox, more scales covering his body the longer they fought. Knox twisted, watching the king shake off the venom. He wasn't sure if he'd broken the skin or not, but the barb was still on his tail so he didn't think so. He had to try again.

He angled his tail as he reached up to grab the king's hands in solid scale-covered claws. The king wrapped the burning whip around Knox's arms and jerked.

Knox went flying over the king's head, landing on the edge of the railing. Venom splattered on the king's sleeves as Knox landed a few feet away.

He blinked, looking down at the crowd below. There was a clattering and clanging of battle, but he couldn't tell which side was winning.

Knox groaned and blinked the pain away. He shook his head trying to clear it of the ringing, then rolled to his side to find Gastone.

The king was already on his feet. He brought his boot down on Knox's throat. Knox grabbed his foot and twisted, his heart beating wildly. His tail twisted out to gain leverage for a strike.

"Die... already," Gastone panted, his nose bloody and one eye swollen shut. He raised his shaking hands, blue flames flickering as he reached for more magic.

Vines twisted around the king's back leg and jerked. A sputtering fireball shot out, disintegrating the vines even as the king stumbled. He hit the edge of the melted stone wall and wavered on his feet as Knox stood.

A feminine cry rang out, "No!"

The king stumbled to his knees, his eyes rolling back in his head as he fell to the stone. Knox didn't stop as blue flames still covered Gastone's hands. He dove again, stabbing down with his tail and puncturing his throat.

The king's mouth opened and closed like a fish on a hook, and Knox jerked his tail back. A small pinprick barb was buried in his neck, a trace of green ooze around it already dripping down. It would take a few minutes, but Knox breathed a sigh of relief.

Then his tail was jerked back.

An unseen force had gripped Knox's tail like a vice, flinging it away from Gastone like a giant hurtling a boulder and sending Knox flying over the edge of the balcony.

Wind rushed over him as he blinked, his heart racing as the Edge called to him. He shouldn't have pulled so much magic to make the vines grow so fast and so tall. There was no way to summon them from the sides of the castle to catch him fast enough.

A lower gabled roof rose closer, and the stark reality of his situation pressed on him like a weight driving him faster down to his death.

His body ached all over, and when he landed several stories below, he knew it would be all over.

He closed his eyes and accepted his fate, letting the Edge draw nearer and welcome him, seeing Eirwyn in the Beyond. The wind and freedom blew over his skin, scales, and horns, and he relaxed.

Chapter Forty

Eirwyn raced over the flames of the forest to the castle and sucked up the air around the flames to put it out. For once, it started to work, but she couldn't stop with just the forest. Too soon, she was flying over the burning houses to the castle. A large group of villagers led by Scarlet pushed through the castle gates as she circled her former home. They fought the guards, but many guards just tossed down their weapons and held their hands up until another group of soldiers poured out of the barracks. Then the fighting started in earnest.

Eirwyn looked up at the balcony above them and saw Bella's familiar yellow dress. Eirwyn flapped, pushing a gust of wind to gain altitude to see–

She gasped. Knox and Gastone wrestled on the balcony, and Bella screamed and reached out a hand. Knox slammed back and fell over the railing. Eirwyn gasped, then shot through the sky like an arrow.

"Knox!" Her cry pierced the air. Eirwyn flew like an

avenging angel on wings of shimmering light, wind wrapping around her to keep her airborne.

Her heart raced faster. The next balcony was rapidly approaching as Eirwyn slammed into him, changing their trajectory to a closer roof.

She wrapped her arms and magic around them to slow their fall, wind and shadows swirling. Magic wouldn't keep them from being splattered on the cobblestones below, and adrenaline race through her as she prayed to the gods.

With her arms around him, she couldn't use them as wings. Knox was limp in her arms, and they slammed onto the roof with only a small bubble of air to cushion their fall.

They skidded along the tiles toward the edge. She gasped, digging in her heels and sending a burst of wind to slow them. She pulled on the waistband of his pants to keep him from going over.

They slid to a stop, and she panted as she looked below. Her eyes teared at the near death experience, but when she looked at Knox, she forgot all about it. All that mattered was him.

"Knox?" she gasped, wiping her eyes and shifting slowly to kneel beside him.

Tears pricked her eyes as she felt along his chest, pushing the necklace to the side. His shirt was ripped and blood was everywhere. There was no pulse, and her eyes teared again as she shook her head. "No, no, Knox, don't do this. I'm here. Come back to me."

The soft whisper was lost on the wind, but her heart yearned with all the longing, hope, and love she had to give. She didn't know what to do or how to save him. She began to cry as despair washed over her.

Shadows wove around them, and fear knotted in her

stomach at the lack of light in them. It gnawed at her, beating her down and making tears streak down her cheeks. She didn't care that they'd only known each other a short time. It didn't matter that she was terrified of being under another man's thumb.

All she knew was she couldn't lose him.

She couldn't see for the shadows and pounded on his chest. "Knox, don't leave me. Please, I can't—please you have to stay with me. I love you. You said mates forever. Stay with me forever, please."

Her mouth found his in a desperate kiss that held nothing back. It begged him to stay, and she whimpered.

At the touch of their lips, magic surged through her, weaving their fates together. Her body began to heat and she felt more than saw light, shadows, and wind swirl around them. Her heart thudded wildly, afraid to hope, afraid to think of what this rush of magic meant.

Then his tongue teased the seam of her mouth, and she gasped, her eyes flying open as she trembled above him. He used the moment to sweep his tongue inside. Her eyes fluttered, and her heart stuttered because *he was alive.*

The kiss was more than just a kiss. It was a hello, a promise of eternal mates, and a declaration of love all wrapped up in one.

His lips were soft, and his short whiskers tickled her lips. Their tongues met in a wet, hot slide, and she felt the magic envelop them protectively.

Her heart ached as his tongue dove deeper. She moaned, her hands resting on his chest. Tears trailed down her cheeks at the feel of his heartbeat, the flow of his breath across her face. Their tongues dueled as if speaking some secret language.

She ached for him, and the kiss shifted deeper, wilder,

needier. She bit his lip, and the tangy taste of blood teased her senses. The blood brought another swirl of magic. It lifted her hair around them, and his hands came up to rest on her waist. The kiss—their first real kiss—sent electricity through her veins.

Then his lips changed too, no longer soft and welcoming. His nose grew, forcing them to break the kiss. When she pulled back, his body shimmered as energy swirled, and his skin turning green.

He grew bigger than a horse, her arms no longer able to hold him. She released him, stepping back as his scales shifted, covering his entire body. The change put too much pressure on the edge of the roof, and it collapsed, plunging them through the debris and air.

She screamed, "Knox!" She reached for him, her eyes closing as they plunged into the courtyard below. Magic coursed through her as she spread her arms to catch the wind.

She took another breath and then a third one. A tightness squeezed her stomach, but the falling feeling was gone. The shadows dissipated and finally, she could see.

Massive claws were wrapped around her waist. She looked up and gasped, her hands holding onto his claws. She blinked and looked around as they soared into the air above the castle. The sun was setting but she was in a light shadow.

"Knox?" It was a question, but she knew the green dragon who held her. There was no fear, only joy and relief. His massive head looked down at her in his claws. She spread her arms wide and let her magic create wings, then she tapped his claw that wrapped around her waist.

"Let me go."

He hesitated then released her, and she soared around

him. Her brain took a few seconds to process what she was seeing, and she flapped her arms.

"Oh gods, Knox, you're—you're a full-blooded dragon! I mean, I know we knew you were, but this..." She tilted around him, the wind bearing her up as she circled.

His entire body was covered in brown and green scales thick as a knight's shield. The emerald and gold necklace hung about his neck just like the dragon in the vision. His horns had grown points as long as her arm. He hissed, a puff of green smoke shooting out and dissolving into the cloud.

Higher they rose above the castle, sweeping through the lowest white cloud.

He beat his leathery wings and thrashed his tail as he learned the size of this body and how to maneuver it. Eirwyn laughed and flapped her arms, her shadow and light wings keeping her aloft.

"You're really alive! You're alright," she said, a grin splitting her face.

He looked at her and somehow, she knew what he was feeling, like what she felt from the birds. He arched a large brow.

Seriously, you think this is alright?

She laughed again and flew toward him, raking her hand along his back to trace over his scales. He shuddered and flapped his wings. She felt him, knew he loved her touch, and she laughed as she flew away, the wind from his wings pushing her higher.

"I love you, Knox, and that includes your dragon form too."

He grinned, his dragon fangs dripping the same green venom that had wrapped his tail before. They flew, swirling around each other. Eirwyn laughed, joy shooting through her to know they were both alive.

Then they flew through a gray smoke, and both of them turned to dip under the clouds at the acrid smell of burning wood, buildings, and flesh.

We have to save the forest and makes sure your brother is gone.

Eirwyn nodded. "We need to *save* my brother, but he can wait. Gastone's injured, and Bella is taking care of him, so let's put out the forest first. But how?"

Smother it.

Knox swooped down toward the trees, and Eirwyn admired his iridescent green scales as they shone in the sunlight. Knox beat his wings, pushing wind down on the treetops that burned with a red glow. Eirwyn felt his intent and flew behind him, pushing wind to swirl into a vortex and away from the trees.

Together they worked to suffocate the fire, but it wasn't enough. Eirwyn swirled the wind, but the air just created a fire tornado that began to rip through the trees again.

"Knox, use your breath," Eirwyn screamed, pointing to the tornado.

Knox blew green gas on the fire, and Eirwyn shifted the wind to give it the most impact. The toxic fumes began to suffocate the fire, and they moved to the next section. Tree by tree, they poured green smoke onto the fire while Eirwyn took away the air, suffocating it one by one.

Eirwyn's arms began to shake from the effort to stay aloft. She'd been flying for so long, and it was only her first day with wings. She'd gotten a burst of energy when they'd kissed, but she was already running low in her magical reservoir.

Exhaustion crept up, and the Edge beckoned. Her

stomach knotted. They were almost done. She could make it.

The last of the fire was finally out, and Eirwyn glided down to the outskirts of the burnt forest. She hit the ground and rolled to a stop.

She groaned, laying on her back as the last light faded. The ground shook beside her, then Knox's big dragon head peered down at her.

She smiled and reached up a hand to trace his nozzle. "I'm fine," she said. "Just tired."

The Edge? Do you need a healing potion?

"No, I'll be alright after a rest and a snack. But look at you, Knox. So beautiful..." She trailed off as she stroked his scales.

He snorted and nuzzled her hands. *Yeah, it's been a big day, hasn't it?*

She chuckled as he nuzzled her. "Yes, but we're both alive, and that's all that matters."

I thought I lost you.

Tears burned her eyes as she replied, "Me? I thought I'd lost *you* when you went over that roof. Don't scare me like that again."

He huffed, and the hot wind of his green breath made her giggle and her body perk in awareness.

I won't if you won't. Don't push yourself into the Beyond again or the Edge either. Deal?

She grinned and stroked his scales. "Maybe. Are you going to spank me if I do?"

He snorted a laugh, and a scream rang out from the castle. Knox tensed, his tail raising with barbs out and his head swinging up to stare at the castle.

"Gastone," Eirwyn whispered, as she stood and buried her face against the warmth of his scaly neck.

I need to defeat him. We can't let the people suffer under his rule anymore.

Tears fell, and a weight settled on her chest. "I know, but he's still my brother, my only family. Maybe if we can bind his magic we can get him some help?"

Eirwyn. Knox shimmered and magic swirled in a green haze. Then he stood before her in his pants and boots. He pulled her into a tight hug and sighed.

"Eirwyn, I have to tell you before anything else happens. He's the one who had your parents killed."

Her chest tightened, and she reared back. His emerald eyes burned with emotion, and his arms dropped to his side as he ran a hand over the side of his head.

"There was a vampire assassin. Your parents... were already gone, but he couldn't touch you, an innocent babe."

Eirwyn shook her head, her hands covering her mouth. "No, it couldn't have been Gastone. He always said Glathen hired the assassin. He was only a teenager. I—it was an accident."

Knox shook his head slowly, reaching out for her. She stiffened and danced away from him, her mind whirling.

"I'm sorry, Eirwyn, but it wasn't. Your brother admitted to it when we were fighting."

Eirwyn's head ached and tears streaked down her cheeks. Her chest was too tight, and she couldn't catch her breath. She fell to her knees and buried her face in her hands.

"No, it can't—he—" she choked on a sob, then Knox's arms came around her. He sat down behind her and pulled her onto his lap, rocking her gently.

He didn't say anything, but she didn't need him to. She could feel his worry for her, his remorse... and his determination to kill her brother.

She understood, but she didn't like it. She had denied the truth of it for years, even when she knew Gastone had been trying to kill her.

On some level, she'd ran to the tavern whenever she'd started to feel his sneaky attacks getting worse. She'd gone to the tavern to eat real food that wouldn't make her sick. She'd gone to the tavern for a friend to listen.

And now her friend was on the roof of the castle with her stupid evil brother. Her heart jumped, and her breath caught in her throat as her tears slowed. It ate at her until she pulled back and looked up at Knox's deep green eyes.

She bit her lip, unsure of what to say, and he just pursed his lips and nodded.

"I know," he said. "You stay here, and I'll take care of it. You've pushed yourself too much already. You'll be safe here, right?"

She nodded, tears pricking her eyes as more fears rose. "But what if he hurts her? What if you need me?"

Knox kissed her forehead, and then they stood up, his hand on her elbow. "Then I'll roar, and you'll come flying. But would it make you feel better if I did a pass over the castle courtyard and tried to find Scarlet or the Robins?"

She frowned and pointed at him. "Oh yeah, the Robins. Why didn't you tell me—"

Another scream ripped from the castle roof, and a burst of magic split the sky above. Eirwyn's stomach twisted at the horrible starburst of colors, every color of magic represented.

"Oh no, Bella," she whispered, dread filling her. The fear was eating her alive, and terror left her frozen in place.

Knox kissed Eirwyn's cheek and stepped away. "I'll find her," he said, shifting into his hulking dragon. He bent his knees and lunged into the air, flapping his wings.

She gave him a gust of wind and said softly, "Bring her here so I can protect her, and be safe."

Then he was flying straight to the castle. Worry twisted her stomach, making her feel nauseous as she held her stomach bump, barely filling her palm with the size of it. She could join him, she hadn't pushed herself too much yet, but if she was pregnant... She had to wait for him.

She bit her lip and watched him fly away.

Chapter Forty-One

Running on adrenaline, Scarlet swung the stolen short blade
and hit a guard in the chest plate. The metal clanged, and
the man fell, and victory made her grin. Scarlet kicked him
in the chest and sent him sprawling on the cobblestones of
the courtyard before turning to find the next enemy.

Half an hour ago, she'd been beaten and bloody. But
multiple healing potions, a couple of bites of jerky, and a
quick talk with the Robins, and she knew what she had to
do. Her emotions were raw from the torture, and she
desperately wanted the comfort of her daggers and blades
and the sweet scent of blood and death. She felt naked
without them, but she'd taken down her first guard by hand,
then taken his sword. It wasn't as fun as her daggers, but it
would do.

The king had gotten into her head with his wicked lies,
and it infuriated her. She'd kept telling herself that Knox
would find her. He was as steady as the stars and the best
brother anyone could ask for. And if their roles were
reversed and he was in trouble, she would be there to help.

Another guard ran at her from the side. She stepped back and kicked her leg out, sending him to the ground on top of the other one. The Robins and villagers behind her flooded the castle courtyard, spreading out to find a way inside the castle itself.

One of the Robins, Ashur, pointed up and yelled at another one, Will. She followed their gaze and clenched her jaw. Thanks to her sharpened senses, she could see perfectly fine, even at this distance.

Knox fought with the king on the balcony above. Her blood ran cold, and her heart raced. She'd been a prisoner of that madman for days. Knox was strong, but he couldn't defeat the strongest mage in the kingdom by himself.

She raced past the two big Robins and yelled, "That's Knox. We have to help him."

She made directly for the closest door, but one of them yelled back, "This way."

Scarlet turned and followed behind them, swinging the sword and slicing open the throat of one of the guard officers.

His hand went to his neck as he gasped. Sticky blood seeped between his fingers, but Scarlet ran past him before he even hit the ground.

She followed the two men, barely panting. "Do you know where we're going?"

Will looked back at her and then took off down a hallway. "You'd best stay on guard down here. We'll help Knox."

"Knox can handle himself. He said to save the queen, if she'll let us," Ashur said as they entered the large foyer.

A scream echoed off the walls, "No!"

Together, they sprinted up the grand staircase to the third floor. When they rounded the landing, they saw movement through the ballroom. They ran through the open doors, the two bulky men falling behind her as she sprinted ahead.

Knox was on top of the king on the edge of the balcony, landing blow after blow and stabbing with his tail. Magic shimmered as the queen reached out her hand and cried out.

Scarlet changed course and ran to Bella. She couldn't let the queen hurt Knox either; he was handling himself at the moment. The queen saw Scarlet coming out of the corner of her eye, and turned to face her.

Her glowing hands flew up, and a shockwave of magic blasted the air, smacking into the tile with a burst of light. Scarlet jumped, but the Robins behind her were too slow, their boots sticking in the melted tile.

The blast slammed into Knox and sent him over the side of the railing.

"No!" Scarlet cried, racing to the edge. Frantically, her eyes searched the ground, but she didn't see him splattered below. Her heart raced too fast, and she started to panic.

A motion to her right had her turn. The princess had shadowy magical wings, brilliant colors reflecting off the solidified air, her arms wrapped around Knox as they crashed into a nearby roof. They rolled but came to a stop on the edge.

Scarlet took a deep breath of relief, but the queen cried out behind her.

"No, no, no, no, no. You're alright. Come on, my love. Let's get you a nice healing potion, yes?"

Scarlet turned to see the queen kneeling beside the king, reaching out to help him sit up. He held his head, eyes glassy and dazed. One eye was already swelling shut, and blood dripped from his nose.

The king jerked back with a hiss. "Get off me, hag."

The queen gasped and scrambled to her feet, following the king as he stumbled to the door of the ballroom. Ashur and Will still struggled with their boots melted into the tile, but Scarlet followed the royals on silent feet, staying just close enough to overhear.

"Scarlet, no, wait for us," Ashur whispered.

Her heart raced with adrenaline, her eyes on the couple as they went through the ballroom. Seeing no response at the whisper, she motioned for them to stand down.

Will was unlacing his shoes while Ashur still struggled. Scarlet stayed in the ballroom shadows, waiting for the couple to leave. Then she sprinted along the wall to see which way they were going.

Bella hovered a step behind Gastone, her hands raised just in case she needed to catch him. He swayed on the stairs, and her stomach twisted with worry. "Gastone, please, let me help. There's a healing potion in—"

"No," he yelled, turning to her on the stairs and stumbling like a drunkard. "You can't help. There's only one thing that can help me now."

"What? How can I fix it?" Bella cried. Her entire world was crumbling, but there had to be a solution. There was always a solution.

The sconces on the stairwell flickered in between each of his mounted trophy heads, light shifting with magic as she walked by. The cries of cowering servants below were ignored as more of the rebels breached the castle doors.

She paid no heed, her only focus on Gastone, the only

one who'd ever taken a chance on her, the only one who'd given her everything she'd ever wanted.

She'd never seen anyone this beat up, even when she'd helped Lailant with healing house calls. "Fysica protect–"

"The old gods aren't part of this," Gastone yelled, stumbling to their chambers. "Borga may side with the rebellion, but I will win the war. The one with Glathen and the one on our own people."

He hit the wall, and Bella cried out, throwing magic at the wall and changing the painting on the wall to a pillow.

"Leave the gods out of it, woman. They've turned their back on me, even though the mirror said I was divinely chosen for such a time as this. The mirror is never wrong. Only the mirror can help now. He'll have a way to fix this."

Gastone rambled and stumbled through her doorway. Her heart raced with fear as he sank to his knees. The mirror on her vanity shimmered with magic, and Bella gasped, her hands going to her lips.

"Magic mirror, hear my plea, who is better than me?"

King of nothing, your rule is through. Everyone is better than you.

Bella gasped, stepping back. No, what magic was this? She'd spent a lot of time around that mirror the past few months. Gastone had said nothing when she'd had it moved from the library to her bedroom.

She shook her head and backed all the way to the hallway wall. A shadow caused her to blink, and the ranger woman from earlier stalked inside on silent feet, barely glancing at Bella.

She wore bloody, ripped, and dirty clothes, black pants and a green shirt. Her hair was matted and covered in mud and the gods knew what else. And the smell—Bella had smelled better from the pig pen out behind the tavern.

Anger coursed through her. She was the queen now, but

once again, she was being ignored like a servant. She blinked, adrenaline pumping and hands shaking as she gathered magic.

"No," she gasped, her voice barely a whisper as she followed the silent, dirty woman inside. Nothing good could come of her being here.

Gastone sank onto his haunches, his movement drawing her gaze. She stepped back into the room to find his face pale and jaw slack as he stared up at the mirror in supplication. He glanced over, but he too ignored Bella. He snarled and narrowed his gaze on the ranger a few paces inside the door.

His jaw snapped shut, and his eyes glittered, blood still dripping down from his temple.

"You," he growled, lurching to his feet. He swooned where he stood. "If you would've killed that bitch like I hired you to do, none of this would've happened."

The woman shifted on the balls of her feet and stepped to the side of the room, away from Bella. Thank the gods she was at least unarmed. Bella watched her like a hawk to see if she was gathering magic to attack him.

"Me?" the dirty woman asked as she pointed a bony finger. "If you hadn't gone power-hungry and tried to kill your sister, none of this would've happened."

Bella gasped, looking from one to the other. Her stomach twisted, yet somehow she didn't doubt the woman's words. "What?" she whispered, her fingers on her mouth.

The woman looked over her shoulder at Bella. "He hired me to kill Eirwyn, and I didn't do it."

Bella held her hands to her lips and shook her head in horror. Not Eirwyn, not her friend and the only little sister she'd ever had.

"No, he wouldn't do that," she whispered, shaking her head.

A blast of magic hit the ranger. With a grunt from Gastone, the woman fell to the ground and magic swirled.

Bella jumped in surprise, her heart racing as she flew to the woman's side to feel for a pulse. "Oh gods, did you kill her too?"

She breathed a sigh of relief. The woman was shimmering with magic, her bones and body transforming into some kind of woodland creature.

"There are worse things than death. A polymorph spell is the next lesson for you to learn. She refuses to be my Hunter? Fine, she'll never hunt again. She'll be the prey now," Gastone said as he laughed maniacally. The laughter faded to a coughing fit, and Bella scrambled back as the woman finished her transformation.

Bella shook her head, looking back to Gastone, terrified to her core of the man she'd married. He wiped blood from his mouth and slung his fingers, throwing blood and sparks from his hand. He glared, his bloody grin scaring her even more.

She didn't know him at all. This whole time, he'd been cultured, intelligent, and listened to her opinions. But he'd judged this woman for sparing a life? And not just any life. His sister's. If he could kill his sister, what would he do to his wife?

She jumped to her feet as adrenaline flooded her body, fisting her pale skirts and backing out of the room. Gastone was unhinged. Eirwyn had been right all along. They had talked about him for years, but she had forgotten. The past was all hazy.

And she'd married the madman. How could she love such a beast?

She had to get out of the castle. He made the mess, and now he could clean it up himself. She'd been running interference for him for months, trying to placate the nobles, the priests, the Chancellor, and the General. She'd even tried to talk to the Council on his behalf. She'd been so busy working on his image that she hadn't stopped to see what he truly was.

Bella stopped before she could reach the hallway as the man from the balcony entered the room. He'd left his boots below, trapped in the tile, and a twinge of guilt licked her spine.

The Robins had finally come for the king. Her heart raced, and she glanced over her shoulder at Gastone. If she left him here, magic depleted, he'd die. Could she live with herself if she let that happen?

Fire flickered in his hands, and he grunted, weaving from side to side as he widened his feet to fight again, the same crazy grin on his face. "Ah, another party. How fun. Well, come on then, Robin."

Gastone made a come hither motion with his fingers and coughed again. Blood dripped down his chin, and his eyes burned with hatred.

Bella ground her teeth, her decision made. She jumped in front of Gastone and held her arms wide at the stranger.

"No, don't touch him," she demanded in her most queenly voice.

Still, it warbled with fear. She didn't want him to die. He was still the king, still her husband. He'd given her the entire kingdom and had laid it at her feet for her help. Without him, she was nothing, and she couldn't let him go.

Chapter Forty-Two

"I won't let you kill him," Bella said, gathering magic in her hands. Her voice shook, but she was determined to stand and make Gastone proud.

The man frowned, lifting his own hands up and palms out, no magic shimmering on them. He was a regular human then, but still, she didn't relax. He was a big brute of a man, and she'd been overcome by his type before.

"We're not going to hurt him. We're going to arrest him, heal him, and put him on trial for all the treachery he's caused this—"

A gurgling sound echoed behind her, and Bella looked over her shoulder again. Another barefoot man stood behind Gastone, his dagger drawing away from her husband. The king gargled, spitting bloody froth and phlegm as his hands came up to his neck.

Bella screamed, but the blood didn't stop. She threw her hands up to send healing Vitaron magic his way, the shock and horror slamming into her full force.

Gastone tripped to the left, saw his attacker, and threw

out a hand. The second stranger burst into flames, blue and crimson hellfire bursting out of the Robin as the fireball slammed into him.

The explosion hit Bella like a wave of heat from the fireplace, and she stumbled back a step, and the other Robin caught her under the arms. The attacker screamed, beating his face as flames engulfed him. The other Robin shouted and jumped forward to help his compatriot, leaving Bella on shaky feet as she stared at the scene.

Stop him. Kill them both.

She threw out her hand, tripping him with the rug as it jerked under his feet. The blazing attacker should die for his treason, and she would not let this one stand in the way.

He lied to you. He was never going to arrest Gastone.

The king turned, one hand on his throat and the other bloody hand rising shakily with flickering sparks on his palm. He glared with wild eyes at the other Robin, prepared to burn him alive, too.

Hide. He's done for.

Bella trembled, fear flashing through her mind as she ducked. Fire shot through the room from Gastone as he slid to his knees.

She choked on the fear like a fist down the throat as the burning attacker fell onto her bed. He had slit the king's throat. He had ended all of her plans to help her friends with one swipe of the blade. Anger burned hot in her stomach, and she twisted her wrist. The sheets and bedding wrapped around him, but instead of putting out the fire, it squeezed him tighter as they, too, burst into flames.

The man exploded and tears streamed down her face.

Liquid rubies of flesh and bone rained like ghastly treasure from the bed. Guts splattered on her headboard, on the window, and across her body, slamming into her with a sickening crunch. She panted as blood splattered across them all.

She looked down. A bone wrapped in ripped flesh rolled near her shoes. The scent of blood filled the room, making her stomach twist.

Shock rippled through her, her body going cold, then hot, then cold again as she realized what she'd done. She analyzed the situation like an experiment, detaching her overwhelmed mind from the horror of the scene before her.

Strangely, there was no guilt like she'd expected. She'd never killed a man before. Instead, a cold sense of calm and numbness settled on her.

He had it coming. You were within your rights to avenge your husband.

Bella's head swung to where Gastone lay on the floor. Her own body was now cold as ice. Blood and gore dripped down her cheek and clung to her hair. Her heart still raced.

"It's too late," Bella whispered, sinking to her knees beside her husband. She pulled the curtains down with magic, dissolved them into ash, and settled them over his body to put out the fire.

His gorgeous eyes stared unseeingly at the ceiling.

She threw her head back and screamed, throwing magic out in a pulsing arch. The transformed woman and the other Robin in the room groaned, and then she registered them scrambling to the door. She heard their footsteps, but didn't open her eyes, too lost in her grief.

The echo of Gastone's heartbeat hit her like she was inside a drum.

Thump thump. It's not too late.

Thump thump. You can keep him with you, learn his magic, and grow stronger.

Thump thump. Isn't that what you want? To keep a part of him with you forever?

Thump thump. To learn all he knows and be better than all the naysayers?

"Yes," she cried, tears streaming down her cheeks and mixing with the blood of her enemies.

Put your hand on his chest and repeat after me. Thump thump.

She followed the mystical voice as if in a trance. Gastone's jacket and shirt ripped apart as she repeated the words, magical words that had no meaning in modern society and language.

It was all gibberish, but she watched in horror as his chest was neatly sliced open.

Thump thump. Take out his heart.

She shook her head. This was awful, it was the exact opposite of everything Lailant had taught her about saving her fellow man. This was destruction, not salvation.

Except you're not a normal human, are you? You're the most powerful mage in the land. Isn't that what you want to be? All the power and knowledge at your fingertips, at the mercy of no one.

"Mercy of no one. They can't hurt me," she whispered the mantra like a prayer.

All you have to do is reach out and grab the heart.

Her hand followed, and she struggled to pull it back. It seemed to have a mind of its own. Her fingers clasped the slippery, sticky, pumping organ and pulled. Magic severed the arteries as she lifted it above his limp, smoking body.

Now go to the vanity. You have all the tools you need to make this potion. Go.

Her body seemed to flash with an inhuman speed. Her pulse raced as if trying to catch up with her body. Her hands flew through the vials and bowls on her vanity, things she'd been collecting over the past few months, things that didn't make any sense but brought her a sense of comfort when she'd laid them on the desk.

Horror and terror clawed at her stomach, and she pushed down the nausea as she squeezed the heart, blood dripping into the bowl. Then she put the heart in the bowl too. It burst into blue flames, and she blinked, turning away from the blinding light.

The light faded, and the mirror rippled with magic.

Now drink it.

She picked it up, the spicy cinnamon smell making her lick her lips. Her body had a mind of its own as the horror and guilt over this entire nasty day seemed to float away. All that was left was her pain, heartache, anger, and rage.

She tipped her head back and chugged the drink, the spice burning her lips like she was swallowing flame. She slammed the bowl onto the vanity, and the mirror rippled again.

She smacked her lips, wincing at the after taste. Her stomach twisted, knotting with pain as she bent double.

Now let it all out, dear. That's a good girl. Let the anger flow.

The good girl sent a stab of pain through her chest, making her gasp. Her father had always said that. It'd always made her feel safe and like she was making him proud. Then he'd gone to war and was probably dead.

She screamed in pain, coming to terms with the fact that none of the king's men had located her father. He was lost, just like her husband. She thought she'd finally found someone to hold her tight and tell her it was alright. A charming husband like Gastone was exactly what she'd needed. He'd praised all her accomplishments the past few months, celebrating with each new spell learned and magical level gained.

And the fucking cretins had killed him. She howled with rage. He'd given her everything!

How dare they kill her husband? She was the fucking queen. In destroying Gastone, they thought they could destroy her, too?

Over her dead body. She'd done nothing but bend over backward in that tavern for twenty-five hellish years. The blood, sweat, and tears that went into that business, and for what?

The little selfish pricks still wanted handouts. They wanted free food and free drinks and thought they should get a discount just because they'd fought with her father in the bloody war.

Oh no, they didn't. She stood over her husband's body, the rage a roiling, magical thing that swept her up. Magic swirled around her until she felt near to bursting.

Then she did burst.

She screamed her rage, throwing more magic out of her body than she'd ever felt before. The potion transformed her, and the absorbed magic from Gastone needed a release. Her body wasn't meant to handle the power and magic of a drakin. She was just a human with magic from her healer mother.

But her mother had died too, long ago when she was just a child. The pain and rage of growing up in a tavern without the calming and sheltering influence of a mother ripped from her, too, sending another pulse of magic.

Her scream echoed off the walls, the grief finally finding the outlet after all these years of keeping it bottled tight within her. The magic twisted her body into some grotesque, hideous monster that could hold all the new magic.

Scarlet hopped down the hallway, her eyes wide with fright. Why was everything so tall? She had to find the safety of the forest. She had to burrow in a hole and hide.

She raced to the stairs and saw servants running and screaming through the foyer below. She slammed into the wall, still unsteady on her new feet.

New feet? She looked down, and her eyes widened. She had soft brown paws for toes and the long feet of a jackrabbit. What the hell was going on?

The stark contrast between the humans below and her own body confused her. She wasn't a rabbit. She'd hunted and eaten rabbit. She couldn't do that if she was a rabbit.

Her stomach twisted at the memory of the roasted rabbit, and she gagged. What sorcery was this? Who was she?

She turned with wild eyes to look at her paws. She sat on her haunches like a rabbit. Her hands were paws like a rabbit, her body was covered in a soft coat of fur like one. A shining object caught her gaze, and she looked over. A mirror had fallen to the ground and was propped precariously on one corner, leaning against the railing of the stairs.

She hopped closer and turned this way and that, her mind racing to catch up with her reality. Eyes wild with fear, she wiggled her little pink nose. Whiskers wobbled as she leaned closer. Large floppy ears hung down her back, mixing with a red tuft of hair between.

She tilted her head, her green eyes shimmering in the

light from the broken window. Her eyes... Those *were* her eyes! She was Scarlet, the daughter of a ranger and a druid.

She'd never had magic before, but she felt the tingle of it flowing down her spine as she realized what and who she was. Her ass itched, and she turned to the side. A fluffy white tail shook.

She sneezed, swiping a paw to her nose as she twisted and pursed her lips and nose. She was a human, but now she was a rabbit. How had this—the king. Her body grew cold, and she shivered.

Then, a scream ripped through the air, making her jump. Her heart raced as she leaped down the stairs, terror licking at her heels.

She was a fucking Hunter. Why was she running? The row of animal heads on the wall of the stairs made her heart race in terror. Her breath caught in her throat as she tripped over her too big feet and went tumbling down the stairs.

Pain raced up her spine as she rolled to a halt. Her tail and whiskers twitched as she blinked past the pain, a prized stag with a giant rack of antlers lay on it's side on the floor, staring at her with blank eyes.

Heavy steps followed her down the stairs, and she threw herself under the stag's antlers and curled into a ball against the wall as the monster came chasing after her.

Except he jumped over the last step and landed with a crash, not even seeing her. The walls shook as more screams echoed above them. A crash made her peek between her paws. Wood and plaster fell over the front door, blocking it as servants and Robins tried to escape. The monster who followed wasn't a monster at all, but one of the Robins. Her mind knew it in a fuzzy way, like a remembered dream.

A blast of magic ripped through the air, and everyone in

the foyer screamed. Scarlet felt her body twist with magic again. Bones crunched, and pain made her gasp as she shimmered.

Her arms lengthened, and she shifted back into her human body. She was relieved, but fear licked at her heels along with anger at being naked. She had already felt off-kilter at having none of her weapons or gear, but now to be naked in the foyer of the castle with a room full of strangers...

She scrambled to her feet and ducked into an adjacent room, falling onto her face at the heaviness on her head. The formal receiving room was dirty, and a maid rocked in the corner crying. Scarlet raced to the debris along the far wall, yanking a curtain that had crashed to the ground. Her head began to ache, and her mouth was dry.

Yet she couldn't stop. She looked for a way out as she wrapped the curtain around her, tying it at her shoulder. She grabbed the gold tie-back cord and used it like a belt, her hands flying in fear of what would happen next. Her eyes scanned the room, searching for a way out, but there was nothing but the whimpering and crying servants in the corner.

She ran to the door and peeked out. More servants poured into the foyer, each talking over the other with more wailing and crying. But they all said the same thing. The doors and windows were blocked.

Screams and vibrations pulsed from upstairs, and Scarlet jumped, diving to the side and crouching into a ball beside the maid. Fuck, what was wrong with her? She didn't hide. She was a fighter.

"Over here," a deep voice yelled. "We can get out through the cellars. Hurry, tell everyone you can find."

"The cellars? Are you mad?" someone yelled.

"No, I'm not," the big man yelled over the others. The walls shook, and more debris fell from the ceiling, crashing around her. She jumped, slamming into the wall behind her. The woman next to her rocked, wailing loudly.

"We don't have time for this. I'm a Robin, and so help me, Borga, if you want freedom, you will go to the cellars. Now!"

His voice boomed, and everyone scrambled to follow his command. Everyone except Scarlet. She cowered in the corner, her spirit wanting to fight but her heart wanting to run and hide. Maybe if she crawled under a table, she would be safe.

The big man came into the room and knelt in front of them, a frown on his stony face. She blinked up at him, hope warring within her even as she trembled in fear.

"Scarlet?" he whispered. "It's alright. We're getting out of here. Are you ready?"

He held out a hand to the maid, and Scarlet wiggled her nose and mouth in fear. He smelled of stone and rain. Another scream from above had her scrambling to her feet to follow him and the maid, holding her head as the weight of it threatened to tip her over.

At another scream, she grabbed his other hand, jumping in fear. She felt bolstered by the touch, and she frowned as he led her down the hall after the servants. Her hand felt so small in his.

What was she doing? She wasn't this little child who needed to be led around by the hand. She stood straighter as they entered the cellar. Voices rose in panic, and the big man dropped her hand.

She flattened herself against the wall as he strode into the crowd and pointed them down the tunnel to freedom. This was familiar somehow.

Her nose twitched, and apprehension pressed on her chest. She walked to a different door, past everyone else, and down into the dungeon. She glanced down at her feet and hands.

She had hands again. Barefoot, she strode down the dark, dank hall to face her nightmare. Memories of her tortuous time here flew through her mind, anchoring her in her human body.

She wiped her forehead, her heart racing. She felt her head, her face. Her heart froze in horror.

She still had the giant ears of the rabbit, but now she had a giant rack of antlers too. She still had the whiskers and a different nose. How long had she wished to be magical and different like her grandmother, like Knox?

But not like this. She never wanted this. What *was* she?

A pain in her ass as she walked made her pause halfway down the dungeon's walk of death.

She reached back, feeling her tail. She grabbed the curtain and ripped just under the belt. Her tail popped free, and she sighed in relief. Then she stiffened, feeling the tail. It wasn't a rabbit's puff tail anymore, but it wasn't a deer's tail either.

It was coarser, like a coyote or wolf. Her fear made her heart race, and her teeth hurt. She felt her mouth, finding sharp canines perfect for tearing into flesh.

The changes made her angry. She stomped the last few feet to the cell at the end and pushed the door open with a creak. The walls shook, and stones tumbled to the floor, but it was muted this far underground.

She stared at where she'd been held for days. She'd cried for ages. She'd been locked in the dark, smelly pit of despair while the king had prodded her, burned her, and cut her, all the while asking questions about the Robins and Knox.

The walls rocked again, and she somehow knew that the king was dead, that he could never get to her again. But the need for revenge lit a fire in her chest. Her tail wagged behind her at the idea, and she grabbed it to hold it still. How could she get revenge if he was dead?

She slammed the door shut on the cell in anger, and it clanged, echoing off the walls. She shut the door on her fear and refused to give in to the childish terrors of the dark.

Long ago, she'd been afraid. Afraid of the dark. Afraid of the monster that visited her every night in her dreams. Afraid of the future.

Then she'd lost her mother and years later, her father. Now her entire world was crumbling around her.

She turned and clenched her jaw, her hands fisting at her sides. She would not be some weak-watered woman who couldn't fight, couldn't defend herself, couldn't forge her own path in life.

So what if she was a rabbit, stag, wolf abomination, an anomaly of nature, a monster unlike any other? She still was who she was. She would not be ruled by this nightmare.

She strode through the cellar and into the tunnel to freedom.

Chapter Forty-Three

Knox flew away from Eirwyn and the edge of the forest, his stomach feeling strangely empty. The ashes of the homes still smoked, but there were no more flames. Some of the younger people ran through the streets toward the edge of the city. A crowd followed, all of them going toward the forest and as far away from the smoking, vine-covered castle as they could get.

He turned his head to see Eirwyn waving to the people. From above, he saw them turn toward her, and he looked back at the castle. An inky blackness began to seep down from the top of the castle, and the walls shook like an earthquake. His chest ached as worry gnawed on him.

He couldn't go to the castle and kill the king. He looked back at Eirwyn. What if the people went crazy with fear? What if they took out their anger and fear on Eirwyn? Who would protect her if he went to the castle and died?

They were pointing at him. He could see their faces, shocked in horror. Several screamed, and a few fainted in the streets.

This was his worst nightmare and exactly why he wore the hood. But he couldn't hide anymore. Not with this giant dragon body, but it wasn't just him anymore. Eirwyn was alive, and he had to find a way for the people to accept him, for her sake.

He dipped a wing and did a slow circle over the city, then flew back to Eirwyn and the edge of the forest.

Eirwyn was walking along the edge to the Lone Road to meet the people leaving the city. He landed in front of her, cutting her off from the crowd that now congregated at the entrance of the forest.

Knox landed with a thud. Would they attack him? Dragons had been hunted down hundreds of years ago. Every face held a mixture of fear, awe, and something he couldn't identify.

Knox stomped his foot, his massive claw digging into the earth as the crowd came to a stop.

Get behind me.

Eirwyn ducked under his body and reached up a hand, resting her palm on his neck. "No, I can help. These are my people."

She came under his other side to stand in front of him, and he looked down at the crowd. He gave a small flap of his wings as he settled nervously. He waited for an attack, but his head told him it was unlikely with children in the crowd.

Several children tried to race forward, curious and full of awe. Their questions tripped over each other, and their parents tugged them back with frowns of worry and fear.

Eirwyn held up her hands. "Please, please, we're going to be alright."

"But princess, what's going on?"

"Who is that? Is that a real dragon?"

"What's happening in the palace?"

"Our homes!"

Eirwyn raised her hands, but the crowd just kept pressing forward, asking questions. Knox flapped his wings, and the air shimmered green. He grew cold, blinked, and then he stood behind Eirwyn.

He was acutely aware of his missing shirt, but he stepped up beside Eirwyn and raised his voice.

"Enough," he demanded, his voice carrying through the field as the crowd continued to gather from the city, growing into several hundred, if not more. "We don't know what's going on at the castle, but if you'd like to seek shelter in the forest–"

The crowd grew antsy, their replies echoing over each other as they cut him off.

"We can't go into the Feral Forest!"

"I've heard there are magical protections."

"We're all going to die."

Knox snorted, and green smoke curled around his nose and sank to the ground. His tail raised to wave behind him, commanding attention.

The crowd grew silent as he stood tall and reached for Eirwyn's hand. He drew comfort and strength from her presence but had no idea what to say. He pleaded with her silently, hoping she would jump in.

Eirwyn lifted her chin. "We're not going to die, not today. I've been in the forest for several days, and Knox can and will protect us as the rightful king of the Feral Forest."

The crowd paused, turning to stare at him. He felt the heat of their gaze and heard the whispers. They didn't know who he was or how he could help. They didn't trust him, and he might not have time to earn their trust, based on the inky blackness seeping over the castle.

He linked his fingers with Eirwyn's and said, "Any who seek safety in the forest will be taken to the village known as Vidrland, the home of the Robins."

The murmurs rose, eyes widening and several people looking around as if waiting to be arrested. But even the guards in the crowd stood still, unsure of what to do or where to go.

Knox continued, "Several of those who were formerly arrested by the king have already been moved to safety, protected by the Robins and the forest's magic. Those who were in the dungeons this morning have already been evacuated from the castle."

Two men pushed through the crowd, and Knox recognized them as Robins he'd sent into the city with the distraction team. They nodded to him, hit their chest with a fist, and bowed.

"Master Warden, what can we do to help?"

Knox's spine straightened as the whispers intensified. He took a deep breath and said, "Tell them what I speak is true. Tell them who I am."

The taller of the two-faced the crowd, his gaze stern as only a former soldier's could be. "It's true. The Master Warden taught us how to travel safely through the forest. He's our dragon king and deals more fairly than the Buspartan king. We vote on all major decisions."

"Not another king."

"I knew I saw a dragon."

"Do you really get to vote as a commoner?"

Knox's brows furrowed as he watched the castle. "Yes, now if you want safety, let's go."

He stepped onto the Lone Road with Eirwyn. The two Robins began to follow along with a handful of others. But most of the crowd stayed on the edge of the forest, talking with each other as they weighed their choices.

Another scream ripped through the castle, and the crowd turned to stare. The white marble turned black as they watched, and many gasped. Mothers pulled their children closer.

"It's a curse."

"The black death! Look!"

"Heavens preserve us."

The murmurs of the townsfolk echoed around them. Knox swallowed hard and rubbed his head. It was time to face who he was. It was probably the only way they'd go with him and escape whatever was going on at the castle.

He wiggled his finger and let go of Eirwyn's hand. He stepped onto the stairs of roots to gaze across the tops of the people. People began to tug on sleeves and point up at him. When every eye turned away from the castle and back to him, he cleared his throat.

"I am the leader of the Robins. I am the king of the Feral Forest. I am a full-blooded dragon, and I will protect what is mine. That includes any who seek safety and follow the rules as set forth by the Robins. You can either come with me into the forest or face the curse that's rapidly approaching."

A few villagers in the back of the crowd began to point to the city. The buildings that still stood closest to the castle were turning black and disintegrating into ash. A blanket of black was slowly creeping toward them.

"How do we know you won't treat us like slaves like the mad king?" came a shout from the back of the crowd.

Knox snarled, green gas blowing from his nose and seeping into the vines at his feet. "Gastone was poisoning the princess her whole life. He paid an assassin to kill their parents. You're right, he was mad, and I killed him."

The murmurs grew, and several people stepped away from him. Hells, this was harder than he thought. But if they wouldn't trust him, maybe they'd trust their darling drakin princess.

He looked down at Eirwyn and said, "You need to show them you can protect them too, princess."

Her brows rose as she asked, "How?"

"Reach for your magic. The mate bond has changed us both."

Eirwyn arched a brow skeptically but reached out a hand. She frowned, concentrating. Then she shook her head.

"I can feel the magic, but it's chaotic. I can't grasp it."

Eirwyn stood in the middle of the broken circle, shadow magic pulsing under her skin, but her breath came short. Her fingers twitched, her mind spinning like a storm. She could still feel the residual pull of the mating bond, her magic reshaped, her body humming with new life—and now this curse, thick and sticky like smoke, crept across the floor toward the edge of the warded space.

She tried to center herself, but her focus kept sliding. The storm inside her wouldn't still.

A small hand tugged at her cloak. "Miss?"

She looked down, surprised to see a boy—barely past toddlerhood—holding something out to her with both hands.

"My wand," he said solemnly. "You can borrow it."

It was short, chipped at the end, with a faint spiral etched into the wood. Eirwyn blinked at it. A child's wand. Nothing more than a training focus, a toy, really. She hadn't touched one in years.

"Thank you," she whispered, bending to take it.

As her fingers closed around the little wand, a tiny pulse of warmth flickered up her arm. No power. Not really. But the gesture... the trust behind it... it grounded her.

She remembered her first wand—light as a feather, but it had taken weeks before she could pour even a trickle of magic into it. That was the whole point. Wands didn't *make* magic. They *helped shape it.* Until the day it wasn't needed anymore.

And here she was, standing in the aftermath of battles and dragons, struggling like a novice again. Her spine straightened. She refused to be the weak link ever again, tired of being pushed to the back to make room for Gastone.

She closed her eyes, held the wand like it mattered, and breathed in.

The threads of her magic settled. She could feel the curse now—its shape, its rhythm.

"Thank you," she said again, louder this time, and turned back to the spreading blackness with steady hands.

She shook the wand dramatically, then pointed at the trees on the side of the road and flared her magic. Her hand shook and lights burst around her head. Then shadows snuck through the trees and turned hard as stone, creating a solid wall where the burned trees had just been still smoking. The crowd gasped, and she sighed in relief. She'd done it! She'd made something lasting with her magic, something that would help protect her people.

Knox grinned, pride spearing through him as he held out his hand to her. She joined him at the top of the vine stairs.

"Eirwyn is your darling princess and my mate. If you

won't follow me to safety, follow her." Knox looked down at Eirwyn and bent his lips to hers.

His mouth was tender, his embrace sure and he tried to pour all his love into it. When the quick kiss broke, they both stood back on the ground, the stairs gone and the foliage creeping back into the forest.

Several of the people began to walk cautiously along the Lone Road.

Knox kissed her forehead. "Take them into the forest. I'll bring up the rear. There should be a dwarf named John with dozens of escaped prisoners somewhere ahead."

Eirwyn frowned at the castle. "We need to find out what's going on there. If Bella is hurt—"

He nodded and sighed. "I know. I'll do another pass over the city and go to the castle to see if I can save her."

She gripped his forearm. "Whatever you do, don't land. The blackness—it has to be a curse. If Gastone died and had some sort of spell set to destroy everything, or Bella got caught up in it, or..."

She trailed off, biting her lip and staring at the castle.

He smiled and kissed her forehead, his chest tightening to see the emerald ring on her finger. He had loved her at first sight, but it was deeper now that he could feel her emotions, now that he knew *her*.

"Don't worry, love," he said. "There's so much we have to talk about and explore."

Her eyes sparkled, and she winked as she grinned. "That's right. Don't go doing anything stupid."

Chapter Forty-Four

The crowd parted, and Lailant walked slowly toward them, leaning heavily on her cane. Some had ventured down the Lone Road with the other two Robins, but most villagers hung back. The adults watched warily as the old woman stopped in front of Knox and Eirwyn.

She stabbed her cane into the dirt twice and tilted her head as if listening to something.

Eirwyn looked at Knox, but he just shrugged and waited. Rope burns wrapped around his torso and arms. She traced the one on his bicep, and he turned to her, pulling her into his arm in a side hug.

Knox's body was stiff, and his chin lifted. A surge of pride went through her that he wasn't afraid to show his face anymore. The scales and horns on the side of his head had reverted to his normal, along with his tail shrinking in size to how it'd been before.

Lailant nodded, "You're right. The king is dead."

The crowd gasped, and Eirwyn felt a weight lift from her shoulders even as a tightness squeezed her chest. She blinked, her mind racing to process and her emotions threatening to overwhelm her.

"How—"

Lailant's rheumy old eyes peered at her, the seer glaring at her. "The how doesn't matter, child."

Knox cleared his throat, looking at Eirwyn with a frown. "I'm sorry, Eirwyn, we were fighting, and I stabbed him in the neck with my tail barb."

She sighed, burying her head in his chest, the pressure on her chest threatening to drown her and only slightly eased by his arms wrapping around her. "Did—did you have a choice?"

She felt his head shake against her hair. "No, if I hadn't, he would've killed me."

She sighed, her eyes closing. "I——that's what I was afraid of. I'm upset, and it'll take time for me to come to terms with it, but it's not your fault he was power-mad and hell-bent on killing us both."

She closed her eyes and breathed deeply, drawing strength from Knox even as she grieved the brother she'd always wanted. It wasn't so much grief for Gastone. It was the fact that now, there was no hope of him ever becoming the brother she'd always wanted.

Lailant continued. "The queen is going to have a hard time adjusting. The curse is settling on the castle as we speak."

Knox's arms tightened around her as she stiffened. "What curse? What's going on? Is Bella alright?"

Lailant nodded toward the city. Still, more people were fleeing, several running toward the forest now as the crowd grew along the road. Eirwyn's throat threatened to close up with worry, and she clung to Knox. Several of the townsfolk listened while still more moved along the Lone Road.

Lailant sighed, resting both hands on her cane.

"The queen has unleashed a power she doesn't under-stand and can't control, a foul incantation born of Nekrosan. She's gained in her magic lessons by leaps and bounds since moving to the castle, but in her grief, she's brought down a curse on us all. It's like an explosion. We're seeing the immediate impact, but the destruction will spread."

Knox's voice was hard when he asked, "How far will it extend? Is it just the city or will it extend to the forest?"

Eirwyn frowned. "What about the rest of the country? What about those still in the capitol and along the coast?"

Lailant frowned. "I'm not sure how much her power will stretch. Knox, you need to change the protection spells on the forest. You can't brand the entire town that comes in like you did with the Robins. There are hundreds, and there's not time, not when you need to extend the wall of the forest too."

Knox stiffened and raked a hand over the side of his head. Eirwyn's heart was heavy, and she bit her lip.

"We don't know that I *can* change them." He looked at the castle and city. The buildings immediately around the castle were gone, nothing more than black ash. Even the trees and stones were gone. The blackness still crept through the city, buildings falling slowly but with terrible force.

"I read about it with Leopol, but it's all in the books. I'm not sure if I can remember it correctly."

Lailant's eyes brightened. "Leopol, you say? How marvelous. He survived."

Eirwyn frowned, and Knox shook his head. "No, he's a ghost. Or he was. He disappeared after we fought the dragon skeleton."

Lailant blinked and cleared her throat. "Ah, the magic

of Hartsgrove is such that I cannot see what happened or what will happen. So you'll have to tell me all about this ghost and dragon skeleton on the way to Vidrland."

Lailant pointed her cane and said, "Change the spells as best you can, and we'll find the books and a solution to stop and reverse the curse. Go on, Your Majesty."

Knox jerked beside her, his eyes going wide. "King? I'm no king."

Eirwyn put her hand on his chest, feeling the rope burns. Anger at her brother flooded her, and she glared at him. "You're more of a king than my brother ever was. You've organized these people, given them shelter, put out the fire. You're *my* king, Knox, now and forever."

His hard gaze softened, and he dipped his head to kiss her. Their lips barely brushed when Lailant began to walk away onto the Lone Road with a chuckle.

"Come along, Eirwyn. Your shadows should weave through the trees along either side of the road to protect the people from the forest while Knox takes care of the protections against the curse."

Eirwyn softly pet Knox's chest then smiled, worry settling in her chest. "Please be careful," she whispered.

He smiled softly and cupped her cheek. "Don't worry. We have our whole lives ahead of us, and I'm not about to jeopardize that. You heard the medicine woman. I'll see you in a few minutes?"

Her chest tightened, loathe to see him go. She'd lost her brother and her best friend today, although she wasn't sure if Bella was truly lost or not. She didn't want to see him walk away, especially with her stomach so tight with nerves and something more.

The possible pregnancy hovered in the back of her mind, and she worried that the battle had caused a problem. She only had Lailant to ask, and now wasn't the time. Tears threatened to fall.

He cupped her cheek with both hands, his eyes serious as he said. "By the gods, we're alright, Eirwyn, and we'll be fine as long as we're together. I'm not going to leave you again, but I do need to protect the forest. I love you, and the thought of leaving you makes me want to scream, but I'll stay inside the bounds of the forest, alright?"

A rush of heat flooded her, and she smiled as a small breeze blew past them. "I love you too, Knox. Don't take too long, alright? I—I don't want to be apart from you either."

Lailant turned and jerked her chin, a group of children running in a circle around her and trying to get a rise out of the old woman. "Come along, princess. We've work to do."

Eirwyn let Knox's hands fall from hers as she stepped onto the road and pulled out the borrowed wand. One child took her other hand as she began to weave shadows through the wall of trees down the road, using them to close the gaps.

She looked down at him, and the small thing pulled his thumb out of his mouth to ask, "Are we really going to live in the forest now?"

She nodded, the crowd beginning to thin as they followed her further into the forest. "For a while, yes. It seems like it. It's going to be a great adventure, don't you think?"

The little boy nodded and stuck his thumb back in his mouth.

She ushered past people, loathe to lose sight of Knox. The little boy dropped her hand and said, "I'm going to my Mama, but when you're done with the wand, I want it back. Mama says it's the most expensive thing we've ever bought."

Eirwyn promised to return it, then he continued on with his parents as everyone followed behind her.

Eirwyn worked quickly, her forehead beading with sweat. When the crowd was spread out, she walked back the way she'd come, weaving shadows through a wall of trees along either side of the road.

She knew this part of the forest, as the secret entrance to the castle was just ahead. She focused on the excitement of learning new magic, but as she worked, so many questions popped into her mind.

Was it all because of their mate bond or had some of it been because of the apple? Or was it simply because her brother was no longer poisoning her? Her chest ached at the thought.

Lailant walked over and began asking questions about Hartsgrove, Leopol, and more. Eirwyn bit her lip as she finished cocooning them with the magical wall, and finally broke down. She told Lailant everything, much like when she'd been a child and had escaped to the tavern. She'd often stop at Lailant's apothecary shop first and vent while she sipped on a potion or two.

At the end of the story, Lailant's rheumy eyes stared over the crowd as she pursed her lips and hummed. Eirwyn was used to it after all these years, but she finally turned to Lailant.

She turned from the crowd. "One question though," she said softly. She put her hand on her stomach, pulling the loose over-sized dwarven shirt tight.

"Is this what I think it is? Is it going to be alright with the battle and stress today?" Eirwyn asked.

Lailant's eyes softened as she smiled, then she stepped up to put a hand on her stomach. Her eyes shifted to solid white, then back again so quickly Eirwyn wasn't sure if it had actually happened or not.

"Aye, this is the start of a new era. The scales of justice are shifting in our favor."

Eirwyn tilted her head and tried to make sense of Lailant's cryptic words.

Sure enough, Lailant continued, "What do you know of dragon pregnancies?"

Eirwyn shook her head. "Just the little that I read in a book, and all it explained was why this happened." She snorted, pursing her lips.

Lailant laughed, her hand dropping and resting back on top of her cane. "The pregnancies are strange. There's not really a *normal* like human pregnancies and births."

Eirwyn groaned and sighed, but Lailant grinned and shook her head.

"Now, now, don't worry too much. For most dragons, once the mating ritual is complete, they will have a honeymoon period. During that time, the egg will grow and be fertilized."

"Fertilized?" Eirwyn asked, her brows rising. "Haven't we already done that?"

Lailant frowned. "Perhaps. I can't quite remember. We'll need to consult the books. What I do remember is that it could be a few weeks or a few months. Then you will give birth to the egg."

Eirwyn's jaw dropped. "Weeks?"

Several of the townsfolk looked over at her sharp tone, but Eirwyn smiled at them and turned back to Lailant.

"The egg will need to incubate for almost a year. During that time, you won't look pregnant, but you'll have all the same symptoms of a dragon pregnancy. Your life still is tied through magic to the babe's."

A movement over Lailant's shoulder drew her gaze, and Eirwyn shifted to peer around a tree. She saw someone coming through the secret entrance to the castle.

She glanced at Knox, still straining as he created a taller wall to slow the spread of the curse. Then she nodded to the entrance.

"We have more refugees," she told Lailant, walking through the small gap in the wall that she'd left open for Knox. The familiar woods and secret entrance were no longer her secret hiding place.

She stopped on the edge of the glen, her brows raising in surprise. A man knelt on the ground, his hand extended down to help someone up the ladder. He was bigger than Knox and looked to be made of solid stone. Her jaw dropped as she saw the stone wings on his back. He was slightly familiar but she couldn't put her finger on it.

He glanced over, then grunted, "Ah, you survived. Excellent."

Her mind reeled. "Um, do I know you?" she asked.

He turned away from the entrance, stood, and offered his hand.

She shook it as he said, "Name's Ashur. I'm a Robin, Knox's second in command. He was anxious about you. Did he survive too?"

Ashur frowned and looked around, and Eirwyn knew he was anxious about Knox. Eirwyn nodded, and he sighed, his face relaxing slightly as he knelt in the dirt once more.

"Great, that's good. Now I don't have to handle this mess. He can." He began pulling the next person up the ladder. Eirwyn gasped as the first one up was the downstairs scullery maid at the castle, except she'd been changed by magic.

"Oh Molly, you poor dear." Eirwyn hugged her, the

feathers on her head making Eirwyn sneeze as Molly began to complain so quickly, Eirwyn could barely understand.

Eirwyn walked her to the edge of the glen and pointed to the gap in the wall of the road. She directed Molly through then turned back to help.

Ashur led more and more people through. Eirwyn kept directing traffic, checking on them, seeing what they needed, and reassuring them they were safe now.

She kept a calm smile on her face even though each person who came through was cursed with twisted features that mixed objects with their bodies. One had table legs instead of real legs, and one had a torso twisted like a wardrobe. There was even a little boy who seemed to be made entirely of wood. Several looked like animated caricatures of furniture.

Every person who came through made her worry about their lives. How would they eat, how long could they live like that, how quickly could they find a cure or curse reversal?

And she worried about Bella. If the state of these people was any reflection on the mental status of her friend, she needed to be there to comfort her. She smiled and listened to the next person, offering reassurances.

She kept glancing back at Knox to see if he was alright. Her gut told her he was growing weaker, spending too much magic.

A familiar woman stepped up the ladder, her round cheeks red from exertion. "Gods preserve us," she muttered, her eyes wild.

Eirwyn raced over to her. "Helga, you're alive," she said, wrapping her arms around her former nanny and maid.

Helga grunted, then hugged her back. "Oh Eirwyn, I've been so worried about you. You're alright?"

Helga pulled back, inspecting Eirwyn. "Well, you look right enough. Unlike myself."

Helga pulled the cap off her head. Her hair fell down around her shoulders, but it wasn't actually hair. Instead, it was leaves. Eirwyn frowned and ran her fingers over one.

"It's tea leaves, dear. What am I supposed to do with tea for hair?"

Eirwyn snorted, her brows rising. "Make tea?"

Helga rolled her eyes and stomped after the last of the people moving through the forest to the road. "There better be some type of civilization in this god-forsaken forest, or I swear..."

Eirwyn shook her head and turned back to the stone man.

The man ducked his head into the hole and said, "Hurry. We need to collapse this tunnel to prevent the curse from entering the forest."

Eirwyn frowned, worry eating at her. She wasn't sure if collapsing the tunnel would work, but it was a different thought that nagged at her. "Scarlet! Have you seen Scarlet? She was with you earlier when you stormed the castle, yes?"

He pursed his lips and nodded. "Yes, she took the brunt of the curse, and it's affected her worse than most of us."

"She's alive then?" Eirwyn asked, her brows rising as she looked around. "Where is she?"

Grimly, he nodded and pointed, but the next person he helped up wasn't Scarlet. "If she's in the crowd, we'll find her. She told me to lead them out and she'd bring up the rear."

Eirwyn felt her heart race, and she bit her lip. The line of people no longer needed her direction so she stepped closer to meet Knox at the end of the Lone Road. She

could feel that he was almost done, and he needed to know
about Scarlet.

Chapter Forty-Five

Knox raked a hand over his head and stared at the village as the blackness began to grow closer. He hoped he could remember what he'd read in the book when talking with Leopol.

He lifted his hands and vines and trees began to grow thick from either side of him. A few more people stumbled toward him, and he kept a break in the living wall to let them through.

He pictured the living wall and extended it in his mind along the forest's edge to the north and south. He wasn't sure how far the curse would extend, so in the north, he took it all the way to the mountains.

In the opposite direction, he stopped at the Southern Road, just in case others in the kingdom tried to flee into Glathen. He wanted them to have a way out if necessary.

His arms began to shake as the magic wove through his veins. The trees grew into massive monoliths, extending four times higher than before and the trunks growing so wide they were as big as houses. He wove vines in the gaps, then pulled up helrose hedges too.

When there were no more movements in the village and the inky blackness was just a few feet away, he pushed the helroses toward the black creeping sand. The blackness stopped when it touched the helroses and receded a foot.

He tested more of it with vines, and just before the inky blackness crept toward his feet, he stepped into the gap behind him and closed the magical living wall.

A sigh of relief echoed through the quiet of the forest, and he turned to see Eirwyn leaning against a tree. She smiled tightly and then bit her lip.

"I was worried about you," she said with a shrug.

Knox smiled, his shoulders relaxing somewhere. "Where is everyone? Did you have any problems?"

She nodded along the road. "I've walled off the road on both sides, and we've decided to camp on the road for the night. It'll be safer to travel to Vidrland tomorrow during the day according to your Robins."

Knox sighed in relief and took a few steps along the road. Not many people had stayed near the edge of the forest, but he could see down the road as people began to congregate into groups. Some were setting fires in the middle of the road, and Knox waved his fingers, pushing the overhanging foliage back so nothing accidentally caught on fire.

"I need to warn you about something," she said, walking up to him and linking their fingers.

He wiped his sweaty brow and walked on shaky legs beside her, drawing strength from her touch.

She looked up at him with a frown. "Are you alright? Did you use too much magic?"

He shook his head. "No, pushed myself but I'm alright. Are you?"

He'd gotten a surge of energy when they'd kissed earlier. He pulled her to his side and wrapped an arm around her waist, lowering his lips to hers. It was tentative at first, but when their tongues dueled, he felt his strength returning.

He broke the kiss, not sure if he was stealing her strength or if being together just caused them both to grow stronger. There were so many questions about this dragon life of his, and Leopol wasn't here to answer.

She smiled up at him, then led him off the Lone Road toward the secret entrance they'd snuck into earlier that day. "Are you alright," he asked again.

She sighed, "I'm fine, just glad you're alright."

He squeezed her hip. "Come on, out with it. It doesn't sound like you're fine. What's bothering you?"

She sighed again as they neared the familiar glen and waved a hand at the sight before them. Lailant stood next to the secret entrance to the castle, the grate open as Ashur helped pull people up the ladder.

Knox frowned. "I thought all the prisoners would've been out of there by now. What's going on?"

Ashur looked up. He looked like he'd aged in the hours since they'd been separated. He turned back to help someone else up through the grate.

Knox blinked. It wasn't really a person though, was it?

The heavyset man heaved through, another voice grumbling behind him. But the man had clock hands for a mustache. His hair looked like the curling wood of a grandfather clock. He stepped to the side and opened his jacket, popping the buttons on his shirt.

"Hobbs!" Eirwyn gasped, running to the man and touching his arm in comfort.

He began to curse. "Hells, your majesty, what am I supposed to do with this?"

Knox rubbed his head but before Eirwyn could answer, the next person came through the grate.

"You're a clock. That's not so bad. Look at me, for drake's sake."

"Miere! Oh thank the gods, I was worried about you two. Cookie is safe. Did you see her come up? She's just gone through to the Lone Road where we've set up camp."

Knox looked at the thin man, his hair dripping wax as a flame flickered from the top of his head. Two more flames rose from his shoulders, and he turned and blew one out.

It relit itself, and the two men began arguing over whose curse was worse, each seeking Eirwyn's counsel as she led them to the road. She smiled and nodded, but just let the men talk. She handed them off neatly to a large woman with an apron.

Lailant stood to the side of the glen, and Eirwyn walked back to her with a frown and began to whisper to the old witch. Knox wanted to wrap an arm around her waist, needed to touch her.

He looked back at Ashur as he handed someone else up from the ladder, but he didn't appear to need any help. So he followed his heart and stepped over to Eirwyn, wrapping an arm around her shoulders.

Eirwyn asked Lailant, "They were caught in Bella's curse? Did it change *all* the people in the castle into something else?"

Lailant nodded. "Yes, the poor girl's gone quite mad in her grief. She's mixed her illusions with transmutation and who knows what else."

Eirwyn's voice shook as she asked, "Did she really love my brother, then?"

Lailant looked at them both. "She thought she loved him, mostly because of that awful mirror."

At the mention of the mirror, Knox's mind whirled. What was so important about that? It nagged at him, but he was too tired to remember what was so familiar. He raked a hand down his face.

Ashur began to close the grate, but Lailant stabbed the ground with her cane.

"Wait, gargoyle. There's one more."

Ashur rubbed his head, and his hair didn't move. Knox blinked, but Eirwyn snapped her fingers. "That's it. That's why you look so familiar."

His friend had been cursed too. His skin was as marble, and his brown hair now looked to be chiseled in stone. Wings hung heavy behind him.

"Did you say gargoyle?" Knox asked, his brows high.

Ashur glared at him, then reached a hand inside the hole in the ground. "Don't start, mate," Ashur growled.

Eirwyn said, "You look just like the gargoyle's that were on the roof of the castle. I used to pretend they were my friends when I was a child, before I learned to escape."

Ashur shook his head with a sigh and pulled a woman up. Knox was tired and still trying to comprehend the change that had come over Ashur, but his heart ached for the little girl Eirwyn used to be, and his arms squeezed around her tighter.

Eirwyn gasped, stepping out of his arms. He immediately went on alert, needing to protect her. He battled with his possessiveness while looking around for danger.

"Scarlet, are you alright?" Eirwyn pulled her forward, grabbing her forearms to check her over.

Knox jerked back to the secret entrance, his eyes shifting to Scarlet in shock at seeing her in a one shoulder dress made out of one long piece of cloth. Apprehension washed over him, clawing at his stomach as his eyes met hers. She had been changed too, and she was not happy about it.

Antlers stuck up on top of her head between two long floppy ears, a wide rack that he wasn't sure how she fit through the escape hole. She had white freckles on her cheeks along with her regular freckles, whiskers, and a pale pink nose. When she turned slightly to hug Eirwyn, he saw a wolf's tail poking through her awkward dress.

Knox stepped over. "Red," he said softly, a knot in his throat. "I thought you'd gotten out with the prisoners."

He pulled her into a hug, lifting her feet off the ground. She stiffened, then slapped his back and rested her head on his shoulder with a sigh and a sniff. His arms grew tighter along with the pressure in his chest.

She sniffed again and said into his chest, "I took a few healing potions, then jumped into the rebellion. What the king tried to do with Eirwyn—it wasn't right."

"But are *you* alright?" he asked, gently setting her on her feet.

"I'll be fine, Knox," she whispered, not letting him go and keeping herself tucked under his arm as she wrapped her arms around his waist.

That's when he knew she was more upset than she was letting on. She never accepted physical affection or comfort, not since her dad died. He held her in a loose side-hug and watched as Ashur jumped back into the hole. They heard banging and the ground shook, then a puff of dust and dirt flew out of the escape hatch.

Scarlet leaned back and they all stepped closer.

Knox crouched at the opening, "Ashur? Ashur!"

The gargoyle's head popped up with a grimace. "I'm here, gods. Back up so I can get out, will ya, mate?"

Knox breathed a sigh of relief and stood, backing up as Ashur pushed himself out of the hold, banging on the wall as he went. More dirt flew up, and Knox waved the women back. Eirwyn stood flanked by Scarlet and Lailant as they all watched Ashur cave in the escape route.

When Ashur stood and began to dust himself off, Scarlet walked over to him with a glare and punched him in the bicep.

He grunted out of instinct, but his skin was tougher now from the shifting scales, so he barely felt it. "Hey, what's that for?"

She put her hands on her hips. "You're the leader of the Robins? This whole time, and you didn't tell me?"

He shrugged and ran a hand over the side of his head sheepishly. "You're a Hunter, Scarlet, and you've stayed away from the forest for a long time. I wasn't sure where your loyalties lay, so I thought it was better to leave you in the dark."

She glared at him and crossed her arms. "Pa would've joined the Robins long ago. Maybe I would've too if you'd have shared about it. We'll never know, will we?"

She shook her head and crossed her arms, cocking a hip and wiggling her nose and whiskers as she glared at him. "I knew there was something going on with you, but it took a rebellion for me to find out."

He shrugged. "I'm sorry, Scarlet. But are you really upset or just chewing me out so we avoid talking about your —ahem..."

He trailed off, and Scarlet's cheeks flushed. It'd been years since he'd seen her blush that brightly. His brows rose.

"I'm not going to talk about it," she said, tilting her head up, then shifting her head forward abruptly as the added weight of her antlers threatened to make her stumble. She huffed and stomped through the glen to the Lone Road.

Eirwyn walked beside Scarlet, chattering and trying to comfort her. "It's not that bad."

Lailant looked at him and said, "She's going to need you a lot more in the coming months. We all will. Seal that hole up to stop the spread of the curse, then start leading your people, Your Majesty."

She nodded, then turned and walked away.

Knox raked a hand over his head and stretched his neck with a sigh. He had so many questions, but he just shook his head, his mind fuzzy from the use of so much magic. It was easier to just do what she said.

Ashur tossed the grate onto the misshapen metal hole with a bang, making him wince.

Knox shook his head, dizziness swarming him. He straightened his shoulders and waved his hands, weaving vines over it and then growing a tree from seed over it for good measure. His hands shook with the effort, then dropped to his side.

Ashur slapped him on the back when he was finished, and Knox almost went sprawling. Ashur jerked him upright and grinned sheepishly.

"Sorry, mate. Don't realize my own new found strength. You going to the Edge?"

Knox thought about it as he straightened. "No, I just need some food and good night's rest. We might need to hunt for some of these people. If any of them pushed themselves in using their magic to escape, they'll need something warm and hearty. They're safe for tonight, but we'll need to set up patrols anyway. It's still Growlers mating season, after all."

Ashur grinned and crossed his stony arms.

Knox raised his brows. "What?"

Ashur shook his head. "Nothing. It's just... you're going to make a great king."

Knox stiffened but didn't argue as they went back to camp, his mind trying to organize and plan what their next steps needed to be.

"Will's dead," Ashur said quietly.

Knox stumbled, and Ashur grabbed his arm again. He straightened and turned at the entrance to the camp. He watched Eirwyn move among the people, smiling tiredly. She made sure those who needed a hand were paired with someone strong who could help. Her eyes met his, and she frowned. He felt a wave of concern, and he shook his head.

She went back to helping the people. John sat on his horse, probably taking inventory with his strange writing tablet as the former prisoners talked animatedly with the refugees from town.

Perhaps it wouldn't be so bad being the leader of all these people, since he had his mate with him. They loved her, and so did he. He swallowed hard past the lump of emotions in his throat.

"Tell me what happened," Knox demanded. Ashur explained how they'd stormed the castle, found the king and queen, and Will's last mission.

"So he killed the king like he always wanted," Knox said softly.

Ashur nodded, and they both stood in silence as they honored their fallen friend.

Chapter Forty-Six

Eirwyn rubbed her back and yawned for the third time in an hour. She was exhausted from flying and yesterday, her mind on autopilot. All day, she and Helga had spoken with each and every person to maintain morale, with Helga noting their needs in a notebook.

The walk to Vidrland was long and arduous, but Eirwyn was in awe of Knox. Sure, the people had no problem talking with her, and she kept the children entertained with shadow and light stories. But Knox...

Last night, a dispute had broken out between a priest and two nobles when they tried to get the first hammock he made for the people. Knox had listened to both sides argue their case on why they should get the first on and resolved it fairly by giving it to the boy who had loaned his wand to her.

This morning, a few nobles had pushed ahead in the line for the meager breakfast provided by the Robins and the castle's cook. The commoners had grumbled, but Knox had stepped in and sent them to the back of the line.

Everyone was talking about this new idea of equality and fair treatment. Some nobles had threatened to go to Glathen, and Knox had told them to go ahead. Eirwyn smiled, still finding it funny.

Then Knox had helped keep the peace and worked with the Robins to transport those who couldn't travel alone. He was a natural leader, and as the day went on, she was more and more impressed.

She could tell the people were too. At dawn, John, the dwarf, went back to Vidrland and gathered carts and volunteers. They'd arrived around lunch with enough food to feed the hundreds on the road.

Soon after lunch, they'd turned off the Lone Road and onto a hidden side road that led north to Vidrland. Knox had ridden ahead, shifting the protection spells so that anyone who stayed on the road would be safe.

He came back with a cart and picked up more families with small children. Then he handed the reins to a Robin and walked to Eirwyn.

She smiled, arching her back and stretching. Her feet ached, and she still hadn't told Knox about the pregnancy.

He let the rest of the crowd pass, then he led her to the south side of the Lone Road. Directly opposite of the small track that went north to Vidrland, he waved his fingers.

The wall of trees began to revert back to normal. Her fingers laced with his, and she followed him just off the southern side of the road. There lay two boulders about the size of a bench. The symbols of three of the gods were neatly carved into both of them. Behind the boulders stood an old tree, blooming with familiar purple-blue flowers.

A heaviness pressed on her chest as she stared at the boulders, so reminiscent of grave markers.

His voice was deep and reverent. "This is where your parents died."

She sucked in a breath, but he just held her hand and continued.

"I was ten when Olive and I went on the annual pilgrimage to the southern ruins. We came upon the carriage accident in the forest."

Her eyes misted, and she looked up at him. "You were there?"

He nodded, not looking away from the stones. "Until then, Olive had kept me away from the Lone Road. I'd never seen anything like that accident before. You were crying, and Olive used her magic to calm you, sneak you out of the carriage, and get us all away from the vampire as he finished draining your parents."

She choked, and he wrapped an arm around her shoulders and kissed the top of her head.

"I held you as a tiny babe and didn't even know what you'd mean to me someday."

The tears ran down her cheeks, and she turned her head to bury it into his chest. Someone had given him a shirt, so sadly he hadn't gone around bare chested all day. Finally her tears slowed, and she stepped forward to lay a palm on each of the boulders.

"You put these stones here?"

He nodded, then he wiggled his fingers. The tree by the boulders lowered a branch. He reached up with his other hand and snapped off the purple-blue flowers.

"I recognize these. You've given me these before." She looked up, the scent flooding her nose as she inhaled deeply, the wind blowing through the leaves.

"This was the perfume she had on that day. The closest

I could find in nature, anyway. She was so beautiful. You take after her."

Eirwyn closed her eyes, another tear rolling down her cheek as she turned to face him. "Thank you for saving me."

He ran a hand over the side of his head and looked away. "I couldn't just leave you there."

She stepped closer but paused, not touching him. "Not just for saving me back then, but for saving me from my brother too. I would've been dead by now if not for you."

He looked down with his glittering emerald eyes, and he reached for her waist. "I will always save you, Eirwyn."

He kissed her forehead softly, then he pulled her into a hug. "But you saved me too. Holding you as a baby made me feel the need to protect you. You lit a fire in my soul that day. If I hadn't met you, I wouldn't have transferred those feelings to the forest. I wouldn't have become the Master Warden of the druids. I wouldn't have saved the wounded soldiers from the war and created the Robins. I wouldn't have stopped your brother from trying to invade the forest."

He trailed off, and Eirwyn let the peace soak into her bones. She longed for a nap under a tree in the late summer sun.

He kissed her cheek and stepped back, looking at her with a frown. "You're tired. I can feel it."

She yawned and nodded. "I've been feeling your emotions too. Do you think it's the mate bond?"

They'd talked about losing his third in command Robin last night when he'd finally crawled into the hammock beside her. Then she'd held him as she'd felt his heart breaking.

Knox looked up and frowned. "I can shift and fly you to Vidrland. I don't know why I didn't think of that sooner."

She shrugged and stretched. "I can fly myself too,

remember? I just haven't felt like I had the strength back to do it."

He tugged on her hand, and they went back to the Lone Road. She gave one last look behind her before stepping through the forest. The boulders and tree were completely hidden from the road.

Even if she and Helga would've made it all the way to this spot of the road all those months ago, they never would've found it.

Knox shifted into his hulking green dragon, but he was smaller than he'd been in the battle. Now he was just slightly larger than a horse.

He laid on all four paws like a dog, his stomach on the ground. She ran her hands over the scales on his head, and he shivered.

Go on. Climb between my wings.

She smiled slowly. "In a minute. I want to explore."

He whipped his head to see her out of one eye, and she grinned and wiggled her eyebrows.

I don't think that's a good idea, Eirwyn.

She ran her hands down his neck to his chest, then turned and walked around him. Slowly, she trailed her hands over his flanks and wings. He twitched but otherwise didn't move, even though his breathing began to grow shallow.

She walked around to his tail, trailing her hand down most of it and rubbing her hand over the dripping tip. He shuddered, the green venom coating her palm as he swung his head around to watch her. She pulled on the waistband of her pants, tugging her homemade belt loose so they barely stayed up.

Then she rubbed her ooze covered hand down her

mound and cupped herself. The warm liquid made her gasp and her nipples pebble.

"We could make a fortune if this worked as an aphrodisiac for everyone," she gasped while touching herself.

He growled. *I don't care about anyone else, just you. I'm going to shift back.*

"Don't you dare." Eirwyn trailed her other hand down his tail to his back leg as he raised onto all fours. He was taller than a regular horse. He'd have to lay on the ground for her to ride him.

But he could ride her first. She slid her hand around to cup his balls, his dick already lengthening and growing even more.

Hells, Eirwyn, I'm holding on by a thread here. I don't want to get violent.

She gulped and set up a furious rhythm in her own pants. "Just do what feels right, Knox, and I'll tell you if it's too much."

She ducked between his back legs and took his dragon dick into her hand.

She jerked in surprise, leaning back and reaching up with her other venom coated hand. "Knox, what the hells is this?"

Both hands wrapped around two different dicks, both coming out of the same base. Knox breathed on her back, and she moved to the side to show him.

Fuck, I have two cocks.

She laughed at his tone of voice. Tone of thoughts? Whatever, she lubed him up with the ooze from his tail and licked her lips.

"Well, this is going to be fun. It just so happens I have two holes, one for each of these big boys. Good thing your tail prepared me for this, huh?"

Knox snorted a laugh, blowing green gas between his legs as he shifted. The scent made her eyes roll, and she squeezed her hands. His laughter choked as he stomped a back foot.

She smiled slowly, anticipation racing up her spine. She couldn't close her fingers around the green and brown ridged lengths. One was longer and thinner than the other, the other as thick as her wrist, but both had wide, flaring tips. The same bumps and ridges that he had on his head in his human form were on his dragon dicks.

When she ran her hands up and down slowly, he oozed green and white pre-cum. Her mouth watered, and she licked the tip of the bigger one. It grew harder than she ever imagined and jumped in her hand. Her mouth stretched wide as she took more of him in. She wasn't sure that she'd be able to get the entire bulging tip in.

But she wanted to feel that painful stretch in her pussy. Excitement raced through her at the idea of him taking her ass and holding her down. She needed it with an ache unlike any she'd ever felt before.

I know what you want, Eirwyn. I can feel it, hear your thoughts. This is a dangerous game, my love.

Green gas billowed around her, and she grew dizzy with desire. She breathed hard through her nose and used both hands to squeeze and stroke as she took his hot, thrusting cock into her mouth.

He began rocking his hips and grunting. He thrust a little too hard, and she fell onto her backside.

She giggled, then tugged off her boots and pants. She spread the pants on the ground to keep from getting too dirty, then rolled onto all fours. She wiggled her ass and reached back to grab one of his cocks. It jumped in her hand, more pre-cum filling her palm to swirl around the tip.

Oh gods, Eirwyn, are you sure? Last chance.

"Please, Knox." She slid him closer. She finally felt him stretch her entrance, the other sliding up her crack and nestling between the globes.

"Go slow, but please don't stop." Desperation clawed at her, and she closed her eyes as she panted.

He briefly paused at her words, then pushed in a gentle rocking motion. In and out, he teased her, the flared tip too wide to go in at first. Her hand let go of his cock, and she fell onto her elbows and knees.

The changed angle helped him slip the tip inside, and her silky heat captured him. She groaned, resting her forehead on her forearms and widening her legs as far as she could.

He stroked the furnace within, and his girth stretched her, finally popping inside. She gasped and jerked in surprise, the sensation overwhelming her.

"Gods yes, that's it."

He gave shallow thrusts but they were becoming more forceful. The green gas blocked her view, intensifying her awareness of him and making her body relax and take it. With each slow and careful thrust, his other cock teased her ass, sliding up the crack and never where she wanted it. Her arousal spiked, and she reached back to grab the other cock.

He froze behind her, his cock jumping within her.

Are you sure? It's bigger than my tail.

She nodded and panted, the pre-cum lubing her and driving her mad with need. He pressed slowly into her ass, and she whimpered, shaking her head. It was too much, she needed a moment to adjust.

But he didn't stop, pushing past her dark ring and making her scream and try to claw away. A claw pressed on the back of her neck, holding her down as he slid inside, stretching her too wide. She tensed and whimpered with every ridge.

This is what you want, isn't it. It's what your mind screams at me, demanding I take you like the animal I am.

She spasmed and jerked underneath him at the thoughts. "Oh gods, yes."

That's what I needed to hear, my precious little cum princess.

Then he slowly eased both cocks all the way inside until his balls slapped against her. She screamed, the pressure and pain sending her straight to an orgasm that took her by surprise. She spasmed which made the tips flare within her and more smoke billow around her.

She was speared by him and so incredibly full. Lights burst around them as he began to withdraw, then thrust back inside.

The flared tips prevented him from withdrawing all the way, making her flinch and moan. She screamed again, writhing beneath him, his claw holding her down between the shoulder blades.

Words tumbled out but sentences were beyond her. "Oh gods, oh gods, oh gods."

She needed more. He was so big, impossibly huge, and it hurt so good. Her walls tightened around his shafts, milking him in an age-old animal mating.

Her legs began to quake and tremble as he rode her body with the passion of a beast. The raw rhythm shifted, and he began to slam his hips, his body hard and primal against her.

More? Gods, yes. I'm going to destroy you in all the ways you want, Eirwyn. You're mine, my mate, my love.

He shifted, cocooning her body between his legs and under his belly. A hump of soft grass and flowers rose to meet her stomach, holding her hips in place. The angle changed as the ground rolled under her, and she moaned, gasped, and writhed.

The slapping of flesh made her whimper and go wild. "Mmph. Ysss."

Words escaped her, only the pleasured cries sweeping through her, mixing with his feral animal grunts of desire. He took her with a pounding need and a driving harder, their hearts beating, bodies melding as she opened herself to him heart, body, and soul.

She was so close, just a little further.

Further. He grunted, more gas making her body relax even as she approached the crest of orgasm.

He stretched her to the limit, and her inner walls rippled against him. Each hard thrust sent her reeling, and he pistoned harder, his shaft slicking in and out.

Her jaw dropped as she reached the peak, and a soul-shattering orgasm robbed her of her senses. She screamed into the forest, tension inside her exploding. Birds flew away in fright, and her body shook as she gave into the moment with total surrender.

Heat streaked through her. Her body went taught, and she erupted. There was no thinking. There was no time or space or anything except the joining of their two bodies.

Her body spasmed around him, lost in the throes of pleasure until his body tensed around hers. Then she felt the tip flare even more.

He went savage. The claw on her neck pushed her down into the dirt. He slammed into her with a ferocity that left her screaming. Her body shook and her pussy ached from the relentless pounding.

His hips hit her backside, roughly sending her forward. She thrashed under him, and he held her neck down.

Being confined made her go wild. She met him thrust

for thrust, stroke for stroke as her orgasm just kept rolling, wave after wave of intense pleasure that made lights burst all around her.

The fury of his deep thrusts filled her, and she craved his release. She was desperate for it, and she whimpered. She couldn't take much more of this animal rutting, the stretching making her clench in pleasure with every thrust. Her vision began to dim on the edges.

Still she wanted more. She widened her legs, drawing him deeper and making tears sting her eyes from the deep painful pleasure.

Something tickled her mouth and she opened wider, his dragon's tongue thrusting inside like that first night when she'd sucked his cock. A similar taste to the venom on his tail made her suck harder, moaning as she swallowed the sticky liquid. The kiss distracted her from the pain until all that was left was pleasure at the triple penetration. She hummed and screamed, garbled sounds of mindless ecstasy.

He tensed and his thrusts slammed her into the ground. His release was hot and violent, savage like him, and she gloried in it. With a roar and scream from them both that sent more birds flying from the trees, his hot seed coated her insides, filling her holes like lightning.

Green gas filled her nostrils, paralyzing her with plea-sure as she sucked on his tongue and swallowed the deli-cious ambrosia. At the explosion and heat, her entire body shuddered. A final scream ripped from her throat as her silken sheath clenched around his hot ridged members.

A raw, rippling wave washed over her from breasts to thighs. It washed her mind clean of all reason as she spasmed and writhed under him. She stiffened and convulsed, a cry of satisfaction on her lips. Her vision went white, and she closed her eyes for endless moments of pure pleasure.

Still, he flooded her in pulse after pulse of lava-like spurts, his body jerking hard and driving her further into the dirt. Each spasm of his sent off a chain reaction in her as they fueled each other's climax. Their bodies were fused in one shared release that defied all probability.

Eirwyn panted, her body shaking softly as he slowly pulled away, releasing his hold on her neck and removing his tongue. She sucked one more time, drinking the nectar from him before he pulled completely away. His head moved back, and she hissed as his flared tips lodged inside.

Am I hurting you?

He moved again, shifting the grass and flowers under her to cradle her body as he tried to pull out once more.

"Gods, just wait, Knox. Just, give me a minute. Be still."

He froze at her words, his dragon body still locked into her ass and pussy as he cocooned her.

Hells, I'm so sorry. Are you alright?

She laid on the soft grass with a sigh and nodded, hoping he could feel her emotions because she wasn't able to form words right now. She smacked her dry lips together. "I'm —I'm just so full and too sensitive for you to move just yet."

She just wanted him to stay inside for a while.

I'd stay here all day if you'd let me.

He chuckled, the vibrations of it making her gasp and another ripple of aftershocks flowing through her wet core. She was replete, more satisfied than she'd ever been.

She grinned as her breathing slowed. "I have no problem with that."

I love you, Eirwyn.

415

I love you too, she thought as she yawned and slipped into a dreamless sleep.

Chapter Forty-Seven

Knox stood in the lodge later that evening to meet with his trusted advisers, his mind clear and his body relaxed from loving Eiwryn in ways he'd never imagined.

John had a map of their current buildings, tents, and treehouses. Knox ran a hand through his head as they planned how to expand so that everyone would have shelter for the upcoming winter.

They'd all made it safely to Vidrland, except for Scarlet who had decided to go straight to Olive and seek advice.

Knox felt a renewed energy from sleeping with Eirwyn earlier in dragon form. It had taken nearly an hour for his tips to deflate enough to slip free without making her wince.

Then he'd carefully cradled her in his claws and flown them both to Vidrland. She'd slept through the entire thing, which he was grateful for. She was exhausted. Was it just three days ago she'd been in the Beyond, so close to death?

He'd tucked her into the treehouse he normally stayed in, covering her with blankets in the hammock bed, then had gone to see how to help get everyone settled.

Now that dinner was ending, several others were trickling into the main lodge. He kept catching snippets of conversations as he talked with John, Ashur, the two old druids, and the other half dozen trusted Robins around the table.

"He lets just anyone listen in on political meetings? How original."

"What's this voting thing about? How does that work?"

"Did you see him fly into town this afternoon with the princess? Wait, is she still a princess or is she a queen? Is this a town, a city, or a village? What are we?"

The last one had made his lips twitch as the teenager had hit the nail on the head. What were they?

Just then Lailant tapped her cane on the floor where she sat at the table. She'd insisted on joining them at the table and listening in.

Lailant looked at Knox. "Are you ready to assume the mantle of responsibility you were born to?"

Knox nodded silently, his jaw clenching. She must've heard the teenager too, but it was the best way to protect Eirwyn and the forest.

Then Lailant nodded her head and arched a brow. "Then you know what to do."

He sighed and rubbed his head as he looked over the growing crowd. Eirwyn walked through the door in a beautiful red dress, smiling and nodding as she listened to one of the cursed castle servants. A human watering can who seemed to leak water out of his sleeves.

Knox consulted with the others at the table, then he lifted his voice to the crowd and said, "We're going to have our first public meeting in one hour. Spread the word. Anyone can join but we need to outline some rules, policies, and procedures so all remain safe here."

Eirwyn came to him, and he leaned down and kissed her cheek.

"How are you feeling?" he asked softly as people began to stream out the door to invite others to the meeting.

"Sore." Her wide grin and twinkling eyes made him pull her closer to his side.

"Have you eaten dinner?" She nodded so he continued. "In that case, let's take a quick dip in the hot springs. John, we'll be back in half an hour. You have the agenda drawn up with our talking points?"

John nodded, so Knox placed his hand on the small of Eirwyn's back and led her through the bustling crowd. Before they walked through the door, a stray thought had him turning. He took in the large room. They'd never be able to fit everyone inside.

Eirwyn seemed to know what he was thinking because she squeezed his hand. "In the capitol, there's a colosseum with rows of bench seating. Could you make something like that in here?"

He ran his other hand on the side of his head and nodded. He took a deep breath and waved his fingers. On three sides of the building, he built rows of benches, angling them down toward the center of the room with the least amount of head room where the wall and ceiling met at the very top of the benches.

He created three sets of stairs and aisles but left a wide area around the central oval table and near the massive fireplace on the fourth wall. Those still inside yelped at the shifting floor and walls, but none of them fell.

When he was done, he sighed, and Eirwyn looked up at him, pride shining in her eyes.

"That was amazing." Her voice was awed, and he felt his cheeks heat.

"Wait until you see how we're going to build up the town." He grinned and led her outside.

He was going to need to push back the wall of trees around the growing town, but it would have to wait until tomorrow. They approached the S path entrance to the hot springs. It was tucked in a secluded glen, and he was grateful to see it empty. Everyone was scrambling to prepare for the meeting.

He wasn't worried, though. With his mate by his side, they could handle anything.

"You're rather quiet tonight," he said softly.

She sighed and leaned her cheek on his arm as they entered the glen. "I know. It's just a lot to take in. My brother is dead, my friend is... well, I don't know what Bella is anymore. And Scarlet—"

"Will be alright. She's tough, a survivor, and she has Olive's help."

Eirwyn sniffled and nodded. "I know, but she's stuck in the forest now unless she goes into Glathen. Some refugees are Hunters, did you know? What will they do for income? How are we going to feed all these people through the winter? And there are so many Growlers to the south."

Knox waved his fingers on the edge of the hot springs and formed a bench. He sat and cupped her face, wiping her tears away. "It's going to be fine. We're going to build up Vidrland into a proper town and protect the people. That's what our meeting will be about tonight. I'll explain how we're going to build shelters, where we'll find food, and how we'll set up a trade network with Glathen, with your help that is."

Her brows rose. "My help? Really?"

He nodded and sat back with a smile. "Absolutely. I

can't lead people without you, Eirwyn. You can help negotiate a treaty and convince Glathen to recognize our reign."

A stab of apprehension flooded him at her stunned
expression.

"Our—oh, Knox, I love you so much." She wiped the
corner of an eye then threw her arms around his neck.

"I love you too, princess. Although I should probably
call you my queen now, huh? Can we have a coronation
ceremony tonight? I'd like to claim you in front of the entire
world, if you'll have me? I don't have fancy jewelry or a
crown, but will you marry me, be my mate, my Feral
Queen?"

Eirwyn gasped and pulled back, her eyes shining with
excitement. "Oh Knox, I'd love to. You know, I've always
hated the idea of matters of the state. Politics was always
something I despised, possibly because I always felt lacking
around Gastone."

He frowned and turned her around to unbutton her
dress. Where she'd found a dress that fit her reasonably well
he had no idea. But the soft blue and red cotton was perfect,
gathering under her breasts and hanging to her toes. It was
a simpler style the women in Vidrland had adopted over the
years, as they needed more movement than the tight bodices
of Busparia or Glathen allowed.

"If you don't want to be involved, that's alright too. I
was thinking we can rebuild Hartsgrove and live there? If
you'd like, that is. Maybe even a town around Hartsgrove
manor, if I can find a way to shift my mother's protection
spells. Would you like that?"

He wasn't a fan of towns but since he'd stopped wearing
his cloak and hiding who he was, it didn't make him anxious
anymore. Perhaps a town where everyone accepted him
wouldn't be so bad.

Eirwyn clapped and nodded. "Yes, we can raise our children there!"

Knox's eyes widened at her exuberance, and he swallowed hard. "Kids, yes. I hadn't ever thought of having kids before."

She bit her lip and dug her toe in the dirt as she looked down, suddenly apprehensive. He felt it come off her in waves. "Do you want kids?"

Her erratic emotions gave him whiplash. "I think so, but I'd like to wait a while though. We need to get Vidrland built up, Hartsgrove rebuilt and a town started, and convince Glathen to recognize us as a nation, sign a treaty, and establish a trade agreement. That's probably going to take some negotiating with the Growlers too."

He undid the last button on her dress and let it fall to the ground. She turned and put her hands on the hard knot that was her stomach. "Well, I think that ship has sailed because we're pregnant."

He stared at her stomach and blinked, his jaw dropping. "Are you—are you sure? Oh gods."

His mind raced as he leaned forward and put his hand on the small bulge, feeling how hard it was. It was the size of an apple, but definitely something that hadn't been there a few days ago.

She bit her lip then rushed out, "Lailant confirmed it, yes, plus the book you left at the dwarves mentioned how likely it was, which definitely helped me stop panicking when I woke up with it."

"Oh gods, how long do we have to prepare? My egg was the size of a human newborn. How are you going to give birth to that and survive? Humans are slippery and long, but an egg is wide, and you're so petite—"

Eirwyn chuckled and kissed him, stealing his breath. He

swallowed and invaded her mouth, making her moan. She teased his tongue, dueling and teasing him with her plump lips.

His panic over her safety shifted into racing desire, and his balls grew heavy. He pulled her closer, reaching for her body. But she pulled away, breaking the kiss and looking up at him with raised brows.

"Take a deep breath, that's it. Now for the rest of the news."

He gripped the sides of his head and turned to pace in the confined space. "There's more?"

Eirwyn's throaty chuckle made his tense shoulders relax. "Lailant said dragon pregnancies aren't like human ones. We're mated though, so my body has changed. I'm suited for this, Knox, and I'll be alright."

He breathed deeply through his nose. "I just need to protect you and keep you safe, my love."

She smiled and cupped his cheek, running her hand up and over the scales at his temple. "I know, and I love you for it. We'll get the books from the dwarves and Hartsgrove and find everything we need to know. And if that doesn't work, we'll see if we can find answers in Glathen or Busparia's capitol libraries, assuming Busparia is safe to enter."

He pulled her head to his chest and breathed slowly, just holding her and ensuring she was safe. He wanted to be like this always.

"Is—are you upset?" Her voice was small and vulnerable, and he pulled back and looked into her blue-gray eyes as he sank to his knees.

"I'd never be upset over this, Eirwyn. This is a miracle that I never expected to have. Thank you."

Knox kissed her stomach reverently, and some of the tension in her shoulders eased as she smiled. His chest felt near to bursting with joy, and he swept her up in a hug that brought her off her feet.

She laughed and wiped a tear from her eye. "I didn't think I'd ever want to settle down. I didn't want some man telling me what to do, but then you came along."

He nuzzled her neck, holding her naked body in his still clothed on. He kissed up her cheek to her lips. "I will never treat you like your brother did."

"I know," she said with a soft smile, her eyes so full of trust.

He kissed her forehead. "I'm ready to settle down with you too, Eirwyn. Settle down into the sweet, wet depths of your pussy."

His words made her giggle, and his dick hardened as he nipped her bottom lip. Now that he was back in human form, he was down to only the one cock, but that was alright with him as long as he could still satisfy his queen.

"Knox, we don't have time," she gasped and giggled, squirming against him and rubbing herself up and down.

He groaned, kissing her lips softly. "I know, I know. Just a kiss."

He swooped in to steal a kiss. He devoured her, a promise of what he intended to do later tonight. She kissed like an angel and fucked like a demon. He never wanted to stop holding her, touching her, being near her.

When they finally broke the kiss, they were out of time to dip into the hot springs. He helped her pull her dress back up, but his hands must've wandered too much because she was laughing and slapping him away. She finished the last few buttons herself, then they walked arm in arm back to the lodge.

Eirwyn chuckled again, surprised by ringing truth of their conversation. She really was ready to settle down now, be a mom, a wife, a queen. It's funny how she wanted to fly free of all the responsibilities just a few weeks ago.

And now her life was completely different. She could literally fly and escape anytime, but the responsibilities, rules, and structure of society didn't weigh on her shoulders like it did before. Perhaps it was because they were forging a new society in the forest. They could set the rules so that they were fair and logical for all. Her voice mattered now, and she was useful.

When they walked into the lodge, a hush fell over the crowd. It was packed and standing room only, even with the addition of the benches that were angled almost to the ceiling. They walked down the newly made center aisle hand-in-hand to the oval table in the center of the room.

Lailant sat along with the dwarf and gargoyle. Two old druids sat along with six others whom she assumed were former soldiers and Robins.

Knox pulled out two chairs side-by-side around the table, and they sat. Ashur stood and turned to the crowd as Knox took her hand in his.

She hadn't ever attended a Council meeting with her brother, so she wasn't sure what to expect. But somehow, she doubted it was quite like this.

John slid two pieces of paper over to each person on the table. Eirwyn read through each line as Ashur spoke.

Ashur outlined the Robin's code, the core rules that governed them all. He explained how he'd come to be in Vidrland and how he and Knox had formed the Robins. Then he explained how Knox had been born from an egg.

Eirwyn flipped the page, her brows rising as she read the agenda and plan for the fledgling nation.

"He *is* a dragon, the first this world has seen in hundreds of years, but that's not something to fear. All his life, he has protected this forest and its people, well before he realized it was his birthright. I would like to formally nominate Knox to be king of the Feral Forest. Do we have anyone to second?"

One druid said, "Aye, I'll second the motion."

Ashur nodded and proceeded. "All in favor will say aye and all opposed with say nay. All in favor, say aye."

Ayes chorused around them, the loudest coming from the Robins. Then Ashur said, "All those opposed, say nay."

A louder group said nay. Knox squeezed her fingers and stiffened in his chair. Ashur looked at Knox, and Knox nodded, his voice projecting even though he didn't stand up or release his grip on Eirwyn's hand.

"If anyone has concerns to voice, do so now. There will be no repercussions."

Someone shouted from the crowd, "We just got rid of one tyrant. We don't want to exchange it for another."

Knox nodded, and several others murmured their assent. She could feel his disappointment and frustration. He just wanted to protect the people, but if they didn't let him...

She bit her lip, bouncing her leg as an idea began to take root.

Chapter Forty-Eight

Eirwyn squeezed Knox's hand and leaned over to whisper. "Can I try something?"

He nodded, and she stood. She was used to telling stories for the tavern, but this was a much larger crowd. All eyes turned to her, and she took a deep breath.

"It might help to show you what the plans are of the— are you called a Council?"

One druid pushed up his glasses and said, "We prefer Confederation."

She nodded and threw a kaleidoscope of lights into the air, then twisted her hands to form shapes. "The Confederation is the law governing body and will be composed of the king, the druid judges, and the ranking members of the Robins. They have come together and created a plan for economic and political stability. Let me show you."

She showed the map of Vidrland as it was now, throwing the map onto the flat wooden ceiling. Then she led them through each step that was on the papers John had passed out.

"First, they will build shelters. This—"

Knox interrupted her, "We."

She looked at him, and his brow rose. Her heart fluttered as she looked back up at the ceiling.

"Yes, we will build shelters like this to expand Vidrland. See, the market district will be here and the houses here. All house lots will be the same size, so there will not be a ghetto or a noble district. You can build whatever house you want as long as it fits on your lot."

"Aye, but we ran into this god-forsaken forest with only the clothes on our backs. How are we going to *pay* for these houses?" someone shouted.

Eirwyn shifted the dancing lights, shrinking the town to show a map of the forest and surrounding nations. "Excellent point. We have two primary options and a third, longer option. First, we can set up a trade agreement with Glathen. I almost had them ready to a peace treaty, before the Chancellor of Busparia shut it down."

Murmurs rose in the crowd, and Eirwyn sent a burst of light to get their attention. When they quieted, she continued.

"Once we get them to formally recognize us as a nation-state, we will have access to their resources. We have a monopoly on the lumber industry, but did you know that the mountains to the north are full of gems? Gems that have been inaccessible for hundreds of years."

Excited chatter echoed through the room as Eirwyn showed them the vision as she understood it.

John pointed above their heads. "There used to be two mining operations by Glathen and Busparia, but when they killed off the dragons, they lost access to the mountains right there. See that valley? We could develop a mining town there on the shores of the river."

Knox pointed to another spot on her map of lights. "There are also technology items that the dwarves have invented. We can set up an assembly line factory to produce those technology items and sell them. There's a way to put a spell on each item so that no other nation can duplicate the technology."

He summarized half a dozen items they'd used on their way to Hartsgrove, and Eirwyn threw a light burst at the ceiling for each one, showing the crowd what they looked like.

Then Knox pointed to another spot. "This is Hartsgrove Manor. It's the castle built by my ancestors and my birthright. Even if you do not elect me as king, I will keep that castle, the land around it, and what is mine."

He gave a hard stare across the crowd and some murmurs died to whispers.

Lailant slammed her cane on the floor twice and said, "To serve and protect is his birthright. To ask him to do neither is like telling a fish not to swim."

Eirwyn showed them the next steps to a treaty with the Growlers and a port in the treacherous northern border to export goods through the mountains.

"So there are plans in place to make money, and the opportunities are solid businesses. If you put in the work, you can absolutely afford a house."

"I just want to go home," a woman cried out.

Eirwyn frowned and nodded sadly. "I know, me too. But we might not have a home to go back to. We need to research so we don't walk back into a death trap. There is also a proposal to send delegates into Busparia via the Southern Road to see how far the curse spreads. We—Knox and I—have books in Hartsgrove that might help us find a reversal spell. If not, then we intend to ask Glathen for access to their libraries."

"We can't trust Glathen," someone shouted.

Eirwyn shrugged. "We don't know yet if we can or not. But these plans are moot if we don't have a leader. They won't recognize a Confederation of citizens all united as one. The kingdom needs a face to represent us to the world, someone with a strong hand and a brilliant mind, someone who will listen to concerns and take action to solve problems."

"That would be you, princess," another cried.

Eirwyn laughed and the lights on the ceiling danced in a rainbow of colors. "I'm more than willing, but I've never been a leader. Gastone kept me out of politics. The only way this is going to work is for Knox and I to rule together."

Ashur banged his hand on the table, and papers jumped. "Aye, on that note, I would like to make a motion for both Knox to be proclaimed King and Eirwyn to be our Queen of the Feral Forest until either of them cannot perform their duties, at which time we will hold another election."

There was a brief pause, and no one seconded the motion. Then John said, "Perhaps we will get more support if we put a limit on it and hold re-elections? Say every five years?"

Ashur nodded. "Same motion as before but changed. Knox will be King, and Eirwyn will be Queen for five years, at which point we will vote to keep them or to elect new representatives. All in favor, say aye."

The crowd's voice rose as one. Then Ashur grinned. "All those who oppose, say nay."

Less than half a dozen said nay, and Ashur banged his fist on the table again.

"The ayes have it. Congratulations, Your Majesties."

Eirwyn released her magic with star bursts of colorful lights, and the crowd clapped as she sat back down with a smile and reached for Knox's hand again. He grinned and leaned over to kiss her.

When they broke apart, John was sliding a canvas bag across the table to Ashur. He flipped open the top of the bag and pulled out two simple golden crowns, the metal twisted and carved to look like wood, both with a single green emerald.

He walked to stand behind Knox and lifted the larger crown. "I have known Knox for a decade, and I doubt I'll see this on his head much. He's not one for putting on airs. He's a good man, a hard worker, and a protector to his core. I think you're going to like having him as king."

Knox froze, sitting straight with wide eyes as Ashur placed the crown on his head. "I decree in the presence of those here and by the authority granted to me by the Confederation of the Feral Forest and the gods themselves that you are Knoxious Clawson, King of the Feral Forest. All hail the king."

The crowd chanted, "All hail the king."

Then Ashur moved to stand behind Eirwyn with the smaller crown. Apprehension made her sweat. It had all happened so fast tonight, but she wouldn't let go of Knox's hand. If they were together, they could do anything, even lead a country.

Ashur repeated himself, saying, "You are now Eirwyn Clawson, Queen of the Feral Forest. All hail the queen."

The crowd picked up the chant, alternating between calling them queen and king. Knox stood, tugging Eirwyn to her feet, and lifted their hands in the air as the crowd roared. Eirwyn threw more light bursts into the ceiling, adding to the festivities as she grinned.

Knox then pulled her into his chest. She gasped, and he swooped in to steal a kiss. The crowd's roar threatened to deafen her.

You amaze me, Eirwyn. Where I am weak, you are strong. Thank the gods, you're my mate because there's no way I could do any of this without you.

She felt a tingle and thought, *I wouldn't do this without you either, Knox. I wasn't kidding earlier. I never wanted to be part of politics, but together—*

He interrupted, *Together, we can protect our people and reverse the curse on Busparia and Scarlet.*

And save Bella.

His tongue dueled with hers, and her thoughts fractured. She wrapped her arms around his waist, and the kiss deepened. The wind swirled around them, and magic flowed through her veins.

Ashur's voice brought them back to reality, and they broke the kiss.

"Thank you all for coming to the meeting tonight. We are going to set the plans in motion tomorrow. If you have questions, come to the lodge. We'll have the plan written out and posted on a bulletin board by the door, but you can always ask us anything. Also the list of rules of Vidrland are posted by the door too. Please review it, as we'll discuss any changed the people want made at the next public meeting."

The crowd began filing out to find a place to sleep, and the Confederation began talking quietly while John cleaned up the papers on the table.

But several dozen looked like they wanted to approach, so Eirwyn smiled at them. They bobbed curtsies, and she chatted as they talked about how excited they were about the gems. Everyone was tired, but most had a smile on their faces. Two nobles met with Knox, and he listened and nodded.

A tug on her skirts had her bending down, and a child handed her a wilting flower. She took it in her hand and slowly and gently fed it magic. The flower bloomed, perking up. Then she handed it back to the child who grinned and took off to his mother, handing her the flower.

Her entire world had changed in just a few short months. No more living in fear, no more being sick. She now had new magic, a new place to live, and a new fated mate. What would the next few months bring?

Her stomach twisted, and she frowned as the last of the people walked away. For once, it wasn't from nerves. She glanced down and bit her lip.

"Knox, the baby," she gasped, her hand going to her stomach. The bump had grown. It no longer fit in the palm of her hand. Knox put his hand over her bump, his eyebrows raising. It barely fit in the palm of his hand.

Lailant walked past them, leaning heavily on her cane. "Ah, I see you've fertilized the egg. Keep doing that until you deliver it."

Eirwyn looked at Knox, her mind racing back to their mating earlier today. She felt her cheeks heat, and Knox grinned wickedly. She giggled.

There should definitely be more of that in my future, she thought.

Knox swept her into his arms and strode for the door. "Happy to serve, my queen."

Next in the Royal Oath Series

vinci-books.com/oathofrevenge

A cursed Hunter. A wounded Growler. An alliance neither wants—but both need.

Hunter Scarlet stumbles upon a wounded Growler in her grandmother's cottage. To break her curse and reclaim his tribe, they must work together.

Turn the page for a free preview…

Oath of Revenge: Prologue

The old woman's medallion glowed brighter with each minute she hesitated to answer the summons. She didn't want to face them again, not yet, not until she had fixed this. But there was no time for delay.

With a burst of energy that contradicted her age, she quickly tossed the special blend of herbs into the stone hearth along the wall of the one-room wooden cabin.

Purple and green flames flashed, and she closed her eyes as smoke billowed from the fireplace. Her mind spun, and she felt like she was falling. The magic pulled her apart, cell by cell, knitting her back together as she tumbled through the portal. A silent scream ripped from her throat as agony filled her. The burning flow of magic twisted and turned, offering no relief until she slammed into the floor, breathless and disoriented.

She lay there for gods knew how long, staring at the glowing medallion shape that matched her necklace on the door in front of her. She focused on her breathing and the glow, willing the pain to recede.

The magic listened, healing her by the time the light faded from the emblem on the door and her necklace stopped burning her skin. The sweet, citrus air that was only found in her homeland filled her nostrils as she slowly sat up.

Carvings as old as time itself adorned other doors like hers along the open-air corridor. She eased onto her feet and brushed her shaking hands down the white silk dress, thick stacks of golden bracelets jingling with the motion. The sight of the large, vibrant tree in the courtyard brought a pang of nostalgia. Birds swooped and played in the branches, but her gaze didn't stop to watch them.

There was an excessive amount of overgrowth. A quick glance down made her frown. Vines and weeds grew thick around the base of the tree. Her father never would've let this happen. The ache in her chest drew her gaze through the thick foliage to the corridor on the oppo-site side of the square building. That corridor housed only two doors, and she yearned to see the white and gold one restored and not this hacked and chipped, lifeless monstrosity. All life and magic had drained from it, just like her father.

Her chest burned with emotion as her gaze swung to the other door. Solid black, apart from the gold and red veins swirling along the surface as it vibrated and threatened to come off its hinges. Fear snaked down her spine and sent her down the hallway to the great room.

There was only one reason for a summons like this, and dread made her stomach twist as she went through the wide, tall marble archway.

The meeting room stretched the entire length of the building and it, too, was open to the elements. That used to be a good thing in this land of perpetual spring, where it never rained or snowed... but that was back when her father was alive.

Now, vines and ivy grew around the columns between the open windows, threatening to choke out all life. She paused in the doorway, the signs of decay and overgrowth driving her fear and anger into overdrive. Magic pulsed just under her skin, making her itch and want to expel it for relief from the raging emotions.

But she wouldn't—couldn't—do that.

If only her father and uncle had controlled their own emotions... They'd all be together, eating family dinners along the long, low table in the center of the room. Mother would sit at Father's right hand, and they'd both laugh with her brothers, sisters, cousins, aunts, and uncles.

Her gaze turned to the far end of the table where *that* uncle had always sat. No matter how clean, open, and airy the room was, the sun had never shone on his end of the table. Many in the family drew straws to see who would sit next to him. Someone always ran away in tears or tried to flip the table in anger before the end of the meal.

But Father had always diffused the situation with a laugh until that fateful day that she had tried to forget for hundreds of years. Tears pricked her eyes as birds flew in and out of the open arches. She focused on their movements, willing herself to calm. Stay rational, think logically, detach her emotions.

All wasn't lost like it had seemed all those years ago. The tree was still alive. Magic still flowed throughout the room, the gold pulsing occasionally over the floor and walls in ribbons so small one had to know they were there to see them.

A movement from the table drew her gaze. Almost directly in the middle sat one of her sisters, arms crossed and frown in place as she stared into the bowl of fire in the center of the marble table.

The fire couldn't quite diminish the smell of ripe ambrosia on the vine, and she breathed deeply as nerves assailed her. This summons—the first in centuries—meant change was in the air. It made her nervous, but she strode to the table, tightening her control on her dread, fear, and anxiety.

Her sister looked up as she approached, and the frown turned to a small smile. Druexxa touched her right thumb to her forehead and pulled it away in a salute. "Well met, Fisica."

Fisica smiled at her lyrical voice, and the nostalgic memories of their childhood flooded her mind. Back when all was as it should be, their mother had tended the garden, singing in such a similar voice to Druexxa while their father played games with the boys.

Her limbs grew heavy at the peaceful memories long gone as she sat on a brightly decorated cushion. The pulsing golden veins in the table caught the light of the fire, casting the entire room in a warm glow. The white columns shimmered with gold between the vines as the light dipped below the horizon.

Druexxa's face eased with relief. "Thank the gods you're here too. It's been a long time."

"Too long," Fisica said, returning the gesture with her thumb to her forehead. "How many of us were summoned?"

Druexxa's frown returned, her tight curls full and rounded, perfectly framing her glowing face. They shared the same wide nose, high cheekbones, nearly white hair, and dark skin of their mother, Gaiana.

"Better yet, who summoned us?" Druexxa asked.

"I did," another voice echoed from across the doorway. They both turned to see their sister Honifery floating toward them, her light pink and white silk dress flowing behind her. "And it's just the three of us today."

Some of the tension in her shoulders relaxed. If they were the only three, perhaps things hadn't progressed quite as badly as she feared.

They greeted each other with thumbs to foreheads and soft murmurs as Honifery sat beside Fisica, her loose, long, blond curls flowing below her shoulders as she settled on the cushion.

"To what do we owe this meeting, Honifery? Is it time to act? Are we safe to meet like this?" Druexxa's lyrical voice asked. She uncrossed her arms to reveal golden veins glowing like intricate tattoos, bright against the dark skin as she sat her hands daintily on the table. Fisica breathed a sigh of relief to see both her sisters' magic flowing so strongly along their dark skin, the gold lines pulsing with life.

Honifery sighed, a wrinkle marring her smooth features. "We are safe if we keep this meeting short. I have distracted our uncle with a minor problem in the Deep at the moment," she said, pausing at the word uncle and clenching her teeth.

"Those who normally search for us have been recalled to Hells to stop the problem, so we're relatively safe," she said, pursing her lips and continuing. "Are your identities still intact?"

Fisica nodded, but Druexxa sighed and said, "There are four who know me like this, but they are my champions in the coming war. It was necessary to reveal my hand."

Silence met her pronouncement, and Honifery leaned

forward to whisper furiously, "You know how dangerous that is, Dru. If he finds us, you know what he'll do."

It wasn't a question. Fisica's arms pebbled at the thought of it.

Druexxa crossed her arms and wrinkled her nose, "I haven't forgotten what he did to Father."

"Or what he'll do to the rest of us!" Honifery whispered furiously.

Druexxa leaned forward and lowered her voice. "It's certain death, I know. These four are my champions. I have blessed them, and they will fight with us when the time comes."

Honifery leaned back, her chest heaving with emotions as she breathed. "You better hope so, because the war is coming faster than we thought."

"What do you mean?" Fisica asked.

Honifery turned to her. "Exactly that. My sources in the Deep say he's planning to open a route straight to Eoni's surface. He wants to use it as a base to attack and destroy Paradise."

Fisica frowned as her stomach knotted. "He can't do that, can he? He's not strong enough."

Druexxa snorted. "We didn't think he was strong enough to take down Father either and look what happened there."

Honifery took Fisica's hand from the table, her touch instantly soothing. "No one knows you as Fisica?" she asked softly.

As a child, Honifery always protected her, but Fisica hadn't experienced any coddling in hundreds of years.

Her back stiffened as she shook her head. "No one, although I also may need to act in the coming months.

Events are unfolding and will soon come to a head, events that will change the Asshole's hold on this part of the world."

Druexxa chuckled at the nickname for their uncle, but Honifery just wrinkled her nose in disgust and released her hand. She'd known her prim and proper eldest sister wouldn't like the term, which was why she'd used it.

"Why would you need to put yourself in danger like that?" Honifery sighed and rubbed her forehead, but Fisica twisted the silk of her dress and kept quiet.

Druexxa said softly, "She's not a child, Honi. If she needs to take action, she needs to take action."

Honifery sighed and her shoulders sagged. "I know. Why don't you tell us what's going on, then I'll share my news and plans," Honifery said, her genuine curiosity making some of Fisica's tension dissipate. Perhaps admitting the events of the past few weeks wouldn't disappoint them as much as she thought it would when she'd first received the summons.

Fisica waved a hand to the fire bowl on the table. The smoke changed to show a bedchamber. A woman kneeled beside the dead body of her husband, crying and wailing as she pounded on his chest. She kept the sound off for now, but they all could feel the emotions, Fisica more than the others.

Fisica swallowed past the lump in her throat to explain. "This is the queen and my protégé, Bella. She has been heavily influenced by the mirror, which held the trapped soul of Hanzel Crookilius, the wizard. On the floor is her dead husband, the former king. This happened only a week ago."

"Hanzel Crookilius? Why do I know that name?" Druexxa said, tapping a long, golden nail to her chin.

Fisica crossed her smooth, toned arms and said, "Because he's the one who caused all the problems three hundred years ago. The last time I saw you. That was him. After he partnered with your Sea Witch, he slowly took over this continent and staged a coup that led to the dragons being nearly destroyed."

Druexxa's eyes narrowed, and her magic flared as a storm cloud gathered above her head. "She wasn't *my* Sea Witch. She made a deal with our uncle."

None of them needed to ask which uncle, as only one was obsessed with deals and contracts. Fisica nodded and waved her hand, a white and gold tea tray appearing on the table with them. She carefully poured three cups as she talked, keeping her tone friendly and even to calm her sister.

"I know, I'm sorry. I simply meant that she was on your side of the planet. Thank you for dealing with that problem, by the way. I saw the mermaid princess and her mate at the queen and king's wedding. Are they your champions?"

Druexxa nodded, her eyes narrowed until Fisica said, "You picked your champions well."

Druexxa relaxed as she took her tea, the cloud slowly dissolving into the air.

Honifery sipped hers silently, always watching and waiting, and then said, "Continue, Fisica. Tell me of your champion, the queen."

Fisica pointed her own golden nail at the bowl of fire, her hands and body now back to her normal, youthful, immortal self. Reluctantly, she said, "Watch."

The queen worked quickly at her vanity, tossing ingredients into a bowl. Then she sank to the floor and hovered her hand over the king's dead chest. The look of horror on Bella's face sent a twist of pain to Fisica's heart. She should've protected the girl better, blessed her with more magic, taught her more spells.

Fisica took a deep breath and watched as her heart broke all over again. Pain at failing the dear girl, frustration that she had to keep her identity a secret, and apprehension at telling her sisters of this whole mess made the hair on her arms stand up with barely contained magic.

Her foot bounced as they watched, and she fed her magic into the spell.

The king's shirt ripped open even as the queen cried and shook her head, tears pouring down her face as her mouth formed the spell to remove his heart. Still shaking her head, she stood, blood dripping from her hands, and put the heart into a bowl. She ground it with the pestle and added it to the potion.

In silence, they watched as she drank the potion, tears streaming down her face.

Honifery sighed. "Oh, dear."

Fisica simply nodded and held onto her magic, her lips pursed as the queen's body shook. She didn't want to watch this again, but she forced herself to stay in the moment. Poor Bella had survived it; watching was the least Fisica could do for failing her.

Energy and magic swirled under Bella's skin, making it ripple and move like a cat beneath a blanket. The queen's soundless scream sent a shiver up her spine, and her heart ached for her dear apprentice.

Her sisters would not be happy about this next part or Fisica's role in it. A pulse of magic shot from Bella's body, covering the room in an inky blackness.

"That's the curse that has infected thousands," Fisica said softly.

Another pulse of golden magic flashed in the room,

then the queen's body shifted and morphed into a red-scaled horned monster. A row of horns spiked back from her temples and went down her back, growing bigger and bursting from her dress.

Honifery sat forward with a frown. "What is—"

"Dragon scales," Fisica interrupted. She had to explain, hopefully make them understand why she'd interfered. "Her human body couldn't handle the drakin king's magic. This was the only way she would've survived."

"Did you cast the spell?" Honifery's brows rose in surprise.

Fisica nodded as the queen in the fire image tried to scratch her back. Her hands shifted into claws as she held her head, digging into her skin and drawing blood before scales covered enough to protect her from herself.

Fisica's stomach twisted along with Bella's movements as she tried to escape her own body. She slammed into the vanity and the mirror wobbled. Fisica winced.

The light reflecting off the mirror caught the queen's dilated, reptilian eye, and she turned to it with a snarl. She grabbed both edges and threw it to the ground.

It shattered, and a burst of magic slammed out, throwing the queen against the vanity. She hit her head on the corner and sank to the ground.

But her spirit held onto the vanity, shaking and heaving. A black curl of smoke shot from the busted mirror on the floor to the drakin queen's body, and it began convulsing.

The pale blue spirit of the queen hovered over her body with a confused frown, even as the king's body turned to ash. Her eyes never left the convulsing body on the floor. It stilled, and Bella just stood there panting. Slowly, the drakin lumbered to its knees.

The queen's blue-tinted spirit backed up, yellow skirts

swishing. Fisica waved her hand again to hear the sound, infusing double the magic into the spell. She simply hadn't been able to stomach hearing the screams again, but this they needed to hear.

"What—what is this?" Bella asked softly.

Her body stood, breathing rapidly and expelling smoke through an elongated snout. Black, beady eyes stared at Bella's spirit, then it threw its head back and laughed.

Fisica wasn't the only one at the table who winced at the grating sound. It was eerily similar to their uncle's and sent a shiver of fear up her spine.

A gravelly, deep voice boomed, making even the table vibrate with its projection. "*This* is magic. I'm finally free from that cursed mirror, and for that, I thank you."

The queen's body glanced at the pile of ash and waved its hand. It coalesced into a pile. From the ashes grew a tiny, green plant shoot.

Then the drakin twisted a wrist and whispered ancient words that made Honifery and Druexxa gasp. A golden strand lifted from Bella's spirit and dipped down to the rose, merging with it until the green bud glowed.

When it faded to normal, the drakin queen grinned, too many sharp predator teeth exposed. "Consider this a thank you present. You may remain here in this precious castle of yours until that rose dies. Then you'll go to the Deep with the others."

Bella's spirit lurched, her arms swinging wide as she somehow lost balance. It should've been impossible as a spirit, but it was a big transition. One that Bella never should've gone through, if Fisica had done her job right.

Regret twisted her stomach as she watched.

Bella gasped, finally gaining control of her new corporeal form. "What? Why? Where are you going?"

The queen's body stepped toward the door. At first, it was just a drunken stumble, but each step became smoother. "Oh, I have plans. Promises to fulfill that are long overdue, my dear."

Bella floated to the door and held her arms wide. "No, wait! You can't leave me here and just take off. That's my— my body."

The drakin arched a brow and smirked. "Are you sure you want it back? I mean, just look at how hideous you are. No longer the beautiful queen. No, I think I'll hold on to it for now. It's been years since I've had a body, and I intend to fully use it before upgrading."

Then the drakin walked through the floating Bella, who screamed. The drakin's chuckle echoed off the shaking walls.

The smoke cleared from the table, and the image dissipated.

Fisica glanced at her eldest sister. "That was Crookilius. Three hundred years ago, he made a deal with our uncle for power."

"What kind of power?" Druexxa asked sharply.

"I don't know yet. I'm still researching. There are two remaining dragons. One has just become king of the forest."

"And the other?" Druexxa's sharp eyes looked so much like their mother's, it hurt.

Fisica reached for her teacup, but her hand shook so badly, she pulled it back to her lap. "The other dragon trapped Crookilius in the mirror. I've talked to him, and he explained Crookilius' plan."

"Why do I hear a but in there?" Druexxa asked.

Fisica wrinkled her nose and inclined her head. "But if Crookilius' plan is still the same, he is going to lay waste to the entire continent. It was part of his deal. If he controls the continent, then the Asshole can begin his campaign to take over all Eoni."

Her sisters stared at her in horror, their faces almost mirror images as they paled.

Honifery rubbed her temples and shook her head. "This is what I was afraid of. My contact in the Deep has shown me that our uncle is trying to create a portal to release his daemon army upon Eoni. We must stop him at all costs."

Fisica nodded. "To stop our uncle, we must stop Crookilius. I am keeping watch on my champions but might need to reveal myself. We will need them in the coming war."

Honifery shook her head. "I don't think that's wise. Maybe Dru's champions can go help?"

Druexxa shook her head. "There is another sin lord in the Zands that has recently come to power. My champions are going to find out if this one also made a deal with our uncle."

Honifery took a deep breath. "Always with the deals... Very well, help your champions however you can, but be smart about it. Try to keep from being seen by our uncle, because I don't want to lose either of you."

Honifery took her hand again, and Fisica squeezed it.

"We'll be fine." Druexxa sniffed and looked away as she blinked quickly.

Honifery released Fisica's hand. "However, that brings us to why I've called this meeting..."

Hours later, Fisica blinked past the pain in her body and the burning medallion on her chest. When her eyes adjusted to the dimness, she found herself back in front of the fireplace in her new cabin, flat on her back.

She looked at her hands and sighed. Her smooth, dark skin was now tan, wrinkled, and spotted with age. The golden veins of magic weren't visible in this form, but more than how she looked was how she felt.

Her back ached from where she'd slammed into the dirt packed floor on her re-entry to this plane. She got up slowly and laid on the bed. Someday, this old body wouldn't be necessary. But first, she had a war to stop and champions to save.

Oath of Revenge: Chapter One

Wulfric snarled and snapped at Brody, anger coursing through him. "How dare you," he growled. "I'm the alpha of the Ironpaws, damn it!"

Brody grinned maniacally and circled him in the small clearing on the edge of the river. "Correction. You were. I'm taking over."

Wulfric shook his head, blood splattering from where it dripped into his eye. He lunged, snapping his elongated jaws. He didn't have time for an alpha challenge, as illegal as this one may be.

It was his job to see the tribe through the winter. The Elders had said it was going to be the worst winter in centuries, and they'd been right so far. They still had weeks to go before spring.

Brody twisted and clamped down on his shoulder. The stupid pup wasn't trained enough to manage a throat attack, but Wulfric turned and took advantage. His bloody teeth latched awkwardly onto the back of Brody's neck and ripped the wolf off. Brody's jaws tore a chunk of Wulfric's fur and flesh as he went flying.

Wulfric didn't whimper. He'd fought many wars over the years, not that he could remember any from the time before. Pain was as familiar as food and almost as necessary. Both would keep him alive.

He limped back, watching Brody warily as he mentally assessed both their wounds. His head pounded from where the wolf and his two friends had ambushed him with a club. One of them was dead and the other lay near a tree, staring silently as he either bled out or healed.

Logically, he knew he'd only been defending himself. But his chest ached at the deaths of his people, the betrayal, the confusion.

Wulfric focused on Brody. "But why?"

Brody shook his head, his eyes glowing with rage as he stalked back to Wulfric. "You don't get it, do you? You walk around like a god, lording your power as alpha over the rest of us. We're tired of it."

A stab of anger made him growl. He played with the young ones, led the youths on hunts, trained the warriors, kept the peace with the other tribe leaders, and took care of the Elders. When had he lorded power over any of them?

He rolled his shoulders, testing his weight on his injured front leg. Pain stabbed him like a knife, but he refused to take his eyes off his opponent. "How was I abusing my power as alpha? Who thinks this?"

Brody howled, the sound echoing off the dark trees. "Butch, for starters, and now he's dead, thanks to you."

He winced and panted, staying as still as possible. He didn't want Brody to realize how injured his foot was or how much those words hurt. He had worked for years to

451

protect and honor the people who had taken him in and loved him unconditionally, if harshly.

He would not be goaded into feeling guilty. "Butch's death is on your head. What did you expect when you ambushed the alpha?"

"I expected more than this!" Brody roared, blood dripping from his fangs as he prowled back and forth with hackles raised. "When I signed on to be a Growler, I expected more than this isolation and tyranny."

Wulfric arched a bushy brow, the movement barely visible in their wolf forms. New Growlers were welcomed with open arms because it was an instant family. "What isolation? Our family is enormous. We fill the entire lower half of the Feral Forest."

"And that's the fucking problem," Brody snarled, shifting onto his back legs as he prepared to pounce. "We've outgrown the forest. We're bursting at the seams. And on top of that, we're not family, are we? I miss my actual family, my flesh and blood. I'm tired of hiding, of giving up who I am."

Brody lunged half-heartedly, testing Wulfric's reaction times. "The time for hiding is over. Busparia's defenses are in ruins, the soldiers have all fled back home—except for us! We want to go home!"

Wulfric jumped back, wincing at the pain as he balanced on three legs. "The Growlers are our home now. You knew that when you accepted the blessing of the Elders."

Brody barked a laugh. "A blessing? Not if it keeps me from my family."

Wulfric froze, confusion and blood loss making his head pound. "What family are you talking about?"

Brody didn't give him time to ask more questions. He

launched into the air with a roar, and Wulfric twisted to the side. A massive paw landed a lucky blow to his temple, sending him out of the controlled roll. Wulfric hit a tree and grunted in pain, coming up on three weak legs.

Brody prowled closer, drool dripping from his muzzle. "Busparia's new queen has nearly destroyed the country, and we're worried about our families. They're no longer safe. Now is the time to strike, to save them, yet we can't just bring them back here. We're too cramped as it is, but in Busparia... they're still waiting for us. The land is ripe for the taking."

Something within him twisted at the mention of Busparia. Faint feelings of a past he no longer remembered threatened to drown him in sorrow. "No," he said to the memories.

"No? That's it?" Brody growled. "See, this is why you're a terrible alpha. How I've survived five years like this is beyond me."

"We're not going anywhere." Wulfric shifted to keep the tree on his bad side. It would help protect him. If Brody was smart, he'd attack the weak leg.

Wulfric tried to diffuse the situation. "We need to talk this through rationally."

"There's no more time to lose. Home is right there on the other side of the forest, and they may need us to save them from the queen or her monsters." Brody's mouth twisted in anger, his features harsh in the cold, crisp sunlight.

He snarled and leaped in the air, but Wulfric spun behind the tree, pain lancing through him. Brody hit the pine, the sharp whine of pain piercing his ears.

Wulfric winced, that sound an echo of his failure as a leader. He was supposed to protect them, not harm them.

"Stop before you hurt yourself. Remember the gift and be grateful for a second chance at life."

Brody snorted. "I know, I know. We were all dying soldiers who otherwise wouldn't have made it home."

Brody stopped, and his beady, black eyes peered into Wulfric's gaze, the emotion and yearning making Wulfric's breath catch in his throat.

Then the anger returned to Brody's face as he lowered his muzzle. "And what's the point of a second life if I can't see my family ever again?" Brody spat vehemently, anger burning hell-hot in his gaze as he clambered slowly to his feet.

The pressure on Wulfric's mind increased, memories fluttering just out of reach. He shook his head and relayed the message they'd heard over and over since being turned. "We can't go into Busparia. They'll hunt us down and destroy everything we know."

"Not everything." Brody's lip curled in disdain. "I know a lot more than just this damn forest. In fact, there are several of us who kept our memories, *alpha*."

He sneered the word and spat blood on the ground, turning to face Wulfric, stretching to test his injuries again.

Wulfric's body shivered in the cold, but his mind was frozen on the words. How had he kept his memories? That was the price of being turned into a Growler. The Elders had been performing that ritual for hundreds of years, but somehow Brody hadn't paid the price?

It didn't make sense. His head ached, and his body seemed to slow even as his heart raced at the danger.

He should end this farce of a battle. It wasn't worth calling it an alpha challenge, as it wasn't within the bounds of the law. Wulfric's shoulders stiffened, and he lifted his head, breathing deeply through the pain as he circled the tree. The pounding in his ankle kept his mind in the moment, even though it tried to draw him into the yawning chasm of darkness.

Damn it, he was supposed to uphold the law and keep them safe, love them as they loved him. Wulfric took a shuddering breath, the scent of blood flooding him, calling to him to turn feral.

Focus, Wulfric, focus. Try to reason with him.

"If we go into Busparia, we'll either kill or be killed. And we're not going to attack innocent civilians outside the forest who may see us as a threat. That will just keep the fear of Growlers going."

Brody took two steps closer, blood dripping steadily onto the pine needle covered ground. "The new queen and the general are taking control of more than just the capital. This winter is the perfect time for us to finally leave these cursed woods and go home."

"It's too cold."

"Exactly! It's keeping everyone inside, so we can slip into the country unnoticed. We're protectors, soldiers, and warriors, but we're stuck hiding in these woods like outlaws when our families are being killed in their own homes."

Wulfric shuffled on his feet, keeping his weight on his three legs as the dizziness increased. "That's not our home anymore. There's no home left for us in Busparia."

Brody's toothy grin widened, red with blood. "Perhaps not for you...but if you won't lead us home, I will. Step down as alpha. This is your last chance."

Wulfric shook his head, tightness pressing on his chest as his vision swam. Blood poured into his eyes, and he shook his head again so he could see. But he was too slow.

Brody attacked, and this time, his aim was true. His jaws clamped around Wulfric's neck as he viciously ripped at flesh and fur. Claws dug into muscle. Wulfric twisted, rolling them both on the ground.

He pinned Brody and dislodged him, smacking him into the dirt with a whimper. Then another wolf slammed into Wulfric's wounded side, sending him sprawling. Spots swirled with white lights behind his eyelids, the gurgling of the river the only sound to be heard over the pounding of his heart. No birds, no woodland chatter. All else was still.

He blinked, seeing double. No, two more wolves had joined the fight and paced beside Brody as he rose to his feet.

"Finish him," Brody said.

Wulfric's breathing grew ragged as his head spun. He'd seen these two wolves with Brody in the past. Why hadn't he opened his senses to inspect the area in a wider arc? They prowled to him, and he assessed his wounds, the situation, his surroundings.

He wouldn't be able to take on two more uninjured wolves. He needed to find medicine or magic. They wouldn't let him, and it wasn't guaranteed that the Elders would help him, either.

Even though the alpha challenge wasn't official and was completely illegal, he had no way of telling if the Elders would even side with him. They would likely say it was the will of their patron goddess and let him bleed out.

Where could he go? The gurgling river was the only sound in the night. The river. It would take him further from the Elders and their medicine, but he would at least be away from Brody and his minions. It was his only chance.

Oath of Revenge: Chapter Two

"Mistress Scarlet, welcome back," said the butler as he took her cloak. "How was your mission?"

"It wasn't as successful as I'd hoped." Scarlet stomped mud off her boots just inside the door of the castle. Every step made her head vibrate and bob side to side as she tried to keep her head upright.

"Oh?"

"It's hard to be inconspicuous with fucking antlers, bunny ears, and a wolf's tail," Scarlet scowled.

The butler sniffed and held her cloak, "Tell me about it."

He waved his two extra arms, which were really just two feather dusters that stuck out from each side of his ribs. Even as he shook out her cloak, the dusters were busy cleaning the dirt on the door and wall.

From his hips extended a broom on one side and a dust pan on the other, which also didn't stop moving.

Scarlet sighed and a stab of guilt made her stomach

twist. "I'm sorry, Hobbs. I know this curse is hard for you too."

He smiled and nodded his head to the wide hallway. "They're in the library, miss. I'll send in some refreshments."

"Thank you," she said, the weight of responsibility added to the heaviness of her antlers. She might have more curses than the others, but she was the one who'd been appointed to solve the problem. They were all relying on her, even though most of the others avoided her.

She walked down the wide, marble hallway. In the past six months, the haunted Hartsgrove castle had been cleaned and rebuilt from an attack by the skeletal dragon.

Now it shined good as new, thanks to Hobbs and the castle's ghost, Leopol. She looked around but didn't see the wispy man as she entered the library.

Her brother, Knox, stood behind his wife, massaging her shoulders. Eirwyn sat in one of the plush chairs in front of the fireplace, feet propped up with a forgotten book in her lap.

Her family turned at the sound of her boots on the floor and smiled. They were so damn happy and content together.

She didn't envy them, she really didn't. She'd never wanted to live the domesticated life, barefoot, pregnant, and reliant on a man. Her dad had raised her to be independent. Plus, there was her love for adventure and that sense of fulfillment from a job well done.

Even if that job was slicing the throat of some noble scum or making an abuser disappear. She was a hired Hunter, but she had standards.

The past few years, the hunt had been getting stale, though. She didn't want a home or babes, but she did want someone to have her back. She was so lonely, especially with these fucking curses.

They'd put a stop to almost all of it. Now she had responsibilities. People relied on her. She pushed down the rage that burned in her soul at the injustice of the curses and fear of failure at being unable to break them.

Knox smiled. "Scarlet, you're back! How was the trip? Did you have any trouble?" His smile turned into a worried frown as she stepped closer.

She sank into the opposite cushioned chair, turning sideways and dangling her legs over the armrest.

"Of course I had trouble. I can hardly ride through the forest without getting this fucking rack tangled in the trees, much less meet with the other Hunters."

She sighed, knowing they would think she had no propriety when in reality, this was just the most comfortable position for her giant-ass antlers.

The housekeeper, Helga, came into the room pushing a cart and swiping her tea leaf hair out of her face.

Eirwyn shifted on the seat to sit up. "Oh, tea is here. This will make you feel better. I'm sure you're hungry after getting all tangled up and traveling all this way."

Knox put his hand on her shoulder and shook his head. "No, you stay here. I'll serve."

Helga fussed, and Scarlet pulled out her dagger to pick at her nails. They weren't dirty, but making Helga glare at her put a smile back on Scarlet's face.

The housekeeper's hair kept falling into her face, and she kept blowing it away. But the tea leaves had a mind of their own.

Eirwyn had confided a few months ago that Helga had taken scissors to them repeatedly, but they always grew back like weeds overnight. So she'd put her curse to work and had packaged tea into bags to transport to the other two new villages in the forest.

Scarlet sighed and sat up, taking the offered tea from Knox. At least the tea leaf hair made a relaxing drink, she thought as she sipped.

"How is the little dragonling and the queen?" Scarlet asked.

Knox pulled up another chair as Helga parked the cart at Eirwyn's elbow.

Eirwyn rubbed her stomach protectively, shadows and light swirling around her as her nerves went higher. "Eh, as well as expected I suppose. Lailant says it's going well, but I would feel better with more information. We have read almost every book in this castle, and Leopol has been very helpful."

Although a ghost, Leopol was the only one who was an actual dragon, other than Knox. He knew what to expect from experience, if not the books in the library.

Scarlet sipped her tea as Knox stared at his wife with concern. She swallowed, the heat burning her tongue. "Yet you're still worried?"

Knox pushed a plate of olpertine closer to Eirwyn and moved a second plate between himself and Scarlet on a low side table.

He nodded. "Wouldn't you be? But everything will be fine. This has been done for thousands of years before, remember?"

Eirwyn nodded, distracted as she practically inhaled the olpertine's sugary fried dough.

Scarlet met Knox's worried gaze and understood. It was like watching her dad ride off to war, not knowing if he was going to come out unharmed or not. The reminder of her dad sent her own worry and frustration sky high.

She took a deep breath and tried to control herself. Her antlers weighed her down, causing a throbbing headache like always. Every damn day, she pushed her body, pushed past the pain and tried to live a semi-normal existence.

She could live with the tail and the nose. The antlers were the biggest problem. They spread as wide as her shoulders and had twelve points. Was it any wonder she was cranky all the time?

Not as cranky as Eirwyn. Thankfully Scarlet wasn't the one carrying a giant egg. That honor fell to her dear sister-in-law.

"Just ring if you need me, Your Majesties," Helga said, dipping a curtsy.

Knox and Eirwyn both nodded but didn't look up as she left. Scarlet smirked. She never would've thought her big brother would become king, but it suited him. He'd taken to it like a fish takes to water.

Unlike herself and the curses. She just couldn't accept that this was her life now.

Other villagers both here in Hartsgrove and over in Vidrland were cursed too, like Helga and Hobbs, but they all gave Scarlet a wide berth. She was used to setting people on edge when they found out she was a Hunter, but this was something completely different.

She'd had months to get used to these cursed changes in her body, but every time someone looked at her in horror, the hair on the back of her neck stood up. Anger seethed under her skin, making her scratch behind her long ears to find some sort of short-lived relief.

Eirwyn frowned, rubbing her stomach absently. "So what's the news in the capitol? Did you find out what's going on? Is Bella alright?"

Scarlet reached for an olpertine and popped it into her

mouth to keep from snapping about the queen. The confectioners sugar dissolved on her tongue as she chewed the fried treat, and her nose twitched as if phantom whiskers were tickling her cheek. She shivered at the memory and took a drink, re-centering the weight of the antlers.

Thankfully, the whiskers hadn't made a re-appearance since that day at the castle.

She cleared her throat. "Of course I found out what's going on. I may be a freak, but I'm still the best Hunter in the land."

"You're not a freak," Knox said. "You're just cursed like nearly everyone else here."

She almost crushed the next olpertine and glared at Knox. "No one else has multiple curses here. I'm the one who sticks out in a sea of weirdness. I'm the abomination in a crowd of tea ladies and candle and clock men. Of all the people who've been merged with inanimate objects, you can't seriously think that I'm just like everyone else."

Knox crossed his arms and leaned back in the straight chair. *He certainly looks royal enough with that stern stare.*

"It's not like you to have a pity party, Scarlet. You know we're going to break the curse."

Scarlet drowned her rage with another olpertine and drink of tea, but the roiling emotions finally broke free. "Yeah, yeah, that's what you've said for months."

"We're not giving up," he said.

Scarlet shot back, "Easy for you to say when you look so normal."

They both glanced in surprise at each other, then burst out laughing.

Knox scratched at his temples where green and brown scales spread around the back of his head. Brown hair grew on the top which he kept in a thick braid. But for years, he'd hidden his scales beneath a cloak and stuck to the shadows of the forest, rarely going in public.

"Well, that's a first. Never heard anyone call me normal before," Knox grinned.

Scarlet chewed another olpertine. They'd fought like this as kids a lot. Quick, heated words, then a laugh, and it was over. It was good to hear him laugh about his own appearance now.

The love of a good woman would do that to a man, though. At least, that's what she'd seen in her short thirty-five years.

Scarlet swallowed and drained her tea. "Well, as normal as you'll ever be," she teased.

Eirwyn had eaten almost her entire personal plate of olpertine and finally stopped long enough to chime in. "You're not normal, but normal is over-rated. You have to accept who you are, Scarlet. Embrace your curses and use them to your advantage, like Helga."

Scarlet arched a brow at her friend and sat her empty porcelain cup on the cart. "Queenie, some curses are easier to accept than others. I appreciate your optimism, but I need my old body back."

"And if you can't get it back?" Eirwyn asked softly. "What then?"

Scarlet stared into the fire, the food settling like a knot in her stomach as her lips pinched. Her heart pounded in her ears, too fast like the scared little rabbit she worked so hard to bury deep inside her.

She had beaten that fear within her for six months and made it her little bitch. But it was a constant, daily battle with her multiple instincts. Run like a deer, fight like a wolf, or hide like a fucking scared little rabbit.

That's what she'd been reduced to with these fucking

curses. It wasn't all about the physical differences. It was about eliminating that fear for good. The only thing that had helped keep it at bay was channeling it into anger, but that anger needed a focus, a release.

Her eyes burned with rage as she turned to stare at Eirwyn.

"I'm going to kill the queen, Eirwyn. Gods help me, if she doesn't fix this, I will kill her."

The silence was only broken by the crackling of the fire in the fireplace. A tear rolled down Eirwyn's cheek, and Knox sighed, handing her a napkin from the cart.

"You can't just kill her," Knox said, the disappointment in his voice making Scarlet's stomach twist.

But she just arched a brow and crossed her arms and ankles. Stretching her legs in front of her toward the fire, she took a deep breath. Her mind wandered as Eirwyn handed her empty plate to Knox, who tidied up the cart.

The silence was tense. She needed to make them see it was a last resort but maybe the best option.

"It's not just about the curses," she said quietly. "There are other things going on in Busparia. We thought the old king was a bad ruler because of the taxes and the war with Glathen? This is worse."

Eirwyn's shoulders sank at the mention of her brother.

Knox sat forward, his tea forgotten as he frowned. "In what way?"

"The king would throw suspects into the dungeon and torture them or hold them ransom until someone paid their taxes, right?" Scarlet's spine tingled at the memory of her own time in the dungeon, but she pushed the emotions away.

She continued. "The queen doesn't. Any infraction leads to sudden and instant death."

Eirwyn gasped, and Knox took her hand.

Scarlet shook her head. "That's not all. Every town in the country has a curfew. No one roams the streets after sunset. There are reports of monsters killing anyone caught in the darkness. Cattle and livestock are found every morning slaughtered and ripped to shreds."

"Monsters?" Knox asked.

Scarlet nodded. "I didn't believe the reports at first, but my team of Hunters and I barely made it into an inn our first night on the road. We could hear the flutter of wings and the growls."

"Growlers?" Eirwyn asked.

Scarlet shook her head slowly, staring once more into the fireplace as her spine tingled. "No, I don't think so. They didn't sound like Growlers. This was something entirely different."

She looked up and met their gazes one at a time, trying to make them see how bad it was outside of the relative safety of the Feral Forest.

"The queen is wielding that fear like a double-edged sword. She claims that those who die are those who oppose her rule and break the laws. It's no coincidence that the so-called monsters only descended on the villages and valleys after the queen passed through on her grand-tour of the country."

"How can the Council just let this happen?" Eirwyn asked.

Eirwyn was the former princess of Busparia. Her brother had ruled with the Council for decades before his death six months ago. That's when their entire world was turned upside down.

Scarlet replied, "I don't think the Council has a choice.

Between Bella, the General, and the Chancellor, it's practically martial law in Busparia."

She rubbed her temples, her head hurting yet again from the balancing act of antlers.

"The Chancellor is a yes-man. He'll do whatever he has to stay in power," Eirwyn said.

Scarlet nodded, "That power has finally settled in the capitol. There haven't been elaborate, fancy balls, but she has begun to wine and dine the nobles and the Council. Those who oppose her disappear, and it's not the Hunters still in Busparia responsible for it, either. Most of the Hunters who remain are no longer getting contracts. When we arrived at the Guild house, they asked us for guidance and help."

"What did you tell them?" Knox asked.

Scarlet shrugged. "Exactly what you said. There's shelter in the forest for any who swear fealty to the two of you."

"And what of the war? Any word on that?" Knox put his empty tea cup on the cart and stepped behind Eirwyn to massage down her arms. Scarlet sighed, ignoring the pain in her chest as she watched the two of them together.

It was almost nauseating to watch all the love between them. The little touches. The heated glances. The tender care.

It reminded her too much of her parents and of what she would never have.

Grab your copy...
vinci-books.com/oathofrevenge

About the Author

Jane Poller read her way through middle school. Romance books got her through countless life changes... moves, degrees, having kids, deployments, teaching high school, international living, health coaching, running a wellness business, homeschooling, and more. She finally gave in to the characters in her head demanding their stories be told. She's an avid reader of historical romance but writes primarily fantasy romance and contemporary small-town romance. Look for the fantasy romance series on her website. The Crimson Creek series is a contemporary steamy small-town romance set in a fictional town in Texas. Speaking of, she lives in Texas with her middle school sweet-heart. He's her real-life hero, Army veteran, and the inspiration for her stories. His interest in Role playing games inspired her love of fantasy romance too. Without him, the fantasy stories wouldn't exist. When she's not doing all the things, she's reading and writing. Or arguing with her characters, who refuse to do what she wants. But that's par for the course, since she's currently raising teenagers and two dogs. Those reviews really brighten her day and are much appreciated.